LORD OF SILENCE

LORD OF SILENCE

Mark Chadbourn

SOLARIS

First published 2009 by Solaris
an imprint of BL Publishing
Games Workshop Ltd
Willow Road
Nottingham
NG7 2WS
UK

www.solarisbooks.com

ISBN-13: 978 1 84416 753 1
ISBN-10: 1 84416 753 4

10 9 8 7 6 5 4 3 2 1

A CIP catalogue record for this book is available from the
British Library.

Designed & typeset by BL Publishing

Printed and bound in the US.

1
MELLIAS IS DEAD

IN THE VAST Store of the Ages, the ghosts never rested. From the pools of unyielding shadows that gathered between the sputtering torches, their sly, sibilant whispers promised terrible answers to haunting mysteries, forgotten knowledge and secrets that should never be brought back into the light. They were present in the crumbling parchments and mildewed books, written in languages no longer understood, in the artefacts whose origins were lost generations in the past, in the great paintings signed by artists no one remembered, in the fine statues of unknown personages, in the pieces of pottery and bone, the shards of broken weapons; in all the fragments of memory waiting to be pieced together.

Those ghosts were no threat to Tomas, Apprentice Keeper only three years into his post. He had accepted the calling to work among the echoes of the past, and to heed those voices as a way to reach some understanding of the long, mysterious history of ancient Idriss, City of Lights. It was a thankless task, he knew; to the people of Idriss, the past was a luxury compared to the hard grind of the present. No one cared. No one wished to remember. No citizen ever, ever ventured within the Store's thick, protective walls, even though it could not be missed, looming over the city on the Mountain of the Heart, the highest hill within the city's boundaries, a monolithic structure of grey stone, silent and imposing, and older perhaps than any other building in Idriss.

The ghosts that concerned Tomas were the ones that had been moving through the great, ringing halls under cover of darkness, night after night for the last few weeks, searching for something they never found. He had heard their soft tread, but never saw any stranger. And if no one ever came to the Store of the Ages, what else could those visitors be but ghosts? That night he had even heard voices, more footsteps, some with a measured step, others hurrying insistently.

What did it mean in a place where there was only ever silence?

There was never enough light within the Store of the Ages, as if the gloom was symbolic of the people's view of the work carried out there. Plucking a torch from the wall so he could search more easily, Tomas hurried through each room, casting an anxious gaze all around.

A distorted shadow of a man was thrown against the far wall of the next hall as he entered. Tomas called out in shock: it appeared to be reaching out for him menacingly. But when he realised it wasn't moving, he edged closer until he saw that the shadow was cast by a statue of the Shepherd, a religious figure that some of Idriss's residents still worshipped, arms held aloft in a manner that Tomas guessed was supposed to be devotional.

His sigh of relief was audible, but it was cut short by the wet stickiness of his footsteps and a rich iron aroma. Lowering the flickering torch, he saw that he was standing in a large, dark pool. His heart burst into a thunderous rhythm and he leaped to one side, knowing full well what it was. Whimpering, he prepared to run in search of one of the Senior Keepers, but instead he was drawn inexorably to the source of the blood.

The body lay immediately before the statue of the Shepherd. The shock of the discovery made Tomas's consciousness see-saw, images flashing in random order as he struggled to process what he saw. It was a man, muscular, blond hair, armed with a sword. Blood. He swallowed, thought he might vomit as his attention skittered over the most striking details, not wishing to see it at all, knowing he would always be seeing it. Both of the eyes had been gouged out. The mouth had been slashed on both sides, giving the victim an insane, bloody grin. His shirt had been torn open and a ragged circle with a line piercing it had been carved into his chest. Tomas couldn't bring himself to dwell on the rest of the body; it looked as if an animal had been at it.

Staggering back a step, he tried to raise the alarm, but the words died in his throat as he realised he knew the identity of the slaughtered figure.

Mellias.

His horror was washed away in a flood of grief. As the tears streamed down his face, he dropped to his knees and pawed at the body as if he could shake life back into it.

Mellias, the White Warrior. Idriss's greatest hero. The most honourable, the most noble, who had single-handedly defeated three-score enemies at the Deeping Gate, who had ventured into the great forest to save the young daughter of a merchant from the horrors that lurked within, who had given more blood for

Idriss than any other inhabitant and had asked for nothing in return. Mellias was Idriss. Mellias was the embodiment of hope for the future in a city that was permanently on the brink of extinction.

What did it mean for Idriss, now Mellias was dead?

Tomas rested his head on the corpse's cold chest and sobbed.

Wrenching himself to his feet a moment later, Tomas broke into a lurching run back the way he had come, leaving a trail of blood in the dust of the Store of the Ages.

'Mellias is dead,' he said to himself in disbelief; and then finally he found his voice: 'Mellias is dead!'

ADMINISTRATOR ASHUR SURVEYED the body for long minutes. His young assistant, Carlo, roused from his bed by the alarm, could not begin to divine his master's emotion, for the mass of scar tissue that kept Ashur's face white and frozen gave nothing away, and the Administrator had made no comment since he had been delivered to the body. Wiping away his own tears, Carlo noticed the small group of Keepers showing the degree of emotion he anticipated everyone in Idriss would be feeling once the news leaked out. There was sobbing, and prayers, and cries for deliverance, and who could fault them? Mellias was dead. Even the statue of the Shepherd appeared to be passing judgement on the terrible scene.

'It is a lie! It cannot be true!' The crackling, paper-thin voice of King Lud floated across the dry air of the chamber. Supported by his two assistants, he took slow, faltering steps from the shadows at the rear of the hall. The King appeared even frailer than the last time Carlo had seen him, his skin yellowing and wrinkled, his pale, half-blind eyes seeping, his frame bowed and twisted like an ancient tree on a wind-blasted hill.

'Your highness, it is true. Darkness threatens to engulf the great City of Lights.' Ashur's rigid facial muscles delivered the words in an unnerving gravelly voice that also rarely revealed any emotion.

'Never!' the King said. He looked down at the body for a fleeting moment before staring deep into a dark corner of the hall, his eyes luminous in the torchlight. Steadying himself, he said quietly, 'Idriss will never die, even though the heart has been torn out of this great city.'

Ashur allowed the King a moment's reflection, and then said in a manner that was all the more chilling for its lack of passion, 'What kind of beast is at large in Idriss? The mutilation here – it sickens me.'

'It is the work of a madman, nothing more. It should not concern us. It is not greater than this terrible loss... this shattering...' The King swallowed the final word.

'What will the people think when this news reaches them? Not only have they lost their favourite son, but the greatest warrior of our history has been slaughtered as if he were a lamb. When they realise that a thing that can plumb these depths of depravity still walks among them–'

'We must act quickly before panic begins,' the King interrupted. 'Our enemies lie everywhere across Gardia. We have stood resolute against the threat from the forest. We shall not be brought down by despair from within. Raise the alarm!' Lud cried, his trembling, arthritic arms reaching to the sky. 'Ring out the tolling bell! Our great hero has been murdered, and Idriss will not rest until the killer has been made to pay for this most terrible of crimes!'

Ashur nodded. 'There is one other matter,' he began hesitantly. 'Who will take Mellias's place as leader of the Crimson Hunt?'

'There is only one candidate,' the King replied, puzzled.

'Not Vidar! The people will not accept it!' Carlo was shocked by the sudden revelation of emotion lurking within Ashur's icy character.

'How could we expect them to see a great hero like Mellias followed by a murderer, thief, and rake, not to mention his band of cut-throats and criminals? A man without honour, or morals. We would be putting the defence of Idriss in the hands of a devil.'

'Vidar has been loyal.'

'As long as he is well paid–'

'That is unfair, Ashur. You know he has proven himself many times over.'

'He commands ghosts! He drinks the lives of others to survive! He is a monster, not a man.'

'He is afflicted with a terrible curse,' Lud said in a tone that brought the debate sharply to a close. 'Now, let the word go out that Idriss shall not rest until Mellias has been avenged. There will be blood for blood. Idriss abides.'

Ashur gave a curt bow, but once the King had shuffled away, he marched over to Carlo and said with a hint of anger, 'Find that damnable Vidar, wherever he might be, and bring him here.' Then he swept out of the chamber in seething silence.

Soon after, the alarm bells began to sound in the tower above the King's palace, each toll a nail driven into the hearts of the people of Idriss.

'You can torture me all you want, but I will never tell.' After so long in his cell in the dark depths of the Palace of Justice, the filthy, wild-haired man shielded his eyes from the glare of the torchlight.

'Torture you? You tease me with possibilities. However, on this occasion I am fated to be disappointed, for you have another role to fulfil.' Flamboyant and urbane, Cheyne prodded the prisoner with his rapier until he stepped into the chamber. Cheyne was red-haired, with a close-clipped beard and moustache and carried himself with the air of an aesthete, though a dark shadow of damage and corruption lay just beneath the surface.

'Where is this?' the prisoner said as he suspiciously looked around the luxurious interior. Though the furnishings were elegant and expensive and far beyond the dreams of most residents of Idriss, the quantity and haphazard placement made the chamber resemble a cave of spoils.

'The quarters I share with my brave comrades-in-arms.' Cheyne sniffed. 'And quite befitting our status in the Crimson Hunt.'

'Who do we have here, Cheyne?'

The prisoner jumped at the growling voice emanating from the shadows in one corner of the chamber. A figure leaped by him, lithe and low like a wolf, muscles hardened by a childhood in the desolate northern mountains, the wild hair and beard adding to the bestial appearance; two fingers were missing from his left hand. A deep joy appeared to be permanently on the brink of bursting out of him.

'A traitor, or somesuch.' Cheyne sighed and waved the question away with a flourish. 'The gaolers found him in the depths of that foul place.'

The prisoner eyed them. 'I will never tell. I am loyal to my city.'

'Yes, yes,' Cheyne said dismissively. 'Asgrim, will you show him through? I fear I cannot stomach the smell any longer.' With mounting horror, Cheyne noticed a black smudge on his shirtsleeve. 'Damn him. That will never come out. Do you know how much this garment cost me on Cantolet Street?'

'Cheyne, you would sell your mother for a pair of Feegrum boots or a silk kerchief.' Asgrim swept his arm to invite the prisoner towards a door at the rear of the chamber.

The prisoner hesitated. 'What is this trickery?'

'Trickery?' Asgrim said with mock affront. 'We invite you into our home, and you accuse us of deception?'

Cheyne sighed. 'If you attempt to escape through the window in the adjoining room, we shall be forced to come after you. Of course, the chance of locating you among the swarming populace of this great city is slim, to say the least. But be warned, nonetheless.'

The prisoner's eyes gleamed. Still unsure, he shuffled towards the door, and with a backward glance stepped through it.

It took a second for his eyes to adjust to the gloom. Only a thin sliver of light leaked through the heavy covering at the window, but he saw it was a bedroom. In the centre stood a four-poster bed, its curtains drawn tightly. As he padded eagerly towards the window, a low moan rolled out from the bed. The prisoner hesitated, but his curiosity got the better of him and he gingerly pulled back one of the curtains to see what was within.

On the bed lay a man so frail he must have been only a breath away from death. His parchment skin was dry, and his bones showed through here and there like bruises. Though barely thirty, whatever illness afflicted him made him look twice his age. His long, black hair hung lankly on the pillow and his eyelids flickered half-shut.

As the prisoner made to turn away, he noticed a faint glimmer. Curious, he gradually eased back the sick man's shirt to reveal an amber jewel as large as a child's fist embedded in his chest. Deep within it, the faintest flame danced, and seemed to flicker eagerly as the prisoner's hand hovered over it.

Movement on the edge of his vision distracted him. In the shaft of light breaking through the gap at the window, twists of mist appeared and faded, becoming more substantial with each passing second. He was mesmerised by the movement, until suddenly the mist billowed out into the room, separating to form shapes.

Shrieking loudly, spectral figures materialised, bathed in a pearly lustre, five, more, swirling like rags blown in a gale. 'Kill him!' they cried. 'Kill him now, while he is weak!'

Terrified, the prisoner scrambled back, half on to the bed, as the fearful apparitions loomed around, tearing at their hair and faces in their anguish.

'Strike now!' the ghosts cried. 'Save us from our misery! Save yourself!'

Rooted, the prisoner returned his attention to the bed. The sick man's eyes were now open and what the prisoner saw in their dark depths chilled him. A slight smile, hard, triumphant. The knife lanced up in a blur from where it had been hidden beneath the covers. Arterial spray gushed across the white sheets as the prisoner made a futile grab for his neck.

On the bed, the man arched his spine with a shimmer of pleasure. Head thrown back, a faint sigh escaped his dry lips. The spectres wailed and moaned, and slowly faded back into the shaft of light; too late.

Vitality flooded the bedridden man's frame as quickly as it drained from the prisoner. His skin grew taut across strong muscles and bloomed with life. His breathing became deep, the dark hair lustrous. Retrieving his sword from beneath the covers, the man swung himself from the bed and landed athletically on the balls of his feet. 'All praise Idriss, the Strong, the Great,' he said wryly, as the prisoner fell backwards on to the floor. 'I am Vidar, Ghost Warrior, Lord of Silence, Stealth, and Vengeance, and I thank you for your gift.'

The prisoner tried to speak, but no words would come.

'Hush now,' Vidar said. 'Enjoy this moment of repose. You are about to join the ranks of my ghosts, and from now on there will be no rest.'

As the prisoner gasped his last, Asgrim bounded in. '*Lord of Silence, Stealth, and Vengeance,*' he mocked. 'I only gifted you the name of one of my gods as a joke. I did not expect you to try to live up to it.'

'It's a nice fit. I'm comfortable with it. Cheyne…?'

'Is attempting to scrub a speck of dirt off his fine shirt. Best not to talk to him for a while. His mood is less than perfect.'

Eyes closed, Vidar enjoyed the rush of vitality, and then said, 'The alarm bells?'

'Ah, yes. Death and terror have been let
loose across our fair city. A crisis looms. Your
time has come, Vidar. You are needed.'

WITH THE ALARM bells still tolling, Cheyne
and Asgrim waited with the clutch of grim-
faced guards at the entrance to the Store of the
Ages, swapping stories and rumours by the
light of a single lantern, while Vidar made his
way quickly through the still, echoing corridors to the gallery on the fifth floor. The
chamber was alive with whispers. In the flickering light of a score of torches, a huddle of
people had gathered. Vidar could just make
out the body.

A woman wearing the forest-green cloak of
the Order of Inquisitors broke away from the
crowd to join him. Though she still wore her
hood, Vidar could tell it was Rhiannon; she
carried herself with the confident grace of an
athlete. Her tongue could be sharp, and when
she directed her humour at him her eyes always
sparkled defiantly, urging him to retaliate.

Her eyes unsettled, her mouth fixed with
unease, she pulled back the hood to reveal her
strong, dark features and the blue tattoo of the
Order on her forehead, the upright staff of justice criss-crossed by five shorter lines
representing truth, strength, honour, justice,
and equality.

'It's Mellias?' he asked. 'The guards downstairs said that was the rumour.'

'Who would kill him?' she replied, forcefully but quietly to avoid being overheard.

'Who *could* kill him? I've seen Mellias single-handedly down four men.'

'Examine the body. It has been laid out in ritual form.'

'Then it's murder?' Like the first tremors of an earthquake, he could already feel the repercussions rippling out across the city.

'Worse than that.' A shudder ran through her. 'There is something…' She struggled to find a word that would do justice to her thoughts. 'Inhuman about this killing. It speaks to me of a cold intellect, one that sees us not as people, but as cattle. Something new is loose in Idriss.'

Vidar was surprised at what he saw in Rhiannon's face. She was hard, and had dealt with some of the worst crimes in the city. 'You're saying a lone attacker killed Mellias?'

'It appears that way.'

He searched the faces of the guards and the King's advisors who hung over the body as if it was some strange artefact from the Store's vaults that they could not comprehend. Emotions churned there – revulsion, disbelief, worry, but most of all fear.

'The people will find it hard to recover from this blow,' Rhiannon said. 'Mellias was a symbol of their security. Mellias was Idriss. Now none of us are safe.' She glanced back at the blood-spattered leg protruding from the crowd. 'I thought he would never die.'

'You and he were–'

She shook her head. 'Not Mellias. But I feel I knew him as if he were a member of my family. We all did. We loved him because he gave everything for Idriss, for us. And when the manner of his passing reaches the inns and the market–'

'Someone has to fill that void quickly. The way we live our lives, the people need someone to believe in.'

'You are the only option.'

He laughed.

'Surely this is not a lack of self-belief?' she said sharply. 'You certainly have had no issues in that regard before. Or do you feel it would interfere with your ability to line your pockets? Certainly it will encourage the women of Idriss to see you in a more favourable light, and that can only please you greatly.'

'You've been listening to all the wrong people.'

Somebody in the small crowd began to sob loudly. Rhiannon leaned in so close that Vidar could smell the scent of her hair. 'There is more here than a death, however great and devastating that death may be. I fear this is a sign of something terrible ahead.' She paused. 'And if you are Mellias's replacement, I fear for you.' Before he could ask her what she meant, she said, 'I must give my initial findings to my superior. Meet me later, on the wall at the Deeping Gate.'

Vidar watched her until she had left the room, then joined the small crowd around Mellias's body. Fearful eyes turned towards him before the group parted to give him access. The whispered conversation stopped as they waited uneasily for his reaction.

The placement of the body, legs together, arms out and up, had a ritual aspect to it, as Rhiannon had suggested. Everything about the killing had been arranged to send a message, though what it was Vidar did not know. Mellias's golden hair lay about his head like a mane, and even in death his face still held the nobility that had drawn many to him. But the atrocities that had been inflicted on the corpse diminished him. His sword was still sheathed. He hadn't even been allowed to fight. His own knife lay near his body.

Vidar was surprised at a sudden spurt of raw emotion. He had always thought himself removed from the adoration Mellias received, but the White Warrior deserved more than a dishonourable death, broken and abused so that he appeared a lesser person, where the manner of the death meant more than the person who had died.

'Vidar. Come to me.' It was Lud, resting on the arms of his assistants.

'Your highness, I'm sorry,' Vidar said. 'The White Warrior was like a son to you. He was a hero to all of Idriss. He won't be forgotten.'

'He was a son to us all, the first and the last. And I know he was a good friend and mentor to you, Vidar the New, and your band will not be the same without him. This is a terrible loss for us all.'

'We'll still defend Idriss.'

'Of course you will, for your name carries the weight of fear in a way that the White Warrior's never did.' Lud searched Vidar's face. 'I know this saddens you, but it is your greatest strength, and your curse. And that is why you must now lead the Crimson Hunt in Mellias's place.'

Vidar bowed his head. 'That's an honour. For someone who is new–'

'You have proven yourself a thousand times. You have earned the trust of all Idriss.' He gave a hacking cough, then smiled. 'One day, perhaps, you will remember the generations who came before you and your place in Idriss will be secure.'

'Perhaps.' Vidar kept his voice clean of any emotion.

Lud eyed Mellias's body. 'To see such a crime committed within the walls of Idriss, where we should be safe and secure from the terrors of this world...' He turned to Vidar with an intensity that belied his great age. 'The people of Idriss need you, Vidar. If they are to sleep peacefully in their beds, they must feel sheltered from the terrors beyond the walls. They must have complete trust in their guardians. And your name already carries the greatest respect. We must move quickly to prevent the spread of the unease that will automatically arise from this terrible tragedy. The people must not begin to doubt our ability to protect them.'

Vidar hesitated before saying, 'Mellias knew his murderer.'

'How do you know this?'

'His sword is sheathed.'

The King nodded. 'He was taken by surprise.'

'Why would the White Warrior be here, in the Store of the Ages? I'd be surprised if he'd ever crossed the threshold before. He was meeting someone.'

The King teetered and almost fell. The assistants gripped his arms tightly. 'I am sorry. I am very tired, and this business has struck to the heart of me. I must rest.'

'The Order of Inquisitors has already opened an investigation,' Vidar said. 'I'll mobilise the Crimson Hunt. Between us, we'll find the killer.'

With a feeble gait, the King was helped out of the gallery, each step a sign of an impending destabilising sea change for Idriss. The King's bloodline had always ruled the City of Lights, but he had no heirs and he was clearly in his last days. Idriss's survival was built on stability. Vidar was uneasy about what lay ahead.

As he returned to Mellias's body, his very presence drove back the worried onlookers. He could understand their fear, but it angered him nonetheless, and his mood was darkened further by the whispering of the ghosts in the back of his head. Most of the time they were silent, but in moments of stress, their voices rose up in an insane chatter, every single one that he had killed to stay alive since he had wandered blankly into Idriss from the unending forest. Hundreds of them. They bided their time, waiting to manifest, to wrong-foot him into disaster or encourage his enemies to kill him. They wanted him dead, and who could blame them? There would be no rest for them until he was gone, and perhaps not even then.

He had seen many corpses, but Mellias's unsettled him on some level that he couldn't comprehend. The empty, gaping eye sockets.

The unnatural placement of the body. The symbol carved into the chest. Pulling up his left shirtsleeve, he examined the blue tattoo on his forearm. He couldn't remember getting it, but had always thought it was supposed to represent some runic charm. Yet it also resembled the position of Mellias's corpse.

What did it mean? Why did it feel so important that he knew?

As VIDAR EXITED the Store of the Ages, Cheyne was engaged in flirtatious conversation with two of the many prostitutes who plied their trade on the Mountain of the Heart. Asgrim prowled along the marble balustrade above the public gardens, his eyes glinting golden in the moonlight. They both joined Vidar instantly.

'The rumours are true?' Asgrim snarled.

'Mellias is dead. Murdered.'

They fell silent for a long moment, until Asgrim said, 'He was a good leader. He always treated me fairly.'

'Ah, well.' Cheyne sighed. 'It could have been worse.'

'How?' Vidar asked.

'It could have been me.'

When Vidar eyed him coldly, Cheyne made a contrite gesture that couldn't have been more insincere.

'So we have a vacancy at the head of the Crimson Hunt,' Asgrim noted.

'The King's asked me to take his place,' Vidar said. He tried to hide the surprise he still felt, and it was clear too in Cheyne and Asgrim's faces. He narrowed his eyes at them, and they laughed and congratulated him with claps on the shoulder.

'Fame,' Asgrim mused.

'Riches,' Cheyne agreed. 'And women, by association, of course. We will remain your faithful comrades as you wander the city. Why, this could work out very nicely indeed.'

'We have a job to do,' Vidar cautioned.

'Yes, justice for Mellias... and Idriss,' Asgrim said. 'Certainly. Top of the list.'

'As long as the people are ready for someone who scares them more than the terrors roaming the forest just beyond the walls.' Cheyne shrugged. 'Just saying.'

'The Inquisitors have already begun their enquiry into Mellias's death,' Vidar said.

'Is the lovely Rhiannon heading that enquiry?' Cheyne asked. 'I presume you would quite enjoy the opportunity to work with her, Vidar.'

Asgrim chuckled. 'We have seen how you look at her.' He sang a few mocking lines of a salty love song from his northern homeland.

'Nothing's going to happen,' Vidar said bluntly.

'Oh, why not?' Cheyne asked.

'Because anyone who spends time around me is probably only a few steps away from feeding the Vampire Jewel.'

Cheyne and Asgrim were uneasily silent for a moment, before the northlander said, 'You would kill your friends and loved ones?'

'I would,' Cheyne said. 'I'd kill anyone, if the need was great. Well, perhaps even if it was not so great—'

'I'm not about to take the risk,' Vidar replied. 'When you're close to death and survival takes over, who knows how any of us would react?'

'*I* know,' Cheyne continued blithely. 'Death for those around me. No doubt about that.'

'So you condemn yourself to a lifetime of loneliness?' Asgrim pressed.

Vidar didn't respond.

'It seems fortuitous that your curse and your current job are a perfect fit, then. If you were doing any other work the Inquisitors would be hunting *you* down.'

'I try to make the best of the hand fate has dealt me,' Vidar said. 'Now, to work. The walls must remain guarded in case this is a precursor to an attack, but bring together whatever men we can spare. I want the Crimson Hunt on the streets within an hour. Once the news of Mellias's death breaks, the people are going to need reassurance that we're doing something. If the Order of Inquisitors identifies a suspect, we have to be prepared to act.'

'You think this is the first act of an invasion, then?' Asgrim asked.

'Mellias is dead,' Vidar replied bluntly. 'Who knows anything any more?'

As VIDAR STEPPED back into the Store of the Ages, his way was briefly barred by a flow of onlookers and mourners shepherded out by three members of the Inquisitorial team. Through the small crowd, Vidar caught sight of Administrator Ashur and his entourage leaving quickly by one of the side entrances. As he exited, Ashur glanced back, his gaze briefly locking on Vidar, but whatever lay behind his eyes was unreadable.

No love was lost between them, but then Ashur was neither liked nor respected by anyone who knew him. The King's nephew, he had been hideously scarred as a teen by whatever lurked in the forest beyond the walls, trying to prove his bravado to his friends by advancing twenty paces into the trees. He had barely escaped with his life, and hovered on the brink of death for weeks. The attack damaged him just as much inwardly; he became cold and withdrawn, revealing no kindness, no compassion, no sign of anything remotely human. Instead, he devoted his life to the King, carrying out the dull daily tasks of the affairs of Idriss in the hope that his uncle would see fit to choose him as an heir in the absence of any children of his own. But it appeared Lud had long since made up his mind that Ashur could never win the support of the people, and so Ashur became more sour, more driven.

In the gallery, the Inquisitors quietly questioned the Store's Keepers, and searched for blood trails and discarded weapons. One thing struck Vidar instantly: Mellias's body was missing. He knew the Inquisitors should be examining it in situ for any evidence of the White Warrior's assassin. Chief Inquisitor Serena appeared puzzled too. A hard-faced woman with long, silver hair, she said, 'It was removed for funerary preparation.'

'On whose orders?'

'Administrator Ashur's.' A flicker in her eyes betrayed her suspicions.

'I'll talk to him,' Vidar said. 'The body will be of some use to you?'

'If we can discern the weapon from the cuts, we may be able to divine the assassin. Butcher's knife, hunting knife, scythe, or one of the specialist tools used by the guilds, perhaps.'

Noticing a curious exchange between one of the Keepers and an Inquisitor, Vidar went over. The Keeper, Xiang Chai-Shekh, frantically searched a row of dusty shelves packed with historical artefacts and small works of art.

'What's wrong?' Vidar asked.

'One of the artefacts is missing.' Xiang checked a large codex he clutched tightly in his arms. 'A small, carved block of unknown material.'

The Inquisitor exchanged a dismissive look with Vidar. 'Is this important?' she asked.

'You're saying it was stolen during the murder?' Vidar pressed.

'It was here during the last accounting period. I correlated it myself.'

'So it could have been stolen before tonight.'

Xiang sighed theatrically. 'No one comes here. No one has any interest in the wonders we preserve. Only the Keepers walk these halls and we know and love the artefacts. We would have no reason to steal one.'

'Why would anyone want to steal a worthless piece of ancient waste?' the Inquisitor said dismissively. 'No one would kill for such a thing.'

Xiang glared at her. 'Everything has a value, if only one can see it.'

The words troubled Vidar on some level he didn't quite understand. Moving to the window, he looked out over Idriss, the lights blazing for miles in all directions until they met the walls and the sea of darkness beyond. Somewhere in those claustrophobic, ancient streets, hidden among the teeming population, lurked a killer with the instincts of a monster, who could slaughter the greatest warrior the city had ever known. The death alone was troubling enough, but the mutilation and the ritual placement of the body hinted at some secret pattern that was still unfolding.

Below, he could see the Crimson Hunt fanning out across the city, watched fearfully by the gathering crowds woken by the constant tolling of the alarm bells. Vidar understood the anxious thought rattling through all their heads. Nothing would ever be right again. Mellias was dead.

2

IDRISS

On the cobbled streets, a tumult had erupted. Vidar pushed through the crowds of anxious residents searching for answers to where knots of the Crimson Hunt searched doorways, questioned passers-by, and delved into the depths of the darkest alleys. They moved with stone-faced efficiency, answering no questions, demanding only answers, but that only added to the tide of apprehension.

In the mêlée, Asgrim caught up with Vidar, shouting to be heard above the clamour of the crowd; some people had taken to wailing and crying that the city was under attack, or that a new plague had been identified.

'We have had reports of a man covered in blood running through the streets of Ten Bells,' Asgrim said. 'It could be nothing – the fights up there are regularly brutal – but I have despatched a unit to investigate.'

'Good. No witnesses around here?'

Asgrim shook his head. 'We will do what we can, but the culprit could be anywhere by now.'

'Then let's hope the Inquisitors can turn up something we can use.' The Hunt did not have enough warm bodies to defend the walls and quickly and efficiently search a city the size of Idriss. A clever killer would already have disappeared into one of the slums in Greatstock, Vidar knew, or faded into the maze of alleys around the Rezshinnia. 'I have a meeting that may bring us more information. In the meantime, keep the pressure on. I'll take a report at dawn.'

Nodding, Asgrim headed back into the dense crowd, and Vidar pushed his way through towards the quiet streets leading to the Deeping Gate, relieved that he would at least find somewhere quiet enough to order his thoughts.

FROM THE EASTERN wall, near the Deeping Gate, the dark sea of trees stretched to the horizon where the faintest glimmer of dawn warmed the sky. Vidar searched the treetops intently, and every now and then was rewarded with a glimpse of movement, a swaying of branches, a sudden flight of birds.

Stories of what lurked in the depths of the forest were many and varied and told on a daily basis, in the inns and market, to frighten children, by traders desperate for a route through the trees, by academics and military planners trying to make sense of the threat. Some claimed grotesque, enormous beasts roamed the woods. Others said they had seen figures, golden-skinned and beautiful, but that they were an illusion to lure the unwary to their death.

Whatever lay within the forest had shaped Idriss as much as the people who lived within the city walls. The ever-present threat pressing hard against the protective stone shield was like a shadow on the heart, lying at the back of every thought of tomorrow, of every action taken, of every new birth. Idriss was strong, and its people proud and honourable and fierce fighters, but the city survived only as long as the walls stood, and everyone understood that fragility.

'It will be a beautiful day. And a terrible day. Everything has changed.' Rhiannon had come up silently behind Vidar. Watching the reddening sky, she pulled her cloak tightly around her against the pre-dawn chill. Vidar thought how beautiful she looked, with her eyes sleepily half-closed and her face raised to the coming light.

'What's the news from the Order?'

'I have been made Chief Inquisitor in the Mellias enquiry.'

'Congratulations.'

'Perhaps.'

Vidar tried to understand her hesitancy. As long as he had known her, she had never been fazed by any task. Indeed, her drive and competence had seen her advance rapidly through the ranks of the Order, so that she was constantly spoken of as a future leader.

'A lot of people would say that was a great honour.'

'It is. And a great responsibility. This enquiry is more important than any other the Order has handled in recent memory. An enquiry that will affect Idriss in so many different ways. So why give it to me?'

'Your winning personality?'

'At least you are not encumbered in that regard.'

'Seems like an opportunity to me. Finding the murderer of Idriss's greatest hero should buy you a good future. Fame. Gold. Wine. Or whatever it is that excites you ascetic Inquisitors.'

'Ah, Vidar. Always focusing on that opportunity for personal advancement,' she said laconically.

He shrugged. 'What else is there?'

'Honour. Duty. A responsibility to a greater calling.'

'I've devoted my life to Idriss. There's room for a little comfort.'

'But what happens when you have to make a choice, Vidar? Will it be you, or will it be something higher? The gutter or the stars?' He didn't like the suspicion he saw in the flash of her eyes.

'I can see I'm not going to convince you with words.'

'So we will wait to observe the answer in your actions. And then we will judge what kind of a person you are.'

'I'm not that much of a mystery.'

Leaning on the wall, her thoughts turned back to her situation. 'There are more experienced Inquisitors, ones who would be eager to use this opportunity to advance their own standing. They are adept at the politics of the organisation, and so it would be valuable to them and they would manoeuvre to get the assignment. I do not care about the politics in the slightest and it is handed to me without a second thought.'

'You think there's some other agenda?'

She considered her response. 'Idriss is restless at the moment. Familiar patterns of behaviour have been subtly altering. I think it is wise to pay close attention to every decision until you are sure of the motivations.'

'You're a very suspicious woman.'

'I have a right to be. The city is ruled by men. Come, walk with me.'

She set off south along the broad, flagged walkway. Idriss sprawled away from them, misty in the distance where the fields and farmsteads nestled on the city's northern and western fringes. As dawn lit the rooftops, smoke drifted up from the first fires of the day as the early-rising workers prepared their breakfasts. With the thick, towering walls defining the city for all time, space was at a premium and the houses were cluttered against each other in jumbled, incomprehensible street patterns that only the locals knew. In Greatstock, the most crowded, and poorest, quarter, new storeys were added at an alarming rate, some of them regularly crashing to the ground due to the inadequacy of the materials and the haphazard construction techniques.

In the centre, the grand, old buildings provided a sharp counterpoint. Set among tree lined avenues and sun-drenched courts where the educated and well bred met to talk of the great issues of the day, they rose up in proud testament to the long glory of Idriss. Intricate carvings and breathtaking works of art covered the exterior of the palace and the law courts, and the Temple of the Shepherd with its gleaming white dome spoke of quiet reflection.

A snaking silver river bisected Idriss and curled around two islands where the most ancient buildings lay, including the tower of the sorcerer Greer an' Lokh. The flashes of light and foul smells that occasionally issued from the top of the tower added to the fearsome reputation of its sole inhabitant, but Greer an' Lokh was mad and mostly left alone until times of need.

'Do you ever wonder who built this city?' he asked.

'There is no point. The beginnings of Idriss were lost long ago. It is said that when the foundations were established for the new homes in the Ironrack Quarter, the builders drove through twenty levels of development and still found no end to it. You know how the song goes – *ancient Idriss, beautiful Idriss, strong Idriss, always and for ever.*'

'We know barely anything about the place we live in. Who built the walls. Who founded the city. All the struggles that have shaped it over the years.'

'Life is about surviving in the here and now, Vidar. But there are stories out there, if you want to waste your time sifting through them. It will not make tomorrow any easier.'

How could he explain to her that knowing those things would make his own days easier?

The same sense of dissolution didn't trouble her – she could count her own family back through two hundred generations. Instead, he slowly surveyed the mad, vibrant, passionate city, filled with many different cultures, all influencing each other, making Idriss greater than the sum of its parts.

Rhiannon noticed his heartfelt gaze. 'Idriss has become a part of you in the last three years, as it becomes a part of all of us.'

'I owe Idriss everything. When I staggered out of the forest, my memory gone, the Vampire Jewel sucking the last of the life out of me, it would have been easy to keep the gates shut. But Idriss took me in and gave me a place–'

'And now here you are, one of the greatest heroes in the city,' she said sardonically. 'Idriss cares for all its people. We stand together, or die alone – that is the saying, is it not?' She glanced briefly at the trees, but returned her gaze quickly to the lights that still burned brightly in the streets. 'Individuals cannot survive in this harsh world. We find strength in each other, and by coming together are stronger still.'

'That's going to be put to the test. Mellias's death will shake a lot of people.'

'Somebody has to take his place in the hearts of the people. Will it be you?'

Unable to read if she was being sarcastic, Vidar opened his shirt to reveal the amber jewel. It flared in the dawn light. 'With this? Not a chance. Everyone in Idriss knows it takes death to keep me alive. However much they give praise for my help in keeping Idriss safe and secure, they secretly fear they could be the next meal that gives me another day of life.'

'You are a man of many contradictions,' Rhiannon said acidly. She reached out towards the jewel then withdrew her fingers sharply when it glowed in anticipation.

'See. Even you're scared.'

'The only thing that scares me about you is your easy morals.' She examined the jewel curiously. 'Where did it come from?'

'No idea. Maybe I was born with it. Greer an' Lokh is convinced it's magic–'

'Of course it is. What else could it be?'

'He's been doing all kinds of rituals up in his tower, but even he hasn't learned any more. All I know is, it gives me life and strength from another person's life force, and when that force is used up, it starts to leach off my own. I grow weaker, until I can't resist any more...' The words caught in his throat.

'Then you should be thankful that the King, and Idriss, still have enemies that need punishing.'

'So far. But what happens when they're used up? Do I turn on the people out there? Do I turn on my friends, the people close to me?' He paused. 'A lover? Do I have a right to live while others die?'

'How long,' she asked, 'before the jewel demands another life?'

'There aren't any rules I can see. Sometimes it's weeks, sometimes months. And sometimes it's so hungry I can't keep it fed. When the raiding party from Vost made their way through the forest to storm the gates, the jewel burned so brightly I thought it was going to set me on fire. In that heat, each life only lasted minutes.'

'Your curse is Idriss's boon.' A hint of compassion softened her voice. 'A warrior fuelled by death itself. Many in your trade would relish a reputation like that.'

'Mellias had a reputation too. A good one, not like mine. That didn't help him either.' Vidar studied the sprawl of streets, then shook his head at the scale of the task facing them. 'You said in the Store of the Ages that something new has come to Idriss.'

'No one here would have killed Mellias in that manner. And...' She hesitated for a moment, then cast a quick, unsettled glance towards the forest. 'Those injuries. I have seen atrocities in this city, but the element of ritual, and the type and extent of the injuries...' She shook her head. 'I find it hard to believe a human could have done that.'

Vidar laughed. 'Devils and demons and monsters? You've been spending time in the Greatstock inns.'

Her cheeks coloured, and she looked away across the city.

'Idriss has a lot of enemies. Cities across Gardia that want some of our scarce resources. More likely they've sent an agent here to destabilise us before an attack.'

Rhiannon snorted. 'How many could get an invading force through the forest? The ones that have tried were decimated by the time they arrived.'

Vidar shrugged. 'It would help if we knew what cities are out there. How many enemies. How powerful they are. It would help if we knew anything about the land beyond the walls that didn't rely on half-told stories and gossip and rumour. If we only had a map–'

'How many times have you heard that in this city? If only. There will never be a map. The forest is too dangerous to explore. Anyone who survives it does so by good fortune, and nothing else.'

'A map would change the world.' He looked into the forest and thought of freedom.

'We all need maps. Four in total to know who we really are. We have to understand where we stand in the land from which we come. We need to comprehend our place in history, our heritage. We need to know the map of our life so we can see how we have been shaped. And we need a map of our heart. Only then are we whole.'

'You're very perceptive,' he said.

'I am an Inquisitor. If I was not perceptive, I would not be good at my job.' She came to a halt and looked across Idriss. He followed her gaze to the Temple of the Shepherd, its white marble reflecting the hundreds of torches that surrounded it so it resembled a sun in the very heart of the city.

'Ready to pray for some easy answers?' he asked wryly.

'You are not a believer.'

'Are you?'

'I would like to be.'

'That's not quite the same thing, is it? I don't believe in anything. There must be at least five hundred gods worshipped in Idriss. They all promise salvation from the hardship of this life. They all have their sacred texts and their rules and regulations, and their stories of the manifestations of their gods' powers. And yet the followers of each god believe only their god is the true one. It seems to me more likely that none of them are true.'

'You may be correct. But sometimes the most important thing is not that the god exists, but that the worshippers believe it to be so.'

'What are you saying?'

'A painting hangs in the Temple of the Shepherd – *The Supplicant Praises the Power of the Visitant*. Have you seen it?'

'I'm always in the Temple poring over works of art when I get time off from the slaughtering.'

'A little quiet reflection may help with your substandard education.' Focusing on the temple's dome, she weighed up whether she should continue. 'The supplicant in the painting lies at the feet of the Shepherd in exactly the same way that Mellias's body was laid out before the statue of the Shepherd in the Store of the Ages.'

'You're saying a follower of the Shepherd murdered Mellias?'

Rhiannon didn't reply.

'The great hero, idolised by all, murdered by the followers of one sect,' he said, thinking aloud. 'If that were true it could tear Idriss apart.'

'You see why I chose to tell you in this lonely place, where we would not be overheard.'

'So that was the reason.'

'Would there be another?'

'Why are you telling me? You're the Inquisitor. I just kill people for a living.'

She looked deep into his eyes. 'The connections and complexities, the potential threat, are too great for the Inquisitors. I spoke honestly when I said Mellias needed to be replaced.'

'And I spoke honestly when I said it couldn't be me.'

'If I am right, only the people's hero can prevent this from turning into a catastrophe for Idriss.'

'I'm no hero.'

'Apparently not. But Idriss still needs you.'

She held his gaze for a moment and then moved quickly back along the wall to the Deeping Gate.

Before Vidar could follow, there was a disturbance along the wall at his back. A guard had grabbed a youth in his late teens who had a rope around his chest, the other end fastened to an iron spike embedded in the wall. In a rage, the youth tried to throw the guard off.

'Let me go!' he shouted.

'What's going on?' Vidar demanded.

'This little idiot is trying to take his own life,' the guard growled.

'I am not!' the youth said. 'It is this city that is killing me! The streets always the same, narrow and clogged, people pressing on every side all the time! This is not life. It is a prison!'

'That's one way of looking at it,' Vidar said. 'Not many would agree, admittedly. But if you're thinking of going out there, you really are giving up on everything.'

The youth glowered at him.

'Take him back to the street,' Vidar said to the guard. 'And if he comes up here again, send him to the cells for his own good.'

Before the guard could respond, the youth shoved him roughly in the chest and leaped over the wall. Vidar threw himself after the youth, but missed him by a hair's-breadth. The youth slid down the slight incline until the rope brought him to a sudden halt, and then, gasping, he released the knot and fell the final few feet. Picking himself up, he zigzagged rapidly into the night.

The guard shook his head. 'Lunatic! He has killed himself.' He cast an uncomfortable glance towards Vidar. 'Do you want me to get some men together–?'

'It's too late,' Vidar said. 'At this time of night we'd only be sending them to their deaths too.'

Nodding, the guard carried on with his patrol. Vidar continued to watch the forest, listening intently, but there was nothing to hear.

* * *

EVERY RESIDENT OF Idriss appeared to be out on the streets, demanding answers, whispering the stories and rumours that Vidar knew would run out of control in the workplaces throughout the day. They watched uneasily as the Crimson Hunt continued to search the winding streets and the boarding houses, the cellars and the isolated warehouses. Vidar could feel the tension in the air increasing by the moment.

By the river, Asgrim and two Huntsmen hauled up a blood-covered man in his early twenties, his eyes wide and fearful. His appearance frightened the crowd, who began to hurl missiles until Vidar despatched a unit of Huntsmen to calm them.

'The one from Ten Bells?' he asked. He could smell the wine on him.

'We found him sleeping off his night of excess in a storm drain.' Dismissively, Asgrim motioned to the blood-soaked clothes. 'In his cups, he fell into one of the sluice-pits at the abattoir.'

'Question him anyway, just to be sure.'

As the Huntsmen dragged the man away, Asgrim said, 'I fear this will be a long day with little result. We will continue to search, but the trail grows colder by the minute.'

Vidar glanced towards the tower rising up from one of the islands in the river. 'Let's see if the sorcerer can magic up our suspect.'

* * *

GREER AN' LOKH'S tower smelled of sweet incense, made more sickening by the underlying stink of spoiled meat rising up from the charnel house below. Only one thing made it bearable for Vidar: the views over Idriss from the floor-to-ceiling windows all around the room. Dazzling silver light reflected off the slow-moving river passing just by the tower's base. With the windows open, he could inhale the perfume from the merchants' quarter, and the aromas of the spicy stews of the sellers along the river boulevard, and the subtle fragrance of slowly warming stone and vegetation as the heat of the day began to rise.

The room was filled with star charts and ritual drawings, parchments and artefacts of obsidian, amber, jade, glass, gold, and silver, many others carved from the bone that came from Greer an' Lokh's working material. Symbols drawn in blood, now brown and congealed, covered the flags, and from the low ceiling hung scores of intricate displays constructed from tinier bones; mingled among them were the skulls and skeletons of small animals and birds.

Greer an' Lokh was a skeleton covered with skin, greasy black hair flying all around his face. Vidar had never seen him eat, and tried not to consider what passed his lips when he did. Necklaces and bracelets of small bones clattered continually, and he wore only a loin-cloth made from skin of indecipherable origin. He danced around the room as if the floor was covered with hot coals, plucking objects from table, desk, and shelf, examining them briefly and then flinging them to one side, constantly muttering and whimpering and whooping. He was completely and utterly mad, as many of his kind must be, Vidar believed. It was impossible to do the work he did without a terrible toll being exacted on the mind.

The only person in Idriss to have slaughtered more than Vidar, Greer an' Lokh lived with final pleadings and desperate sobs constantly in his ears, with screams and spurts and bubbling, with the soft whisper of torn meat and the sound of sawing, with garbled lists of the loved ones who would miss and be missed, with prayers to gods, cut off mid-sentence, with blown pupils, vacated bowels and bladders, rattling breaths and expiring whispers, and the quiet spectacle of the light slowly dying in a pair of bright eyes.

'Yes, yes, yes, Mellias is dead,' he whined. 'So what?'

'You didn't see it in your rituals?'

'Why should I? I am not the power that binds all things together. I do not hear and see and smell and touch and taste all. I look for things, as you look through that window, and sometimes I see them, and in this case I was looking towards Idriss's defences. Are you finished now?'

Greer an' Lokh had difficulty remaining around people for too long. It was always as if he saw them, or their state, as an aberration, and his eyes would watch for telltale signs of life coming to an end. When someone caught their breath, or when they stood still to think, he would clasp his hands and wait in anticipation. It did not endear him to any member of the court; that and the smell that constantly accompanied him.

'How does your magic work?' Vidar asked.

Greer an' Lokh sighed. 'Systems, numbers, patterns, that is all this universe is. Learn to see them and you see everything. Control them and you control everything.'

'And how do you control—'

'The life essence! The vital energy! Once released, it has the power of a furnace. But so quickly it goes! So quickly. You have to be fast.'

In the corner, on a hook on a chain, hung the remnants of one of Greer an' Lokh's previous incantations. When he entered, Vidar had tried not to look at it too closely – it was hard to tell it was even a body – but as they spoke the eyes flickered open briefly, ranged with welcome insanity, and clamped shut again.

'Where did that one come from?' Vidar nodded towards the poor wretch.

'Which one?' Greer an' Lokh peered at the hanging bulk, but appeared not to see anything. Vidar decided not to pursue the matter.

'I need to find whoever killed Mellias,' he continued. 'You can help?'

Greer an' Lokh danced, humming to himself.

'His death has the stink of religion about it,' Vidar said, 'but there seems to be some underlying pattern that I can't quite grasp.'

Greer an' Lokh perked up.

'I thought that might capture your interest,' Vidar said.

Greer an' Lokh danced closer with an unnervingly coquettish air. Vidar held his breath as the bitter smell swept over him. 'It is not just the patterns of Mellias's death that interest you.' One jagged, yellowing fingernail brushed the soft flesh beneath Vidar's chin. Greer an' Lokh closed his eyes and sniffed the air, with an orgasmic judder. 'Oh yes, oh yes. You think this might be a key to the greatest mystery of all. Or *your* greatest mystery. The one that troubles too many. Who are you? Why are you here?'

'Mellias's death could threaten the security of Idriss. That's my only interest.'

'You will have more soon.' Greer an' Lokh stared blankly at the ceiling.

'What do you mean?'

'The pattern is shifting. A power grows in the east, a terrible power.'

'An enemy? Tell me.'

The sorcerer waved him away. 'Too soon, too soon. It is just a glow in the mesh at the moment. The life-energy shifts and folds. But someone manipulates it, oh yes!'

Vidar sighed. 'Sometimes I wonder what the point of you is.'

'But there is a point in you, Lord of Stealth and Silence. A point of light. A point of power.' Snickering, Greer an' Lokh danced away a step. 'Show me,' he said.

'This isn't the time.'

'Show me, show me, if you want my help, show me!' Greer an' Lokh squealed.

With irritation, Vidar unbuttoned his shirt to reveal the amber jewel. He thought he heard it whisper as it met the light. The charge from his last victim was already beginning to expire.

The gleam reflected in Greer an' Lokh's eyes. 'Oh, yes,' he whispered. 'Here is the real key.'

'You've examined the jewel a hundred times,' Vidar said. 'If you haven't found any answers by now, you never will.'

'Not true.' Greer an' Lokh threw himself at a bookcase like a wild animal and tore through the contents of the shelves until he located a parchment wrapped around an ash spindle. 'For ten days, I searched through the depository in Effrey Street until I found this.' He ran his green-tinged tongue along the edge of the parchment, tasting the years. 'Some say this comes from the time of the wall-builders. I think, no. I think it is older still. Perhaps even from the days of the Shepherd.' He eyed Vidar slyly. 'You do not believe in the power of the Shepherd?'

'I believe in myself.'

'Good, good. We are all gods after all. The power burns within us, waiting to be released.'

'What do you know about the jewel?' The snap in Vidar's voice gave away too much of his emotion, and Greer an' Lokh offered a greasy smile in recognition.

'All we have in Idriss are stories. They are what we cling to in place of a history. No truths. No facts. Stories, and gossip and rumours, imaginings and dreams. A map might find a path through them, but in its absence we must feel blindly for the way. And one of those stories is of twenty great objects of power scattered across all Gardia. Whoever holds all those objects holds the fate of the world in his hands.'

Vidar glanced down at the softly pulsing jewel. 'This is one of those objects?'

'Who knows? Perhaps this is an imagining, or a dream. But I like to think that, perhaps, it is a truth. They are rare and beautiful and filled with riches, like jewels, like that jewel.'

'One of twenty objects of power? Why would I have something so valuable? How did I come across it? Is it sucking my memory, as it sucks lives?' *Eating me alive*, Vidar thought. It was something he always feared. While it consumed his life force when its energy was low, was it also secretly stripping away his essence in the background all the time, and his memory was just the first part of it? What would be next? His rational mind? His motor skills?

He caught Greer an' Lokh studying the thoughts playing across his face. 'Do you want to know who you are, Vidar? Do you want to find your place in this great mystery?'

'You know I do.' Greer an' Lokh's words released a desperate rush of longing that he thought he had suppressed ever since he had wandered into Idriss. It was destabilising, like the after-effects of strong wine, and he could have allowed himself to be lost to it if he had not caught an odd note in Greer an' Lokh's expression. 'You're not interested in the jewel for my sake. What do you want?'

'Whoever holds all those objects holds the fate of the world in his hands,' he repeated, making no attempt to hide his desire.

'If you can find a way to get it off me, you're welcome to it,' Vidar said. 'In the meantime, start looking into Mellias's death. Find those patterns. I want to know what it all means. And if something... someone... has come to Idriss, I need to know that before anyone else.'

Greer an' Lokh sighed. 'Oh, my work is never done.' He flexed his fingers and plucked a small silver sickle from the table before shimmying towards the hunk of flesh in the corner.

VIDAR WALKED FROM the tower into the cauldron of activity and emotion filling the streets and alleys of Idriss. Women wailed from open windows, and men muttered darkly in groups of two or three. Crowds gathered in the squares and along the merchant routes exchanging lies, half-truths, and imaginings, but no dreams, only the hint of potential nightmares.

The musicians along the Rolling Road were already trying to make their day's earnings with sentimental fiddle songs with titles such as 'Lament for the Fallen Hero who Made Idriss Great', or the simpler but no less saccharine 'Mellias is Dead'.

Asgrim prowled up and down the steps of the barracks along the broad, leafy Avenue of the Unknown Warrior where the Crimson Hunt was billeted, his constant movement a sign of his anxiety. Asgrim nearly always rested when they were not on duty, conserving himself for the lethal bursts of energy that had earned his reputation.

'Couldn't they have kept the death quiet for at least a day?' Vidar snapped. 'Everyone is going to be asking questions now, and we have no answers.'

'Ashur announced the Ceremony of Remembrance when dawn broke,' Asgrim replied. 'The body has already been prepared, ready for the pyre in the Fire Gardens.'

'It still needs to be examined,' Vidar said, frustrated. 'And for a hero of Mellias's stature, it should take a week to organise his Ceremony of Remembrance.'

'Ashur wants it over and done with quickly. A prolonged mourning period may make the people realise what they have lost.'

'Isn't that the point?' Vidar could see Ashur's logic; get the ceremony out of the way quickly and people could return to the struggle of their daily lives. There would be no time to dwell on the vacuum Mellias had left in Idriss's daydreams. But the circumstances of his death would never go away. They would live on, twisted and warped beyond all reasoning, in the stories told in the inns and markets, and who knew what imaginings would eventually emerge, what repercussions would spring from those imaginings. 'Has anyone begun to talk about how Mellias was killed?' he asked.

'Not yet. Ashur first announced that it was a sickness, but that only started rumours of the plague returning, and so he has now issued another decree stating that Mellias slipped and fell down a flight of stairs in the Store of the Ages, breaking his neck.'

'Those tales will come back to haunt him.'

'Who is the enemy here, Vidar?' Asgrim balanced perfectly on the stone balustrade that edged the steps. 'I like to see the pulse of blood in the throats of my foes. It unnerves me when they hide in the shadows.'

Inside the barracks, the atmosphere was solemn and still. The night shift was already asleep in the dorms and the day shift was out patrolling the walls and showing their presence on the streets, their crimson shirts a comforting sight to the population whenever they raised their heads from their daily tasks. Striding through the shafts of sunlight breaking through the high, arched windows, Vidar considered the stories that the building had once been a place of learning, but that could only have been long ago, when study held some value.

As they prepared to climb the stairs to their offices, Vidar was overcome by a wave of exhaustion and briefly clutched the stone banister to steady himself.

Asgrim caught his elbow. 'The jewel's energy is waning already?'

Vidar noted the underlying hint of suspicion that Asgrim might be the jewel's next victim. 'There's still plenty of time before I have to feed it,' he lied.

'You should rest. If there is to be an attack on Idriss, you will need all your strength to lead us.'

The exhaustion passed quickly, but he was still feeling the tremors and the chill when he reached the top of the stairs to find Ashur and three advisors talking in quiet, intense tones outside his room. The sunlight flooding from Vidar's room made the scar tissue of Ashur's face even whiter.

'Vidar,' he said, the facial muscles barely moving. 'The King informed me that he has made you the leader of the Crimson Hunt. Congratulations.'

His bloodless voice revealed no subtext. He could have been mocking Vidar contemptuously for all Vidar knew.

As if in recognition of the troubling aspects of his appearance, Ashur always surrounded himself with extremely handsome men; indeed, some had cruelly whispered that he chose his advisors more on the squareness of their jaws than the sharpness of their minds. But luckily for Ashur, one, LeStrange, had both wit and looks and was renowned throughout the court for providing the best counsel in Idriss. He nodded politely to Vidar and added, 'A fine choice. Idriss will be better for it. If anyone can replace Mellias in the hearts of the people, it is you, Vidar.'

'Do not fawn over him,' Ashur said. 'He saved your life. That is all you owe him. Perhaps one day soon he will see fit to take it back, when his hunger grows too great.'

Vidar knew there was little point in responding. Ashur had been suspicious about LeStrange's gratitude ever since Vidar had ridden into the forest in the middle of the night to save him from an attack on the remnants of a caravan that he and two guards had been trying to guide to Idriss, after Greer an' Lokh had discovered it in one of his rituals. It was carrying much needed food supplies from some city to the west at a time when the crops had been poor and Idriss was struggling to feed its own. The caravan had been part of some desperate expedition, and had been set upon by some force within the forest. LeStrange had been the first to rush to its rescue. He understood most clearly the needs of the starving people and weighed his own life against that.

Vidar had ridden out soon after to find the guards dead and the last few wagons of the caravan riding wildly for the gates, the drivers almost insane from what they had witnessed. LeStrange was left behind.

With the wild cries of the beasts drawing closer, Vidar had found him, weak and bloodied, and brought him back inside the city. LeStrange had been instrumental in Vidar's rise in the King's eyes ever since.

'You moved swiftly to prepare Mellias for the Ceremony of Remembrance,' Vidar said to Ashur. 'Some might say too swiftly. The Order hasn't finished its enquiry.'

'I discussed the matter at length with the King,' Ashur replied as he led the way into Vidar's room. 'I appreciate that the Order may have been able to find some evidence of Mellias's killer on his body, but it was outweighed by the possibility of unrest in the city. There are many shortages at the moment and tempers are already running high. We have not been found by a caravan for a long time. Nothing comes down the river save rotting branches and corpses.'

'They will come. The merchants' love of profit always wins out over their fear of the forest, whatever city they hail from,' LeStrange noted.

'Sadly, I do not share your optimism,' Ashur said. He pulled up a chair without being invited. 'I seek your counsel, Vidar. In your opinion, does Mellias's death presage an attack on Idriss?'

'It's possible.'

'You are, then, making plans to repel any assault.'

'Of course.'

'Do not let Mellias's murder distract you. I know he was a mentor to you–'

'To all of us in the Crimson Hunt.'

'Certainly. You have my word that the Order will not rest until they have found his murderer. A crime of this magnitude strikes a blow beyond the killing. It hits at the very heart of Idriss. We are strong. We are unbeaten, unbroken. Idriss can never be defeated. This attack is designed to shift the earth beneath our feet. It must not be allowed to do so. And for that very reason, Mellias's death has to be linked to a potential attack. We have an unseen enemy, Vidar, prepared to attack from without and within.'

Vidar said nothing.

'You do not agree?'

'I'm just a simple weapon of Idriss. Point me in the right direction, I kill our enemies, then return to the inn and my bed.'

Ashur sized up Vidar, and appeared to have his suspicions confirmed. 'I do hope we can have a healthy and close relationship now you have attained the heights of the leadership of the Crimson Hunt,' he said, rising. 'My door is always open to you, Vidar. A constant exchange of information will benefit both of us.'

'If I hear anything, you'll be the first to know.'

Ashur paused at the door. 'There are some in Idriss who bemoan your rapid ascent. I am not one of them. Your family is not one of the oldest in Idriss, like LeStrange's here – why, it takes him half a day to recount the names of the ancestors he learned in childhood. You are New, and though Idriss welcomes all wanderers committed to its principles, and offers equal opportunity to attain high office to all, still some carry a weight of prejudice against you. Perhaps because you cannot name even one generation. Perhaps for that thing that simmers beneath your shirt. Do not give them any ammunition. Idriss needs its heroes, particularly at this difficult time, and there is more at stake here than your reputation, or your life.'

He nodded curtly and left. LeStrange hovered in the doorway for a moment longer, making silent apologetic gestures, and then hurried in pursuit of his master.

Asgrim began to speak, but Vidar could not hear him. The ghosts in the back of his head were howling excitedly.

IN THE SHAFT of sunlight falling through the brothel window, the mass of scar tissue that covered Cheyne's chest and arms looked raw. He sat on the edge of the bed in his undergarments, hands clasped in his lap. His exquisite shirt and breeches, made from the finest cloth in Idriss, were folded neatly on the sheets beside him.

'Still nothing?' Manda lounged back in a pile of silk cushions, lazily combing her dyed black hair. She was naked, the folds of her flesh merging with the material on which she lay.

Cheyne shook his head.

Footsteps thundered along the corridor outside. A raised voice. Cheyne jerked from his recollections, glanced towards the door as if they were coming for him.

'Nothing?' Manda said.

He looked at her blankly. 'Nothing.'

'We can try again tomorrow. You are a strange fish, Cheyne.'

He nodded. 'I am broken inside. There is not a single person in this city whose life I would spare if pressed. I would kill my brothers-in-arms, the people I drink with, the girls

I spend the night with, the healers who stitch my wounds and tend to my fevers. And I would not give it a second thought afterwards.'

More footsteps ran past the door. The distant voices were punctuated by a shout, then another. Manda laughed at his words disbelievingly.

'And I would kill you. In a minute.'

Her face fell. 'After all the nights we've spent here?'

He stared at her.

She chewed a lip, her gaze ranging across his face for some sign of comforting deceit.

He watched the dust motes for a long moment, then slowly began to dress himself. 'We shall try again tonight.'

'Any time you want, dearie. If you've got the money, I'm here for you.'

The hubbub echoing from beyond the door almost drowned her out. The shouts had grown louder, and a woman was now giving a keening cry, rising and falling so that it sounded almost mechanical. Cheyne wondered if it would ever end.

'What is going on out there?' Manda slipped on a transparent dressing gown and threw open the door. Three of the prostitutes' children ran by, eyes wide, followed by the ashen-faced madame. She paused briefly to stare at Manda, her face filled with conflicting thoughts. Her mouth opened and closed like a fish and then she hurried on after the children.

Manda lurched in the direction of the outcry while Cheyne slipped on his boots and sauntered after her. Pressing through the bodies jammed into the winding corridor, they arrived at a room where the door hung open. More people crammed inside, standing in a circle, heads bowed. The keening woman continued her siren call.

Cheyne saw Manda clasp her hand to her mouth before his eyes fell upon what was before her. One of the prostitutes lay in the centre of the room, naked, her eyes cut out, her arms arranged so that her body lay in a Y-shape.

Another prostitute, a girl still in her late teens, crouched next to the corpse, her face torn into a ragged expression of disbelief. 'What has happened?' she said. 'We are safe here in Idriss.' She looked around the others for support. 'We are safe here.' She returned her gaze to the pooling blood. 'And now we are not. First Mellias, now this. A killer is abroad.'

Cheyne raised his eyes from the scene to see Manda staring at him with a questioning gaze. A shadow crossed her face and she swallowed.

'What has happened to us?' the teenage girl whispered.

3

THE TEMPLE OF THE SHEPHERD

IN THE MISTY silence after dawn, the guards on their patrols noticed a ragged bundle in the middle of no-man's-land between the walls and the forest. As always, the Huntsmen had kept watch throughout the night with their unwavering, dedicated attention, but no one had seen the bundle deposited, nor had any idea who could have left it there. Fierce debate raged for more than an hour before one brave volunteer dashed out to examine the mysterious deposit.

He returned with the remains of the youth who had leaped over the wall the previous morn, though they were so mangled it took the guards a while to realise what the bloody pulp had been. The Huntsmen all knew that the body had been left as a warning for the people of Idriss, underlining a message that had haunted them for generations: entering the forest is death.

TWO MARBLE PILLARS flanked wrought-iron gates topped with a skull and crossbones, their scale both a celebration and a cautionary warning to those who passed through them. Shrouded by ancient yew trees, the Fire Gardens lay on the edge of the municipal quarter, within easy walk of the forum and the palace. It was a quiet place to meditate upon the great who had given their lives in the service of Idriss, and thereby to consider how Idriss was great. A long, polished black wall flanked the western edge of the gardens, carved with thousands of names across the generations. No one recalled what kind of people those names represented, or what great deeds they had achieved, but the sheer volume of the names was in itself a testament; to what, Vidar was not quite sure.

He felt a little stronger. Perhaps the jewel had been tricking him earlier, and the energy of its previous victim would last a little longer. Close to the hissing heat of the eternal flame that gave the gardens their name, it was easy to fade out the wearying drone of the succession of faceless dignitaries praising Mellias's great victories, the defence against the raiding party that emerged from the forest, near mad from fear, or the time he sailed up the river to save a barge filled with supplies that had been set upon by enemies unknown, the crew dead, and the things in the forest moving closer.

Everyone loved and admired the White Warrior. Vidar could understand that, and his own grief burned as hot as the flame for a while, but gradually the irony of the situation crept over him. While so much attention was being paid to the remembrance of a hero, and the great stories that gave shape to his life, soon they would be twisted in the telling, perhaps even his name lost or distorted, and all that would remain would be a single word carved on the great wall, which no one would read because it meant nothing.

Asgrim caught his eye. Cheyne had appeared on the periphery of the crowd, pushing his way through the bodies with a swaggering disregard. As one of the three people closest to Mellias, his absence at the start of the ceremony had been starkly noted by the dignitaries.

'Couldn't come until you had the perfect little silk ribbon for your forearm?' Asgrim mocked quietly when Cheyne slipped in next to them. 'Shopping for a new jacket with just the right number of buttons?'

'Had it been for sartorial reasons, my tardiness would have been perfectly reasonable. I was detained for questioning by the Order.' Cheyne tugged at his sleeve, a tic that was his only sign of anxiety.

'Crimes against common decency?' Vidar said.

'There has been another murder – a doxy at the Four Staves, her body carved and arranged like Mellias's. I had the misfortune to be in the inn when the body was discovered and, knowing of my particular predilection, those small-thinkers in the Order decided it was worth talking to me.'

A lone drummer began the beat of the funeral procession, quiet at first, growing louder. All heads turned towards the gates. After a moment, they swung open to admit six members of the Crimson Hunt in their distinctive robes and hoods over leather and steel armour. Carried on their shoulders was Mellias's body, swathed in the Hunt's colours, a splash of blood among the black mourning cloaks of the crowd.

Vidar watched the procession move slowly past, keen to devote his thoughts to his friend but already distracted by troubled notions. Another death meant the killer was still in Idriss. Yet there appeared to be some purpose to Mellias's murder, however obscure, while the death of a prostitute suggested a random victim of primal urges.

'When was the girl killed?' Vidar enquired.

Cheyne shook his head. 'She was in her room all night. The others presumed she had a special client.'

'So she could have been killed before Mellias, or long after.'

Cheyne sighed. 'Do not exercise yourself so, Vidar. Leave it to the Order. We have more important things to consider – like Mellias's wake. Will they have those little pastry cases with creamed mushrooms in them?'

'Many women admired Mellias,' Asgrim mused. 'They will be at the wake, seeking solace.'

The bearers carried Mellias's shrouded body to the pyre where the court's Chief Funerary Officer accepted a blazing, tar-dipped torch.

'No religious observer,' Vidar noted. 'What religion was Mellias?'

'I never heard him mention any belief,' Cheyne replied. 'He bore no witness to his gods before battle.'

'Did he not go to the celebration for...' Asgrim struggled to recall the name. 'Hera? That warrior goddess the olive-skinned people worship?'

'He was invited as part of his duties as leader of the Crimson Hunt.' Vidar watched the tar-soaked wood of the pyre go up with a *whoosh*. From the nearby trees, crows screeched into the sky in a thunder of wings ahead of greasy, black smoke billowing up to swallow them. 'He wasn't a follower of the Shepherd?'

'One of the little lambs?' Cheyne snorted. 'Mellias? What was his final body count – three hundred and fifty? That is almost as many as yours, Vidar.' Cheyne pressed a perfumed handkerchief to his nose.

Heads went down in silent supplication as the body was consumed by the fire. Soon the blackened bones would be picked over and cleaned and deposited in the catacombs with the other unfortunates who did not merit a public funeral. The drumbeat silenced and the bright morning was filled only with the crackle of flames.

Yet beneath it rose the sound of troubled voices drawing closer. A crowd was gathering beyond the gates, workers from the fields in their threadbare clothes, tanners and foundry men and candle-makers, even a few merchants.

'What is this?' Asgrim said with irritation. 'A shortage protest, at Mellias's funeral?'

'They must be protesting the lack of eastern silk.' Cheyne sighed from behind his handkerchief. 'It is impossible to find a good shirt these days.'

Several representatives of the Order among the funeral group rushed to hold the gates as the mob pressed against them. Three of the women drew their swords to rap the knuckles of those trying to force the gates open. Two others dropped back and levelled their bows, but the crowd did not relent. Vidar could hear their chants now, the fear that underscored their anger.

'Word of your dead doxy has got out, Cheyne. After Mellias's murder, it was only to be expected. People have started to realise that the great walls not only keep out the threat from the forest – they also keep in what's here.'

A cry of alarm rose up as a rock arced over the gate and crashed near the party supporting the frail King.

'Come on,' Vidar said. 'We're needed.'

Drawing his sword, he thrust through the mourners with Cheyne and Asgrim close behind. By the time he reached the gate, the ranks of the Crimson Hunt stood at his back.

'Return to your work,' he commanded.

'You are not Mellias!' someone shouted in response. 'We need protection!'

'Mellias's death was not an accident,' another called. 'There is a killer loose in Idriss. None of us are safe!'

Another rock glanced off Vidar's temple, drawing blood. Instantly, he felt the familiar, sickening bubbling at the back of his head as the ghosts rushed out from wherever they lay. The air around him shimmered, faces appearing in swirling, pearly mist, their mouths yawning wide in shrieks that echoed a moment later. As one, the mob recoiled in horror.

'Kill him!' the ghosts screamed. 'He cannot protect you! He will eat you alive!' Their grasping hands reached through the gates, but they could not escape whatever gravity trapped them. Not realising the ghosts' impotence, the crowd turned and ran back down the cobbled street.

'Well, that is one way to disperse a mob.' Cheyne sniffed. 'Though not quite the Mellias way.'

Angry at his own inadequacy, Vidar let himself through the gates and marched to Rhiannon who had just arrived from the direction of the Four Staves. Her face was set.

'Keep your man Cheyne out of view for a while,' she said, 'at least till this business is concluded. His reputation is starting to take an unfortunate turn in the stories spinning out of the Four Staves.'

'We can go into hiding together,' Vidar spat.

'Feeling unloved?'

'I'll get over it. Not too sure I can say the same for the population at large.'

'Heroes come in all shapes and sizes.'

He couldn't tell if she was mocking him. 'The girl was definitely killed by Mellias's murderer?'

'The same knife strokes on the body, as far as I can tell without a proper examination of Mellias's corpse. At least this time we will have an opportunity to carry out a more detailed enquiry.'

'Why was she killed?'

'Why is anyone killed? Love, sex, money, power.'

'You're looking into her client list?'

'Are you telling me how to conduct my work?'

'No.'

'Because I have some views on the defence of Idriss if you are interested—'

'I apologise. You're very prickly.' The Crimson Hunt marched by with Cheyne and Asgrim bringing up the rear. Cheyne flashed him a knowing wink, Asgrim a lascivious grin. Vidar positioned himself so Rhiannon didn't see.

'With this latest death, there is an added degree of scrutiny that I could do without. The King and his advisors are already paying close attention and this will only make it worse,' Rhiannon said.

'Religion always has the capacity to pit people at each other's throats. The number of competing faiths in Idriss naturally means there's a chance of major upheaval. With the King aged and no obvious successor, there's already a sense of insecurity. He's bound to be worried.'

Rhiannon glanced down the cobbled street to where it met the maze of shadowy alleys that edged the artisans' quarter. 'That little group of complainers was motivated by one murder and the rumour that it was linked to Mellias's death. How many will rise up if there is another killing? How will that volatility interfere with your ability to protect Idriss if an attack is imminent?'

'The people will rally round if we're attacked. This is Idriss.'

'Idriss is not used to facing a threat from within. We are on unknown ground.'

A gloom fell across the street as the smoke from Mellias's pyre obscured the sun. The calls of the birds grew quiet. The mourners began to file out from the gardens, their usual post-funeral exuberance replaced by apprehension. Ashur nodded to Vidar as he passed slowly by, the King clutching his arm. Lud's cheeks were still wet with tears.

'Big shoes to fill,' Rhiannon noted.

'I'll survive.'

'I know you will.' She left without looking at him, disappearing quickly into the midst of the throng of black-cloaked mourners.

* * *

DEEP IN THOUGHT, Asgrim balanced on the end of the bed in the room he shared with Cheyne, and used to share with Vidar before he had moved his belongings into the leader's suite.

'Will you stop doing that?' Cheyne snapped as he entered. 'You remind me of some animal. You already smell like one. I have had to double our order of scented flowers.'

'Where have you been? Vidar wishes us to review our defence strategies. He fears an attack sooner rather than later.'

'At the Four Staves.'

'The Order wanted you to stay away from there,' Asgrim noted.

'How remiss of me.' Cheyne plucked from his bag a dirty shawl and tossed it to Asgrim. 'I have need of your nose.'

Asgrim sniffed the air, savouring the complex layering of scents. He could discern a subtle change in emotion from the quality of sweat secreted, the telltale sign of musk interacting with perfume or soap, the freshness of clothes, food on breath. He buried his face in the shawl and then snatched it back with a shudder. 'What is this?'

'Our dead doxy's prized possession, poor cow. She was wearing it when she died.'

Tentatively sniffing the shawl, Asgrim winced at the sour odour. 'The one who killed her is on here.'

Cheyne gestured expansively. 'Applause, please.'

Asgrim screwed up his nose. 'Why are you wasting your time on this, Cheyne?'

'To find whoever committed this atrocity,' he replied with faux concern.

'The Inquisitors will locate the killer.'

'Being a filthy beast with no pride in your appearance, you clearly could not be expected to understand. I have no problem with being branded a killer. Indeed, I take pride in my calling. However, I will not be accused of slipshod despatch or brought to account for messy handiwork when it is not my own. My reputation for finesse will not be sullied.'

Asgrim laughed. 'You fear the Inquisitors will interfere with your lifestyle while they carry out their enquiry.'

'The matter must be brought to a conclusion quickly and efficiently, and if I can contribute to that result, all the better.'

'A scent is no good in a city the size of Idriss.' All aromas were unique to Asgrim, but there was something troublingly out of the ordinary on the shawl, too bitter, neither animal nor human yet unmistakably some kind of musk, the kind released at the height of arousal.

'Which is why I spoke to Madame Beaufort and gained descriptions of two men, one seen entering the doxy's chamber shortly after Mellias would have been killed, and another visitor observed leaving just before dawn. They both wore dark cloaks. And Feegrum boots.'

Asgrim sniffed again, forcing his way past the sickening bitterness. 'Yes,' he said, 'I smell it – breakhorn spice, rare and expensive.'

Cheyne nodded. 'The kind sold by a merchant who could afford hand-stitched, aged Feegrum boots. I knew those flaring, lupine nostrils would come in use some day.' He waved a dismissive hand. 'Go on, then. Do your business.'

'You owe me for this.' Asgrim bounded towards the door, clutching the shawl to his chest.

'Cheyne always pays his debts.' He grinned. 'Bring me back a trophy.'

Asgrim paused in the doorway, his excited senses now picking up a complex mix of signals. 'There is fear in the wind. And suspicion. Vidar is thrust into his new role at the worst possible time, isolated in a rapidly changing landscape. We must watch his back.'

'Of course we will watch his back, you hirsute carrion-eater. He is our friend. And frankly you need all the friends you can get. Now leave me and allow my delicate senses a chance to recover.'

Snorting, Asgrim padded out of the door and into the corridor where the day watch was just lighting the torches, his last task of their shift. Through the windows, the sky was red and purple along the dark horizon.

Something in the mix of colours and scents floating in from the city brought back a sharp, yearning memory of his childhood: his father resting a proud hand on his shoulder as the sun set over the mountains, the snow crisp underfoot. The demands of his life barely gave him a chance to revisit his past, but whenever he did it still stung him with the powerful sense of something valuable lost for ever. The end of that day he had spent with his father, hunting and talking and revelling in the sense of being loved, was the last time he recalled being truly at peace. He missed his father even now, the words of comfort, the advice, the guidance. He missed his eyes gleaming over the evening fire.

One day later, he had been all alone, everything he valued stolen from him, fleeing for his life over rocks and ice, heading south towards, though he did not know it at the time, Idriss. 'One day I will hear your wisdom again,' he whispered with a pang of grief that never seemed to diminish.

Outside on the cobbled streets, twilight was creeping slowly over Idriss the Strong and the sound of the call to prayer in the Rezshinnia mingled with the nearer songs of the street-sellers offering their spiced meats and broths along the Serpent Way.

Asgrim instinctively kept to the shadows beyond the pools of illumination that the army of lamplighters threw up every dusk. No one in Idriss could bear the dark – it reminded them too much of the forest beyond the walls – but Asgrim found it comforting.

The merchants would be in the process of closing up their shops and stalls, and many would already have departed for the night, but the wealthier would be buying their dinners in the inns that clustered in the streets and alleys around the bank. He sucked in another reminder from the shawl and bounded towards Red Hill.

The main thoroughfare thronged with public carriages collecting and dropping off the well-heeled. The street musicians had replaced their laments to Mellias with jaunty drinking songs, competing with each other for tossed coins, and with the jugglers and dancers, the sellers of hot broth, bread, and roast meat.

Asgrim concentrated as he slipped into the flow of pedestrians, forcing the complex patterns of sensory chatter into the background, focusing on the one odour. Sweat and perfume came and went; urine; the musk of sex from an open window on the second storey. Cloaks flapped around him. Silver-topped canes clattered on the cobbles. Horses snorted, stamped their hooves, and released piles of stinking dung. He moved along the streets, close to the walls, keeping to the shadows wherever possible, invisible, conscious thought just a flicker at the back of his head. He passed through the inns unnoticed, rising above the vinegar-stink of stale beer, the woodsmoke, the shouts and whispers, the pewter, the iron and leather. In the dosshouses and brothels, no one saw him. The cries of pleasure and pain, the moans of fitful sleep folded around him.

And finally, three hours later when night had fully fallen, he caught the singular odour on the breeze of a passing carriage, sour and laced with the hot passion of unpleasant deeds. The hairs on Asgrim's neck prickled erect. He searched back and forth, caught it again, only this time it was mingled with another familiar aroma: the iron scent of blood.

The odour filled his world. Barely seeing the speeding carriages as he darted across the street, he narrowly evaded the crushing wheels. Curses followed in his wake as he pushed through a crowd of drunken merchants urinating in the gutter. The bitter odour came and went, but pulled Asgrim insistently away from the busiest part of Red Hill to the quieter streets on the fringes. The subtleties of the odour began to build a picture in his mind, of desolation and cruelty, tears on a cold day, beetles forcing their way through damp wood-chips, iron scraped along stone, ashes, the cries of the birds that flocked around the Fire Gardens.

He passed the entrance to the maze of alleys that ran behind the inns and doubled-back; the odour was coming from within. The alleys were barely lit, isolated pools beneath inter-mittent torches in a long river of black. Drawing his knife, he entered silently, keeping low and close to the wall.

His acute hearing picked up distant echoes: the scrape of a boot, a rustling exhalation; not near. Loping quickly, he followed the path on instinct, turning this way and that along the narrow, stinking alleys. The sour odour grew stronger, the sounds clearer; the breath was dying.

Finally, he came to a halt against a wall on the edge of a branching alley. The subject of his search was just around the corner, the smell now so powerful Asgrim could have choked. A heavy boot splashed in a puddle; breath that most would barely hear rasped loudly in his ears. From the echo-picture, he estimated that his prey was at least as tall as Vidar, but with a much slighter frame.

A whispered prayer to the gods beyond Bifrost, and then he was out into the mud-splattered alley, knife drawn, ready to launch himself at the soon-to-be victim. The scene caught him off-guard and he skidded, unbalanced, scrabbling for traction.

Captured in the seething light of an overhead torch was the owner of the sour odour, hunched over his victim, a young man barely out of his teens wearing the rough but smart clothes of a merchant's apprentice. Blood pooled around him, glowing in the reflected illumination. His final breath drifted away just as Asgrim launched into view and in that moment, a change came over his murderer, who wore a long, thick, woollen cloak, far too big so that it made his body appear thin and sickly. A short silver knife was clutched tightly in his bony hands.

But it was the face that threw Asgrim off-balance. At first glimpse it had appeared to be a man in his early fifties, skin too pale, cheeks drawn, bright, intelligent eyes, with the perfectly groomed hair of a wealthy merchant.

But in the moment the victim died, the features began to run like a candle placed too close to the fire, pooling, shifting, falling away. What lay beneath held Asgrim gripped: a face as white as bone, the mouth a bloody slash from cheek to cheek, eyes lost in pools of shadows, hair wild and a brilliant, unnatural red. Just as quickly, that face disappeared too, though in reverse, as new features ran up liquidly, drawing together, growing solid: a man in his early thirties, the skin red and chapped by the wind, the eyes stupid, the brow low.

The superstitions of his people gripped Asgrim, and he held back apprehensively. 'What are you?' he growled.

Without answering, the Red Man turned and ran down the alley, his boots echoing off the walls, his cloak billowing behind him like the wings of a giant bat. Ignoring his fears, Asgrim bounded in pursuit, gripping his knife tightly.

Alley merged into alley, some so narrow Asgrim bounced from wall to wall as he ran, twisting back and forth so that all sense of direction was lost. The Red Man was strong and fast, but Asgrim closed on him, bounding over the detritus from the inns, the rotting food and the empty barrels.

With a fleeting backward glance, the Red Man realised he could not outpace Asgrim and as he turned into a broader, better-lit alley that opened on to the heart of Red Hill, he came to a skidding halt before kicking open a door with such force that it burst from its hinges. He darted into the well-lit, smoky interior.

Following close behind, Asgrim found himself in the corridor of one of the bigger inns leading to the main bar area. Prostitutes and men lined the walls, flirting and bargaining, though many were now yelling angrily at the rough path the Red Man had forced through their midst. Asgrim thrust aside any that attempted to block his way, brandishing his knife at the most outspoken.

The hubbub in the bar was even louder. The Red Man had upended a table filled with drinks and was now racing up the stairs. Asgrim headbutted one furious man who barred his way, and snapped at the throat of another, before leaping onto a table and launching himself over heads to the foot of the stairs, where he landed lithely and drove up the steps without missing a beat.

The thunder of the Red Man's boots continued ahead of him, past the first floor to the second and on. Asgrim bowled over prostitutes and clients emerging from their rooms, using heads and chests as launch-pads to attempt to close the gap. On the third floor, one woman lay unconscious, while a man attempted to staunch the bleeding from a jagged wound across his cheek.

On the fifth and final floor, a door hung open revealing a man and prostitute mid-coitus on the bed, the woman yelling obscenities. The

Red Man was just disappearing through the window, hauling himself up and onto the roof. Asgrim ran through the room, cursing loudly; heights terrified him. His people were effective on the flat, open, frozen wastes and shied away from the few vertiginous paths that led through the mountains.

Steadying himself, he leaned out of the window. The alley lay far below. Overhead, the Red Man's boots clattered across the roof tiles. Gripping the flimsy guttering, Asgrim hauled himself up, trying to ignore the creaking protestations of the iron supports. Breathing hard, he made it on to the pitched roof tiles and scrambled up to the top. The Red Man was three rooftops away, leaping from one to another oblivious to the drops, his shadow dancing even more wildly in the light flooding up from the streets.

Asgrim skidded down the opposing pitch, and as he neared the edge of the roof tried not to look as he threw himself across the gap. A tile shattered underfoot, almost throwing him off-balance. As the pieces careened down to the street, he steadied himself and made his way up the slope. At the pitch, it was clear he would not be able to catch the Red Man without taking risks.

Clearing his head of all thoughts, he threw himself down the slope recklessly, leaping almost too late so that his heel tore the guttering from its mounting. With a groan, it crashed into the next alley. Asgrim landed splayed on the next roof, and used the balls of his feet to propel him on.

The pursuit continued for fifteen long minutes. The rooftops of Idriss stretched out all around, islands of dark suspended in a sea of light. The Red Man pushed on relentlessly, away from the merchants' quarter to Greatstock where the poorer workers lived in their ramshackle, continually mutating houses.

The roofs became less steady, and on more than one occasion Asgrim punched a foot through poorly made tiles, tearing his flesh. The blood made his feet slick and less able to keep a grip. Some roofs bowed upwards at a steep incline, and on these he found himself sliding back inexorably towards the drop, scrabbling for purchase with his fingernails, tearing off tiles so he could gain a grip and pull himself up.

Yet he was closing on the Red Man, who was slowed by his larger frame. 'Now I have you,' Asgrim whispered to himself as the houses gave way to a broader street that it would be impossible to leap across.

The Red Man hovered on the edge, looking back and forth for an escape route. But when Asgrim landed on the roof, he felt it creak and give beneath his feet. He held out his arms to steady himself. The roof continued to move, then settled. He was on one of the buildings where upper storeys had been added haphazardly by tenants to provide space for their growing families. Asgrim knew that workmanship and materials were often poor.

The Red Man teetered along the roof's edge, trying to circle around. Asgrim moved quickly to block him. The roof shifted again, the timbers groaning loudly. The Red Man windmilled his arms to keep his balance, only catching himself at the last moment.

Asgrim stopped moving again until the roof settled, but never took his eyes off the Red Man.

'Best give yourself up now,' he called, 'or we'll both be a bloody mess on the street below.'

Ignoring him, the Red Man continued to edge around the roof, closing on a side that provided access to another house. If he reached it, he would be able to disappear back into the interior of the city. As he prepared to leap, Asgrim threw himself over the pitch of the roof, tiles flying all around as he skidded down towards the Red Man.

But his weight was too much for the roof. With a series of pops and cracks that grew louder until they were deafening, the roof lurched to one side and broke free of its moorings. Asgrim was thrown to his side, skidding downwards as the roof slid away from the building inexorably, accelerating.

Asgrim caught sight of the Red Man leaping and catching hold of the safety of an exposed roof timber. And then the roof was free and plunging down towards the cobbled street with Asgrim caught in the disintegrating tiles, laths, and beams.

In the centre of the city, the blaze of light from Idriss's streets turned the twin marble columns at the entrance to the Temple of the Shepherd into spectral sentinels. Vidar paused on the broad steps and noticed for the first time that the building was the largest place of worship in the city. Torches burned permanently on either side of the doorway, above which there was a discreet carving of the religion's symbol, a stylised Y representing the Shepherd standing with arms raised. It set disturbing echoes in Vidar's head, not the least an image of Mellias's body on the floor of the Store of the Ages.

The interior was dark and cool and smelled of sweet incense, barely masking the aromas of great age that appeared to be infused into the stone itself. The space was vast and the only illumination came from candles on ledges along the facing walls. Above them were great works of art painted over the millennia: the Shepherd ministering to the poor and the sick, defeating the demons that lurked in the forest, weaving magic that turned the sky to rainbow splashes of colour. Briefly, Vidar felt as if he was being watched, but it was only the carved figures hanging in the shadows high over his head.

Rows of wooden seats were interspersed with stone columns so that he was forced to walk an odd processional route along the hall, the mysteries ahead glimpsed then hidden. He couldn't see the painting Rhiannon had described, and as he searched the works of art along the walls a figure separated from the shadows.

'The leader of the Crimson Hunt. This is an honour.' It was a man in his late fifties, his shaven head and face covered with fading blue tattoos of swirls, concentric circles, and stars. He wore the purple robes of the religion that Vidar vaguely remembered seeing at some religious festival or other.

'You know me?' Vidar said.

'Everyone in Idriss knows you. The great hero. Chief defender of this ship of light in the vast sea of night.'

'Yes. I kill people for money.' He turned back to the paintings. *And food*, he thought. 'You're the priest here?'

'Something like that. We call ourselves Seekers, and I am the chief of those. My name is Laurent.'

'I'm looking for a painting – *The Supplicant Praises the Power of the Visitant*.'

'Hmm. One of the lesser works. Why that particular painting?'

'No reason.'

Laurent led Vidar to an alcove lost to the shadows. Taking a candle, the Seeker indicated a painting barely two handspans in width, much smaller than Vidar had anticipated. Leaning in, he saw Rhiannon was right. The Shepherd looked to be in his late forties, with long, brown hair streaked with silver. As he loomed over the supplicant on the ground, something in his right hand blazed with a white light. The figure before him lay on his back, legs straight, arms bent, just as Mellias had in his death.

'It doesn't look like the Shepherd is being praised there,' Vidar noted. 'It looks like the one on the floor is scared of him.'

'As we should all be scared in the face of god's power,' Laurent replied. 'To lay down your arms, to bare your throat, to offer up your life and trust in the judgement of the Shepherd whether you should live or die… that is the highest praise of all.'

'What's that in his hand?' Vidar pointed to the white light.

'That is known as the All-Seeing Eye. It casts judgement on the lost lambs.'

'Which are?'

'You. Me. All of us.'

Vidar stepped back, weighing what he had seen. 'This painting isn't important in your religion?'

'No, or we would have given it pride of place on the walls of the temple.' He indicated the great, devotional artworks of the Shepherd, some of them more than twice Vidar's height. 'Very little is known about this work. As you can see, its age is great. It has faded and been retouched. There are some in the temple who believe it is a copy, perhaps a copy of a copy of a copy. But it tells us nothing new about the Shepherd. Yet it is always here, for worshippers to find if they so wish.'

'Do you ever see anyone looking at it regularly?'

'I will tell you what I told the Inquisitor – many people come here to look at the paintings, to find their way to the Shepherd. The representation of the thing is the thing. The Shepherd is here, in all these images, looking back at you. Judging you.' Laurent gestured expansively. 'I can see you know little about the Shepherd or his teachings.'

'You know one god, you know them all. Misery in this life, salvation in the next.'

Laurent smiled, beckoned. Vidar shrugged and followed him towards the darkness at the end of the hall.

'The way of the Shepherd is not the oldest in Gardia, but it used to be the most widely followed in all of Idriss,' Laurent said as they walked.

'I heard the same thing from the followers of some other god. Everyone has stories about how their god is the best, the one everyone used to follow before times got tough.'

Laurent's laugh was low and warm. 'True. And we know what stories are worth here in Idriss! Believe me or not, but what I'm telling you is true. There was a time when almost everyone in Idriss followed the way of the Shepherd. But this is a city that has always offered shelter to travellers from afar. Many brought with them their own gods, and as time passed the numerous voices raised in prayer became confusing. But we are still here, offering guidance to any who come to us.'

Laurent came to a halt before a circular area where a low flame flickered in a pool of oil set into the floor. The flame changed colour – green, red, blue, gold – and made the shadows jump and dance around that secluded part of the temple.

'This is the beacon,' Laurent said.

'Colour-changing fire. It takes a little more than that to impress me.'

'The way of the Shepherd offers more than the other religions you will find in Idriss. It offers salvation in this world. The word, passed down from generation to generation of Seeker, is that the Shepherd will send others to aid the people.'

'What kind of others?'

'More Shepherds. They will walk among us, and save us from the suffering of our lives.' He smiled tightly. 'No waiting for death, Vidar. Here and now.'

Vidar looked around at the worn stone of the ancient building. 'And how many generations have died waiting for salvation in this life?'

'Are you afraid to believe in something, Vidar?'

'I believe in myself. That's all I need.' A surge of weakness flowed through Vidar, and he leaned against a pillar so as not to show it to Laurent. 'Is there any way to recognise one of your religion's followers? Clothes? Symbols? Tattoos? Signs?'

'The followers of the Shepherd move among you, unmarked, unnoticed. We are you.'

'That's what I thought.'

'Perhaps I could invite you to join one of our rituals? You could see the wonder of the Shepherd for yourself.'

'I wouldn't be a very good listener. Short attention span. Not very easily impressed.'

Laurent was not offended. 'Your predecessor joined us on many an occasion,' he pressed.

'Mellias was a follower of the Shepherd?'

'He had not yet found his way. But he had developed an increasing interest in the teachings of the Shepherd.'

'He spoke to you about this?'

'I offered him guidance.'

'What was he searching for?'

Laurent smiled. 'Illumination. I can say no more. These matters are private between the supplicant and myself.'

'And the painting – did Mellias spend any time looking at it?'

'He did.'

Vidar returned to the picture and considered what might have drawn Mellias to it; the White Warrior was not someone who had the time or the inclination to indulge a love of the arts. He trained and killed, ate and slept, killed some more. As Vidar studied the work, he noticed something incongruous that he had missed with his initial focus on the central figures. In the background, along the horizon, were four cubes that resembled dice without the spots. Now he had noticed them, they continued to jar; the painting was realistic in its depiction of the scene, apart from

the four cubes, which appeared to be symbolic.

'What are those?' he asked.

Laurent peered into the image, clearly seeing
the shapes for the first time. 'I do not know.'

'There's nothing in the Shepherd's story to
account for them?'

'No.'

'I presume the artist placed them there
because they're important.'

Laurent shrugged dismissively. 'Who knows
what artists try to say? They deal in symbolism, but often the meaning is lost to all but
themselves.'

Running footsteps interrupted them. Rhiannon appeared with two fellow Inquisitors, her
face drawn. She motioned for the other two
women to stand guard and took Vidar to one
side.

'Another killing. In Red Hill,' she said quietly but intensely.

'Same as the others?'

'This victim was not laid out in the same
manner, but the wounds are similar. The murderer was disturbed by your man Asgrim.' She
held up a hand to silence Vidar. 'He is badly
wounded, close to death.'

'Take me to him. Now.'

'Of course. But first I have a message from
the King. Word of the murder has spread

rapidly from Red Hill. Groups of citizens are gathering in the public places. They are angry and scared, Vidar. The King wants the Crimson Hunt to keep the peace in Idriss. All your men,' she added pointedly.

'The Crimson Hunt are defenders of the city,' Vidar snapped. 'My men should not be used to control the people. This has never been done before.'

'Nevertheless, it is the King's demand.'

'Sent through Ashur?'

She nodded.

Vidar cursed loudly. 'That frozen-faced snake isn't thinking. Tell me this: if the Crimson Hunt are despatched across Idriss to maintain order, what will happen if an attack comes from outside? We could be overrun before the Hunt gets to the walls.'

Vidar could see Rhiannon had already considered this. 'These are dark times, Vidar. I fear for us all.'

4

RED MAN

WITHIN THE HOUR, the Crimson Hunt left their positions on the walls and fanned out across Idriss. Protests were already being reported, in Greatstock near the building collapse where an elderly woman crushed by the falling debris added to the mounting tension; in Fallen Spire, beneath the four-tower monument where a great fire blazed and a large crowd had gathered; and in Borlonwood, Highmost Michael, and Lerose Cross. Under Vidar's strict orders, the Crimson Hunt did not intervene, but their brooding presence on the borders of the protests did not go unnoticed.

Vidar had Asgrim brought to Greer an' Lokh's tower where his broken body was tended by the King's physician and his six-strong team of assistants. The northerner had not regained consciousness, and the physician had told Vidar it was unlikely he would. Though they had staunched the flow of blood, too many bones were broken, too many organs damaged. Cheyne waited silently by his friend's side, keeping a silent vigil, his emotions unreadable.

On a small wooden balcony high up in the tower, Vidar and Rhiannon looked out to the blaze at Fallen Spire.

'Do you know why Idriss is called the Strong?' Vidar said. 'It's not because of the warriors, it's because of the people. This city has always survived on the edge of disaster. Shortages within, threats from without. And it's kept going because of the strength of everyone who lives here. They give Idriss its spirit, not us. But if the people aren't behind us completely we can't defend Idriss. We have no power except what they invest in us.'

'The King is scared that all he has built during his life could be destroyed during this period of tension.'

'We've had trouble before.'

'But not when the King was old and ill. He is afraid that Idriss may not be eternal. That it may fall during his reign because he is not strong enough to maintain control.'

'He's overreacting. This has Ashur's fingerprints all over it. The King used to ignore his nephew's advice when it was obviously wrong. We're in trouble if Ashur is making all the decisions. He's been frightened ever since he was scarred by what lives in the forest, and fear makes you do stupid things.' Vidar fought a wave of weariness as the amber jewel sucked more of the life from him.

'The people will calm once the murderer is caught. Living with the fear of what lies beyond the walls is one thing, but this killer strikes at the very heart of their security.'

'What if you don't catch him? The next thing, there'll be innocent people getting burned alive in Greatstock. Ashur will order the Crimson Hunt in, and everything will go up in flames.'

'Pessimist.'

'Pragmatic, I think.'

She eyed him curiously.

'What?'

'You have an odd turn of phrase, Vidar. I have not heard its like before.'

'I'm one of a kind. Didn't I tell you that?'

'Where is your home, I wonder?'

Rhiannon's incisive gaze made him uncomfortable and he turned away. 'I want to check on Asgrim.'

On the stairway, the stink of death that permeated the entire tower became even more acute, and the deep, uneasy silence of the building was occasionally broken by the distant sound of hammering and indistinct cries. Vidar and Rhiannon both tried to ignore their surroundings as they descended slowly.

'I am sorry for what happened to your friend,' Rhiannon said. 'He was strange in his ways, but at heart he was a good man.'

'He's not dead yet.'

Rhiannon gave a quick look of pity, but said nothing.

'The witnesses said he was in pursuit of the murderer,' Vidar continued. 'He may have seen something that can help us identify our target. We need him to gain consciousness so we can question him.'

Rhiannon nodded non-committally. 'Of course.'

The entire fourth floor had been given over to Asgrim's treatment. He lay on a bed in a large chamber flooded with light from a hundred candles. The King's physician had bound his wounds and given him drops of a potent painkilling solution, but his breath was barely a whisper. Vidar had seen the state many times before when he had looked in the mirror; the life was leaking out of Asgrim second by second.

'Why did you bring him here?' Rhiannon whispered. 'Surely he could have been given more comfort at the court in his final hours?'

They were interrupted by Cheyne who carried a bowl of warm water and a cloth to mop Asgrim's brow. 'I will do my rounds of the stations shortly,' he said.

'There's no hurry. The captain reported back – it's tense but quiet out there. Take as long as you want here.'

His face impassive, Cheyne nodded. He went to the bedside and began to wipe the sweat from Asgrim's sickly, yellowing skin. 'I gave him the killer's scent and asked him to pursue the matter,' he said.

'That was the right thing to do,' Vidar replied.

'I did it to protect my reputation. No higher motives.'

'You couldn't have known what would happen.'

Cheyne meticulously squeezed every drop from the cloth, then resoaked it. His attention to detail was meditative.

'You've been friends a long time?' Vidar asked.

'Ever since he arrived in Idriss, a wet-furred beast from the north, face still stained with carrion.' He thought for a moment. 'Ten years now. Ten.'

'I know you've always looked out for him. Those bodies that turned up in the river last year... the ones who'd attacked him when he was drunk in the Four Staves...'

Cheyne remained silent.

'He never knew?'

Shaking his head slowly, Cheyne added, 'He is unfortunately corrupted by decency and honour, and needs protection from these harsh times in which we live.'

Vidar understood. Cheyne had found in Asgrim something missing in himself, and that had helped to form such an incongruous friendship. Those bonds ran deep, though neither of them acknowledged it; instead, they masked it with bickering and taunting.

Cheyne didn't appear to want to speak any more so Vidar returned to Rhiannon, who waited respectfully in the doorway. He noted how tautly she held her shoulders, the uneasiness in her face; the weight of her investigation lay heavily on her.

'There's nothing we can do here,' he said, 'not until Greer an' Lokh eventually emerges from whatever twisted business he's engaged in right now.'

'You do not want to keep vigil for your friend?'

'What use would that be? If you want some help, I'm available, and I've got an idea what we can do.'

Through one of the windows, Vidar's attention was suddenly caught by shimmering lights in the sky. Peering out, he tried to make sense of them. They were nothing to do with Greer an' Lokh's magics, and appeared to be manifesting over the Fire Gardens. He thought he could see images and colours in the smoke that still rose from Mellias's pyre.

Rhiannon stared in wonder. 'What does this mean, Vidar? Is it a sign from the gods that Mellias is greater even than we believed?'

'I don't believe in signs from the gods. But when the people see that, they'll be thinking the same as you. Mellias the great hero being murdered is bad enough. The killing of a man favoured by the gods is worse. They'll be asking themselves who would have the power to kill someone so favoured. And why he is still at large.'

He watched the shifting lights for a long moment, seeing troubling patterns that he tried to put down to his imagination, and then he left quickly, with Rhiannon close behind.

ANGRY CRIES ECHOED occasionally across the sleeping city, and from the steps of the Store of the Ages, Vidar could see torchlit groups moving through some of the streets. He knew it wouldn't take many more murders before the people decided that their protectors were not up to the task with which they had been charged.

'How old were you when you started your preparation to be an Inquisitor?' he asked Rhiannon as they entered the silent building.

'Are you really interested?'

'Passing the time.'

She shook her head dismissively, but still replied, 'Ten.'

'You all start so young?'

'The mind needs to be trained to see the connections presented by an enquiry, and to appreciate the moral framework of the post. It is a calling. Life's work.'

'You should start hiring some men. You'd find your casework clearing up a lot quicker.'

'Oh yes, that would be an advance,' she said sarcastically. 'Women are interested in justice, not judgement. And justice takes time and reflection.'

The fifth-floor gallery where Mellias had been killed was now silent. The wooden floorbricks had been scrubbed clean, and the glass cabinets washed of all spatters.

'Why are we here?' Rhiannon asked. 'The enquiry at this location has been closed.'

'I want to find out about the artefact that went missing.'

'There are no connections between it and Mellias's death. The White Warrior was assassinated to rob Idriss of its hope. With him gone, the defence of Idriss is severely weakened, and we are ripe for invasion.'

'When you say it like that, it almost makes sense. And I appreciate the vote of confidence in my abilities, by the way. You checked the missing artefact against the codex?'

'Of course,' she said sharply. 'It is worthless.'

Carrying a lantern, Keeper Xiang Chai-Shekh moved like a ghost among the cabinets. He bowed to them. 'How may I be of assistance?'

'I want to know about the missing artefact,' Vidar said. Xiang was clearly pleased by this line of questioning; Vidar guessed no one ever asked him about his work. 'You said it was a carved block of unknown material. Like a die, yes? Six sides?' He could feel Rhiannon's probing gaze upon him.

'That is correct. Very, very old.'

'Are there any more like it here?'

'No.'

Vidar thought for a moment. 'Where did it come from?'

Xiang excitedly unlocked the heavy volume he carried under his arm; a small chain fastened it to his wrist. 'Everything is here, recorded for all time. Few appreciate the need for the Store of the Ages, but now, you see, now… What we keep here is wisdom in material form.' He riffled through the pages until he found the entry he wanted. 'It was found by the honoured Keeper Pietr al Monquessant, twelve generations gone, when the Stumbling Way was recobbled.'

'Near the Temple of the Shepherd,' Vidar noted thoughtfully.

'It was in a layer of detritus that the honoured Keeper believed to date back many generations further still.' He read: '"Possibly for use in a dice game played by children."'

'Satisfied?' Rhiannon said.

'You're confident this disappeared on the night of the murder?' Vidar asked, ignoring her.

'Certainly. It could not have been taken at any other time. Indeed, who would have taken such an item? It was barely visible in the cabinet, lying amid a pile of various other items of uncertain origin.'

'But you noticed it was missing.'

'I walk this gallery a hundred times a day. These old things are the scenery of my life. I notice every new cobweb, every sprinkling of dust. Every echo is familiar.'

'Thank you, Keeper Xiang Chai-Shekh. You've been invaluable.'

The Keeper bowed and left. Rhiannon wagged a finger at Vidar. 'Why do you think Mellias wanted such a worthless item?'

'I don't think it is worthless.'

'And you believe the murderer stole it?'

'No.'

'You are an infuriating man.' Her jaw set, and she glared at him.

'I believe the murderer came here to steal it, but Mellias stopped him.'

'What evidence do you have?'

'The murderer is still at large in Idriss. If he had what he was looking for, do you think he'd still be around?'

'*If* he was looking for this. Why would Mellias give up his life to prevent the killer leaving with this… this die?'

'Good question.'

'If the murderer did not take the die, where is it now?'

Vidar considered teasing Rhiannon further, but the look in her eyes deterred him. He walked over to the statue of the Shepherd and gestured to where Mellias's body had been laid out. 'Remember the scene,' he prompted. 'The body had been ritually displayed by the killer, yes?'

'Of course.'

'The eyes cut out. Symbolic, perhaps.'

'Symbolism? What kind of a warrior are you, Vidar?' Admiration mingled with suspicion in her face.

'Pay attention. The mouth slashed. All ragged cuts–'

She followed his line of thinking. 'But the symbol carved in his chest was not. It was carefully done.'

'Almost as if by a different hand. Because Mellias did it to himself. You saw his knife nearby. Would the murderer have been able to take the knife from Mellias, even if he knew him?'

'No?' she said hesitantly.

'No. Not from Mellias,' Vidar insisted. 'Mellias left us a message, cut into his own body, next to the heart. A message of truth that could not be wiped away.'

Rhiannon closed her eyes and pictured the scene. 'A circle, with a line cutting into it. What does that indicate?'

'A sealed space, being entered.'

Rhiannon sighed. 'And?'

'Let's find out if I'm right.'

THE GREASY SMELL of burning still hung over the Fire Gardens. Though Mellias's body had been consumed, the core of the pyre was still red hot and a trail of black smoke twined up into the night clouds. The lights Vidar and Rhiannon had witnessed earlier were gone.

The gardens were bathed in a glow from the torches that burned on every column along the perimeter wall, allowing them to find their way easily to the funerary enclosure.

'You realise the gardens should not be entered until three days after the ceremony, out of respect for the departed?' Rhiannon said tartly.

'I have more respect for Mellias than anyone. But in three days the morticians will remove the bones and take them to the catacombs, and clear all this up. That'll be too late. It may already be too late.'

With his sword, he began to rake through the remains of the pyre, scattering glowing chunks of wood across the marble dais. Rhiannon was horrified. 'Vidar! What are you doing?'

Charred bones tumbled out of the ashes, the smoke billowing all around them. Vidar was forced to back off as the flames winnowed up when the embers were disturbed.

'Vidar!' Rhiannon hissed.

'Trust me. I'm not doing this on a whim.' He paused and looked along the iron spikes on the perimeter wall.

Rhiannon followed his gaze. 'What is it?'

'I thought I saw something.' He continued to watch cautiously, but there was no sign of movement. The trees around the gardens shifted in a slight breeze, their shadows edging back and forth.

'Most officials will be preoccupied with the unrest, but if any of the people find you desecrating the remains of Idriss's great hero, your feared reputation will be the least of your worries,' Rhiannon noted.

'I know the risks.' Vidar watched for a moment longer and then returned to the fire. His instincts were usually right, but there was no reason for anyone to be around the Fire Gardens at that time of night. When the flames died down, he poked around in the ashes some more. Finally, he located an object and scraped it out with the tip of his sword. It was the die, each side about as big as two thumbnails.

'Mellias swallowed it to keep it away from the murderer,' Vidar said. 'It was the only place he could guarantee his killer wouldn't search.'

Rhiannon gaped for a moment, then said, 'The fire did not destroy it? Of what is it made?'

The die cooled with unnatural speed, and once Vidar could pick it up, he examined it closely. All six sides were smooth and devoid of any marks or inscriptions. It was impossible to discern the material from which it had been shaped; not wood, certainly, not stone nor bone.

'Why?' Rhiannon said simply.

'Mellias thought it was important. The painter of your picture in the Temple of the Shepherd did too. There are four of these illustrated in the background.' Vidar turned the die over in his fingers, but could see nothing that gave any value to it. 'This whole affair is starting to make me feel uneasy. Nothing makes sense.'

They were startled from their contemplation by the sound of shattering glass and voices raised in anger as some street protest got out of hand. The bonfire at Fallen Spire appeared to have grown larger. Not far away his friend was dying, and the King who had ruled Idriss for so long was dying too. Vidar couldn't escape the feeling that everything was falling apart.

Rhiannon took the die and slipped it into the bag hanging from her waist. 'I will study this. But we tell no one how we came across it. Agreed?'

Vidar nodded.

They left the Fire Gardens quickly. As Vidar moved along the cobbled street away from the gates, he was overcome by another feeling that he was being watched. He glanced back and a shadow loomed across the street, along the walls, and was gone. There was no sign of what might have caused it, and all around was still and silent. Vidar waited a moment longer and then hurried Rhiannon away.

* * *

AT GREER AN' Lokh's tower, Asgrim's condition had worsened. Cheyne grimly continued to minister to his friend, but the physician and his assistants had given up making anything but the most cursory attempts to help the northerner. Troubled by the circumstances of the die's discovery, Rhiannon returned to the offices of the Order to consider how the new information could possibly fit into her enquiry, leaving Vidar to pace the silent, stinking chambers with anger born of unease.

Eventually, he heard the bolts drawn and the door thrown open to Greer an' Lokh's ritual rooms. Vidar found the sorcerer naked and smeared with black grease dancing a jig to music only he could hear.

'Vidar, Vidar, Lord of Silence,' Greer an' Lokh sang quietly, 'he leaves no trace in his passing. God of the northern men, who is not a god, just a man, and nothing more.'

Vidar restrained himself, and then said, 'My friend is dying. I need your help to save him.'

Greer an' Lokh came to a shuffling halt. He stared at Vidar blankly for a moment, as if trying to comprehend a foreign language, before waving Vidar away. 'Fetch the physician if you need a life saved. I do the opposite.'

'The physician can't help.'

'And you think I can? I am not a god, either, Vidar.'

'You said we are all gods.'

'I did, did I not?' He thought for a moment, then continued with his dance, which had now become a waltz with an imaginary partner. 'Do you realise, do you realise, do you realise the consequences of me saving a life? Or even attempting to save one?'

'I don't care about the consequences. Just the life.'

'It has been a rule of all the sorcerers of Idriss that we do not attempt to pull the dying back from the edge of their lives. For every action, you see, there is a reaction.'

'A price to pay.'

'If you will.' He dropped to his knees and anxiously began to count the bones that hung around his neck. 'Numbers... patterns... nothing created... nothing destroyed.' He stared at Vidar with hollow eyes. 'Do you not know how this works?' he said desperately.

'You cut up some poor bastard, suck out their life, and use it to change things, or learn something new.'

'Yes, yes, the release of energy. It transforms. But it does so by altering the patterns. A touch here, a push there, one thing shifts, and everything connected to it moves too. But how? That is the question. Who has the eyes to see such a thing? We try and we hope, but we never really know. And to save a life, to mend bones and livers and kidneys, to pull the energy back into every small part, to drive away the fever and ignite the brain – what a shift in the pattern that is. What could it cause, Lord of Stealth and Silence? We are not allowed to take that risk.'

'You have to do it.' Vidar could see that Greer an' Lokh, with his insane drive for knowledge and experience, could not resist, if the barrier was lifted for him.

Greer an' Lokh rolled across the floor, tearing at his flesh and hair, and when he came to rest his eyes burned wildly. 'Then you must accept responsibility for what happens. You must tell the King or his stone-faced little dog that it was not me. Not me searching, pushing at the door, pushing, pushing. It was you!'

'All right. Now what do you need?'

'You know what I need, Ghost Warrior. What you take so freely whenever you hunger.'

'There's a condemned man in the cells–'

'Two, Silent One. Two!'

Vidar hesitated.

'Yes!' Snickering, Greer an' Lokh jumped to his feet. 'Two for a ritual of this magnitude. No less will do! But there are only two condemned men in all the cells, is that not right?' His eyes gleamed. 'Just two, and you were saving them for a little snack at a later date, were you not? If they are both gone, what will you feed on when the amber jewel sucks the life out of you? One of your friends? That Inquisitor who pokes her nose into all the nooks and crannies of my home? Or an innocent off the streets, skipping home to her mother and father, with thoughts of sugared treats and little puppies?' His laughter became a gurgle, then a hacking cough, but he continued to dance around the chamber with glee.

Vidar grew cold. The sorcerer was right: if both condemned men were given up for Greer an' Lokh's ritual, he would have no option but to take an innocent if he wanted to survive.

'If you do not sanction this, your wild-haired friend will die, no doubt,' Greer an' Lokh jabbed cruelly, revelling in Vidar's dilemma. Vidar half-thought about taking the sorcerer's life instead – of all the people in Idriss, he had inflicted the most pain and suffering, and if Vidar had to choose a life he would lose least sleep over Greer an' Lokh, but that would leave the city defenceless.

Greer an' Lokh watched intently, as if he could read every thought passing through Vidar's head. 'Do we proceed, Lord of Stealth and Silence? Or is your friend's life no longer so valuable?'

'Get on with it,' Vidar snapped. He marched out of the chamber before Greer an' Lokh saw any sign of his weakness.

* * *

MOVING SWIFTLY THROUGH the Palace of Justice, Rhiannon was taken by how uncommonly busy it was for that time of night. Inquisitors huddled together in corridors, whispering, or waited silently in their rooms, faces hidden in the depths of hoods, brooding by the light of a candle. An intense atmosphere suffused the entire building.

Ashur, his features appearing more frozen by the light of the torches, passed her on his way out of the building, LeStrange and another assistant close behind. She was puzzled to see his gaze flicker towards her as though he knew her, but he was gone before she could read his eyes.

As she was about to enter her chambers, she was summoned into Chief Inquisitor Serena's office, a silver-haired woman with cold, commanding eyes and a jagged scar running from the edge of her mouth to her jawline, which made her appear to be permanently grimacing.

'The Mellias enquiry is not progressing fast enough,' Serena said bluntly.

'It is a complicated enquiry, Chief Inquisitor, and growing more complicated by the day–'

'Not so,' the Chief Inquisitor interrupted. 'It appears perfectly simple to me. An enemy from beyond Idriss is at large in the city. Find them.'

'Yes, Chief Inquisitor.'

'There is some concern at the court regarding the slow pace of this enquiry. Doubts are being cast on your ability to see it through to completion. There have been... rumours that evidence was mislaid, or, perhaps, consciously destroyed to cover your mistakes.'

'That is not true, Chief Inquisitor, and unfair,' Rhiannon protested. 'I carry out my duties to the fullness of my ability.'

'You are aware of the unrest in the city, of course. The death of a great hero like Mellias has understandably left the people bereft. He was loved and respected for all he has done for Idriss. But now stories are circulating that he was murdered, and if the greatest hero in the city can be taken by surprise and slaughtered, then Idriss itself is at risk of falling. There is a belief at the highest level that the unrest will only get worse – that Idriss could be brought down by its own people – unless Mellias's murderer is brought to justice. Quickly.'

'Justice must be weighed carefully, as you well know, Chief Inquisitor–'

'In this instance, justice must be rapid. There is too much at stake.'

'Errors may happen if the correct paths to a solution are not followed–'

'The people need to be soothed and Idriss needs to be saved, Inquisitor Rhiannon. That is the first priority now. And Administrator

Ashur has made it quite clear where blame will fall if this outcome is not assured.'

'I will be blamed?' Rhiannon said, stunned. 'You will take my job? It is my life!'

'If there is any proof that you were complicit in the failure to find Mellias's killer, it may cost you more than your job. In this instance, a case for treason could be made.'

A bitter cold rushed through Rhiannon. She could read every unspoken word that lay behind the Chief Inquisitor's comments.

'The solution is simple,' the Chief Inquisitor continued. 'Find the culprit, and do it quickly. I expect to be kept appraised of your enquiry.'

Rhiannon left the office in a daze. She had feared politics lay behind her appointment to the enquiry from the very first, but she had not expected the outcome to be so rapid or extreme.

Along the marble-lined main corridor, with its busts of Inquisitors past, their names now long forgotten, Assigners were ordering the ranks into small groups and despatching them across the city. It was not the role of the Inquisitors to keep the peace, but as representatives of unending justice they would be a symbol of stability at a time when it was most needed.

Feeling suddenly weary, Rhiannon made her way up the stairs to the first floor. Her footsteps echoed loudly in the stillness. When she had been appointed to the Mellias enquiry she had been given a new chamber to befit her status, large and cool with marble inlays, a high ceiling, and windows that looked out on the Mountain of the Heart. But it was far away from the main bustle of the Order and the comforting chatter of her colleagues. Now, with the first-floor corridor in darkness and all the adjoining chambers deserted, it felt as if her chamber perfectly matched her position: isolated, lonely, soon to be forgotten.

Taking a lantern from the rack near the door to the stairs, she lit it with her flint. Shadows raced along the corridor. Followed by the soft metronome of her boots, she moved through the half-light, her mind sifting the main points of the enquiry. Mellias was killed by someone he knew. The brutalisation of the body, and its ritual placing that hinted at some connection to the religion of the Shepherd. The strange die that was referenced in an ancient painting. Her powerful intuitive ability to find connections that others missed had always been highly praised within the Order, but she was seeing nothing here. Too much was still missing.

Instinctively, though, she knew the Chief Inquisitor was wrong to see it as a straightfor-ward murder by an enemy of Idriss. There was design, and until she could identify that design it felt as if the safety of them all was at stake.

Her chamber felt cold, despite the time of year. Placing her evidence bag on the table, she stood at the window, looking out over the deserted tree lined avenue winding up the hill, her thoughts turning to Vidar. She found him infuriating and stimulating in equal measure. He did not carry the attraction of a long heritage within Idriss, but he was filled with an energy that always drew eyes to him whenever he appeared. She had tried to put it down to a by-product of the unnerving vampiric jewel, but it was evident it was within him. Her fellow Inquisitors felt he was too dangerous for consideration, but she found that a significant part of the attraction.

A clattering on the roof over her head echoed in the stillness. Pressing her face against the glass, Rhiannon peered up, but it was impossible to see anything. Her mind had been trained to perceive intricate webs of connections and already it was instinctively performing its task behind the patina of her conscious thought, sifting subtle signs, the echoes of the sound, suggesting weight, the out-of-place nature, the direction of movement towards the walkway along the roof, with its door that gave access to the building.

She was unsure why it concerned her, but the patter of her heart was responding to some notion that had not yet presented itself to her. Picking up the lantern, she stepped out into the dark corridor and listened. All was still.

Who would want to gain access to the offices of the Order? No citizen, certainly. But with so many secrets and mysteries circling that night, she was not prepared to reach any conclusions. In her training they had called it the Unknown Shadow. The Unknown Shadow in any enquiry obscured not only meaning and motivation, but also potential danger. When the Unknown Shadow was present, an Inquisitor should be on the highest alert and dismiss nothing, no matter how insignificant or ridiculous it appeared.

Rhiannon moved slowly along the corridor towards the stairs to the roof. The heavy door groaned as she eased into the stairwell. The flame of her lantern gave a barely perceptible ripple, but Rhiannon instantly knew what that meant: a draught from the open roof door.

She considered alerting the guards at the main entrance, but by the time they returned, any intruder would have the run of the building. She began to climb the stairs on the balls of her feet, making no sound.

At the third floor, the door was very slightly ajar. Normal passage would see it slammed shut. Someone had crept through. Slipping through the door into the corridor, she listened again: a sound that could have been a faint tread. She looked up and down the corridor, but the lantern light didn't reach the end.

She was puzzled. Two or three people should still have been working on that floor, but the lights in all the chambers were extinguished. Inquisitor Amala was certainly at work, cross-referencing the statements from the Keepers at the Store of the Ages, work that Rhiannon had charged her with earlier that day.

Outside Amala's chamber, Rhiannon smelled the subtlest hint of smoke from a recently extinguished lantern. No movement was visible through the glass of the door. She swung it open, ready for any intruder, but was instantly thrown off-guard by the meaty scent of blood. Amala was slumped in one corner, her throat slit.

Rhiannon checked for signs of life, found none. As her heart thundered, her mind raced through the new information she was receiving, building possibilities and probabilities, a picture that mutated rapidly. The Unknown Shadow was all around now.

Movement flashed past the door, just a glimpse from the corner of her eye. Did the intruder know she was within? Probably not.

Keeping low, she moved quickly around the edge of the room to peer through the glass of the door. The corridor was too dark to see anything. Further along, a shaft of moonlight broke through a newly opened door. The intruder was searching, but for what?

Rhiannon silently covered the distance to the open door, but she could hear no sound within. Balancing on her toes, she was ready to use the self-defence techniques that were second nature to all Inquisitors. Cautiously, she peered around the door jamb. The room was empty.

The scrape of a boot at her back came a moment too late for her to react. A hand clamped across her mouth, and she glimpsed the glimmer of a blade sweeping towards her. A sour aroma filled her senses, hot breath on the back of her neck.

She threw her entire weight backwards, crashing her head into the face of her attacker. A snarl, unsettlingly bestial. The knife missed her by a fraction and caught in the folds of her cloak as she continued to drive backwards. Her attacker overbalanced, removed the hand from her mouth, and clawed at the wall for support.

Rhiannon rolled over the body, landing on her feet, the tips of the fingers of one hand brushing the floor for balance, and then she was up and moving. Never stay still, that was the prime rule. Inquisitors never carried a weapon, but she had always found her well-trained physical defences just as effective.

The attacker was just a bulky shadow in the dark of the corridor, but as it edged around the shaft of moonlight she saw it was a bulky man in a thick woollen cloak, balding on top, hair thin and grey and long around the ears. His lips curled away from his teeth in another snarl that was more animal than human.

He launched himself at her, the knife arcing. His speed belied his size, and he was strong. Rhiannon barely managed to dance out of his way, catching him a fleeting blow on the side of his head with a stiff forearm. It had no effect, and even as he was moving past her, he changed the direction of the knife and tore it along the length of her arm.

The pain sent lances of fire into her shoulder, but she didn't cry out; she never cried out. She spun on one foot, swinging her left boot up into his face as he rounded on her. His nose shattered in a spray of blood, his cry even more savage.

Continuing the arc of her leg before stepping back, Rhiannon adopted a defensive posture, but the attacker was already driving forwards. He slammed into her with such force it drove the breath from her and propelled her into the wall. Her head cracked against the stone and she fell to the floor, dazed.

Struggling to regain consciousness, she expected the attacker to slash her throat as he had done Amala's, but instead he began to rifle frantically through the pockets of her cloak.

Realisation came in a flash: *he wants the die*.

The revelation shocked Rhiannon alert. As the attacker tore at her clothing for signs of hidden pockets, she brought her knee up sharply into his jaw. He fell back with a howl of pain, the half-clutched knife skidding along the floor. Rhiannon rolled on to her stomach and was on her feet in a second, running towards the door to the stairs. Blood streamed down her arm and splattered across the floor.

Behind, her attacker's furious breath came like the barks of a hunting dog. She crashed through the door as he reached her, throwing the full weight of it into his body. It slowed him for just a second. Nothing appeared to hurt him significantly.

Careering down the steps, her head spun from the blood loss. The attacker was so close behind she could feel his fingers tearing at her cloak. Desperately, she loosened it at the neck and let it fly behind her. It caught around him and he fell heavily, but was back on his feet just as quickly.

Finally she skidded out into the ground-floor corridor, staggering weakly. 'Guards! Intruder!' she called out, hoping her cries were loud enough to hear.

The attacker emerged into the corridor just as the guards ran towards them, drawing their swords. His eyes flickered from them to Rhiannon as she slumped against the wall, clutching her arm, and in that gaze, she saw a cold hatred with all humanity stripped from it. Rhiannon had the strangest impression that his face was a mask, though it appeared real; it lacked a certain elasticity, a nuance of emotion, as though he had pulled another man's face over his own.

For a second, he weighed his options and then fled back through the doors and up the stairs. As he disappeared, Rhiannon caught sight of something glinting in the corridor torchlight: a heavy silver ring on the second finger of his left hand.

'After him!' she gasped as the guards arrived. 'He will try to escape across the roof.'

Inquisitor Satra ran up, tearing off her shirt, which she bound tightly around the wound on Rhiannon's arm. 'This needs stitches,' Satra said. 'You must come to the physician.'

'Wait,' Rhiannon replied weakly. 'First I must retrieve something from my room.'

'Can it not wait?' Satra said, puzzled.

But Rhiannon was already staggering towards the stairwell door, aware that the die may well be the key to all the misfortune that had befallen Idriss since Mellias's murder.

5

THE WORLD BEYOND THE WALLS

ALL ACROSS IDRISS, eyes turned towards Greer an' Lokh's tower where lightning crackled and purple smoke plumed from the highest floor. The spectacular sight eased the tension that lay tight across the city, for everyone knew that the great sorcerer who had helped keep Idriss safe for so long was now active in their defence. Surely it was only a matter of time before the threat within the city walls would be destroyed, and the people would be safe once more.

Inside the tower, the air seethed with the heat from a furnace blazing in one corner of the sorcerer's ritual space. Sparks flew in golden clouds as Greer an' Lokh plunged mysterious implements into the heat before taking them back to his work on the killing benches. Vidar and Cheyne wore kerchiefs tied across their mouths against the billowing, acrid smoke that somehow still stung their throats and teared their eyes.

'There is no doubting it – he is a master,' Cheyne said as he admired Greer an' Lokh's flourishes. The screams and gibberings could not be heard above the pumping of the bellows and the crackling of the flames.

Vidar eyed the soon-to-be corpses uneasily. The bouts of weakness were coming with increasing regularity, and when he looked in the mirror he saw his cheeks were hollower and his eyes had lost their sparkle. 'As long as he saves Asgrim. That's all that matters.'

'To be frank, this sorcery business unsettles me. I like things I can control, and understand. Hard things I can hold in my hands. This is beyond me. The lives of those two will flow into Asgrim? Is that how it works? Like life flows into your jewel and into you?'

'Greer an' Lokh uses the release of their essential spark as a fulcrum to alter the patterns of the world. It'll change the pattern of what will happen to Asgrim. Healing where there would have been decay. Or something.'

As a spout of blood rose up, then rained down on Greer an' Lokh, he did a little dance as if greeting a spring shower, his face and shoulders painted incarnadine.

'So the furry ball of misery is worth two of other men,' Cheyne said appreciatively. 'If he can identify Mellias's murder, we should start the search through Idriss immediately. The people will help us. They will probably tear the bastard limb from limb. Living in fear of what lies outside the walls is one thing. To have it in their midst, where they are supposed to be safe and secure, is another. Why, I think it would drive them to commit any atrocity on the source of their terror,' he added with a note of relish.

'We don't know how much Asgrim saw,' Vidar cautioned. He could tell the life was beginning to ebb from Greer an' Lokh's two victims, for the jewel in his chest was starting to pulse hungrily.

The array of tools, gems, bone artefacts, chunks of quivering meat, candles and braziers, and roughly painted scraps of parchment arranged around the killing tables made no sense to Vidar, but the items were clearly laid out in some pattern that only Greer an' Lokh could see. Smoke surged mysteriously as the sorcerer threw his hands into the air and gave a high-pitched squeal, and as the clouds obscured the final acts of his ritual more bolts of energy lashed across the room so that Vidar and Cheyne had to take cover beyond the furnace. There was a stink of burned iron, and a sound like a metal door being wrenched open, and then Greer an' Lokh ran from the smoke.

'Quick! Quick!' he shrieked. 'Let us see!'

He weaved past Vidar and Cheyne, out of the door, and down the stone steps, whooping and singing as he went.

Vidar and Cheyne found him bent over Asgrim, head pressed against the northerner's chest, listening intently. 'Yes, yes, I hear the change,' he breathed. 'A push here, a shove there. The wheel turns, the cogs fall in line. What would be is not, and what could not be, is.'

He roughly forced open Asgrim's eyelids. At first there was no movement, but then a tremor ran through the eyes, and finally they ranged around the room. After a moment of stillness, Asgrim spasmed, then flailed his arms wildly so that Greer an' Lokh had to pin him down to stop him throwing himself off the bed.

'Vidar! Do not kill her! Do not consign us all to hell!' he raved.

'They sometimes say the strangest things when they come back from the brink,' Greer an' Lokh said sheepishly.

Ignoring him, Vidar rushed to Asgrim's side. Cheyne roughly thrust Greer an' Lokh away now his work was done.

'Leave us,' Vidar said.

'No thanks?' Greer an' Lokh asked slyly.

'I would leave now,' Cheyne said quietly, 'before I see if I can match you in expertise at the killing tables.'

Unfazed by the threat, Greer an' Lokh watched Cheyne for a long moment as if considering the sounds he would make at the end, and then he turned and scampered like a monkey out of the room.

Vidar watched as Cheyne checked Asgrim's vitals with a tenderness he rarely exhibited, and then he smiled and nodded. 'Alive, still, and growing stronger. It worked.'

'Good. It could have got unpleasant at the Fire Gardens. All that hair – he'd have gone up before they lit the tinder.'

They sat silently next to the bed for a long hour, watching as Asgrim visibly recovered. But Vidar couldn't shake Greer an' Lokh's warning that there would be a price to pay for his sorcery, and he had an inkling what that price would be. His bouts of debilitating weakness had become more intense with each brightening of Asgrim's condition, as if life was draining from one to the other. If he hadn't been sitting, his state would have been obvious to Cheyne, who had seen the decline on many occasions. But for the first time things were different. There were always murderers and rapists kept in the cells for the moments when the jewel demanded replenishing, insurance the King had agreed to when Vidar had proven his worth to the Crimson Hunt. Now there was none, and with his life dribbling away, sooner or later he would be forced to find a victim.

He had asked the question of himself many times: how far would he go to survive? Soon he would know the answer.

As dawn broke through the windows in gold and purple, Asgrim finally came out of his febrile state and looked around with clear eyes.

'You are in Greer an' Lokh's tower. He wants to hang you on a hook in his ritual chamber,' Cheyne said. 'We are currently negotiating to see what we can get in return for this pile of bones and fur.'

Asgrim saw through his words. 'Drive a good bargain, assassin. My pedigree is priceless.' He tried to lever himself on to his elbows, but fell back.

'Rest. You're still weak,' Vidar said. 'If we had time, we'd leave you to recover, but we need to know—'

'About Mellias's murderer.' He nodded. 'It is not what you think, Vidar. He is not human. Some kind of… demon.'

'What did you see?'

'He had claimed another victim in the alleys of Red Hill. As the poor fool died, the murderer changed his face–'

'He is still feverish,' Cheyne said.

'No.' Asgrim gripped Cheyne's wrist. 'By all my gods, it is true. He took the life from his victim, and used it to alter his appearance. And in between the two faces, there was another... his real visage. Face as white as the bones in the sorcerer's charnel house, a bloody red slash of a mouth, and his hair red too, a bright, brilliant red, like the summer sun. He is a demon, this Red Man. A demon.'

Vidar and Cheyne sat in silence for a moment, and then Vidar said, 'And his new face?'

Asgrim shook his head. 'I barely glimpsed it. But if he has killed again, that face will be gone and a new one will sit in its place.'

Cheyne shook his head incredulously. 'How can we catch him, if he can be anyone?'

'And when the people find out there is a killer in their midst who could look like their friends, their family... that they can trust no one... what then?' Asgrim ruminated.

'Chaos,' Vidar said. 'We can barely contain them now. With the threat outside the walls, they need their security within. Take that away from them and the whole structure of Idriss will fall apart.'

'What, then?' Cheyne said. He and Asgrim looked to Vidar.

'We keep this to ourselves.'

Asgrim shifted uneasily. 'Not tell the King? Or even Ashur? Keeping secret things that relate to the security of Idriss may well be considered treason.'

'*Will* be considered treason,' Cheyne insisted. 'Our heads will be on spikes at the Deeping Gate, and my complexion is too delicate to be exposed to the elements.'

'We don't know who we can trust,' Vidar said. 'And you know the court. Every secret is soon spinning out of control in the inns and markets. Our loyalty is to Idriss. If we want to keep the city safe, we can't risk this information getting out.'

'Hmm, noble,' Cheyne observed.

'Yes. Who'd have thought it?'

'Then what do you suggest?' Asgrim asked. 'That we hunt this bastard down ourselves? A killer who could be anyone?'

'But think of the reward when we catch him,' Vidar said.

'*If* we catch him.' Asgrim closed his eyes wearily. 'Before we get stabbed in the neck by someone we think is our trusted friend.'

'Or before Ashur finds out,' Cheyne said. 'Still, I like the sound of that reward. I have a few gaps in my wardrobe that need to be filled.'

'Get some rest,' Vidar said to Asgrim. 'We need to develop a strategy to deal with this. And your ability to scent your prey is going to be the key.'

THE MOUNTAIN OF the Heart was flooded with sunlight, quiet in that peaceful time before breakfast had been completed and the day's labours begun. It was set to be another beautiful early summer day, but Rhiannon could only see the Unknown Shadow clustering around the edge of her mind. Her arm ached where the physician had put in a row of ragged stitches; she felt sick from the herbs he had given her to numb the pain, weary from hours without sleep, weak from blood loss, and on edge at the thought that her life was in jeopardy if her enquiry failed.

The sensible thing would have been to retire home to rest before throwing herself back into work, but she felt instinctively that time was critical. The guards had failed to catch her attacker before he had escaped across the rooftops. If he was prepared to storm the very stronghold of the Order to attempt to reclaim the die, it would not be long before he tried again.

Not so long ago she would have reported the importance of the die to the Chief Inquisitor, but now she wasn't sure she could trust her not to use the information against Rhiannon in some way she couldn't yet perceive. She was on her own.

Or was she? Vidar was self-interested, dangerous, and decadent, but strangely she felt she could trust him. Plucking the die from her evidence bag, she rested it in the palm of her hand. It was insignificant, yet it appeared to have odd qualities. It made her skin tingle, and there were times when it appeared to be reflecting light from no obvious source. She considered her options, then returned the die to her bag and left quickly.

The eyes of the guards and other Inquisitors appeared to follow her as she left the Palace of Justice, although she wondered if that was her own paranoia. Even when she was lost in the winding, quiet streets, she didn't drop her guard for a moment, her eyes searching every alley and doorway, continually scanning the rooftops.

The Temple of the Shepherd was, if anything, even more peaceful than the awakening city. At that time of day, with its main doors aligned to the east, the building was flooded with sunlight, so that the walls and every column appeared to glow with a soft white light. Rhiannon made her way to the tiny picture tucked away in its alcove and allowed herself a moment of stillness. Ever since she had first stumbled across it by accident, it had spoken to her, though she was not sure why. Part of it, she guessed, was that life in Idriss was hard, always on the edge of subsistence, with every effort marshalled into achieving the next day, and the thought of someone who could reach out and save her from those struggles was deeply comforting. But it was the sense that there was something more than this mundane existence that excited her the most. Their lives in Idriss felt so small and contained, so meaningless beyond simple survival. What if there truly was something greater?

Checking no one was around, she removed the die and compared it to the depiction in the painting. Vidar had been right; the proportions were perfect, and the artist had even captured the odd quality of the light that came off it. Whoever painted the picture must have seen the die and understood its importance. More intriguing was that the painting suggested there were four such artefacts. What was their importance to the Shepherd? And why were they so important now that someone would kill to obtain them?

Rhiannon found Laurent meditating next to the flame that continually changed colour. His purple robes and blue tattoos were striking against the white of the walls and columns. He smiled when he saw her. 'Inquisitor. It appears you have found a new home.'

'It is very peaceful here.'

'Have you made your decision to join the little lambs of the Shepherd?'

Rhiannon hesitated. 'I think... perhaps I have.'

'Then we will make arrangements for your induction. I am very pleased. You will be most welcome here.'

'I have a question about *The Supplicant Praises the Power of the Visitant*.'

'I must move that painting into the main gallery.' He laughed. 'It is becoming our most popular work.'

'It shows a very distinctive landscape. The hillside with the tomb in the background. The mountain that resembles a sleeping giant. It looks to me very much like that place exists.'

'That is the wonder of an artist's imagination.'

'You do not think it is real?'

'I do not think it matters. Perhaps it was the artist's home, where he dreamed up this way to praise the power of the Visitant in his own way. What matters are the Shepherd, and his power, and the supplicant before him. That is the essence of our religion. We go bare-headed and weaponless before the Shepherd, and we bare our throats to him, and await his judgement.'

'I do not know,' Rhiannon said, unsure. 'An artist constructs his work like a potter makes a bowl. Everything is there for a reason.'

He smiled, but clearly had no interest in her ruminations. 'Shall we make arrangements for your induction now?'

'Later. I have important business to conduct first.'

She left the temple in a hurry, feeling the Unknown Shadow shift slightly. She had discovered something of importance, she was sure.

ASGRIM'S RECOVERY WAS astonishingly rapid. By mid-morning he was already sitting on the edge of his bed, examining his wounds and complaining loudly about his forced inactivity. Vidar and Cheyne had pinned a large map of Idriss to one wall and had spent the last hour dividing it into sectors for a search once Asgrim had sufficiently recovered.

The familiar sickness overcame Vidar as they debated how to cover the sprawling Red Hill district, and he made his excuses and left. He could feel Cheyne's gaze heavy on his back. Cheyne knew, and soon everyone would know, when he could barely drag himself out of a chair, and his cheeks grew hollow and the flesh hung limply from his bones, and every glance in a mirror was a vision of his death.

He passed Greer an' Lokh as he stumbled down the steps of the tower, pausing regularly to catch his breath. The sorcerer blocked Vidar's way, giggling. 'Oh, it has started again! So soon this time! Perhaps there will come a time when the jewel sucks the life from you faster and faster until taking a life no longer works. What then? Will you embrace the eternal silence, or be dragged into it, screaming?'

Vidar found the strength to throw Greer an' Lokh to one side and careered down the steps until he emerged into the hot sun. The field-workers delivering potatoes from the arable land to the north paused to stare at him as they hauled their cart over the cobbles. He staggered towards the river and rested against the stone wall, fighting the breathlessness and the flashes before his eyes. Nearby a group of children threw stones at some unrecognisable carcass that had floated downstream from somewhere in the forest. It still bore the teeth marks of the carnivorous river dwellers that prevented most passage.

The amber jewel pulsed in his chest, sending cold fingers towards his heart, and the ghosts were whispering loudly in the back of his head. '*Die! Die! This time! Die!*'

Closing his eyes, he steadied himself, but the whispering only grew more intense. The ghosts always appeared to know when the threat against him was greatest; were they sensing that this time he really was in jeopardy?

He looked at the playing children, measuring them, considering how close to death he would need to be to kill one of them; if he could even do it. Turning, he watched the fieldworkers. Could he slit one of their throats? Innocent, hard-working; why did he deserve to live more than they did? There was no logic to survival; just an uncontrollable desire. But where, he wondered, did it end? Would he do anything at all to keep living?

He choked back the poisonous urge from the jewel to rush the fieldworkers and kill them on the spot. His hands shook from the strain. When he looked back at the men, they had hurried on, throwing backward glances as if they could read his murderous intent.

'Vidar? Are you all right?' Rhiannon rested a worried hand on his arm. She had been making her way to the tower from the Palace of Justice.

He was sickened by the combination of desires – the hunger for her life, and the hunger for her love – and for a moment he couldn't look her in the face. Finally, by force of his trained will, he reined in the jewel's hunger.

'Taking the sun. It's been a long night.'

She searched his features for a moment, trying to see where the lie lay, and then she said, 'We have much to discuss.'

As they climbed the tower back to the chamber where Asgrim rested, she told him about her attacker and her belief that he was searching for the die, and that she was convinced the painting in the Temple of the Shepherd not only showed a location that was somehow important, but also underlined the great value of the die – or the four dice.

The period of weakness passed, and Vidar liked to think it was Rhiannon's presence that had brought him back to vitality, although he knew if he gave voice to it he would have sounded like a stupid romantic.

He hesitated about telling her of the Red Man's face-changing abilities, but he valued her incisive mind. 'There's a secret,' he began. 'I know you report everything to your Chief Inquisitor, but this has to be kept between us.'

'Tell me,' she replied. 'I am already breaking the rules of the Order by keeping the die secret.'

'It's dangerous,' he said. 'You could be putting yourself at risk.'

'Ah, so you do care.'

'I'm an honourable man.'

'Really,' she said, not attempting to hide her disbelief. 'Tell me.'

She listened intently to his description of Asgrim's discoveries about the Red Man and then said, 'That explains why the attacker risked such a dangerous assault in search of the die. The Order allows only women into the enquiry rooms above the ground floor. He could not simply swap his face and slip in.'

'As he could at the Store of the Ages,' Cheyne said. 'Or the inns and businesses at Red Hill, or my favourite little brothel above the Four Staves.'

'The die is the key,' Vidar said. 'Let me see it.'

Rhiannon handed it to him. 'But it makes no sense. It is plain and simple. It has no use.'

'Like the Red Man,' Vidar said, 'you can't judge it by appearances. There must be something we haven't yet discovered.' He held it up in a shaft of sunlight and turned it slowly. It was as plain as it had appeared to be in the Fire Gardens; no faint markings emerged in the light. Yet as he lowered the die, it glinted briefly as if it had soaked up some of the sunlight and was radiating it. 'Did you see that?' he said curiously. When he tried to bite it, the taste of iron filings filled his mouth. 'Hard as rock. But light.'

Asgrim lurched over from the bed. 'Let Greer an' Lokh loose on it. He will soon divine its meaning.'

'If this has the value we think, he's not getting anywhere near it,' Vidar said.

They passed it around, suggesting increasingly wild theories. 'Not bone, or metal, or rock, or wood,' Cheyne noted, puzzled.

When Vidar took it back, he brought it close to his chest and it fizzed and sparked in his hand.

'What happened there?' Rhiannon asked in amazement.

Deep in thought, Vidar rolled the die around his palm, but it had returned to its original state. Then, as he slowly brought it towards him, it came to life again, vibrating and throwing off more glints of light.

Asgrim ran his hand uneasily through his hair. 'It is calling to you, Vidar.'

'Not me,' Vidar said. He tore open his shirt to reveal the amber jewel pulsing dully. Holding the die between his thumb and forefinger, he brought it towards the mysterious gem.

When it was a hair's breadth from contact, there was a silent explosion of light and movement spinning all around them. Crying out, Asgrim threw himself back. Rhiannon's hand went to her mouth in shock, and Cheyne was rooted.

All around them misty, three-dimensional images of a heavily forested landscape spun, the colours shimmering with a note of unreality: purples, pinks, and turquoise merging with the green of the trees, and grassy hillsides, and the grey-blue of a river.

'Sorcery,' Asgrim gasped. 'What is this thing?'

Rhiannon reached out and slowly moved her arm through the image. It swirled around her and returned to its original form. 'Just a painting in the air,' she said with relief.

Cheyne was entranced. 'Look,' he said. He reached out, palm first, and advanced. The landscape moved with him, revealing areas that had previously been hidden. 'This is quite wonderful. But what is its purpose?'

Vidar probed into the heart of the image until it revealed a city with soaring towers. Beyond it, the azure sea stretched to the horizon.

'It's a map,' he said, hardly daring to believe.

Asgrim gaped, and then broke into a broad grin. 'A map! Vidar, we are about to become the greatest heroes in the history of Idriss.'

'The world will fall open before us,' Cheyne said, with awe. 'We can establish trade routes. No more shortages.'

'It is small wonder the Red Man would risk anything to get this,' Rhiannon said. 'Why, it is the most valuable thing in all of Gardia.'

'How does it work?' Cheyne peered at the cube closely, but there was no sign of how it projected the image.

'It must be magic,' Asgrim said. 'There is no other explanation.'

'Magic that dates back to the time of the Shepherd,' Rhiannon said quietly. Her face had taken on a transcendent expression. 'Perhaps this wondrous object was a gift from the Shepherd himself. From the god to the supplicant, showing us the path out of the darkness.'

'The painting suggests a direct link between the cube and the Shepherd,' Vidar conceded. 'But why would a god need a map?'

'And why did it take your damnable jewel to make it work?' Cheyne asked.

'Power,' Vidar mused. 'The life-spark, light, heat. You saw how it glinted in the sunlight, ready to be opened. And last night, when it lay in the embers of Mellias's pyre, these pictures played in the sky high over the Fire Gardens. It has no power in itself, but draws on sources in the world around it.'

Holding their breath in wonder, they moved around in the world, following sandy beaches, streams, and rivers, discovering new cities and towns, and tiny, heavily defended settlements in the heart of the forest. They found mountains and downs, salt-marshes and plains in areas where, astonishingly, the trees didn't reach. It felt to all of them as if they had been given a view into another world. They could barely contain the beating of their hearts.

'We're seeing things that have been hidden from generation after generation of the people of Idriss,' Vidar said.

Cheyne had been following a trail through the forest. It came to an abrupt end, and when he backtracked the trail was gone. He thought deeply, and then said hesitantly, 'I think, brothers and sister, that we are seeing a reflection of the world as it is now. This map is not fixed in time. It changes, as the world changes.'

He indicated another trail slowly closing near a city on the edge of a lake.

'That explains why we've never been able to retrace a path through the forest.' Vidar was gripped by the revelation. 'The forest itself, or something within the forest, hides the routes.'

'It tricks those who dare enter it,' Rhiannon said. 'Perhaps it truly is alive, as the guards say at the Deeping Gate.'

'But with this map,' Vidar said, 'we can see the trails that are closing, and we can find new ones – if we can travel between one and the other.'

'Wait,' Asgrim said, puzzled. He had manipulated the map until it refused to move any further. 'There is more beyond the edge here, yet it is impossible to see it.'

'Not a map,' Vidar corrected. 'A part of a map. The painting in the Temple of the

Shepherd shows four cubes. This one reveals one quarter of the land. You need all of them to see everything there is to see.'

They considered this for a while, and then Rhiannon said what had leaped into all their minds: 'What if the Red Man already has the other cubes, and is preparing to deliver the four to our enemies?'

'With this cube as well, the world would be theirs,' Cheyne said.

'That makes it even more important.' Vidar had found something curious in the unfolding image. A spike of white light emanated above the trees in one area. Not too far away were four other spikes close together, one scarlet, one emerald, and two more white spikes. Both sets of spikes were moving slowly in the same direction. 'What do we have here?' he said thoughtfully.

The four of them studied the moving lights for a while, but could not identify what they represented. 'Everything else is clear,' Asgrim mused. 'Forests, rivers, coast, hills. What else is there?'

'Unless,' Vidar suggested, 'the map was designed specifically to track something. Or someone.'

'Three thousand years ago?' Cheyne said. 'And it is still moving?'

They watched the gradually moving spikes of light for a while longer until Vidar said, 'It looks as if the only way we'll find out is to go there ourselves.'

Cheyne, Asgrim, and Rhiannon stared at him in horror. 'Travel through the forest? That jewel has sucked out your brains,' Cheyne said.

'And on a whim?' Asgrim added. 'When there are no lives at stake? This is the first and hopefully the last time I need say this: I agree with Cheyne. You are addled. With all due respect to my honoured leader.'

Rhiannon levelled a piercing gaze at him. 'You are not serious?'

'Just a thought. If a map this astonishing was designed and built to track these things, I'd say they would have to be valuable. Possibly priceless.' The lanterns ignited sudden sparks of interest in Cheyne and Asgrim's eyes. 'But, of course, you're right–'

Asgrim plucked at his beard thoughtfully. 'It is true to say that the dangers in the forest are beyond our imagining, and the chances of our survival – even with the map – are next to nothing. But priceless, you say? Why, recovering such a thing for the glory of Idriss must be considered.'

'Dismemberment,' Rhiannon prompted. 'Death.'

'Of course,' Cheyne said, 'and I am second to no man in the preservation of my appendages. But still… glory for Idriss, the King, and the Crimson Hunt… This deserves further consideration.'

'You are all mad,' Rhiannon said.

'There's no point discussing it until we find out where this map is showing us,' Vidar continued. 'It could be on the far side of the horizon.'

They continued to study it, moving through the constantly unfolding images with as much exhilaration as if they were actually travelling abroad, until Rhiannon said reluctantly, 'The river.'

'Of course!' Vidar responded. While Asgrim and Cheyne stared at him blankly, he moved rapidly through the map until he found the broad, shining river. 'Is it ours?' he said. Eagerly, they traced it until they reached the edge of the map.

'That looks like the bend just beyond the walls,' Cheyne said. 'See – there is that inlet where the river-monsters live, according to the description of the merchants in Red Hill.'

'I am not sure,' Asgrim said hesitantly. 'It is not wholly clear.'

'That would be sensible,' Rhiannon said sharply. 'To venture out into the forest with a half-identified map, only to discover it is another river far beyond the horizon–'

'But we would not have to venture far to be sure,' Cheyne said thoughtfully.

'It would make sense that if the map was stored here, it would have some benefit to Idriss,' Vidar said. 'Why would someone bring a map from the other side of the horizon here?'

'Oh, I don't know... chance?' Rhiannon said tartly. 'To excite, confuse, and damn some treasure-hungry fools?'

'We would need a good argument to convince the King to allow us through the gates with enough provisions,' Cheyne said. 'And horses, of course. And they are not about to waste those on a whim.'

Vidar closed his hand tightly around the cube and the map winked out. The chamber appeared desolate without the colours and the fresh horizons that had been afforded them.

Rhiannon read his meaning in his glance. 'Keep it,' she said. 'Rather you the target of the bloody killer than me.' Her comment was dismissive, but Vidar knew a deep bond of trust had been forged. For an Inquisitor to give up a vital piece of evidence from her enquiry was unheard of. From that point there would be no going back for any of them.

Asgrim beat his chest firmly. 'Look – I am fit and healthy now.' He choked back a cough sheepishly. 'Get me back to my quarters. I can stand the stink in this vile pit no longer.'

Cheyne snorted. 'Now you see what I have to put up with, with your unseemly body odour and constant flatulence.'

Bickering, Cheyne and Asgrim began to collect the northerner's clothes and make their way out of the tower. Rhiannon held back until they had gone and then said, 'You state your love of treasure loudly, but I am certain there are other matters at play.'

'Like?'

'You feel this map – and the others – may open up the mysteries of your past.' Her piercing green eyes searched his face. 'You see in this discovery not only the solution of the mystery that is affecting Idriss, but also a route to the solution of your own mystery. You want to find your place in the world, Vidar.'

'You see that with your Inquisitor's perception, do you?'

'No, I see it as a–' She bit off the final word. 'Do not drag your friends to their deaths with your own personal obsession. They will follow you to the ends of the world, you know that.'

'They'll get a fair reward for their troubles.'

'You would risk the perils of the forest to discover who you are? It is that important to you?'

At first Vidar wasn't going to answer, but the hints of emotion he saw deep in her eyes demanded too much of him. 'You said it yourself – we need four maps to find out who we really are. I don't have any of them.'

She nodded, said nothing, but her thoughts were clearly deep. As she turned to go, she added, 'There are forces moving all around us, Vidar. Together we are stronger. We should aid each other – to uncover the Red Man, to defend Idriss. And, if you wish, to find your place in the world.'

Her last comment contained too much that was unspoken, and by the time he had attempted to understand it, she was gone.

Vidar followed Rhiannon a moment later. In the shadows of the stairwell, Greer an' Lokh stood silently, turning over everything he had seen in the chamber.

EN ROUTE BACK to his rooms, Vidar was brought up sharp by the sudden tolling of the palace bells. The note of alarm in them had never been heard in Vidar's time in the city. No warning of invasion or of a threat to Idriss – this was something even worse. As court officials broke off from their conversations, white-faced, Vidar ran as fast as he could towards the palace.

His worst fears were confirmed when he entered the cool marble entrance hall, peaceful and welcoming with its bubbling fountain and high, airy ceilings. Women stood around, sobbing, and courtiers passed with dazed expressions. Vidar bounded up the stairs to the administration complex on the second floor where Ashur was locked in deep debate with the senior members of the court. LeStrange emerged with an armful of parchments.

'The King is dead?' Vidar asked bluntly.

LeStrange shook his head, glancing around in case they might be overheard. 'He still clings to life. But the physician says it is only a matter of time.'

'He's named his successor?'

'No.' LeStrange looked as if he had no blood in his face. 'The council has pressed him for a long time, and he has always promised an answer, but never delivered.'

'If the people lose their King so soon after losing their greatest hero, this unrest is going to get much worse. And with no one in line to offer them security—'

'We are all painfully aware of that, Vidar,' LeStrange snapped. He passed a hand across his face. 'I am sorry. These are difficult days. Ashur's demands—' He caught himself.

'The King's conscious?'

'Yes, but Ashur has decreed that no one should see him.'

Vidar smiled. 'In case they persuade the King that they should be the next in line, and not Ashur.'

LeStrange waved a cautioning finger. 'I will tell the King you visited. It will be good for him to know. He always favoured you.'

'I'll brief the Crimson Hunt. They need to know what demands are going to be placed on them in the days to come.'

Vidar made his way back down the stairs. He had only just reached the entrance hall when a breathless LeStrange careened after him. 'Wait! Wait!' he gasped. 'The King...!' Red-faced from his exertion, he caught his breath. 'The King insists that you see him.'

'All right,' Vidar said, puzzled.

LeStrange led him into the King's private chambers. Dwarfed by an enormous four-posted bed, Lud looked like a child at rest. Only the yellow tinge to his skin and the vinegar smell of the room gave away his critical state. His eyes flickered open and a frail finger beckoned for Vidar to come closer. LeStrange retreated to allow them privacy.

'Vidar? Is that you?' the King croaked.

'It is. You should rest–'

'My time is short, I know that, and there is much still to do. I have been foolish in these final years. A successor should have been established long since, but we all feel that we have more time than is truly marked on the map of our life.'

His head lolled so that Vidar thought he had finally expired, but then he whispered, 'I remember when you arrived at the Deeping Gate, Vidar. Wild, ranting, smeared with your own blood, like an animal. The guards on the wall were convinced you were one of the forest creatures and were ready to loose their arrows at you. But I was on the walls that day, inspecting the watch, and I saw something in you, Vidar… a quality that I recognised. Fear. A forest creature would not be filled with that thing which defines us.'

He smacked his lips and beckoned for a sip of water. In the hanging skin, and the rheumy eyes, Vidar saw himself on too many occasions, clinging to the last of life, desperate for just one more minute, one more second.

'You came to Idriss like so many here,' he continued, 'ejected from the world, demanding sanctuary. How could I not take you in?'

'And I'm grateful. I owe you, and Idriss, everything.'

'You are unique, Vidar.' He reached his trembling fingers towards where the jewel lay, then let his hand fall. 'I recognised that the moment they brought you through the gates. A King needs many qualities – strength, wisdom, good fortune, certainly, but most of all, vision. I ensured your rapid rise through our society – for one so New, unimaginably rapid – because

I could see how much you could offer Idriss. And you have, Vidar, you have. And you will continue to do so.'

'You know I'm committed to Idriss's security.'

'I know, and that is what gives me hope. Everything I have done in my life, everything in recent weeks, has been to ensure the security of this glorious city. Idriss the Strong! City of Lights in the vast, terrible dark! But now our security is threatened, Vidar, and you must do whatever is necessary to ensure Idriss continues for ever.'

Lud stared at Vidar with such intensity, it gave him pause. 'What are you saying?'

'A city like Idriss only survives, only becomes strong in the face of such adversity, because of rules. There cannot be anarchy here. The many conflicting pressures within the great protective walls can only be held in place by the age-old structures. But those rules will not be enough to see Idriss through the times ahead.'

Lud gripped Vidar's hand with surprising force. His strength was like that of a man half his age; desperation gave him power.

'It is the curse of Kings to be forced to make choices that would shatter lesser men, for the sake of the greater good. We bear it in lonely silence, for we can never talk about these things to others. And we endure. But there are no absolutes, Vidar. There is, in the end, only survival, and Kings must choose whatever is necessary for the realm to survive. However terrible. However much of a scar it leaves on our hearts. I ask you to do the same, Vidar. I cannot name you as my successor, for the people would never accept it, and who would hear of a King rising from the ranks of the Crimson Hunt?'

He coughed violently, gripped the bed clothes, fighting to hang on.

'Of all the people in Idriss, only you can truly understand my burden, Vidar,' he continued. 'You must kill to survive. You must kill despite the toll it takes upon you.'

'What are you asking of me?'

'To break the rules, wherever necessary. To do whatever it takes to keep Idriss safe.'

'Of course–'

'No!' His nails bit into Vidar's wrist once more. 'These are no feeble requests of a dying man, to be dismissed with platitudes. This is the future of Idriss! You are my legacy, Vidar! And I will have you accept this burden with the greatest gravity.'

The flame in Lud's eyes was shocking. He saw then exactly what the King was asking of him. It was a role that would provide no peace for him, ever.

'Let nothing stand in your way, Vidar. Idriss must survive, and you must be the weapon that ensures it. There is no one else in the city that can carry out this work. Only you, Vidar. Only you. Do not turn your back on Idriss when Idriss has saved you.' His eyes flickered shut and he fell into a deep sleep.

Vidar watched him for a while, bitter at the burden that had been transferred to his shoulders. To kill, always, anyone who stood in the way of Idriss's security. To become death.

The palace bells continued to toll their mournful, warning song until his head hurt and he thought he would hear them for ever.

6

SECRETS

News of the King's impending death served to still the tensions engulfing the city as people forgot their fears and looked to an uncertain future. Vidar knew it was only a brief respite. The moment Lud died the dam would break and a torrent of fear would sweep across the city. With no symbol of security to give the illusion that they were safe, those structures that Lud understood so well would quickly fall, and every desperate urge would be turned inwards.

Despite the looming crisis, or because of it, the council appeared paralysed, unable to agree on a single name to put forward to the King as a successor. Meetings were convened every two hours, sometimes dragging on interminably so they became one long, circuitous debate.

And the bells tolled, on the hour, every hour – *The King still lives. But time is short… short… short* – and the people huddled on street corners, and in the inns at night, and the rich talked in the forum, and everybody waited.

For Vidar, the King's words had brought long-repressed memories back to the fore. He recalled little of the moment when he had been discovered at the Deeping Gate; a desperate scramble through the last few yards of the forest as though emerging from a mist, branches tearing at his face and hair, driven so far off balance by his experiences that he didn't even recognise what the city was when he saw it, didn't understand the strange language of the people shouting down at him from the walls, knew only that he needed to be safe. He remembered the jewel whispering terrible things to him, and he recalled brandishing his tattoo at the guards when they opened the gate, as if it meant something, and ranting wildly. The bonds bit hard as the guards carried him inside the walls and then to the physician, who gave him a foul-tasting drink that calmed him and made him sleep – for three days, they said.

Images came to him in that deep rest, so powerful that he recalled them on waking and had never forgotten them. A gauntlet, silver in the moonlight. A room of glass and steel, and crying, desperate people. Grim exchanged glances. Now those images haunted him once more.

In the heat of the afternoon sun, he stood on the walls and looked out across the forest. Though he had always known there was a world beyond it, the map-cube had forged it into a hard reality, less terrifying in a way, though no less mysterious. More than anything, it helped put the problems Idriss was experiencing into perspective: just one city's struggles, not the end of the world.

The answers he desperately needed – Who was he, really? Where had he come from? Why was he cursed with the jewel? – were out there, not in Idriss, and Rhiannon was right: the map felt like his only chance to uncover them; to mark his place in the world, so he could start moving forwards instead of looking back.

But now Lud had thrown his plans into disarray by dragging duty into the mix. He knew he was cynical and too often in the grip of baser motivations, as Rhiannon accused, but he still accepted he owed everything to Idriss. The city had given him a place when he was adrift in a sea of nowhere, and had allowed him to achieve his potential when he was friendless and, to many, worthless. He respected Lud, but at that moment he felt anger towards the King for placing in his head the suggestion that only he could keep Idriss secure; from now on, all his choices would be conflicted.

Cheyne interrupted Vidar's thoughts, his billowing shirt a brilliant white untainted by the sweat and grime that appeared to be driven into the very pores of Idriss. 'I have identified a merchant who is prepared to sponsor our sojourn in return for unique rights to any trade route we establish. Frankly, I had to fight them off. There is not enough profit in Idriss at the moment.'

'Horses?'

'Four. Not exactly an army, but we could not afford to spare more men with the current situation. So you have decided? We go to our doom?'

'Positive as always. I'm still weighing the right course. I'll decide by this evening.'

'This would not be the best time to leave Idriss. Your leadership may be needed, and tested, in the coming days.'

'I know.' Vidar watched the guards go through their daily ritual of testing the strength of the gate and the secondary and tertiary defences. 'But if we delay, whatever those spikes are could move off the edge of the map.'

'A dilemma, then.'

'There's another way of looking at it. If we can prove the map works and bring whatever is out there back to Idriss, it might be the one thing that could unite the people.'

'Hope, you mean.'

'That we're not trapped here, surrounded by hell. That we can exert some control over the world outside, establish trade routes that would minimise the shortages. It could be a new age for the entire city.'

Cheyne watched the gently swaying tree-tops, a bemused smile lighting his normally serious face. 'After generation upon generation, a way out. That is almost too much to believe.' He thought for a moment, then nodded appreciatively. 'Hope.' When Vidar didn't answer, he added, 'I think I may take an hour of personal time. My loins are enflamed by all this talk.'

After he had departed, one thing preyed heavily on Vidar's mind: soon he would need to kill again to survive. It would be safer to stay in Idriss where there was always a chance that fate would take any decision out of his hands and provide him with another murderer, rapist, or enemy. In the forest, if he did not make it back in time, there were only two choices: one of his companions or himself.

'NOTHING?' MANDA ASKED insistently. Naked, her flesh rippled as she heaved around the room, adding squirts of perfume to the small pots of dried flowers that added such a pleasing aroma to her cramped, sweaty room in the brothel above the Four Staves.

Cheyne shook his head. Hands behind his head, he lay dismally on the bed, staring at the ceiling.

Manda sighed. 'Perhaps another approach. Tell me about your childhood, then, dearie. Little boy Cheyne. There must have been some pain there. No child gets through those days without a little suffering.'

Cheyne watched dust motes floating in the sunlight. The room was warm and the aroma of the perfume comforting, the bare stone of the walls hidden by scarlet drapes. 'I was eight years old,' he began after a moment of deep reflection. 'I am a handsome man, but the little Cheyne was a beautiful boy with curly red hair and an angel's face.'

Manda raised one eyebrow, shrugged, but Cheyne did not see.

'And so there were many boys in my street who were jealous of all the attention I received. One day they attacked me, stripped me naked, then made me wear the dress of one of their little sisters.' He considered this for a moment, then added, 'Plaid, I think. They put ribbons in my hair, and rouge on my face, and made me little girl Cheyne, before dragging me off to the grim side of Greatstock, where the boys hunt in packs, and the hunting dogs are scared of the boys. Naturally, as beautiful as I was, this made me something of a target.

'Soon the whistles rose up, call and response, you know, the predatory sign, and so, being as streetwise as I was beautiful, I ran. You know what lies on the eastern edge of Greatstock?'

'The sewage lagoon?'

'Yes, the excrement of the entire city, where they process it to fuel our fires and fertilise our food. You can understand why that side of Greatstock is called "grim". Almost choking to death, I fled to the edge of the sewage lagoon, rightly thinking it would be a safer route home rather than through the streets. There is a path through the lagoon that some of the boys know, and I followed that. I tell you, I thought I had murdered my nose that day.

'I was halfway across, and the mists had risen, when I heard a sound behind me and turned suddenly, fearing it was the Greatstock Runners. My foot slipped and in I went.'

Manda screwed up her face in distaste.

'I flailed around, trying to reach the side, but the excrement began to suck me down, and that was when I screamed and yelled. As anyone would do. It is not a sign of weakness.'

'Of course not.'

'And who should come running up but my elder sister, Alice. Dear Alice. Alice, who watched over me around the house when my mother and father were working, had heard what the boys had done to me and had come to save me. I cried for her to help me, and without a second thought she waded in. I was sinking fast, and spluttering, and my mouth was barely gasping air, and I was shouting and yelling like a mad thing, for at that moment I was convinced my life was over.

'But Alice came in, without a thought for her own safety, and whispered in my ear, "Hush, little baby, it will be all right." And she lifted me up, even as she sank down, and carried me to the path. I sat there, catching my breath, and suddenly I realised Alice was not with me. The sickening swamp had swallowed her. I ran back and forth, calling her name, and reaching in, but I never found her.'

He paused, letting the memory settle. 'My parents recovered her body the next day, and they wailed and cried, and from that moment on, they were cold to me. And not a day passed when I did not think of my Alice, my protector, and wished she were back with me. And not a day passed when I did not think of my role in her demise.'

Manda let the words settle and then asked once again, with all the tenderness she felt for her client, 'Now, anything?'

Cheyne thought for a moment, and then slowly shook his head. 'This may be our last attempt for a while,' he said.

'Why?'

'I have to disappear for a while. A journey into great danger. I may not return.'

'Oh. You are going back to Greatstock?'

'Though it is hard to believe, there are worse places.' Noticing the puzzlement shadowing her face, he added hastily, 'But enough of those things. Reward me now with the fruits of your passion, for in this hour of my need they will be richer still.'

Smiling, Manda heaved herself on to the bed, and on top of Cheyne, and soon the room was filled with creaks and gasps and release.

VIDAR HAD BARELY arrived back at his rooms when he was summoned to the palace where Ashur admitted him into his private office. Unusually, it was just the two of them, without any of the administrative support. Ashur's frozen face always gave him an advantage in any meeting, but Vidar had taken to attempting to read his eyes, and on many occasions with some success. This time he thought he saw fear there.

'The King summoned you for private counsel,' he said.

'Someone's been talking.'

'Nothing happens within the palace that does not come to my attention. I note LeStrange did not instantly report it to me. On this occasion I will presume that to be an over- sight. The rules were very clear. No one was to visit the King.'

'You're criticising King Lud for inviting me?'

'Of course not.'

'Then what do you want, Ashur?'

'The balance of power is shifting in Idriss. It would be wise to maintain respect wherever possible. You have enjoyed King Lud's protec- tion since you arrived in our city, for reasons that escape me. Sadly, that situation will soon change. I wish to know where your loyalties lie.'

'To Idriss.'

'Yes, that is the correct answer. Now give me the true answer.'

'I'm a simple man, Ashur. A roof over my head, some food on the table, and a few coins to pay for entertainment are all I really need in life–'

'Apart from the occasional ritual sacrifice to keep you alive. Yes, I have heard your glib answer before.'

'I don't play politics. That must be difficult for you to understand. I've served Idriss well, and I'll continue to do so, whoever's in charge.'

Ashur searched Vidar's face for a long moment until the fear in his eyes diminished and the old arrogance flared once more.

'I have a question for you,' Vidar said. 'Why did you rush Mellias's body to the pyre and prevent the Inquisitors from carrying out a proper enquiry?'

'You know why. It was important the insecurity did not drag on and unsettle the citizens.'

'That worked well. We've had two further murders in Idriss. If you'd allowed the Inquisitors time, the killer may have been caught by now.'

'You are blaming me for those deaths?' Ashur leaned across the table, his hands trembling.

'What's your religion, Ashur?'

The question caught him by surprise; his mouth gaped for a second.

'Are you one of the Shepherd's little lambs?'

'My beliefs are my own. I do not have to reveal them to you,' Ashur said, recovering quickly. 'What does this have to do with anything?'

Vidar ignored his questions. Another wave of weakness lapped at him; they were coming too fast now. 'I'm concerned about security. I'm considering a brief expedition outside the walls to search for possible breaches.'

'Into the forest? Are you mad?' Recognising an advantage, Ashur caught himself. 'How many men?'

'No more than four.'

'And how long would you be gone?'

'A few days at most.'

'That would be acceptable.' The brief smile Vidar saw in Ashur's eyes added an unsettling note to his implacable face.

IT WAS PAST midnight when Rhiannon made her way to the Four Staves. She had spent much of the day researching the long, convoluted history of the religion of the Shepherd, sifting through the stories that Laurent told her in the temple in an attempt to discover how it could be driving a series of murders. It appeared on the surface to be a religion of openness, but like everything else in her work, the more she probed, the more secrets she discovered hidden just beneath. Like so many religions, at its heart was the promise of revelation, and it was this one mystery that attracted Rhiannon, and excited her, and which appeared to influence so much else that was loose in Idriss.

Yet despite her hard work, she felt annoyed and off-kilter. Her job demanded extreme concentration, yet she had found herself distracted on too many occasions by worries about

Vidar's safety. She could see why so many Inquisitors chose a life of loneliness and celibacy; the lack of emotional distractions kept the mind razor-sharp. Vidar's bone-headed stupidity only heightened her annoyance. She could understand his desire to uncover his past, but not to risk his life in the forest in the process. Few who ventured beyond the tree line ever made it back, and even with the map the chances of his survival were slim. She hoped that when he had sent a message to meet her in the Four Staves he had changed his mind, but she feared the worst.

The streets were quiet, but the underlying air of tension still throbbed in the background. The weather was not helping. The high temperatures of the day had not dissipated, and the farmers in the north were predicting a heatwave. Summer in the city was always bad. There were too many people, too little space, and too many shortages. No one could escape the stifling streets and alleys, and tempers escalated along with the number of brawls and violent arguments. But when a heatwave blanketed the city, everything lay still for days, or a week, and then erupted at once. It was during the heatwave three years earlier when the Britzak slums were razed to the ground and more than a hundred people burned alive.

The atmosphere in the Four Staves on Regis Street was close and clammy. There was only a smattering of patrons in the inn at that time, most of them from the night staff at the royal palace, a few merchants at the end of a long day, a handful of prostitutes from the brothel upstairs, and one or two drifters. It was dark and inviting, with numerous tiny rooms and snugs for secret conversation, all lit by candles, the walls covered with ancient items that had been left there during its long, illustrious history – weapons, pocket watches, hats and cloaks, pamphlets and books, and numerous objects made from metal and glass whose use had long since been forgotten.

Bursts of raucous laughter from the back room broke the quiet, and that was where she found Vidar, Cheyne, and Asgrim, drinking beer and telling bawdy tales. They paused when she entered, and stood to welcome her.

'It is late to be drinking so heavily,' she said. 'A celebration or a wake?'

'We're leaving at dawn,' Vidar said.

'Oh.' She pulled up a chair and motioned to the barman for some water. 'You are tired of life, then.'

'There's no point us arguing,' he replied. 'Let's enjoy a drink, and a pleasant time among friends.'

She nodded. 'You would not be doing this if you did not think there was a risk you would not be coming back.'

'There's always a risk.'

'Why, it keeps us alive,' Cheyne said.

'You were kept alive by the last three hours in the brothel upstairs,' Asgrim snorted.

Cheyne looked indignant. 'I had to say goodbye to my Manda.'

Certain that she would not change Vidar's mind, Rhiannon stifled her disappointment and resolved not to throw more shadows over his departure. 'When do you leave?' she asked.

'Cheyne and I ride at dawn, as I said. Asgrim stays here to command the Crimson Hunt in my absence.'

'I think you made the wrong choice,' Asgrim said. 'I may still be recovering, but at least if I accompanied you, you would not have to listen to constant whining about stains on my clothes, dirt in my girly hair, and the effect of sun on my parchment-like, red-headed skin.'

'I do not whine,' Cheyne said superciliously. 'I am simply a man with extremely high standards, and I am not about to settle for less. Besides, it is a well-known fact that red hair is a mark of bearing.'

Asgrim took a long draught of his beer and then said bluntly, 'I wonder what is really out there beyond the walls?'

'Stories are all we have around here,' Vidar said. 'No one knows the truth of what really lies beyond the forest. No one even knows the true tale of Idriss's long history. There are only stories and they change in the telling every time.'

'They should be written down, or learned by heart to tell in inns like this, so that everyone knows. If people do not know their place in history, how can they know who they truly are?' Asgrim winced and added, 'I am sorry, Vidar. I did not mean any offence.'

'None taken. People learn the names of their ancestors from generations past so they can cement their place in Idriss's hierarchy, but they never learn who those people were or what they did. Once you die, you're forgotten. All that counts is what you do here and now.'

Asgrim slurped on his beer, already bored with the conversation, but Vidar was talking as much to himself as to his companions. 'People have come to Idriss from all over Gardia, in their ones and twos, making their way through the forest against all odds, bringing their cultures and their stories and their gods. There must be passable routes out there. You travelled here from the north, Asgrim. Can't you remember the way back?'

'I remember running for my life, eating bugs and drinking water from rotted tree stumps, clinging on to my life with my bare hands. Remembering the road back was not a priority.'

'And if the paths change all the time, even remembering means nothing,' Cheyne pointed out.

The bickering and laughter continued for three more hours. Rhiannon couldn't help but be drawn in, enjoying the free-spirited talk in a way she never could in the ranks of the Order. Then, as dawn neared, Vidar rapped his flagon on the table and said to her, 'The Crimson Hunt is built on deep bonds forged over time. We die for our comrades. We made our own ties in Greer an' Lokh's tower when we agreed to keep the secret of the map. We're a unit now—'

'Some would say a conspiracy,' Rhiannon suggested.

'But we haven't got the time to make those bonds deeper, so here's what we do. One secret each. The most important one. A secret you've never told anyone before. And we each vow to keep that secret to our dying breath.'

Rhiannon shifted uncomfortably, but Cheyne and Asgrim, used to the ways of the Crimson Hunt, both nodded.

'I'll go first,' Vidar said. Staring into his ale, he thought deeply before beginning. 'You remember Gorland Krone?' he said to Cheyne and Asgrim.

'The traitor?' Cheyne said.

'Under the rules of the Crimson Hunt. He abandoned his post on the wall and was executed, two years ago,' Vidar explained to Rhiannon. 'If you leave your post, you're a traitor to Idriss, and you pay with your life.'

'Harsh,' she said, 'but understandable. Without the security of the walls, we are all dead.'

'Except Gorland Krone didn't leave his watch because he was scared, or because he was lazy or wanted to get drunk. His boy was sick, close to death with the fever. Gorland had left his wife searching for a physician when he began his shift, but it was the middle of the night and none could be raised. His wife came to the walls, desperate and afraid the lad was dying. Gorland ran from his post, carried the boy in his arms to the nearest physician, kicked down the door, and held a knife to the physician's throat until he carried out treatment. Then he returned to the walls without knowing if his boy had lived or died. The boy did survive. Gorland Krone was put to death.'

'Oh,' Rhiannon said, ' that is a sad story.'

'Normally, when a Huntsman dies in the pursuit of duty, his family receives his stipend for the rest of their days,' Vidar continued. 'But because Gorland was decreed a traitor, his wife and son got nothing. The boy needed constant attention from the physician – costly, as you know – and the wife's work could not begin to meet the fees. She was prepared to prostitute herself to raise more. We do what we have to, for survival.'

'We do,' Rhiannon agreed. She found herself strangely engrossed by Vidar's words.

'Since Gorland Krone's execution, I have given a portion of my salary to the wife and son,' he added. 'Enough to get all the help from the physician they need.'

Cheyne and Asgrim started. 'Are you mad?' Cheyne said. 'If that gets out, you could be executed yourself for aiding the family of a traitor.'

'It won't get out,' Vidar said. 'The only people who know are the wife, me, and now you. So my life is in your hands. Look after it.'

Asgrim tugged at his beard thoughtfully. 'You do not know her. You barely knew Gorland Krone.'

Vidar said nothing. He saw Rhiannon looking at him with puzzlement and asked, 'What is it?'

'You hide your secrets well,' she said.

'That's why they're secrets.' He turned to Cheyne. 'Next.'

Gathering his thoughts, Cheyne stared into his beer, then said quietly, 'I cannot cry.'

Asgrim threw his head back and laughed loudly. 'That is a secret? Why, you have no feelings at all!'

Cheyne's cheeks flushed. Rhiannon noticed the hurt in his eyes and stepped in. 'Hear him out.'

And then Asgrim saw the depth of feeling in his friend's expression, and his laughter dried up immediately. 'Tell us more,' he said quietly.

'When I was a boy, my friends and parents used to joke about it,' Cheyne began. 'The boy who could not cry. Even when he fell and tore his knees. No punch from a bully, no loss of a toy could make the tears come. I was paraded as the bravest child in the street, and everyone smiled and patted my head. Then, when I was eleven years old, I saw my father burned alive at the foundry, and still I did not shed a tear. The praise dried up then. *This odd child. This broken child. Not right in the head, not right in the heart.* And then the criticism began, slowly, to turn to fear. *If he cannot cry, if he cannot show remorse*, they said, *what is he capable of?* And they were right, for, of course, I am capable of anything.'

His voice grew so quiet that they could barely hear him. For someone normally so bereft of emotion, Rhiannon found the depth of feeling shocking.

'And I take great pleasure in what I do, that is true,' he continued, 'though some... many... might find it disturbing, but still... but still...' He bit his lip. 'If I cannot cry, I cannot feel, and if I cannot feel, I am a ghost passing through life. Meaningless to those I call my friends. I want to feel. I want to know what it is to be a person. And so I want to cry.'

He took a deep breath to steady himself, so lost to his emotion that he wasn't aware of Asgrim staring at him intently as though seeing his friend for the first time.

'You wish to cry,' the northerner said quietly, 'and I am only too happy to stop.'

'Tell us, Asgrim,' Rhiannon prompted.

Nodding slowly, Asgrim grew glassy-eyed as he remembered. He stared at his mutilated left hand, missing two fingers, before he said, 'I have never spoken of how I came to leave my northern homeland and travel to this place, which is too hot, and too dusty, where the horizons press in against you. Childhood is a hard time here, where you are taught early to survive, and to accept your responsibility to help Idriss survive, through toil and sweat and long hours until you die. Not so in my home. Children ran free in the snowy wastes, playing and exploring and learning what it means to be alive. And I learned most from my father, known as Grim in the language of my people, a false name for a man who laughed louder and longer than any in our village. He taught me to hunt, and the skill of the scent, and he told me the best stories of our people, and he listened when I spoke. And he loved me, for love is valued among my people. It is the glue that binds us together and makes us stronger. And I loved him in return, doubly so, for my mother died when I was born, and there was just the two of us, helping each other to survive.

'In the winter of my fifteenth year, the raiders came to my village and burned it to the ground. My father and I were hunting and we saw the smoke against the late afternoon sky. We knew what it meant. We could not go back, and so we had to travel across the mountains to find another settlement that would take us in. But the raiders knew we were away, somehow, and so they pursued us. We ran and ran, never resting, for three days. We were starving, and there was no prospect of food to come for the mountains were a desolate place. And then, in the middle of a blizzard, my father slipped into a crevasse and broke his leg. He could not move.'

Tears sprang to Asgrim's eyes, and he wiped them away with the back of his hand, unselfconsciously. Cheyne watched the action curiously.

'I stayed by his side, listening to the hunting horns drawing closer, knowing our end was near. And then my father told me to leave him. I could not bring myself to do so, knowing he was still alive, and that he would face a slow, painful death from freezing, and more likely a slower, more painful death at the hands of the cruel raiders, who were known to flay their victims and use the skins as flags on their ships. But he begged me, and he cried, as I cry now, and he told me he would die without living a meaningful life if I gave up my own days so easily. And he said… and he said…' The words caught in his throat. 'That I should kill him, and cut from him meat to take with me to survive over the mountains, for I would surely die with nothing to eat.'

The words caught in Asgrim's throat again and he bowed his head, struggling to contain the fierce rush of emotion. Cheyne rested one hand on his shoulder. 'Enough,' he said softly.

'No, there is more,' Asgrim insisted, but his feelings overwhelmed him, and he looked away, blinking back tears.

Rhiannon rested her hand on his. 'Let me,' she said gently.

He nodded, touched by her quiet sympathy.

'Like all Inquisitors, I was taken from my parents when I was very young to be schooled in the skills of the Order,' Rhiannon began quickly, to deflect attention from Asgrim, who was shaking with repressed feelings. 'The aim of all training is to free the individual from the tyranny of emotions, so all enquiries can be

conducted with cool, unbiased intellect, however terrible they may be. And we encounter
many terrible enquiries. Teachers never look at
the Inquisitor children. They never touch
them. And the children are not allowed to talk
to each other. Sometimes you cry out for the
warmth of human contact. You lie in your bed
at night, crying. But the teachers will never
indulge. And gradually you learn to be apart,
to rise above emotions, and to look down on
the world dispassionately.'

She sipped her water; the memories brought
an involuntary tightening of her throat, even
after so many years. Vidar was watching her
curiously, although she always found it difficult to read him; he was adept at presenting
faces that were expected of him to hide his true
feelings.

'During those early days, the only time we
were allowed outdoors was in a tiny courtyard, barely bigger than this room, with
buildings on every side, so only a thin, grey
light made it down to us. We would tramp
round and round in circles, speaking the legend of the Order – *truth, strength, honour,
justice, and equality* – and if we dared to look
up at the sky, the teacher would hit us across
the shoulders with her staff.

'One day I thought I could take no more.
My eyes burned from crying, and my limbs

were so heavy I could barely walk. I was ready to leave the Order, even though it would have brought dishonour on my parents. They would also have lost the stipend they received for giving me up.

'And that was the day I broke the first rule of the Order: obey.' She bowed her head, shamed.

'Rules are meant to be broken,' Vidar said.

'Not in the Order. In the kitchens was a large range, and beside it a flue that I knew was accessible, because the boys had cleaned it only the week before. For the next half-hour I worked my way up the system of flues, choking back soot, black from head to toe and gasping for breath in the claustrophobic space, until I emerged from the chimney on to the roof.'

Closing her eyes, the memory washed back, still pin-sharp and bright. 'It was another world up there, above the city. I could breathe. I could see the sky in all its glory. And as I looked out over the gleaming rooftops of Idriss, I understood the grandeur of the place, and I realised that wonder was the most important thing in me: believing in something larger than myself, something that touched the soul. I stayed up, watching the sun go down, charting the shift of colours into the black, and only then did I climb back down. I was filthy, and beaten for allowing myself to get into such a mess, but I never told anyone what I had seen, and what it had given me: the strength to survive. Whatever the Order did to me from that moment on, I would always have that memory to keep me going.'

A shadow crossed Vidar's face, and she regretted talking about memory, but he soon smiled and said: 'It's done. Now we all share something vitally important to each of us. Pain, joy, doubt, whatever. This sets us apart from everyone else in Idriss. They can beat us, torture us, but now they can never tear us apart.'

Cheyne and Asgrim nodded in agreement. 'Whatever lies ahead, they can never tear us apart,' they said together, a chant, a ritual, complete.

When they went to the bar to fetch more drinks, Vidar said, 'So you'll miss me?'

'The air will be fresher without the reek of male bravado.'

'You'll miss me.'

'Try not to bruise your ego on those low-hanging branches.'

He grew serious. 'Use Asgrim. There's no one better for tracking. The Red Man has attacked you once and he'll probably do it again. Make sure you get him first.'

'I intend to.' She paused, confused by her thoughts and feelings. 'Do not take any unnecessary risks, Vidar. Stupidity only works as a shield for so long.'

'I aim to be back before you know it.'

He had the practised grin of a cocky teenager, but in his eyes Rhiannon could see that he understood completely what lay ahead, and that the chances of returning were slim, but it was a risk worth taking. It would have been cruel of her to break the illusion.

They drank some more, and when the first hint of sunrise brought silver to the horizon, they made their way to the Deeping Gate where two members of the Crimson Hunt waited with the horses and provisions. Vidar was already distracted by the job to come, inspecting the saddles, briefing the two Huntsmen, checking the weapons. The serious, driven man emerged easily from behind the irritating boyish façade, and Rhiannon understood why she had grown to like him.

When the Huntsmen went on to the wall to survey the tree line, she stepped forwards and kissed him briskly on the cheek. 'Good fortune,' she said. 'You will need it.'

Their eyes met briefly, and the silent communication surprised each of them. But as she turned to go, a distant tolling brought her up sharp. The tone was duller than the palace bells, but Rhiannon immediately recognised the call of the Order to all Inquisitors.

'Your people?' Asgrim asked.

She nodded. 'A major disturbance.' She listened to the cadence, counting the spaces between the tolls. 'Death, times five.'

WITH A SENSE of foreboding, Vidar watched Rhiannon and Asgrim moving swiftly over the cobbles towards the heart of the city before he focused on what lay ahead and turned back to the gates.

Cheyne looked up the length of the Deeping Gate, towering ten times his own height, the wood dense and seasoned. It had stood impenetrable for generations, looming over the lives of all who lived within Idriss, as comforting as it was ominous, a constant warning of what lay outside, of what lay ahead for all of them. 'There is still chance to back out,' Cheyne said.

'If I didn't know better, I'd think you were scared.'

'I think only of you. I know you would find it difficult to retreat from your position without losing face.'

'Get on the horse, Cheyne.'

The horses stamped and shook their heads as if they could sense the uneasiness. The two Huntsmen were already in the saddle, crimson hoods pulled high so their faces were thrown into shadow. They were both in their early twenties, strong and fearless: Chien-Fu, an axe-man and archer, with sleek, black hair tied into a ponytail; and Abbas, dark of mood and skin, as adept with a dagger in the shadows as he was with a sword in the thick of battle.

'We will miss Asgrim's tracking abilities,' Cheyne noted. 'That nose of his could sniff out danger before we saw it.'

'Idriss needs him more than we do.'

'I admire your confidence in the face of all reason. Do you have the map?'

'Of course.'

Cheyne steadied himself with a deep breath. 'Then I suppose there is no further need to delay. Let us ride, to adventure, riches beyond imagination, and glory.'

'To the future,' Vidar said, before adding quietly, 'To the past.'

He nodded and the gate guards rallied to haul on twin chains thicker than his arm. With seven men on each side, the clanking iron gradually moved, lifting the giant oaken bar and drawing the complex system of locks and bolts with a series of resounding booms that sounded like a martial drum.

When all was done, the two teams hauled on two sets of smaller chains, straining and blowing with the exertion, and gradually the gates ground open. The juddering shriek resounded across the city, and Vidar knew that bedroom windows would be thrown open, sleepy-eyed citizens hanging out to peer south with a sense of awe. Even the guards watched intently, so rarely were the gates opened.

As the gap between the two gates grew, two teams of archers flanked the road, arrows nocked and ready to be loosed. The black slit grew wider still, and faces became drawn, eyes fixed and narrowed, breath held tightly in chests. No one spoke.

Vidar felt a rush of cool air, laced with the aromatic scents of the night-forest, refreshing after the dusty heat of the city but unsettling in its rareness.

And then the gates opened fully with a thunderous boom that shook the ground. Still nobody moved, as they anticipated a sudden rush of all their worst fears, but in the gloom beyond the walls, all was still.

The captain of the guards motioned frantically for Vidar and the others to move through the gates.

'How rude to rush us to our deaths,' Cheyne muttered.

They urged the horses forwards slowly. The flickering light of the torches gave way to deep shadow as they passed under the wall, and the silence grew even more intense. They were barely outside when there was keen activity behind them and the deafening rattle of chains and creaking of wood, which ended with one final boom as the gates closed and the bolts, lock, and bar fell into place. Only then did the quiet return.

'No going back now,' Cheyne said. 'Not that I want to, of course.'

They moved halfway across the grassy no-man's-land and came to a halt. The silver sliver on the horizon was slowly transmuting into gold, allowing the trees to emerge from the gloom like ghosts. The night's silence fell away as the chorus of birds rose up, shrill and unsettling, from the dense wall of leaf and branch. Vidar scanned the entire tree line; nothing moved, although he couldn't escape the uneasy feeling that they were being watched. The moment of his birth from the forest came back to him in full force, the fear looming at his back as he ran with the trees clawing at his hair, his face, the constant shriek echoing through his mind, driving all conscious thought from it. He remembered flashing sensory pictures, his breath searing in his chest, the ache of his legs, rain spattering, the smell of leaf-mould, but nothing from before that moment except a single spectre, an emotion: despair.

'Let's go,' he said. He flicked the reins, and they moved forward, one by one, towards the trees.

* * *

THE INQUISITORS MILLING uneasily around the reception hall at the Palace of Justice directed Rhiannon and Asgrim to an address in Greatstock, not far from the building collapse that had almost killed the northerner. The streets were narrow and stinking with refuse and excrement, and the buildings with their ramshackle, amateurishly constructed upper storeys towered so high barely any sky was visible.

At that time, the quarter had the stillness of a new day, which was why it was such a shock when Rhiannon and Asgrim rounded a corner to be confronted by a vast crowd, completely silent, all their faces turned towards the second storey of a half-timbered boarding house with overhanging eaves. Rhiannon tried to read their expressions, but the blankness was truly unsettling.

They pushed through the crowd to the front door, and once they had stepped into the cramped, damp-ridden hall, Asgrim sniffed the air. 'Sour,' he said, nose wrinkling. 'The Red Man has been here.'

Inquisitor Sian guarded the foot of the stairs. She was barely out of her teens, her complexion too pale, her hair a shining black. From the flicker of uncertainty in her eyes, Rhiannon saw she hadn't yet learned how to mask her feelings. 'Inquisitor Rhiannon,' she said.

'We have requested the Crimson Hunt for crowd control, but they have not yet arrived.' Her eyes flickered towards the door, assessing its strength.

'They are calm enough out there,' Asgrim said, distracted by the scents that were drawing him up the stairs.

Sian made to stop him, but Rhiannon held out an arm to block her. 'He accompanies me,' she said. Sian failed to hide her puzzlement.

As they climbed the stairs, Asgrim's face grew darker, the breath choking in his throat intermittently. On the second floor, another Inquisitor waited outside a door, which she quickly opened to reveal a room that reeked like a butcher's shop and where five other Inquisitors were moving meticulously around, examining the floor and furniture.

As they rounded the door, Rhiannon saw the source of the smell. Along one wall, five bodies had been arranged in an unnatural manner to present a strange tableau: an old man and a young woman were kneeling, heads bowed; two young men had their faces raised, mouths gaping, arms outstretched; the final victim, a man in his thirties, was curled into a foetal position, his hands over his head. They all bore the familiar wounds of the Red Man.

After her initial shock, Rhiannon's attention was drawn to an ungrammatical legend smeared on the wall in lantern soot above the bodies. It said: *These are the one what tell you.*

Rhiannon was so absorbed she jumped when Inquisitor Fabienne came up behind her and said, 'What does it mean?' She was beautiful but hard, her cheekbones sharp and her eyes piercing.

'It means that he is sending us – or someone – a message.'

'The alarm was raised by others in the boarding house. He went through the rooms one by one until he selected this five.'

'So he knew them all?' Asgrim growled.

'Or they fit the picture he had in his head,' Rhiannon said. 'So now the word is out.'

'More than that.' Fabienne set her jaw and led them to the window where they looked down on the crowd. 'Several residents claim they saw the attacker's face changing. That he became someone else entirely. Lies, of course, but once that story begins to circulate, well, you can imagine the response.'

The crowd continued to stare up blankly. Now Rhiannon thought she saw hope there: hope that the Inquisitors would come out and prove that the terrible story they had heard was a lie; that they would have the killer in here, and he would be some stable-boy with a head full of nothing, or a merchant addled on beer and the herbs they sold in the bars around these parts.

Giving nothing away, Rhiannon examined the activity in the room. 'Has anything been uncovered?'

'Not yet,' Fabienne replied, 'but there are bloody footprints and handprints—' she indicated them '—suggesting he moved around the room, beyond arranging the dead. It may well be that he left something here.' She chewed her lip, unable to hide her concern. 'I am not in charge of this enquiry, but this looks like the kind of thing the killer would do. I sense an intelligence here that is twisted beyond the range we are used to. Have you seen the like of this before?'

'No.'

'Then I ask again, what does it mean? For there is clearly meaning here, but its currents run deep, beyond my ability to understand. It troubles me, for I think the meaning may be worse than the crime.'

Rhiannon turned back to the five bodies, their odd positioning, the carefully printed message, and felt a shiver as the image spoke to her; and what it said made her blood run cold.

7

THE EMERALD WORLD

UNDER THE DENSE canopy of the forest, it was another world, framed in a thousand different shades of green. Amid the reverential stillness of a temple, shafts of sunlight broke through the leaf cover to illuminate patches of moss or tangles of fern, or lichen-mottled boulders, occasionally shimmering off tinkling streams like beacons in the primeval gloom. The densely packed trees were so ancient they resembled alien life forms, craggy-skinned, bent this way and that, trunks so thick it would take five men to encircle them. They were the lords of that silent world, barely noticed but always watching, their power deep in roots or spreading through branches high overhead. The forest breathed slowly, and waited.

Progress was cautious as Vidar and the others guided their horses along a circuitous route through the trees, the soft leaf-mould muffling the sound of hooves. At first, chests had been tight with anxiety, every trembling leaf and swaying branch a sign of an impending attack. But gradually, over an hour into the trees, they had settled into a steady rhythm of watchfulness. No one spoke, for the jarring sound of human voices would carry far in the quiet. An attack would come – it was just a matter of when.

Sometimes they could almost forget the background throb of incipient threat, the weight of dark anticipation, and the never-ending half-light that lay heavily over everything. The forest was so different from the city, it felt like freedom after the choked streets, and the dust, and the refuse, the constant noise of voices and anvils and looms and cartwheels on cobbles, the feeling of wrappings pulled tighter and tighter around the chest. The quiet and the clean, verdant scents refreshed the senses as if they were waking after a long, troubled sleep. The play of light and dark, the nuanced sounds, were almost magical. But the most liberating thing of all was the realisation that there were no walls, only a horizon that went on for ever. Was this what it was like for their ancestors, Vidar wondered? Not cut off from the world, but a part of it. On occasion, he even convinced himself there was an intelligence in the trees and the greenery, and the birds and woodland creatures that scurried through the undergrowth. One mind tentatively welcoming them back into the fold.

But as soon as he relaxed into the beauty of their surroundings, he was jarred out of it by the realisation that the forest was as dangerous as it was magical, and that they were not being welcomed back but tolerated, until they no longer were.

The environment rekindled more trace memories of Vidar's frenzied flight to Idriss – a leap across a craggy outcropping, a plunge down a fern-covered bank – which gave him hope that the amber jewel had not consumed them, but only locked them away, while at the same time haunting him with hints of what had led up to the moment when his past disappeared.

His energy levels, too, appeared to be responding to either the returning memories or the tense atmosphere, escalating cycles of weakness slowly eroding him. He wondered how long it would be before the signs became clear to his companions. Could he make it back to Idriss before he became too weak to move? Then he would need to rely on the others to help him, and to find him the life he needed. In the forest, the options were limited, and he was sure they would probably leave him to die rather than risk their own lives. That meant he would need to kill before his weakness reached that late stage. He eyed Cheyne, Chien-Fu, and Abbas, felt a dismal guilt wash through him: none of them deserved such a fate. But sooner or later he would have to make a very simple decision: live or die.

He was convinced Cheyne knew every thought he entertained, could feel those pale, piercing eyes on his back, weighing carefully. No wonder he felt so alone; even those closest to him were suspicious of him.

The flatlands surrounding Idriss gave way to a steep incline, where rocks burst from the surface and shattered along planes, crumbling banks revealing the strata created by millennia of violent upheaval. But the trees had gained a foothold even there, with long, probing roots curling and prying for a secure position.

Dismounting, they led their horses by the reins, searching for a safe path among the folds and crevasses hidden by dense shrubbery, where one wrong foot could send them plummeting on to the rocks deep in the dark of the earth. Soon the exertion left them slick with sweat and dry-throated, and they were assailed by clouds of midges that congregated in the blocks of sunlight that were more prevalent in that area.

A distant shrieking cry brought them to a sudden halt, and left their hearts pounding and a cold wash on their hot skin. It was answered by another, and then another. Vidar and Cheyne exchanged a glance; silently they wondered what kind of beast could make such a sound.

Their path wound back and forth along the hillside until they reached a sunlit area where the bank had been torn away raggedly. Roots protruded like grasping fingers from the coloured striations of the revealed subsoil, but their attention was caught by the view across the forest. It stretched to the horizon, a sea of dark green, the waves moving lazily in the faint, cooling breeze. Idriss was not visible from their vantage point, so they were left feeling isolated; the only people alive in a hostile world.

After the oppressive mood beneath the trees, they enjoyed having the sky above them for a while, watching the birds dip and soar, until Abbas caught Vidar's arm urgently and pointed towards the bottom of the exposed bank among long, yellow grass.

Now they could see it, it was hard to believe they had missed it before: bones, everywhere they looked among the grass, human in the main, but some animal ones also: skulls and femurs and tibias and ribs and collarbones and shattered spines, some brown and honeycombed with age, others that looked almost new, picked clean and white in the sunlight.

Vidar and Cheyne inspected them closely, but there was no clothing, weapons, or jewellery, no distinguishing features whatsoever.

Cheyne picked up a long thigh bone and examined the ball joint. 'No teeth marks,' he whispered. 'Or tool marks. What happened here?'

Vidar looked over the spread of bones. 'Is this a midden? A feeding ground? A nest?' The lack of evidence for all those things made the discovery even more disturbing; the mystery tugged their minds to areas they didn't want to visit.

'I would say one thing is clear,' Cheyne continued. 'This is not a place we should tarry.'

Their skin tingling, they both looked around, seeing the landscape with new eyes, listening intently with new ears. But there was only the breeze sighing as it moved the grass and the leaves and branches.

Vidar motioned for them to continue on their way, but the atmosphere had grown more intense. Abbas removed his knife from its hidden sheath and gripped it tightly as he picked up the reins, and Chien-Fu adjusted his quiver for easier access.

'I wish whatever is here would attack. I am sick of the waiting,' Cheyne said quietly, adding, 'Actually, I now regret saying that.'

They continued the slow climb. At the top, the land levelled out again before plunging them back into the gloom beneath the trees, and here there were hardly any shafts of sunlight to illuminate their way. They came across a clear stream sluicing over a rocky channel disguised by heavy fern growth, and beyond it a large dark pool surrounded by reeds where insects flitted in the half-light. The sound of the running water was just loud enough to prevent them hearing any approach.

Vidar signalled for them to stop, and ordered Abbas and Chien-Fu to water the horses, while he led Cheyne off through the trees to a hollow edged with a dense bank of bramble. They used their swords to cut their way through until they reached the bottom.

'I need to check the map,' Vidar said quietly. 'We should be able to pick up one of the channels through the forest nearby.'

'If they did not all close up the minute we stepped beneath the trees,' Cheyne muttered. 'I expected to reach one of them quicker.'

'So did I,' Vidar admitted. He had examined the map just before they left the city and had identified a route nearby, but it already appeared to have gone.

'How do the channels move?' Cheyne asked, looking around uneasily. 'Are the trees themselves alive, as some of the fieldworkers say when they are in their cups?'

'Trees are trees,' Vidar said. 'It's things with fang and claw we need to worry about.'

He removed the map-cube from a purple velvet bag and held it in his palm for a second, where it buzzed gently before he brought it towards the amber jewel. A second later, the hollow was filled with the rich, swirling colours of the map with Vidar and Cheyne at the heart of it. Vast tracts of dense forest, the distant mountains, the shining sea beyond, all perceived as if they were in it, or above it; it took their breath away as much as the first time they had seen it in Greer an' Lokh's tower.

Carefully, Vidar manipulated the map to bring it into alignment with the bend of the river they had tentatively identified as being close to Idriss.

'Still certain?' Cheyne asked.

'I never was,' Vidar replied. 'But look...' He indicated a white spike and an orange spike above the trees. 'That would appear to be us.'

'Really?' Peering in closely, Cheyne tried to make sense of what he was seeing. 'Which one am I?'

They pondered the relevance of the colours for a while, and then Vidar shifted the map around to get a better view of what lay ahead. The other spikes of light hoved into view, one white on its own, two whites, a scarlet, and an emerald not too far from it. Vidar got his bearings, then indicated north-west. 'We're on course. They look as if they're moving in a straight line so we should be able to intercept... here.' He marked a spot on the map. 'And the nearest channel through the forest is... here.'

There was a clear, winding route among the trees to the south-west that would take them close to their destination.

Cheyne rubbed his chin, frowning with uncertainty. 'That is more than half a day's ride from here, I would say. We would be in the thick of this damnable place when night falls.'

Vidar shared Cheyne's concern. From his earlier viewings of the map, he had anticipated reaching a channel much sooner, but it had slipped tantalisingly away, as though drawing them on.

'We have also progressed much further than I expected without a fight,' Cheyne continued. 'Perhaps the forest really is not as dangerous as we all feared. Or perhaps whatever lives here is letting us get just far enough away from

Idriss so we cannot get back home when the attack happens. Which begs the question, how far is too far?'

'Stop letting your imagination run away with you. We've got a job to do. Focus on that.'

'Yes, let us all pretend we are not in the middle of hell.' Cheyne sniffed. 'How could we possibly have forgotten the picnic basket?'

Vidar cupped the cube and the map winked out. Back at the pool, they found Chien-Fu with an arrow nocked, turning slowly as he peered into the trees. Facing the opposite direction with knife drawn, Abbas squatted, ready to move fast. Vidar and Cheyne instantly drew their swords.

'Where?' Vidar growled.

Chien-Fu nodded. 'Far off in the trees. Movement. On two feet. Just a shadow, then gone.'

Vidar scanned in a slowly turning arc. Nothing moved. 'Passing by, or watching us?'

'Impossible to tell. It was gone too quickly,' Chien-Fu replied.

'Fill the water bottles and let's move on.'

'I told you,' Cheyne whispered as he passed.

Abbas caught Vidar's eye, and Vidar nodded in response. As Chien-Fu filled the bottles from the still waters, and Cheyne and Vidar tended to the horses in a manner that would draw attention to them, Abbas slipped off into the vegetation, keeping low. Barely a fern frond moved to mark his passing.

'He is good,' Cheyne said quietly and with admiration. 'I think perhaps he could match you for stealth and silence. I saw him slip through the cellars of that house near Fallen Spire where the Black Hand Revolutionaries were holed up. Six of them were dead before they even knew he was in the building.'

Vidar pretended to be engrossed in grooming his horse's flank. 'If he can get us any intelligence, it would help. We're not going to be able to ride hell-for-leather in this terrain. Any retreat will always be compromised.'

A minute passed and then the quiet of the forest was torn by Abbas's agonised cry, cut suddenly short.

'Guard the horses!' Vidar barked to Chien-Fu. Sword drawn, he sprinted through the undergrowth with Cheyne close behind. They found Abbas's ragged form splayed in the branches of a hawthorn, arms spread wide, bones broken in many places, blood dripping from numerous wounds.

Cheyne cursed loudly. 'So quick! What did that?' He moved back-to-back with Vidar, their swords held defensively as they slowly circled, searching the forest vegetation. There was no sign of movement, no sound at all.

'We get out of here fast,' Vidar hissed.

They dragged the body down and carried it rapidly back to the horses where Chien-Fu waited, arrow nocked. He took in Abbas's corpse without a hint of fear, his face cold. Replacing the arrow in his quiver, he touched his forehead with his index finger in the Crimson Hunt mark of vengeance to come.

Throwing Abbas over his horse, they quickly mounted, weapons at the ready, eyes never slowing in the search of their surroundings.

'How could it kill so fast and leave no mark of its passing?' Cheyne said.

'It's still here, watching us,' Vidar said.

'How do you know?'

'Because it has no reason to be afraid.' Vidar chewed his lip, his mind racing. He urged his horse on as quickly as it could move through the trees. Cheyne and Chien-Fu kept close by. 'No mere animal, that,' he added. 'There's intelligence in the way Abbas was displayed. A message to us.'

'A warning?' Cheyne said.

'Contempt, I think. It said, "Look at this. There is nothing you can do."'

Cheyne's jaw set. 'Silent, fast as quicksilver, so brutal it can destroy a body in seconds, clever, and sly. One of its kind would be a trial. Let us hope there are no more.'

Vidar recognised that both Cheyne and Chien-Fu understood the bitter truth of their situation. Whatever moved through that emerald world was so deadly, it could pick them off without any of them seeing it coming.

'We ride for the channel,' he said, 'and we don't stop until we get there.'

ON OCCASION THEY had to double-back, where fallen trees barred their way or the soft leaf-mould turned to marsh, filled with sucking pools of brackish water where insects hovered in clouds. In the thickest patches, they had to dismount and hack their way through the undergrowth, and even in the clearest parts of the ancient forest, the trees were so closely packed it was impossible to step up the pace beyond a trot.

A slight gradient led them to a ridge which they crested and then began a slow descent down steep banks into a deep valley with a river running along the bottom. Here the sunlight was comforting, but Vidar was frustrated by their slow progress, and they were all growing exhausted from the intensity of their constant watchfulness. They had seen no sign of whatever had killed Abbas, but Vidar instinctively felt it was shadowing them, just a heartbeat beyond the point where their eyes failed to pierce the gloom. They moved fully into the sun on the stony bottom of the winter flow channel and rode a little faster.

'The promise of treasure is starting to lose some of its allure,' Cheyne said.

'No point going back now,' Vidar replied.

'There may be no going back at all,' Cheyne muttered.

Shielding his eyes from the glare off the water, Vidar said, 'We need to find a crossing point. The map suggested there might be a ford a little further on where this broadens out.' Now they were in the light, Vidar's mind turned to the incipient guilt that had dogged him since Abbas was killed. The death would be on his conscience, a sacrifice in his search for identity, and though he had been the cause of many other deaths, this one hurt more than most. Abbas was a good and honourable man who deserved to die with some glory. He had no family, but Vidar knew he had been seeing a girl in Ironrack for nearly two years. He tried to tell himself that the expedition was to Idriss's long-term benefit, but he was aware of the truth, and his attempt at self-deception didn't assuage his feelings.

It wasn't long before the sun began to sink behind the trees, casting a dull, reddish light among the lengthening shadows. With it came a sound that chilled the blood: a long, high-pitched shriek like the one they had heard earlier, but with a different note of hunger, and unnervingly close. It was soon joined by another, and then another, and as the sun slowly faded away, more and more bestial noises joined in: barks and howls, some that sounded like a crying baby, others that whistled, and roars so loud it felt as if they were making the trees shake.

Instinctively, they rode closer together and faster, but the noises were unnerving the horses, which had to be continually restrained and guided. The forest, so still and quiet for most of the day, now appeared to be filled with unseen creatures. Glancing from side to side, they could see nothing in the darkness beneath the branches.

Nearby a tree cracked loudly and fell like thunder. Cheyne looked towards the sound and said, 'How big–?' before catching himself.

'We need to get away from the river,' Vidar said.

'Back under the trees? Are you mad?' Cheyne exclaimed. 'If I am going to die, it would be good to have the sky and the stars above me, instead of that damnable, suffocating canopy.'

'They will be coming down to the river to drink.' It was the first time Chien-Fu had spoken for hours, and that somehow gave his quiet words a terrible intensity.

Another tree cracked and shook the ground with its fall, closer this time.

'Ride faster,' Vidar prompted.

On either side of the river the treetops began to shake and the branches and bushes along the edge trembled with increasing force.

'Ride!' Vidar ordered.

They spurred on their horses as fast as they could along the uneven, shifting shale, lying low over their necks, eyes darting all around. The sun was almost gone, the shadows reaching out hungrily from the tree line, the orchestra of beast-sounds deafening. Another tree crashed to the ground, this time so close that the tip protruded into the river behind them.

Terrified, the horses' eyes rolled, and the riders had to fight to keep them under control. The one carrying Abbas's body broke free and galloped back the way it had come. They heard an explosive emergence from the trees, a roaring that made their ears hurt, and frightened whinnying cut short, followed by a ravenous rending and tearing.

Rounding a bend in the river, they came upon the ford. The river pooled into a shallow basin, and Vidar instantly drove his horse into the water; there was no time to check if it was the correct path and he knew he risked them both being swept away. As the water surged up around him, Cheyne and Chien-Fu followed suit.

Somehow they stumbled on to a path where the river only came up to their boots. Once they were on the other side, Vidar estimated the direction of the channel, and then glanced briefly at Cheyne and Chien-Fu. 'If any fall back, the others keep going. No heroics. Agreed?'

Cheyne and Chien-Fu nodded. They all drew their swords, and then Vidar drove into the tree line. The sun winked out the moment they left the river bank behind, and instantly they all realised the hopelessness of attempting to navigate the forest. Even when their eyes had adjusted to the intensity of the shadows beneath the branches, they could only just make out the vague shape of the nearest trees against the dark background. The shrieks and howls caught beneath the canopy were so loud it made their heads ring, and all around they could sense movement of things huge and small, yet see nothing.

The stink of whatever was out there drove the horses into a frenzy. Fighting to keep in the saddle, Vidar decided to take his chances on foot – at least he would be able to move quicker over a short distance. He jumped down and set the horse free, knowing it would not last long.

Cheyne and Chien-Fu were nowhere to be seen. There was only the cacophony and the chaos of movement in the dark. Blindly, he moved forwards from tree to tree. Something bounded by, sensed him, and turned back with a snarl. Lashing out with his sword, he felt it bite through flesh and bone. The snarl died and the beast fell into the undergrowth, but he was already moving on.

Conscious thought was replaced by a blind instinct that protected him against the insanity of the situation, and served him well in slipping through the vegetation to hide in the nooks of great gnarled oaks as things thundered past a hair's-breadth away in the dark. For a long time, he didn't remember breathing, until the burning in his chest was too acute to ignore, and then gradually he began to realise that the noise was diminishing as the beasts made their way past him to the river's edge.

Listening intently, he waited for long moments in the twisted roots of an oak as wide as a house, and then steeled himself and ran as quickly as he could away from the river. Darting back and forth among the trees, dead branches cracking sickeningly loudly under his boots, he covered a quarter of a mile before skidding down an incline into a hollow and coming to rest against hard rock.

Once his breathing had subsided, he allowed himself to listen again. At first, all around was silent, until the sound of running feet appeared in the distance, drawing closer. Mistrusting anything his senses told him in that forest, in the dark, Vidar considered remaining silent, but the light-footed gait was familiar.

When the footsteps began to pass to his right, he called out quietly, 'Cheyne.' The word carried unnervingly in the stillness. The footsteps came to a halt, and then slowly began to prowl towards him. Vidar's hand tightened on his sword. A second later, the footsteps ended again, and however much he strained he could hear no movement.

When there was a burst of activity on the lip of the hollow and a figure propelled itself towards him, at the last second he stopped himself from hacking out. Cheyne crashed into a heap next to him.

'How graceful. And I was making such a good approximation of your stealth and silence.'

'I could have killed you!'

'And I, you.' Cheyne rested back against the stone, sucking a deep breath to calm himself. Vidar could feel his companion trembling against him. 'I always thought the horses were a bad idea,' he added.

'Chien-Fu?'

'I saw nothing, not even my hand in front of my face. But you know Chien-Fu is fleet-footed. He has probably already reached the horizon.'

Even if Cheyne's optimism was well founded, they both knew Chien-Fu didn't stand a chance without the map.

'So here we are,' Cheyne continued as his breathing calmed. 'Stranded in the middle of the forest, with no horses, no supplies, and a hellish distance to cross in difficult circumstances to get back to Idriss. Still, it could be worse.'

'How?'

'Ah. I was hoping you would not follow up on that one.'

The sat silently for several minutes, trying to calm their racing minds. The screech of an owl nearby made them both start.

'Drinking time at the river will be over soon,' Vidar said.

'That would mean we need a plan.'

'I have one: keep going in the direction of the channel as fast as we can.'

'A good plan. The best.'

Vidar froze. 'Did you hear something?'

They both listened for a moment.

'The Lord of Stealth and Silence is frighted by the dark,' Cheyne said, nonetheless lowering his voice until it was barely audible.

Vidar continued to listen, but a night breeze had picked up and the forest was filled with the creak of branches and the rustle of leaves. His ghosts sensed his anxiety, whispering excitedly at the back of his head.

'Did you see any of them?' The unease in Cheyne's voice was unmistakable.

'Shadows moving, that was all.'

'Yes, that was all I saw. Different shapes... some very big indeed.' He paused. 'I thought I saw teeth... a mouth large enough to swallow me whole. Perhaps it was my imagination.'

A wave of weakness washed over Vidar, and he fought to contain it, but his bitterness felt like a knife. He couldn't afford to start losing energy, but he could feel his joints starting to ache and his limbs growing leaden. Through his fears, his senses pricked again. 'I heard something, I'm sure,' he hissed.

Silence held sway for a few more moments until Cheyne said, 'Imagination or not, we cannot stay–' The word caught in his throat.

'What is it?' Vidar asked, concerned.

'This stone at our backs. It feels worked. Here.' He fumbled for Vidar's hand and placed it on what Vidar had thought was a rock. He thought he could feel a linear join between two stones, and another, but it was hard to tell amid the lichen.

'There were some ruins on the map not far from here,' he recalled. 'I didn't pay them much attention. But it might be a place we can hide away till daybreak.'

'Do you remember how to reach them?'

'Even if I did, I'd never be able to guide you through this place at night. But we might be able to follow this…' Feeling along the stone, he came to a hole, half-hidden by overhanging fern. The edges were smooth and completely circular. 'There's something here. Might be a tunnel, a sewer outlet–'

'I do not by any means desire to crawl along a sewer, however ancient and unused, but if it means an escape from this unpleasant hole in which we find ourselves, then I am all for it.'

'I can't see how far it goes, or if there's anything inside that we might not like,' Vidar said, frustrated.

'Let me strike my flint–'

'No! It'll be like a beacon.'

'Quickly. I can shield it with my body–'

'No, Cheyne. It'll still be seen.'

'We cannot sit here all night deliberating!' The snap of his voice revealed how scared he really was. He leaned past Vidar and struck the flint hurriedly before they could debate it further.

The flare of light burned the sanity away from Vidar and Cheyne for one terrifying instant. A dense wall of beasts had gathered around the lip of the hollow, reaching far back into the trees. The fleeting instant of illumination seared a half-glimpsed image in Vidar's mind, of ferocious teeth and seething eyes, of shimmering black skins and lithe, muscular limbs, what could have been insects as big as a horse, or lizards with gleaming scales.

As the glare faded, something flew through the air and landed at their feet, and though it was only barely seen, Vidar knew it was Chien-Fu's upper torso.

Cheyne threw himself into the hole and Vidar followed, cracking his head and elbows on the stone. Behind him, he heard a rush of movement as the things surged forwards.

They found themselves in an ink-black space big enough to stand upright. Feeling around as they lurched forwards, they discovered it was a tunnel, dry and dusty, either a sewer or a storm drain, they guessed, but it was so dark they were blind.

'Move!' Vidar yelled. 'They're coming in behind us!'

'There might be a drop ahead!' Cheyne protested. 'We could go plummeting to our deaths!'

'Stay here and get torn apart like Chien-Fu, then!'

Convinced, Cheyne began to run, holding his arms out to guide him along the walls on either side. Vidar kept up, but the weariness made his limbs almost too heavy to move. Behind them came the sound of the things forcing their way into the tunnel, and then the awful crying baby sound they had heard earlier, rising up from numerous throats until the tunnel was filled with it.

Vidar and Cheyne ran as fast as they could, but the dark was so intense they lost all sense of where they were, so that at times they would crash against the walls, or pitch forwards with the sensation that they were floating in space.

As the beasts drew nearer and Vidar's heartbeat pounded harder, the ghosts finally broke free of the tether in his mind. The shimmering forms appeared all around, tearing at their hair and howling with glee: '*You will die! They will catch you!*'

For the first time, the ghosts were a help, their thin light illuminating the path ahead. Vidar made the mistake of glancing back to see the beasts swarming along the tunnel only yards behind.

'Run faster!' he barked. Cheyne muttered an obscenity under his breath – he was going as fast as he could.

The tunnel continued for half a mile, and then began to slope upwards until it came to a halt at an iron grille with a handle in the centre. It gave and then stuck as Cheyne threw himself at it.

'Rusted!' Cheyne said.

'Just get it open.' Sword at the ready, Vidar turned to face the howling mass.

As the ghosts surged around him, Vidar was thankful that he only perceived fractured glimpses of what he faced. In the half-light, he hacked and slashed, his sword a blur of steel that allowed nothing to penetrate his defences. When his blade bit into one of the creatures it shrieked so loudly he thought his ears would burst. A foul-smelling, sticky liquid squirted from the wounds.

In his hands, the sword felt as heavy as the rag-and-bone carts that came in and out of Greatstock, and he didn't know how much longer he would be able to find the strength to fight; his energy was fading fast.

The screaming beasts drove him back a step, then two, but finally he heard Cheyne grunt loudly and the rending of the grille as it tore free from its rusted moorings. There was a clatter as it fell out into the void beyond.

'Time to stop dancing,' Cheyne called.

Vidar threw one final strike with the last of his strength and clambered into the hole. Cheyne hauled him through, and together they thrust the grille back into place as the beasts threw themselves at it. The force of the attack almost burst the grille outwards, but Vidar and Cheyne put their shoulders against it and managed to hold it long enough for Cheyne to lock it in place with the small wheel at the centre.

As the desolate ghosts winked out one by one, Vidar and Cheyne fell backwards on to stone flags, breathless and exhausted. 'At the moment, the only treasure I am concerned about is a long sleep and some good food,' Cheyne said.

Lying on his back, Vidar let the strength gradually leak back into his limbs. Above him, the sky was filled with a milky wash of stars and a full moon had risen, high and bright. They were in a vast, dusty courtyard overgrown with scrubby trees and grass breaking through the flags. Beyond, crumbling buildings were silhouetted against the night sky. It looked as if it had been abandoned for a long time. Glancing around, he couldn't see any imminent signs of danger, but even if there were he didn't have the strength to fight.

'The weakness has come over you.' Cheyne studied him, reading all the familiar signs.

Vidar nodded, pulling himself up on to his elbows.

'How long?'

'A while. It started getting worse after Greer an' Lokh's spell to help Asgrim.'

'And how much longer?'

'You know I can't answer that.'

'But sooner rather than later?'

'Yes.'

'And there are only the two of us.'

'I'm not going to cut your throat when you're not looking, Cheyne.'

'Oh? I would.' He stood up and held out a hand to help Vidar to his feet. 'Do not rush to stake your position, Vidar. We all act in ways we cannot divine when it is a simple choice between survival and death.'

'I don't see life as survival at any cost. I think I'm better than that.'

Cheyne smiled tightly. 'We all do. But we shall see, shall we not? And in the meantime, you will forgive me if I keep one eye on you and your sword.'

'So do I have to keep one eye on you? You'll do me in before you think I'm going to come for you?'

'Ah, but I have the upper hand. You will only get weaker, but I am a strong, sprightly man who can dance out of the way of your blade.'

Cheyne kept the mood light, but the underlying dilemma continued to weigh heavily on them both. They picked their way over the rubble and through the subsistence-level undergrowth to explore their surroundings. A jagged gash in one wall allowed access to the forest beyond. The debris thrown across the courtyard suggested it had been smashed in from without, possibly by an invading army, Vidar and Cheyne mused. The breach in the defences was unsettling, and they quickly made their way to a keep of yellowing stone. They could now see they were within a fort, perhaps an outpost for some once-powerful city or forgotten empire.

The entrance to the keep was barred from within, but the wood that had been used was ancient and shattered with some effort from Vidar and Cheyne. They resealed it behind them as best they could and located a torch, which Cheyne lit with his flint.

As they moved through the keep, they found piles of ancient bones here and there. 'Starved to death,' Vidar guessed. 'When the walls came down, they holed up here as a last resort. With the fort open to the forest, they had nowhere else to go.'

'We all live a fragile existence with the forest at our doorstep,' Cheyne said. 'A few stones and mortar are all that lie between life and death.'

Emerging on to the roof of the keep, they walked around the ramparts, but could see no lights across the forest that spread from horizon to horizon. They felt more alone than they ever had done in their lives.

'It seems we have come out behind in this transaction,' Cheyne said. 'We have gambled away a prison of a city for a prison of a building.'

'It's not over yet,' Vidar replied. But Cheyne's words resonated loudly with his thoughts. Finding out exactly who he was had always seemed the most important thing to him, but had he now sacrificed everything else to that end, including his life?

As WAS SO often the case when the weakness gripped him, Vidar couldn't sleep and he made his way back up to the roof of the keep shortly before dawn. Where the forest had been a deep, threatening darkness before, he was now surprised to see lights glimmering through the canopy just beyond the fort's walls.

As he prepared to rush down the steps to make contact with what he initially presumed was a caravan, he suddenly paused. The lights were moving in a slow procession, and there was something about their quality that made his skin tingle and filled him with a profound sense of wonder. Whoever carried those lights was not scared of what lived in the forest. There was no urgency, and almost a sense of being at peace in their domain.

His curiosity piqued, Vidar thoughtfully watched the lights until they disappeared from view. What else lived in the forest, he wondered?

IN THE REZSHINNIA on the south-eastern edge of Idriss, the night was filled with the fragrant smoke of the water-pipes bubbling in the crowded shops that lined the jumbled streets around the bazaar. Stories were exchanged over hot, sweet pastries and steaming drinks, ancient histories brought back to vibrant life or the day's gossip dissected and discussed in insistent voices talking one over the other. In the shadowy lanes of the market, shoppers still haggled with sellers sweating beneath the canvas covers of their stalls amid the thick scent of spices.

Asgrim led the small unit of the Crimson Hunt along streets crowded with people watching the belly dancers clattering their zills in time to the thrust of their hips while small boys scrambled for tossed coins.

'It is too crowded, too hot, there's too much noise,' the captain of the unit complained. 'We will never find him here.'

'We have had three reports of a man changing his face in the alleys around the Rezshinnia,' Asgrim said. 'We cannot afford to ignore them.'

Tempers began to fray as the Huntsmen pressed on into the middle of the throng, their attempts to keep in formation sending passers-by flying. Angry voices were raised at their backs and fists shaken in the air.

Asgrim grew uneasy. His own men were short-tempered, hot, and exhausted after a night without sleep and a day being deployed at numerous trouble spots around the city. Their faces were strained, their eyes glowering.

'If we are attacked, no one must respond,' Asgrim said to the captain. 'We retreat to a safe spot and wait for passions to die down.'

The captain nodded, but he was unsettled. 'The goodwill we always enjoyed is fading fast.'

As they skirted the edge of the bazaar, Asgrim somehow caught a trace of the familiar sour smell amid the numerous conflicting aromas that assailed him. He held up his hand to halt the unit and peered into the dark, claustrophobic confines of the cluttered market. A man and a woman argued furiously over a battered urn. A child sat on a pile of carpets, picking his nose. A young woman flirted coquettishly with a lean, muscular helper on a stall packed with jars of herbs.

And then he had it, one fleeting sly glance his way from a balding, overweight man with a thick moustache.

'There,' Asgrim indicated.

The man fled into the heart of the bazaar as Asgrim and the Crimson Hunt gave pursuit. There was barely room for three people abreast among the stalls, and soon produce was spilling across the aisle, glassware was shattered, and shoppers and sellers hurled abuse as they were crushed in the mêlée.

Determined not to lose the Red Man, Asgrim bounded ahead as the Crimson Hunt battled their way through the constricting space. But in the very heart of the bazaar, the overweight man came to a halt next to a stall selling lanterns. Knocking the owner to the ground, he upended the stall to block the aisle and a pool of oil spread across the ground from the tumbling lanterns. Knowing what was to come next but unable to do anything about it, Asgrim watched in horror as the Red Man ignited the oil with a torch and then sprinted away from the soaring flames.

The fire raced through stall after stall in a matter of seconds, the heat so intense Asgrim and the Crimson Hunt were driven back. Panic erupted as thick smoke billowed across the bazaar. Confused, choking stallholders raced wildly, screaming and shouting, fighting with each other to find a way out of the claustrophobic space.

'Fetch water!' Asgrim yelled. 'We must fight this before it spreads throughout the entire bazaar!'

The flames already soared twenty feet into the air, leaping from canvas roof to canvas roof in all directions. But as the Huntsmen scrambled to find buckets and a water supply, scores of men armed with sticks raced into the bazaar and began to bludgeon them repeatedly.

As heads cracked and blood spurted, the Huntsmen drew their swords and turned on their attackers until Asgrim yelled, 'Do not attack! They think we started the fire!'

More men surged into the angry mob so that the bazaar became alive with attackers surrounding the Huntsmen. The blows came faster, harder. Missiles were thrown and then Asgrim saw the glint of knives. The crowd chanted, 'You shall not destroy us!'

'Collect the wounded and follow me!' Asgrim yelled to the captain.

He overturned a stall, and then another, forcing a path through the bazaar to the fringes where they could scramble under the remaining stalls and sprint into the winding alleys that led out of the quarter.

Soot-blackened and bloody, they did not stop until they were outside the Rezshinnia, collapsing breathlessly on the side of the road.

'News of this will spread quickly,' the captain said.

'The Red Man planned this,' Asgrim said, his gaze cold and hard on the flames leaping up into the night sky. 'He wanted to undermine the Crimson Hunt's reputation and add to the mounting panic. It only serves his purpose.'

'And what is his purpose?' the captain asked.

LAURENT THE SEEKER emerged from the Temple of the Shepherd on to the marble steps to watch the fire burning brightly on the south-eastern edge of the city. He could hear the screams and shouts clearly on the hot night air.

For a while he stood there, listening to the clashes rising up in other quarters and feeling mounting despair at what was happening to his city. If only everyone followed the path of the Shepherd, he thought, there would be no trouble, no brutality. There would be hope for them all.

He turned to go back into the temple to meditate some more on what solutions might lie in the Shepherd's teachings, only to be distracted by an unfamiliar smell. A strong, sour smell. It seemed to be rising up within the temple. Curious, he ventured inside to investigate.

8

BENEATH THE TREES, A SHADOW

Two HOURS OF sleep were all Asgrim could allow himself. The captain of the day shift woke him just as dawn began to appear, with a bowl of thick porridge and some water, which he consumed as he listened to reports of the night shift's travails. A protest in Ironrack during which three houses were burned to the ground. A mob confronting a shopkeeper on the edge of the market in Lerose Cross for no other reason than someone had decided the Red Man hailed from that community. And a near riot in Greatstock after numerous conflicting rumours drove the people into a frenzy. The greatest fear spread across the city like a plague: that no one knew anything, and therefore no one was safe.

Patrols around the walls had been severely curtailed to cope with the amount of peace-keeping activity that Ashur had demanded of the Crimson Hunt.

'We cannot do two jobs effectively,' the captain told Asgrim. 'Our first call is to defend Idriss from attack, not to mediate petty squabbles.'

'I would not call the burning of three houses a petty squabble. Or the devastation that's crippled the Rezshinnia.' Asgrim thrust his bowl away from him. He knew there was a reason why he had resisted promotion at every turn. 'And unrest on the scale we are seeing is a threat to Idriss, as surely as if we had an enemy force at the gates.'

'You agree with Ashur, then?'

'I agree that the threat has to be dealt with. But as a good member of the Crimson Hunt, I do not question the orders of my superiors.' He fixed an eye on the captain, who nodded curtly and left. The open dissent was just another problem he would have to manage. The Crimson Hunt under Mellias had been loyal to the King at every turn, even when some of the political decisions had been questionable, but the Hunt had never taken to Ashur. Part of the prejudice came from his appearance – they couldn't read his face and so didn't trust a word he said – but he had on more than one occasion put Huntsmen's lives in danger with ill-considered orders. The belief that the current order went against the ethos of the Hunt only played along with that perception.

Once he had briefed the day shift, and mounted more sentries on the walls, Asgrim sought out Rhiannon. He eventually found her at Fallen Spire, questioning a boy who had witnessed the Red Man tear through the boarding house. The boy had been in hiding for his life since the atrocity, but Rhiannon had tracked him down as she had promised. Asgrim was quietly impressed with her abilities.

When she was finished, she came over to Asgrim, the strain beginning to tell on her face.

'Anything new?' Asgrim asked.

Rhiannon shook her head wearily. 'A description of the face he wore when he entered the house. A description of the change-face, which you saw, and the final face. But what is the point?'

'True. There may be bodies yet undiscovered, and several faces since that one.'

'We will not catch the Red Man through the standard procedure of the Inquisitors – meticulous questioning and thorough understanding of the scenario that led to the death,' she said, frustrated. 'We'll do it by understanding his thinking and predicting what he will do next.'

'If he knows himself.'

'Oh, there is an intelligence there.'

'He kills to gain a new face, to evade capture, so he can continue to spy on our defences for the enemy, whoever they might be.'

'That is one explanation, and the reason for the murders of the woman at the Four Staves and the boy you came across in the alley. But it does not explain yesterday's slaughter.'

'That was a message, you said so yourself. But of what?'

Despite the already mounting heat, she pulled her cowl over her head so her face disappeared into shadow. 'That tableau had religious connotations to me. The way the bodies were arranged spoke of supplication.' She appeared to be weighing how much to tell him before saying, 'I have been to the Temple of the Shepherd to discuss the matter with the Seeker, but he is nowhere to be found. The Inquisitors are searching for him now.'

'The Shepherd?' He laughed loudly. 'I cannot imagine the little, lost lambs chopping up bodies for sport!'

His humour fell flat, and Rhiannon looked up at the four shattered monuments, avoiding his questioning gaze. 'We cannot ignore the possibility that the Red Man is also conspiring to cause the chaos we see around us,' she said. 'Every new death inspires more fear. He plays the city like an instrument. If an attack is imminent, a divided, terrified population would be easier to defeat than the strong and proud citizens of a few days ago.'

'All the more reason to catch him.'

Her shoulders sagged. 'I do not need more pressure, Asgrim. I am aware of my responsibilities. Vidar left you here to help me.'

'And I will. Tell me what you require.'

She thought for a moment, then shook her head. Asgrim had never seen her so dejected. 'I wonder if I am up to this task.'

'Vidar believes you are—'

'What does he know?' she snapped. 'And where is he now? Defending Idriss? No, seeking treasure and fulfilling his own personal quest.'

'Do not speak ill of him,' Asgrim said sharply. 'He has faith in you, in all of us. And he believes this quest will benefit everyone here—'

'You are a fool, Asgrim,' she replied, equally sharply. 'As are we all.' She turned abruptly and walked away towards the river before he could ask her what she meant by her final comment.

* * *

WHILE CHEYNE SLEPT, recovering from the exertion of the previous day, Vidar re-examined the map and fixed in his mind the location of the nearest channel and the slowly moving spikes of light. His exhaustion came and went in waves, with the troughs increasingly close together. The amber jewel's cycling consumption of his energy was a familiar process now it had depleted all its reserves, and to make matters worse, the whispering ghosts of the lives he had consumed were now constant at the back of his mind, so that at times it was impossible to tell his own thoughts from theirs.

On occasion, he'd wondered if they really were ghosts or simply manifestations of his own guilt, given form by the Vampire Jewel. In the end, it didn't really matter. He was haunted; there was no getting away from it.

Cheyne slept half-sitting in the corner of the room, facing the door so it was impossible to creep up on him. Vidar noted the dagger gripped in Cheyne's hand: a warning to him. He'd barely stepped across the threshold when Cheyne was alert, suspicious eyes searching Vidar's face.

Vidar pretended not to know what was going through his friend's mind. 'We can't afford to waste any more time. The morning's half-gone.'

Sheathing his dagger, Cheyne stretched the kinks from his limbs. 'The breakfast at the Four Staves would be welcome at this moment.'

'You'll have to settle for catching a bird or a rabbit en route.'

'While keeping a weather eye out for any immediate evisceration, of course. So we are still moving forwards?'

'There's no going back on foot.'

'And your jewel may find a tasty snack shortly, if those lights on the map are what we think. Which will be a relief for both of us.'

The stillness that lay over the fort was eerie as they made their way across the courtyard to the gash in the walls. In the daylight, they could see its great age and the oddities of its architecture, which bore little resemblance to the craftwork of Idriss. Carvings on some of the blocks of yellow stone that made up the walls and buildings suggested they had been part of some other long-forgotten structure before being scavenged and used in the construction of the fort.

'We aren't that far from Idriss,' Vidar noted. 'I had no idea there were other civilisations so close.'

'The forest makes even a few miles a world away. Who knows what really exists beyond what we can see? Perhaps there really are shining cities of angels and shadow-shrouded demon haunts.'

'Or perhaps there's nothing,' Vidar said, 'except a few out-pockets of people clinging on desperately, waiting to be picked off by what lives in the forest.' He looked around. 'Like whoever lived here.'

As the birds swooped in the clear blue sky overhead, they climbed through the gap in the walls and reflected for a moment on the dark, encroaching tree line. After a day under the branches, the hot sun on their heads felt good, and both of them were loath to return to the gloom. Then, without another word, they slipped out of the heat and into the cool, scented interior. Instinctively, their hearts began to pound, but once their eyes had adjusted and they had scanned the surrounding area, they saw no immediate danger.

They moved at a rapid jog among the trees, skirting areas of dense vegetation or rocky outcroppings that could hide waiting predators, but the density of the trees made it increasingly difficult to get a clear view even a few yards ahead.

At one point, Cheyne signalled for them to stop, and ducked down to press his head against the soft moss underfoot. Vibrations of a heavy tread ran through the ground. Scrambling under the roots of a massive, twisted oak, they buried themselves under leaf-mould close to the base of the trunk as the ground shook more and more. Something enormous passed within thirty yards of their hiding place. They could hear the rasp of its breath and bass rumbles deep in its throat. Every now and then it stopped and tore at the under-growth.

They lay still as the vibrations gradually diminished, but just as they were about to emerge, the scratching of something smaller rose up in the beast's wake. From the sounds it made, Vidar estimated it was the size of a pony, probably hoping to pick up any remnants of food the larger creature left behind.

It passed by their tree and then paused for a long moment. Vidar had decided it had slipped away into the undergrowth when they heard a low growl only feet away. The growl mutated into a higher pitched noise that almost sounded like human speech, though unintelligible. Words appeared to come and go with an insistent tone that sounded by turn pleading and hateful.

It moved closer, scraping gently at the leaf-mould as it probed the area around the tree's roots. Vidar gripped his knife, and knew Cheyne was doing the same.

The snuffling noise came closer and closer until it was almost next to his head. The chattering voice faded, to be replaced by a deep, low growl. Holding his breath, Vidar prepared to drive the knife upwards.

Before he could move, a deafening screeching tore through the air and a burst of tremendous activity exploded next to them. Shrieking and roaring emanated from a furious battle that tore up the leaf-mould all around, and then there was one final screech before silence fell.

His heart thundering, Vidar lay still for several long moments until he was sure there was no further activity. Drawing himself slowly from his hiding place, he found chunks of bloody meat and bone scattered all around, but no sign of what had caused the carnage.

Cheyne emerged a second later, turning the torn flesh over with his knife. 'And this is the second time in a matter of hours that I am thinking more warmly of the Four Staves than I am of treasure.'

'There's always something higher up the food chain.' Vidar brushed himself down, keeping one eye out for a returning predator. 'Probably not a good idea to be hanging around these choice bloody snacks.'

The terrain inclined gradually downwards, eventually plummeting suddenly into a deep valley where it was as dark as night. Among lush grass and thick fern, a fast-flowing stream

gushed along the bottom, where they were surprised to find well-worn stepping stones placed
across the narrowest part of the channel. Vidar
examined them, but it was impossible to tell
how recently they had been used.

The other side of the valley gave way at the
summit to a rocky area where the tree cover
was sparse, before tumbling down again
towards another shallower valley. They
stopped on several occasions to hide from
predators moving away in the forest, but as
they made their way up the valley side, Vidar
caught Cheyne's arm surreptitiously.

'We're being shadowed.'

'A beast?'

'Two legs. Four people.'

'Where?'

'To your left. They've been matching our
progress for a while.'

'And you only choose to tell me now?'
Cheyne sniffed.

'I didn't want you to alert them till I'd got
their measure.'

'And what did you think I would do? Run
towards them, pointing and shouting?'

'Just being cautious, Cheyne. If they can
direct their attention towards stalking us
instead of just surviving in this damned place,
they've got to be as mean and nasty as the
wildlife.'

'It is difficult to imagine any people who could live up to that description,' Cheyne said, unsettled. 'Which suggests they very well may not be *people*. Do you think they killed Abbas?'

'Probably.'

'And they were responsible for the lights you saw moving through the trees last night?' Vidar nodded. 'What could survive out here, my friend?'

'I don't think we want to find out, do you?'

As they crested the valley side, Vidar increased their pace, keeping lower than they had been on the skyline. They came to a large lichen and moss-covered rock bursting out of the ground and ducked behind it, instantly veering sharply to their left before dropping on to their bellies to crawl through the thigh-high bracken.

The terrain fell away suddenly down a steep scree slope to another deep valley. Vidar propelled Cheyne over the edge and they skidded at speed down the sun-drenched bank, tearing through scrubby bushes and cracking knees, elbows, and heads on the shale.

When they landed in a heap at the bottom, Cheyne immediately launched into a tirade of cursing before Vidar thrust him roughly into the undergrowth and forced him to run along the valley bottom before scrambling up another steep bank. Only when they reached the top did Vidar allow them to take a moment's rest.

'Next time, give me some warning!' Cheyne snapped. 'Look – I have scuffed my boots.'

Ignoring him, Vidar shielded his eyes from the sunlight breaking through the branches so he could peer down into the valley.

'We lost them.' Cheyne sighed. 'Come, now.'

A shape flitted among the trees at the foot of the valley, followed by another.

'Let's go.' Vidar's grave tone told Cheyne everything he needed to know.

'I scuffed my boots for nothing? How could we not lose them?'

'Must be some kind of trackers.' Vidar broke into a run.

'They are hunting us?' Cheyne asked breathlessly.

'Stop talking, unless you want to end up like Abbas. It's not far to the channel from here. We'll be able to move quicker there.'

'So will they.'

For the next three hours, every attempt to throw their pursuers off their trail failed, even wading waist-deep across a fast-flowing river, doubling-back further downstream, and then crossing again at another point. The four figures kept on coming, drawing closer with every passing hour. Vidar would glance back and see them briefly silhouetted against the sky as they crested a ridge, or like ghosts deep in the trees. They were tireless, relentless.

'What are they?' The irritation in Cheyne's voice showed clearly. 'And why do they not leave us alone? Are we truly worth all this trouble?'

'They clearly think so.' Vidar tried to get a clear view of their pursuers, but just when he thought he might glimpse them, they would disappear into the vegetation or merge into the background, just another feature of the hazy green world.

At the same time, the predators in the forest were also growing closer. They heard the screeches of unseen creatures flying just above the treetops, from the resonant sound much larger than any bird they had ever seen before, while the ground trembled regularly from the thunderous passing of the largest creatures, hidden by the trees nearby.

A snake with a body as wide as Vidar's torso attacked them on the edge of a dark pool, its gold and green scales gleaming in the half-light. As it lunged, Vidar and Cheyne struck out with their swords, hacking chunks from its flesh, but their attack only slowed it a little and they had to sprint along a precarious path through a sucking bog to escape it.

'Why did I allow you to talk me into this?' Cheyne said, wiping the sweat from his brow.

Fighting back a debilitating bout of weakness, Vidar asked himself the same question.

And with each new obstacle in their path, their pursuers grew closer. Now their spectral forms took on a disturbing hardness whenever Vidar glanced back through the trees.

'Not much further now,' he gasped, his own voice getting lost among the rising cries of the ghosts in his head. They were enjoying the danger, seeing the distinct possibility of his own demise in the mounting threat and doing whatever they could to destabilise him further. He could usually contain them, but they found strength in his weakness.

'... much further?' Cheyne was asking. Vidar noted his friend's concerned glance, politely hidden.

'Over the next ridge and down the other side should do it.' His pale words disappeared into the pounding of his heart.

'Can you make it? Do you want me to carry you?' He added, 'You will have to give up your knives and sword, of course.'

'Cheyne, you are never going to carry me. I'll crawl first.'

'Pride makes a poor companion in the afterlife.'

'You just want a story to tell at my expense in the Four Staves.'

'True. The Day I Gave a Piggy-Back to the Ghost Warrior should earn me a pint or two.'

The roar was so loud their hearts stopped for a second, and it was followed instantly by thunderous vibrations in the ground that made their legs buckle. Trees cracked and fell with resounding crashes as a path was torn through the dense forest towards them.

Vidar and Cheyne exchanged a brief glance and then ran even faster, drawing on reserves of energy they didn't know they had.

Another roar, their eardrums burning with the volume. The monstrous footsteps crashed behind them at a furious pace, moving ever closer. Vidar and Cheyne leaped rotting tree-trunks, threw themselves over lichen-mottled rocks, bounced and rolled, and continued to sprint, their breath burning in their chests. With each deafening roar, they could now feel a blast of hot breath on the back of their necks.

Splashing through a boggy area that threatened to mire them, they reached the lip of the valley side and saw through the trees a sun-drenched path along the bottom far below. As Vidar prepared to propel himself down the slope, in the corner of his eye he saw Cheyne knocked flying.

Gritting his teeth, he drew his sword and turned. Bleeding from a wound on his cheek,

Cheyne scrambled behind a tree as massive jaws snapped shut on the air where his head had been. Looming over them on two powerful legs was a giant lizard four times Vidar's height, its tail so strong it destroyed trees when it thrashed from side to side to balance the beast's frenzied movements. Fierce eyes blazed down at them above a jaw torn wide to reveal rows of enormous teeth that could have ripped a horse in two. Despite its size, it was fast and vicious, tearing and snapping for Cheyne constantly.

Vidar ran forwards and hacked at its leg. The sword bit slightly, but the thick skin dulled the brunt of the attack. Even so, the beast roared and lashed out with its head, the top catching Vidar squarely and sending him flying.

Winded, he rolled out of the way just in time as the hot breath bore down on him and the jaws tore through the turf beneath him as they snapped shut. He came up with the sword again, ducking under the lashing tail to hack at the other leg. This time he cut a large chunk of flesh. Roaring and snapping, the beast turned on him, driving him back so that he had to duck behind trees that splintered as the teeth raked across them.

Recovering from his wound, Cheyne joined in the attack, slashing and then dancing beyond the range of the head and tail. The distraction gave Vidar his opportunity. He scrambled between two tightly packed oaks, and as the beast thrust its head after him, it became wedged. As it strained to free itself, Vidar continued over the edge and down the valley side, with Cheyne skidding and leaping after him.

A tree was torn from the ground by its roots as the beast freed itself, and then it came hurtling down the valley side after them, its enormous bulk smashing through everything in its path.

Vidar and Cheyne lost control of their motion, flipping over and rolling, careering off trees, and bouncing over rocks until they heard a distant drone drawing nearer.

'Bees?' Cheyne gasped. 'At the moment, being stung to death would probably be slightly preferable to bone-crunching and slow digestion.'

Yet there was an unnatural quality to the hum, which had a faint metallic edge to it. From the corner of his eye, Vidar glimpsed a black cloud weaving rapidly through the trees away to his right, dense, not bees, but creatures of around the same size, though moving with seemingly a single mind in a way that he had never seen bees behave. In shafts of sunlight, flashes of emerald and sapphire glimmered as the cloud surged towards the beast.

When he heard the drone become high-pitched and hungry, Vidar caught hold of a branch to stop his descent. Behind him, the cloud of insects descended on the beast. It roared and snapped furiously, but within seconds the insects began to strip it of flesh, bones gleaming here and there as it thrashed around on the hillside. After a moment, it crashed to the ground and lay still, the cloud obscuring it completely.

Vidar and Cheyne exchanged a brief glance before throwing themselves down the hillside even faster. They didn't slow until they could no longer hear the droning.

'This forest is a damnable place,' Cheyne said as he caught his breath. 'Is there not even a second to rest?'

'It seems to me we should be thankful we've survived this long,' Vidar replied. 'Unless we find that channel soon, it's just a matter of time until something or other picks us off.'

'What happened to that message of hope? Thankfully, we are a tough kill, and I plan to maintain my reputation in that area.'

Shielding his eyes against the sun, Vidar scanned the top of the ridge. After a moment, he caught sight of their pursuers emerging from the trees and beginning to descend the steep bank.

'Looks like they were waiting until the feeding frenzy was over,' he said. 'Let's go.'

Cursing quietly, Cheyne joined him at a fast pace along the valley bottom. For another hour, they ran until their leg muscles burned and their breath seared their lungs, skirting bogs, fording streams, clambering over fallen trees twice their height.

As they ran, Vidar always kept one eye on their pursuers, who never slowed, never diverted from their path, until suddenly they were no longer there. Vidar came to a halt, watching the trees for movement and listening for any sounds of pursuit. Not only could he hear nothing, there was an unnatural stillness across the entire area: no birdsong, no movement of wildlife in the undergrowth, not even the stirring of leaves in the breeze.

Cheyne felt it too. He shivered. 'Is it me, or is it colder here?'

'And darker too,' Vidar replied. Looking around, they both realised no sunlight broke through the canopy at all, and in areas it was almost like night. The difference was stark and unsettling.

'I am not a man attuned to nuance, but even I have to say this does not bode well,' Cheyne said. 'Should we retrace our steps?'

'And run straight into our waiting pursuers?'

'Good point. And yet I am concerned at what else this forest is prepared to throw at us. Have we seen all it has, or is there worse to come? Forwards or back? Death or worse? These choices torment me!'

As Vidar weighed their options, a wind blew directly towards them from the gloomy distance, highly localised and shifting branches as it approached so that it appeared as though an invisible beast was on its way. It died before it reached them, and though the stillness returned it was now infused with a dark apprehension.

Cheyne's eyes darted around the forest, and then he slowly drew his rapier, even though he knew as well as Vidar that it would likely be useless.

'Something is coming,' he said quietly.

'It's here,' Vidar corrected.

They were both overwhelmed with a sense of presence, in the trees, the ground, and all the spaces between them. An oppressive dread folded around them until they felt as if they were suffocating, and they had to fight the urge to flee blindly. Something was dissecting them with a forensic intelligence. They couldn't shake the uncomfortable sensation that death was only a moment away.

After a moment of waiting, breath bound tightly in their chests, a figure lurched from behind a tree on the edge of the darkest area. It took a few seconds for their eyes to grow accustomed to the half-light, and then they realised it was Abbas; yet instinctively they knew it was Abbas in appearance only, and in essence something alien and terrifying.

His white eyes stared, unblinking, for a long moment, and then his lips moved, but the words they heard appeared to originate directly in their minds.

'You can never know me.' The voice boomed loudly and then faded away into a distorted squeal.

Something touched the back of Vidar's neck, but when he whirled around there was nothing there. Cheyne experienced the same sensation. The thing that had taken the form of Abbas continued to study them, the sense of threat mounting with each passing moment.

'Why does it look like Abbas?' Cheyne hissed.

Vidar thought for a moment and then said, 'I think it's stolen him from our heads.'

'But what is it?'

Suddenly, Abbas tore his mouth wide and roared, the sound so loud they fell backwards, clutching their ears. Shadows swept all around them, and in them Vidar briefly thought he saw eyes, and once again he felt the full weight of that awful presence before he fell to the ground, unconscious.

BRANCHES TORE AT Vidar's face as he raced through the night-forest. He could still feel the presence all around him, probing his every thought, but he was consumed by fear of what was at his back. A glance behind him revealed he was being chased by the statue of the Shepherd from the Store of the Ages, its arms outstretched, no longer devotional but hunting for the prey that had slipped through its grasp.

The shock of seeing the Shepherd came close to dislodging some of the memories locked deep in his unconscious: who and what he was really fleeing; who he was; the true significance of the amber jewel. And then he burst from the trees, and Idriss was before him, and it was that day when he first came to the city, only on this occasion Abbas stood between him and the gates.

Vidar skidded to a halt. The Shepherd was gone now, and Idriss was irrelevant; there were only Abbas's fearsome, staring eyes, behind which lay such a terrible intellect Vidar could not bring himself to consider it.

As he stared into their depths, he realised he could sense some aspects of the thing that lay before him, as though they were connecting on a level beyond conscious thought.

'You've killed a lot of my kind,' Vidar noted.

'Yes.'

'Are you alone, or are there more of you?'

Abbas didn't answer. Vidar wasn't sure if he even understood the question.

'What are you?'

Again, no answer.

'How long have you haunted the forest?'

'Always.'

The presence pulled a primal fear from deep within Vidar's heart and shaped it as if it were clay. Images churned out of his memory: he was wearing strange clothes, sprawled on a hillside with several men looking down at him; a woman's face, deeply familiar and filled with fondness, although he couldn't recall her name – she was saying to him, 'You are a hero,' and, 'I'll wait for you'; an explosion, a wall of searing heat striking his front, and then the crushing pain of something crashing against his chest, shattering bone, looking down, seeing the amber jewel settle into his body.

With a shudder, he snapped out of the succession of memories.

But Abbas still would not leave him be. 'Look,' he said, pointing into the shadows that continued to swirl around them. Rhiannon lay on the ground, blood splattered about her.

Someone hunched over her, the features indistinct.

'No,' Vidar said. 'Is this happening now? Is it going to happen?'

The shadows swallowed Rhiannon. He glimpsed other things – the Huntsmen carrying a body wrapped in a bloodstained shroud, a city floating on the sea, constructed from galleons lashed together, the Shepherd looming over Idriss, and then a brilliant white light – but it all faded quickly until only Abbas stood before him.

Vidar looked through the familiar face at the thing behind it, and sensed its intention. 'You're going to kill me too?' he asked.

Abbas hesitated, and Vidar could see the hunger behind the thing's eyes, but something held it back. Finally Abbas pointed at his chest where the jewel pulsed, and then it turned away with disgust. Slowly, it walked away, Idriss, the forest, everything falling into the darkness that cloaked it. Just before it disappeared for good, it glanced back at him, a long, glowering look, and its eyes seemed to say it would see him again, in the not-too-distant future, and then the business would be finished.

VIDAR AND CHEYNE woke at the same time on the cool leaf-mould and realised it was early morning. The entire night had passed. Impenetrable gloom no longer lay all around and the temperature was once again warm.

Brushing the twigs from his hair, Cheyne sat up. 'Frankly, I am surprised to find both of us here,' he croaked, coughing. 'It appears there is a use for that jewel of yours after all.'

'That thing spoke to you too?'

'Oh yes, none of which I am inclined to recall.' He stood up and stretched the kinks from his limbs. 'Let us count this as a close call, for if I read that thing correctly, it will be back for a second bite if we tarry here.'

Vidar agreed, and soon they were running through the forest again. Cheyne's spirits were brighter since their escape from what should have been certain death, but Vidar was subdued, haunted by the images the thing had pulled from his memory, and the ones he was convinced were premonitions of a dark future. Though it went against everything he had hoped for over the last three years, he was starting to think he might be better off not knowing.

9

SAM

In the charnel house in the basement of Greer an' Lokh's tower, the great sorcerer lay on his bed, oblivious to the stink of decomposition, and let his butterfly thoughts flutter through his head.

Seeing the map had disturbed him on some level he didn't quite understand. It was a symbol of the things for which he had always quested – knowledge, power – and it was almost in his grasp. Yet he realised it had scared him, and he had not been scared since he was a small child.

And that notion brought back memories of his formative years that he had not considered for a long time. Indeed, not only had he forgotten the faces of his parents, he had for a long time forgotten that he even had parents.

But there they were now, flashing through his mind. In the Rezshinnia, holding his hands as they walked through the bazaar where the merchants paraded the items that had come from distant cities, works of art and ornaments and carvings that were bought and then resold when the owner died, in a constant cycle of reuse, like everything else in Idriss.

He recalled being entranced by a painting of a beautiful woman posing in a red dress, and the merchant had bent down to him, smelling of spices and perfume, and had explained to him how a painting was created. Greer an' Lokh had accepted at that moment that it was his destiny to be an artist, to create, to paint the astonishing and wonderful things that ranged inside his head, and the remarkable things he saw across the glorious city of Idriss, things that no one else appeared to see.

Back at their small house on the al-Abarit, he had eagerly explained his ambition to his mother and father, and now he could see their faces change, like the clouds of a summer storm sweeping across the sun.

He acutely remembered the pain from his father's beating – and again, he did not remember feeling pain at all any more, as if in his childhood years that ability to suffer had been knocked out of him, a blessing from above. And he recalled how his father had dragged him to the abattoir to instil in him the harsh realities of life, and most of all, of survival. He had been locked in overnight with the carcasses, and the buckets of congealing blood, and the intestines and the glistening eyes, and the tongues, and the livers and the kidneys, and he had screamed until his throat was raw, but no one came. And when the morning arrived, and the abattoir workers returned, he had learned a brutal lesson about what meat was, and from where it came, and what death really meant. 'Survival,' his father had told him, punctuating each word with a slap. 'Everything is about survival.'

Why did the map scare him so?

And why, he thought as he dragged a curious finger across his cheek, was he crying?

As SHE MADE her way along the banks of the river, Rhiannon noticed for the first time a disparate collection of religious groups gathered in the morning sun, urging passers-by to join them. Red robes, yellow robes, tattoos, piercings, tall staffs, flickering candles, ornate headdresses, and bald pates. Usually they stayed in their own particular temples and worship-houses, largely forgotten by most of the population who had the more mundane matter of day-to-day existence on their minds. For most, the walls and the Crimson Hunt were the true divine protectors, keeping everyone safe in the face of the utmost threat for as long as any story could recall.

Yet now the religious leaders had found a population more open to their ideas of divine intervention. Everyone was scared – of what lay in their midst, and that the powers that had always protected them could no longer do so. She had heard the stories: that the Red Man was some supernatural force come to torment Idriss, picking people off for their crimes large and small, one by one until there was no one left. And who was to say they were wrong?

More, she understood their urge to believe in something greater than the suffocating world in which they all existed. Hope was the fuel that kept them all going, and at that moment she felt very low on that essential commodity. The sense that powers were working against her behind the scenes was impossible to escape. She was going to be made a scapegoat to protect the reputation of others; and it would probably cost her her life.

The Temple of the Shepherd had often felt like a sanctuary from the thick stew of the city, where she could reflect on the person she truly was, and not the one that she had been beaten into when she joined the Order. But now that bolt-hole had been stolen from her. Every time she stepped across the threshold, all she could see was the bloody hand of the Red Man. Increasingly, she was convinced the religion informed all of the Red Man's killings. The moment she had seen the boarding house slaughter she had wondered if it referenced another painting, but though she had searched the temple she had found nothing. And now Laurent the Seeker was missing. What part did he have to play?

The Unknown Shadow continued to shift around her, revealing things then hiding them again. Those rhythms of her unconscious had become familiar to her, and she knew she only had to be patient for it to reveal its secrets. Yet she knew there was a connection waiting to be made, with the corpse tableau, the Shepherd, and the Red Man. Something she had seen, or heard; something she knew, nestling deep in the recesses of her mind. Wandering around the temple, she examined the paintings in case there was something she had missed, but as she made her way to the tranquil area around the coloured flame, a hand gripped her wrist.

'Come with me.' It was Asgrim.

She exclaimed, but he simply dragged her through the temple and out into the sun. 'What is wrong?' she cried.

'Nothing. With me.'

Before she could question him further, he picked her up and threw her over his shoulder. She squealed as he loped across the cobbles to the nearest buildings, and then cried out in shock as he began to climb the side of one, finding toe- and finger-holds in the faced stone that she could barely see.

'You will drop me!' she said.

'Then stop wriggling and make my work easier.'

Rhiannon screwed her eyes shut tight as the cobbles retreated beneath her, and the spread of the city began to rise up above the rooftops. Asgrim moved rapidly, continually shifting his balance to keep her comfortable, but it only added to the sensation that he was permanently on the brink of letting her fall.

'You have gone insane,' she whispered insistently.

'You would be surprised how often I hear that.'

'That really is not reassuring. Where are we going?'

'To a place above your problems.' She stifled another scream as he leaned backwards at an alarming angle, and then she felt a lurch as the northerner pulled both of them over the guttering and on to the roof. His feet clattered over the tiles until he reached the pitch of the roof next to the chimney where he put her down. Only then did she open her eyes.

The view across the glorious sun-dappled city made her breath catch in her throat. The ancient stone buildings, tall and proud, the gargoyles and the carvings, the towers and the cupolas, the gold statues and the gleaming white roofs down in the Rezshinnia, and the jumble of the houses in Greatstock and beyond.

'Oh,' she said brightly. She glanced towards Asgrim and saw he was gripping the roof tightly, a strained expression marring his features. 'What is wrong?'

'I do not like heights,' he muttered.

'Then why did you drag me up here?' she said, exasperated. 'Is there something I am supposed to see?'

'Yes,' he replied. 'You are supposed to look out and see within.'

Puzzled, Rhiannon followed his gaze across the rooftops, and gradually his meaning dawned on her.

'Even in the darkest moments, there is always light somewhere,' he said. 'Even when we are broken and despairing, we can find a way to rise above it and see our problems, and life, with new eyes.'

'Thank you,' she said.

'You needed reminding of what you learned so long ago.' Shyly, he looked away towards

the vast swathe of green fields that fed the city.
'Do not think badly of Vidar. He is a good
man. Troubled, but good. He carries two great
burdens – the jewel, which forces him to do
things he despises, and his lack of memory,
which also drives him in ways that cause con-
flict and distress. He is stranded, unsure of
who he is and therefore of where he is going,
and that makes him feel like one of the ghosts
that haunt him. A nearly man, almost, almost
but never quite.'

Surprised, she said, 'You are very perceptive.'

'For a hairy, barbaric northerner?' He
grinned. 'That is what Cheyne would say. Ah,
I miss the twisted fop already. Drinking in the
Four Staves is not the same without him. But
do not tell him I said that.'

'You gave Vidar his name, did you not?'

'It was during his first week here in Idriss,
when he had recovered from the madness that
gripped him as he fled the forest. Instead, he
had developed an unpleasant mouth, bitter
and angry and lost. Everyone would tell him to
be silent, and so I started to call him after one
of my gods, the Lord of Silence, in the hope
that he would learn. It was only later that he
realised how apt the name was, when the King
had taken him under his wing and brought
him into the Crimson Hunt. Vidar, the Lord of

Silence, Stealth, and Vengeance. He could slip through the shadows as effectively as my god, and kill with speed and efficiency.'

'He is an irritating man, though.'

Asgrim smiled, but did not look at her. 'That is not your head talking.'

Rhiannon was about to respond when a thought struck her sharply, and then another and another in quick succession. The Unknown Shadow shifted and she saw as clearly as she viewed Idriss across the rooftops. 'You have done me a great service by bringing me here,' she said. 'New eyes. A new perspective. Let us return to the temple.'

She kissed him on the cheek in thanks, which seemed to please him, and then he carried her back down the side of the building. Her excitement kept her fear at bay and when they reached the ground she ran over the cobbles so fast Asgrim had to hurry to keep up.

Breathless, she moved around the temple, examining certain paintings. When she had completed a circuit, she nodded, pleased.

'What have you seen?' Asgrim asked.

'I have been searching for a painting that reflected the corpse-tableau, but I now see that was wrong. Instead, the Red Man arranged each body to echo one figure from each of five paintings. Here.' She indicated a man curled into a foetal position as he floated on a raft on the sea. It was entitled *The Longest Journey*.

Asgrim studied it, nodding. 'He is in the position of a newborn. The title could refer to a sea crossing, or the journey of life.'

Rhiannon eyed him, impressed. 'You are full of surprises,' she said. She turned back to the painting. 'Why these five? What did he mean by *these are the one what tell you*? But we do know another thing: that he has visited the temple regularly to study these paintings.'

'Then I must keep watch. If that sickening odour appears anywhere near here, I will know.'

Rhiannon gently stroked the tattoo on her forehead in thought. 'What will these tell me?' she whispered to herself. Moving purposefully along the walls, she took each of the five paintings down and placed them on the floor side by side. One showed a blazing tree with an old man kneeling before it. The third showed a young man standing with arms out-stretched towards a table covered with objects, as though he was hungry. Another had a young woman kneeling, head bowed, before a long stone box on a hillside. And the final one showed a man with arms outstretched towards a floating orb that glowed a brilliant white.

'Curious,' she said, turning slowly to examine the walls of other paintings. 'These are the only ones that do not include the Shepherd. Then why are they here?'

Rhiannon could see Asgrim was puzzled by the painting with the table covered with unusual objects. Indicating one item almost obscured by a silver gauntlet, he said, unsure, 'There. Is that not Vidar's jewel?'

THEY FELT AS if they had been running for ever. The green canopy had become hallucinogenic as their energy flagged, and they yearned to see other colours, so when Vidar and Cheyne burst through a wall of vegetation and crashed into a wide, sunlit path it was like entering another world. Winded, heads spinning, they picked themselves up and raised their heads to the sun and the blue sky.

'This is it?' Cheyne said in disbelief. He looked along the path among the trees in both directions. 'The channel?'

'Yes!' Vidar said with exultation. 'Now, which way?'

He oriented himself with the map, and then indicated westwards. Unable to keep the grins from their faces, they continued for a hundred yards in silence, enjoying the daylight and the overwhelming feeling of success.

Vidar reached out an arm to halt Cheyne's progress, and they both stopped and listened. They could hear one of the great beasts

thrashing around in the trees just beyond
where they had broken through on to the path,
but it was making no attempt to come after
them.

'Can it be true?' Cheyne said. 'These channels do indeed give safe passage? Are they
magic?'

The path was wide enough to encompass
three men lying head to toe, and continued in
a near-straight line through the trees. There
was nothing out of the ordinary about it.

'The beast doesn't like it,' Vidar said, 'but it
might be a boon to our two-legged pursuers.
We keep moving. Fast.'

He glanced back once along the length of the
path, but there was no sign of the shadowy figures. Fighting off the debilitating bouts of
weariness, he turned and ran, not knowing
how much time he had left.

THEY HEARD THE army long before they saw
it, the booming, war-drum step that made the
ground shake more than the giant lizard and
sent clouds of birds screeching into the sky
from the treetops, the rattle of the armour, the
barking orders of the captain at the head of
the column.

Vidar and Cheyne crawled on to a sandstone
cliff overlooking the junction where the path
on which they had been travelling met another,

wider path. It was along this that the column of warriors was marching. Vidar estimated there were barely more than a hundred – not an army at all, but certainly a fighting unit ready for battle. Their armour gleamed a burnished black, their helmets styled on animal totems: bears, bulls, boars, birds, snakes. Each warrior had a splash of red, a ribbon fastened to the spike on the top of their helmets, which flowed in the breeze like blood streaming from their victims. The captain rode on a black stallion alongside the colours, a red banner with a black lion's-head symbol. But behind him was a carriage hauled by six men, the curtains drawn so it was impossible to see the occupant.

'I do not recognise those colours,' Cheyne mused. He winced as he pulled the makeshift stitches with which Vidar had sewn up the cheek wound he had received from the giant lizard.

'They're not heading towards Idriss,' Vidar replied. 'And they're not a large enough force to attack any outpost. Yet they're risking travelling across the forest. Why?' He thought for a moment before adding, 'They must be the two coloured spikes and the two white spikes on the map. And they're pursuing the other white spike.'

'Which is who, or what?'

They both peered along the channel, but could not see the object of the pursuit from their vantage point. 'Whatever it is, if they want it, so do we,' Vidar said.

Puzzled, Cheyne scrutinised the enemy force. 'What is the significance of the coloured and white spikes? And why do we merit similar spikes on the map?'

As they watched, there was a sudden burst of light behind the curtains of the carriage, pulsing initially, but then shifting around with a familiar numinous quality.

'They've got a map!' Vidar said.

'They have a map, we have a map – that explains some of the spikes,' Cheyne said. 'And if the maps are the white spikes, they are pursuing a third.'

'Of course they are! Get all the maps, you control the world.'

'That does not explain the coloured–'

Cheyne was interrupted by a loud, barked order from the depths of the carriage. The captain held up his hand and barked in response, and the column came to a sudden halt.

'Now what?' Vidar muttered.

The captain leaned from his horse and poked his head through the curtain. After a moment of intense discourse, he withdrew and began to search the trees and cliffs on either side.

Vidar thought for a moment, then said, 'They're hunting for their prey, but he's off their map now and on to ours, so they don't know how near or far they are from him.'

They scurried backwards off the brow of the cliff and scrabbled down the sandy bank to the channel. In the distance, they could already hear the unit breaking into a regimented run, the armour clanging like a tolling bell. The barked orders of the captain floated over the treetops like the baying of a hunting dog.

Vidar glanced back along the channel the way they had travelled. Retreat was not an option; though he had not seen their four pursuers since the previous day, he was sure they were back there somewhere, hiding in the shadows beneath the branches, awaiting their moment. 'That way.' He indicated the new path and the direction of the map-cube being hunted by the mysterious army.

'Ah, we can drive our quarry to ground and relieve him of the map. Though I must admit I was expecting a more immediate form of treasure. Say, one that would allow me to live like a king in the Four Staves.'

'You'll get all that and more if we return with two parts of the map.' Vidar paused, then added, 'Or four.'

'Take on those warriors? I admire your ambition. And perhaps you can feed your little friend in the process.' Cheyne smiled broadly. 'Which would, of course, be a relief to me.'

Maintaining a neutral expression, Vidar tried not to show how depleted his reserves were. But the thought that he might be able to kill one, or two, or more, disturbed him as much as it filled him with a shivery excitement.

The wider channel curved around the base of a large hill and continued to head southwest, through the dense, seemingly unending forest. Somewhere in the distance was the sea, an object that most people in Idriss held in near-reverence, hearing of it only in the stories told in the inns, or from the mouths of newly arrived merchants who had somehow survived their journey through the trees, and lied as much as they told the truth. It left Vidar untouched – water was water, however big the body – but perhaps those being pursued hoped to escape across the waves on a boat.

Though the pursuing warriors were fit and well-trained, they were not expected to catch their prey; their strength lay in their stamina for relentless pursuit. Since Vidar had gained the map, he had watched their slow progress across the terrain, not deviating, not slowing. He wondered if they were pursuing a similar sized group, charged with protecting one of the most valuable items in all Gardia. Who would tire first?

As they ran, they kept one eye on the afternoon sun slowly slipping down the sky. Even though they were on the path, the memories of the previous night filled them with dread. Vidar felt his life would be good if he never again heard the cacophony of hideous beast-calls that had moved through the darkness towards the river, or saw the shadow-thing that had pretended to be Abbas.

With each passing mile, his pace slowed noticeably, but when he briefly paused to check the map, he saw they were closing rapidly on the white spike of light.

'I have a question,' Cheyne said as they ran. 'If or when we gain the second map-cube, what then? Do we come back this way and face the warriors? Do we detour through the forest and risk being torn limb from limb as our good fortune rapidly runs out – I am suggesting "no" to that one, by the way – or do we continue onwards, without food or drink or horses, moving further away from Idriss with each day?'

'I'll tell you soon enough.'

'I take great comfort in the knowledge that you have a plan that will save both our lives. Thank goodness. I foolishly thought we were running blindly into great danger, with no rhyme or reason to our thinking.'

'Good, because I wouldn't like to start thinking your backbone was crumbling. Long odds can be beaten, and we've got a job to do.' Vidar knew if he considered it closely that the whole expedition had gone sour almost from the beginning, but his comment was true: they all knew the risks when they embarked, and they were all prepared to face down the longest odds with grit and courage; that was the job the Crimson Hunt was tasked to do. Never give up, fight to the last, for Idriss, the strong, the unbeaten. And if you could line your pockets on the way, all the better.

'How much longer till we find this damnable army?' Cheyne said, flinging beads of sweat off his red face. 'You would have thought we would have got a glimpse of them by now.'

Neither of them saw the rock coming as it arced out of the slowly setting sun, catching Cheyne firmly on the temple. Stunned, he flew over to one side, almost crashing into the trees. He came to a halt a mere six inches away from the dark shadows under the branches, slumped to his knees, rubbing his head as he fought to stay conscious.

Vidar's sword was drawn in an instant. A squat figure launched itself out of the glare, hoping to catch him off-guard, but Vidar took in the glint of a knife, ducked, and brought his blade up sharply. The flat caught the attacker on the side of the head and he sprawled across the path opposite Cheyne.

Vidar loomed over the figure, sword poised to ram down into its heart.

'Wait!' Then: 'Luke?'

As Vidar shifted out of the glare, he saw the attacker was a man in his late forties with preternaturally white hair down to his shoulders, and a hint of madness in his piercing blue eyes. He was very short, his muscular body starting to turn to fat, and he was dressed in a rough grey shirt and mud-splattered, threadbare trousers. His boots, too, were almost worn through on the soles.

'Luke?' Vidar repeated.

'It is. It is!' The man jumped to his feet in a manner that reminded Vidar oddly of Greer an' Lokh. Barely able to contain his excitement, he raved, 'I hardly recognised you with… with your hair like that…' He gestured vaguely towards Vidar's head and clothes.

A chill ran through Vidar. 'You know me?'

'Come on – it's me. Sam!'

The world swam around Vidar. He was vaguely aware of Cheyne watching him, puzzled, but his attention was locked on the short man with the mad eyes, searching every inch of his face for some sign of recognition. There was nothing.

'Come on!' Sam repeated. He marched forwards and threw his stubby arms around Vidar, clapping him on the back.

Vidar threw him off. 'Get away from me. I don't know you.'

It was Sam's turn to search Vidar's face. Vidar caught a hint of slyness in his features that suggested his words could not be trusted. 'You really don't remember?' He glanced at Cheyne. 'What have they done to you?'

His heart pounding, Vidar grabbed Sam roughly by the shirt and hauled him up until their faces were only an inch apart. 'Don't treat me like a fool,' Vidar snarled.

'I'm not, I'm not!' Sam wriggled free like a stoat and backed off a step, still searching Vidar's face. 'You really don't remember.'

Vidar advanced with his sword.

Sam stumbled backwards, holding his hands before him. 'We all wondered what happened to you–'

'We?'

'The team. The seven of us, Luke. We were inserted into this world to put everything right. The mission! You don't remember the mission?'

'Vidar?'

Cheyne's odd tone caught Vidar's attention. His friend was pointing into the trees beyond Sam where the four figures that had been pursuing them could just be glimpsed deep in the gloom. And they were not alone.

10

THE MUSIC OF OTHER WORLDS

THE SKY WAS afire above Idriss as the world turned slowly towards night. Along the oven-hot streets few people moved, preferring their own barely cooler rooms to the public areas where an air of tension permeated everything. The Crimson Hunt conducted regular patrols, but there were not enough of them to reach everywhere, and the abiding feeling was that sooner or later the pressure would vent. It was just a matter of where. Would it be in Great-stock, where three people had already been killed on the basis of foundless accusations of slightly altering features, a shift of shadows that made cheeks hollower, or a sudden tic that brought a scowl to a placid face? Or would it be in Red Hill, where the merchants' profits had plummeted, and arguments had spiralled into brutal fights? Or in Ten Bells, where the metalworkers and weavers and glassblowers continually turned old things into new to keep the isolated city in goods, and where stories circulated and were themselves reworked in the febrile atmosphere of the workshops?

One event would finally trigger the explosion of seething emotion, and everyone knew what it was: the death of the King. The dismal bell that tolled the hour announced that he was still clinging to life, but, so the stories went, his time was marked in days, if not hours, and then Idriss would be leaderless, and prey to all the threats that lurked just beyond the walls, and now within them.

Rhiannon waited on the stone bench in the airy corridor outside the council chamber, ostensibly watching the patterns the stained glass made on the age-old walls, but her mind was completely detached, turning over the evidence she had already collected. Though she barely dared admit it, it felt as if the Unknown Shadow was receding.

Finally the council broke up – it seemed to be in continual session now – and Chief Inquisitor Serena filed out deep in conversation with Ashur. His frozen face revealed nothing, but his eyes flickered continually towards Rhiannon. After a moment, he peeled away with LeStrange and two of his advisors, and the Chief Inquisitor came over, her face almost as unreadable as Ashur's.

'Thank you for waiting, Inquisitor Rhiannon. The council needed more time to debate potential insurgency and the part the one you call the Red Man could play. Walk with me.'

She led the way along the corridor to the doors in the atrium, and then down the broad, white steps to the sun-drenched piazza. 'I am afraid I have some troubling news,' she said.

'Chief Inquisitor?'

'The council has decreed that the killings represent a fundamental threat to the security of Idriss. The belief was expressed that the failure to make any significant advances in catching the killer can only be down to incompetence—'

'That is untrue!' Rhiannon caught herself. 'With all due respect, Chief Inquisitor, we are dealing with someone whose face can change at will. The moment we draw near, he becomes someone else and fades into the crowds. We have on several occasions been close. Citizens have come forward with useful information, but at the last he slipped through our fingers with a new identity. That is not incompetence.'

'Excuses do not help me, Inquisitor Rhiannon.' The Chief Inquisitor would not meet Rhiannon's gaze.

For the first time, Rhiannon noticed a piece of parchment clutched in the Chief Inquisitor's left hand. 'What is that?' she asked, already knowing from the red seal of Ashur and the black ribbon encircling it.

'I am sorry to say the council's position has only hardened since our last discussion. If the killer is not caught, the fear is that Idriss will be torn apart. The only option the council has to prevent this is–'

'A public death. A line drawn beneath the failure. A fresh start, hoping this will dissipate the tensions.'

The Chief Inquisitor nodded.

'How long have I got?'

'Until the death of the King. The physician believes that could be in five days, or less.'

The unfairness of the decision stung Rhiannon, but there was nothing she could say. Ashur had signed the final proclamation. There was no appeal. 'Five days to find the killer, at least, or I die.'

'For the good of Idriss.'

Rhiannon searched the Chief Inquisitor's face for a hint of sympathy, but it remained a frozen echo of the mood that had descended on the rulers of the city. Rhiannon nodded curtly and walked away, her ears filled with the bell ringing out the King's final hours.

* * *

ON THE MARBLE ledge running above the first storey of the palace, Asgrim sat, unnoticed by those who passed below. It was not so high that it made him feel queasy, and low enough that he could oversee the people passing through the piazza. So still was he, many mistook him for a gargoyle. His initial intention had been to search for the sour odour of the Red Man, but then he had seen Rhiannon exit the building and had overheard every word of her conversation with the Chief Inquisitor.

He bounded down from the ledge and loped across the piazza to catch Rhiannon as she marched purposefully away.

'Trouble?' he asked.

'There is now a deadline on our hunt for the Red Man.'

'Is that all?'

'Does there need to be more?' She blinked away tears of anger.

'Then we must increase the pace of your enquiry. I think it is time to enlist the aid of Greer an' Lokh.'

'Sadly, I agree.' Rhiannon steadied herself. 'His insanity and chaotic approach to life are anathema to me, but my own options have been sharply curtailed. First, though, a brief call at the Temple of the Shepherd.'

Half an hour later they arrived at Greer an' Lokh's tower with the five paintings identified by the Red Man's slaughter at the boarding house. They found the sorcerer spinning around his chamber in a delicate, almost beautiful dance, humming quietly to a tune only he could hear.

Unembarrassed, he sashayed over to them, and continued to twirl slowly around them while they spoke.

'Paintings,' he mused in a sing-song voice.

'From the Temple of the Shepherd. They are of some significance to the Red Man.'

'Ah.' He motioned to Rhiannon to lay the paintings out against one wall while he danced before each one in turn. When he came to the one showing the objects arranged on the table, he halted, swaying from side to side as if hypnotised.

'Do you see anything there?' Asgrim asked.

'I see things on a table.'

'That is not what I meant, as you well know.'

Greer an' Lokh danced over with an enigmatic smile playing on his lips. 'I see many, many things. I see the patterns of the universe, the patterns of life, sometimes even the patterns of hearts. I see here five paintings that are of importance to the religion of the Shepherd, but do not contain the Shepherd.'

'We know that,' Rhiannon snapped. 'Is there more?'

'Perhaps. But that is all for now. Are you finished here?' He appeared eager to get back to the paintings.

'No,' Rhiannon said firmly. 'The Red Man has some connection to the religion of the Shepherd. It dominates his thoughts. Now Laurent the Seeker, who oversees the Temple of the Shepherd, is missing. I must know if Laurent is the Red Man, and where he now hides. Can you help?'

Greer an' Lokh set off on another dance, this time wilder, whirling around so his beads and bones flew, taking in all the corners of his chamber. Finally, exhausted and ecstatic, he returned to them, eyes closed, head back. 'Perhaps I can. Or perhaps I cannot. But certainly, without a life to draw upon… not.'

'There are no condemned criminals left in the cells,' Asgrim whispered to Rhiannon.

She bit her lip. 'Then we are wasting our valuable time.'

Asgrim glimpsed a hint of fear in her eyes as she turned to go, and his heart went out to her. He caught her arm and said, 'Wait here.'

'Why? Where are you going?'

'Wait.' He bounded out of the room.

For a half-hour, Asgrim prowled the streets of Idriss, spying on deals conducted by hard-faced men in shadowy back alleys, listening to the corrosive comments of husbands who brought welts to the faces of their wives, and to the sly-faced smiling people who tried to attract the girls and boys at play in the streets of Greatstock.

No life had more value than another. His father had taught him that at an early age, and it had always been Asgrim's driving force to cleave true to the memory of the man who had shaped him and still lived in his heart. But there he was, weighing lives so he could select one person to die for the greater good, and feel it was not a simple act of murder. But he knew the truth, and he knew what his father would think of him.

Devastated, he made his choice.

IN HIS DREAM, Vidar was running through a deep, impenetrable darkness that may have been the forest, for he was sure he could hear the chilling cries of the predators in the distance. Pulsing in his chest, the amber jewel cast a wan light that guided his way, but with each step his limbs grew increasingly leaden. And then, from nowhere, Sam appeared, his white hair making him resemble a spectre, his welcoming smile transformed by the cruelty in his sly eyes.

'*Don't forget the mission, Luke,*' he said.

Vidar came round with a start. The flood of sensory information overwhelmed his thoughts for a moment as he struggled to place where he was. He recalled confronting Sam on the forest path with Cheyne nearby, and then he glimpsed the figures in the forest. As they started to emerge… something had happened. He blacked out.

The aroma of the cooling forest was heavy around him. Leaf-mould was soft and shifting beneath his fingers as he lay on the ground, and it was dark, although there was a warm golden light from some source he couldn't define. His mouth was as unbearably dry as if he'd spent a night drinking in the Four Staves.

He sat up.

Cheyne and Sam lay unconscious nearby. They were deep in the forest among oaks so twisted and ancient they looked like works of art carved from black stone. Strung among the branches was an array of papery globes in which lights flickered casting a hazy, dream-like atmosphere over the area. Vidar didn't know if it was the quality of the light or the after-effects of whatever had made him fall unconscious, but he felt strangely at peace. It was as though they had been sealed off from the terrors of the forest in a place that had its own peculiar qualities. His heart fluttered with excitement and he felt an uplifting and irrational sense of wonder as though he were on the brink of a religious experience.

People moved here and there with an easy grace, but they were like no people Vidar had seen before. They were tall and slender and elegant, yet exuded a muscular power, and they wore clothes of grey and green and brown that merged with the forest background. Their hair was long and ash-blond or grey, their eyes almond-shaped, and their skin had a faint golden tan. When their hair shifted as they moved, he thought he glimpsed ears that were slightly pointed.

One of them noticed he was awake and came over. His androgynous face was emotionless to the point of blankness, but there was a brittle hardness in his eyes that could have been cruelty or contempt.

Vidar's hand surreptitiously slid to his knife, but he realised he was too weak to use it. Whatever had happened to him since they had left the path had drained most of his reserves. He was now running on the last of his life before the hungry jewel began to exert its final demands.

The stranger stopped before him and looked him slowly up and down as if he were examining a beast of the field.

'Who are you?' Vidar asked.

'The original inhabitants of this land.'

'You live here in the forest?'

'We lived everywhere, until your kind came, and killed, and poisoned, and drove us away from the fields we loved. Until you built your cities.' The final word dripped contempt.

Vidar struggled to his feet. His head spun and he had to steady himself against a tree. 'What did you do to me?'

The stranger stared at Vidar for a long moment, and then turned. 'Come,' he said imperiously.

As Vidar trailed behind him through the trees, he felt as though he was still dreaming, or drunk. Distant music came and went though he could not see where it originated, and rich, complex perfumes drifted here and there, stimulating strong emotions with the merest wisp. Vidar laughed, and then tears came unbidden. His skin tingled with the awareness of infinite possibilities.

The stranger came to a halt in a grove lit with a brilliant white light. The illumination came from something resembling a glass snowflake turning slowly four feet above the ground with no visible means of support.

'Magic?' Vidar asked.

The stranger laughed coldly.

Far away, Vidar could just make out the roar of one of the forest beasts. 'We're not safe here,' he said.

'Nothing will harm us,' the stranger replied with a chilly confidence.

All the time he was talking, Vidar was surreptitiously scanning for possible escape
routes. He reached the conclusion that he
would have to bide his time; there were too
many of the enemy around to try to make a
break into the forest. But if he waited much
longer, the last of his energy would ebb away
and he would be completely at their mercy.
However, the dreaminess of the environment
dulled the edge of his concerns, as it was
meant to do, he guessed.

'What do you call yourself?' Mesmerised, he
watched the slowly spinning design.

'My people have had many names over the
long years. The name we choose for ourselves
would be unpronounceable to you.' He gestured thoughtfully. 'You have stories?
Legends? Myths?'

'That's all we have.'

'Then you may have heard reference to the
Elorhim. In the earliest times, this entire world
was our field. We lived at peace with everything in it, and felt the beating heart of all
there is, and we dreamed. Oh, how we
dreamed! And in our dreams the stars came
down to us and gave us true hope and understanding.' His eyes flashed fire at Vidar. 'And
then your kind came. We embraced you, and
offered you our knowledge, our friendship.
We offered you peace. Do you know how rare

a quality that is? And you spurned it, for you are an arrogant, contemptuous race. And you brutalised us, and drove us back, and back further still, until we had no choice but to give up everything that made us who we were.'

His voice was low, but filled with a potent plaintive emotion. Slowly he reached out and brushed his fingers against the snowflake, which hummed warmly in response as if it were alive. A subtle change in the quality of the light made Vidar feel as if he were being comforted by a parent. Emotions filled his mind, which in turn caused images, of loss and regret, of sadness and dissolution. Vidar briefly glimpsed the people of the forest running and hiding, hands torn apart, eyes wide with fear. He saw fire, and blood, and bodies.

'Why do you do the things you do?' the stranger said.

Vidar couldn't answer.

'For a long time, we disappeared from this place and left it in your brutal hands. And you destroyed the garden. Destroyed it. Until, in turn, it destroyed you. But now we are back, and now you are back, and everything has changed. You have made us into something else, and you will not like what you have created. We do not enjoy what we have become, but this is who we are now, and this is the world in which we must exist.'

Vidar watched the other Elorhim and in their grace and beauty saw echoes of what they once were.

'Your kind can never realise the enormity of what you have done, and through that, what you have lost. There are so many marvels in this world,' the stranger continued. 'Wonders that would take your breath away. It is a place of mysteries and secrets. But you will never find them. We will not allow it.'

'You killed one of my men.'

'We will kill any of your kind we find.' His words were calmly spoken, free of guilt and regret, and thus unbearably chilling. 'We will kill and kill until there are none of you left. You set us in motion, child of man. You must now reap the consequences.'

Vidar realised he still had his sword and his knife. As his hand moved towards his blade, the stranger's eyes fell heavily on him, daring him to proceed. Vidar could see they hadn't removed his weapons because they didn't consider him even slightly a threat.

'Why haven't you killed me?'

The stranger smiled. 'There is always time.'

'There's a reason you didn't kill us straight away.'

The stranger pointed one long, slender finger at Vidar's chest. 'You carry with you a conduit to the beyond.'

'The jewel?'

He looked deep into Vidar's eyes, then said, 'You do not realise what you have.'

'A curse,' Vidar said bitterly, before adding, 'An object of power. One of twenty.'

'One of twenty.' He nodded slowly. 'Power that could destroy everything there is. Or save it.'

'You want it, take it.'

'Oh, we will. In good time. You will not survive its removal.'

Despair washed through Vidar. Did that mean he could never be free of it, even if he managed to escape from the forest? The last of his energy ebbed away and he slumped slowly to his knees.

'Remember this, child of man,' the stranger said. 'When death comes, you do not hear it. There is fury, and then there is only silence.'

CHEYNE'S HEAD STILL fluttered with the fading remnants of a dream that others would have found intensely disturbing, but which, for him, was a natural and accepted part of his life. He had left behind the still-unconscious Sam and prowled through the trees, his sword drawn. The strange, stately people watched him pass disinterestedly, and no one made any attempt to stop him, even though he could have been waiting to kill one of them or attempting to flee.

He found Vidar sprawled on the ground, barely conscious, his muscles already starting to sag, his cheeks growing hollow. Cheyne had seen the signs often enough to realise that Vidar had little time left. There would be a few more occasions of wakefulness, and enough strength to move around, but they would grow farther and farther apart. And then Vidar, the great warrior, the multiple killer, would be like a child, completely dependent on those around him.

Quickly, Cheyne scooped his friend up in his arms, keeping one eye on any movement for the hidden knife, and carried him back to where Sam lay. As Cheyne placed Vidar in a comfortable position, Sam stirred and said, 'What's wrong with him?'

'Keep quiet. Another word and I will cut out your tongue.'

Sam ignored him. He leaned over to raise Vidar's eyelids. Cheyne knocked Sam away with the back of his hand, and would have killed him on the spot if Vidar had not shown an interest in him. Sam eyed Cheyne murderously, then slyly hid it.

'You people know very little about medicine... you know, the physician's work. I could help,' Sam said.

'There is only one way to help him, and you might not be so eager to contribute if you knew what it was.'

Sam pulled himself up and sat at the base of a gnarled hawthorn, where he observed Vidar thoughtfully. Cheyne didn't like the squat man. He had the slippery characteristics of a merchant, and an arrogance without any apparent reason.

'You know Vidar?'

Sam smiled tightly. 'I thought I did. I could be mistaken.' Keen to change the subject, he glanced around until he saw the people of the forest. His curiosity increased as he scrutinised them without any sign of fear. 'Now where could they be from?' he said to himself.

Cheyne was more interested in finding a way out of their predicament. The people of the forest lived in a makeshift camp that could be easily picked up and moved. Small structures made from branches and hide and big enough for a handful of people littered the forest floor on the edge of the area lit by the lanterns. Others, though, appeared to be equally at home in the branches of the trees where they moved as easily as if they were walking on the ground. Cheyne tried to estimate their numbers, but they came and went, small parties disappearing into the forest dark, either hunting or guarding their perimeter, he presumed. There were certainly too many for them to fight their way out. It would require stealth and silence. He looked to

Vidar, who was stirring, the whites of his eyes now yellow-tinged.

Still time, he told himself hopefully. He knew death well enough to see when it was near at hand, and if it allowed them a chance to balance their fortune they could still slip away.

Sam appeared to understand his thoughts. 'You'll never get away from here without bargaining with them.'

'You clearly have never encountered the Crimson Hunt before.' He waited until two of the forest people had passed by and then added, 'If you touch him, I will find you and kill you.' And with that he slipped away into the night.

'WHERE'S CHEYNE GONE?' Vidar's voice was barely more than a rustle, almost lost to the sound of the breeze in the branches.

'Who knows? A suicide mission of some kind. I don't know why you waste your time hanging around with such people.'

'You said you knew me. Is that a lie? Because if it is, you've a good chance of ending up dead very quickly.' Every joint on fire, Vidar eased his way on to his elbows, his desire to learn the secrets of his past overriding the pain. But he was also afraid that he would be disappointed. Every instinct told him not to trust Sam, but they were overruled by his desperate hope.

'For one thing, you're not in any state to start threatening me,' Sam said. 'And for another, you've learned some very bad habits from your new friends.'

Vidar drew his knife with a speed that startled Sam. 'Start talking.'

'All right, all right.' He chewed a lip while he turned over his thoughts. 'But I've got to go slowly, do you understand? You've clearly lost something up here.' He tapped his head. 'Some kind of accident? A fugue state? No matter. If I tell you too much too quickly, it might prove destabilising. A bit at a time, okay? Not too many questions at once. You've got to trust me, Luke.'

'Is that my name?'

Sam hesitated. 'Lucas Kane.'

Vidar turned the name over in his mind for a moment, but it didn't spark any recognition. 'You said we were part of a team?'

'Seven of us. You, me, Joshua, Reichert, Grable, Tyler, and Ben. Grable's dead. He...' A moment of horror ghosted Sam's face, but he waved it away.

Vidar leaned forward with intensity. 'But which city did we come from? How far away is it–?' He was silenced by Sam's enigmatic smile and a shake of his head.

'We were sent here from somewhere else, Luke. Somewhere far beyond what you've been used to in recent times.'

'Where?' Vidar insisted.

'That's a question for later. Now, tell me why you're so ill.'

Frustrated, Vidar hesitated, then opened his shirt to reveal the amber jewel. Its gentle pulse lit Sam's face and sparkled in his astonished eyes.

'The jewel! You have it! Of course you do. Oh dear, what happened?' He carefully examined the scar tissue around the edges of the gem. 'It's bonded with you. They do that.'

'They?'

'The artefacts.'

'The twenty objects of power?'

'Yes, yes.' Watching the slow pulsing, he said, 'The quantum charge is fading. What is it doing? Drawing the energy from your cells?'

'It sucks the life out of me unless I feed it with some other poor devil's life.'

Sam nodded knowingly. 'Our mission is to reclaim these objects, Luke. Their power, together, is beyond anything you can imagine. With them we can... well, that's another of those questions for a later time.'

Vidar fought to understand what Sam was telling him. He had always thought that when he finally unearthed some information about his lost days, the dam would burst and his memory would come flooding back, but there was nothing.

'So you're saying I went to recover the jewel, but instead of bringing it back, it bonded with me and sucked out my memory of all these things?'

'That must be what happened.'

'If what you're saying is true, why didn't you come looking for me?'

'You have to understand, Luke, we were all lost. The entry was more traumatic than any of us anticipated. We were thrown apart, spread across this continent. I don't even know where all the others are. They might be dead, like Grable, or still hanging on, surviving, like you, me, and Reichert, looking for ways to get back together. If I hadn't found the map-cube, I'd probably still be wandering around, trying not to get eaten alive. But that led me to Reichert, and that...' His voice trailed away and he stared dismally into the dark.

'Where is he?'

'Reichert is no longer what he was. On any front. The artefacts... you know yourself – they change you. The quantum effect activates certain unique abilities in each one. I've got no idea of the science involved, but maybe Reichert does. Of all of us, he's the most likely to know. The artefacts bond with a user–' he gestured to Vidar's jewel '—and change that person on some fundamental level. They take on some of the artefact's abilities. Of course, we had no idea of this when we were charged with retrieval. If we had, we would have taken some precautions. But no one knew anything really. We were thrown into the dark and left to fend for ourselves,' he added bitterly.

'And Reichert has been altered by one of the… artefacts?'

'By two of them. Luke, you wouldn't believe what's happened to him. Saying he's gone mad sounds so melodramatic, and that would be my perspective anyway. From his point of view I'm sure it all makes perfect sense. When the first artefact changed him, he sought out the second. Actually looked for it, even though he knew what it would do to his body. I suppose the physical side doesn't matter in comparison to the power he now has at his control. And two artefacts aren't enough — he wants all of them. And not for the reason we were sent here — a good, decent, honest reason. For his own personal gain. I don't think he even wants to go back. Can you believe that? He just wants to rule in hell.'

Vidar began to understand what Sam had said about the new information destabilising him; his head was spinning and he was having trouble assimilating everything he was being told. Some of it was simply beyond his narrow framework of comprehension. *Quantum effect?* What did that mean?

'So Reichert has power–'

'Yes! He's conquered an entire city now, Luke. Berex. He's got thousands of people jumping at his every word. Reichert – that skinny, bespectacled brain! Unbelievable. He's got an army. They've been on my trail for weeks since I found him out and tried to get him to carry on with the mission–'

'He's with that army we saw?' Vidar mused.

'He wants that jewel to add to his collection. And he'll kill to get it, Luke, believe me. Watch out for him. I only just escaped with my life. You see, he wants the map-cube. He has two already. With four cubes, the world is his. He can uncover the Prime Locator, and then he'll find all the artefacts, and then...' He took a deep breath to steady himself. 'It's all over.'

'You have a map-cube?'

Sam hesitated and then allowed Vidar the briefest glimpse of the object cupped in the palm of his hand. He returned it quickly to his pocket.

'The coloured spikes are–'

'Artefacts,' Sam said. 'But they only show up when they're activated. That's why he needs the Prime Locator.'

'And the white spikes are map-cubes.'

He nodded.

'So Reichert will keep coming after me until he gets what he wants.'

'He calls himself Verlaine now. There's not much left of the Reichert we both knew.' Sam wrinkled his nose as if there was a bad smell.

Some of what Sam had said made sense to Vidar in terms he understood – powerful magic objects that could control the land were being hunted by a cruel overlord. The motivations and details didn't matter, Vidar decided. But one thing was clear: the only way he could survive an entire city's forces directed against him was in the heart of Idriss the Strong.

The details of the mission, the artefacts, and the map-cubes were all clearly of utmost importance to Sam, but the only thing that mattered to Vidar was the parts of his life that were still off the map.

'You can tell me who I am? Where I come from? My family?'

'Of course,' Sam replied.

'Later.' Cheyne had returned to them as silently and unseen as he had quickly circumnavigated the entire camp of the forest people. 'We cannot afford to dawdle here any longer. A council of our captors has just broken up. Now they are preparing knives. And other interesting implements which, if I had time to study them, would no doubt bring me joy.'

Vidar tried to get to his feet, fell back. 'You're going to have to leave me–'

'No,' Cheyne said firmly. 'They will only make me pick up your tab at the Four Staves.'

'You won't be picking up any tab because you'll be dead.'

'How negative,' Cheyne said indignantly. He nodded to Sam, and together they grabbed Vidar under the arms and hauled him to his feet. 'At the moment, the only casualty is your pride,' Cheyne continued. 'Let us keep it that way. Besides, if they come after us, we can always throw you to them as a diversion.'

'That's more like it,' Vidar said hoarsely.

'How do you plan to get out of here if we can only move at a snail's pace?' Sam asked. His tone continued to suggest a curt dismissal of Cheyne.

'In their arrogance, our enemy misjudges us. They do not see us as a threat, and so their attention is diverted on to more pressing matters. And who can blame them? A dandy, an invalid, and a fat dwarf–'

'I am not a dwarf! I'm a little shorter than average,' Sam said indignantly. 'And this is all muscle,' he added, tapping his belly.

'Nonetheless, our captors have failed to realise they have in their hands two of the greatest warriors of Idriss.'

Sam sighed. 'That's just the kind of thinking that's going to get us killed. Stupidity masquerading as arrogance. You're as bad as the forest people.'

'Time to move,' Vidar pressed.

'We should get one of them on their own so you can despatch them, and feed that damnable jewel,' Cheyne whispered to Vidar.

'That's too risky. If we don't get it right straight off, the alarm will be raised. Besides, they're not like us. I don't even know if the jewel will accept their lives.'

Cheyne fell silent, and Vidar knew exactly what he was thinking. He cast an eye at Sam, and then whispered, 'You could—'

'No,' Vidar said firmly. 'If we can get out of the camp, my strength should come back a little in a few hours.'

'Yes, for thirty minutes. But long enough to get us back to Idriss?' Cheyne snapped.

'Let's get away from here first.'

Relenting, Cheyne guided Vidar and Sam to a path that led away from the soft light of the lanterns, pausing every now and then to slip behind trees when one of the Elorhim passed nearby.

'They'll raise the alarm soon,' Vidar said, and barely had the words left his lips when a high-pitched whistle rose up from the area where they had been kept.

'Not much farther now,' Cheyne said quietly but insistently, urging Sam with his eyes to take up the strain and move faster.

Eventually they came to a foul-smelling area scattered with bones and the remnants of carcasses, where the Elorhim had removed the hides from animals to construct their makeshift homes. One carcass was still being worked, a different variety of the giant lizard, smaller than the one they had encountered, but with a bulkier body that moved on four legs. A fin ran along its spine. The head had already been removed and the beast had been gutted before the workers had downed tools.

Sam grew excited when he saw it. 'Of course, of course,' he said. 'I'd heard rumours of these kinds of things living in the forest. It makes sense. Lord, I wonder what other marvels are out there.'

'You wouldn't call these things marvels if you were on the brink of being its next meal,' Vidar croaked.

'No, of course not. But still… Amazing! It must have fallen through the cracks, just like your ancestors did.'

'What do you mean?' Cheyne said.

'Why, in generations long past, you all tumbled into this world from your own particular place, like I did. Though your ancestors found themselves here by accident.'

The sound of running footsteps rose up behind them as the forest people fanned out across the camp. After the initial alarm, none of them spoke, their silence a chilling reminder of their ability to disappear into the forest background. Vidar recalled what his captor had told him about not hearing death until it was upon him.

'Inside the carcass with him,' Cheyne ordered.

Before Vidar could protest, they had bundled him into the stinking body cavity. 'What good is this going to do?' he said. 'They'll find us here eventually.'

'Does no one have faith in my remarkable strategic abilities?' Cheyne dragged Sam to the rear of the beast and placed his hands on the carcass. 'Push. And when it starts to move of its own accord, jump in. Or not. I would not be unduly troubled.'

Sam glared at him.

Peering out of the open neck-hole of the carcass, Vidar could just about make out the ground falling away, and the first part of Cheyne's plan became clear.

'Two predators joined together. How fitting.'

Vidar started at the familiar voice floating out of the night. He crawled to the belly-slit of the carcass and saw emerging from the trees the stranger who had spoken to him at the snowflake. Sam cowered against the hulk of the beast, but Cheyne was nowhere to be seen.

'In your pride, you think you have control over circumstances. You have none,' the stranger continued as he marched up. 'You cannot hide from our eyes – we can see the length of the forest, even in the dark. You cannot run, for we never tire. You cannot survive.'

'We're leaving here,' Vidar said. 'Your arguments are all with the past. You have no issue with us.'

'The past never goes away, child of man. Have you not learned that yet?'

Vidar never even saw a shimmer of movement. One moment the stranger was staring at him with baleful eyes, the next Cheyne's long needle-blade was protruding from his ear. The stranger's eyes remained heavy on Vidar as he fell to his knees.

'You will come to regret what has happened this day,' he croaked. 'My people will never rest until vengeance has been taken.' His eyes rolled and his mouth drooped as Cheyne slowly drew the blade from his brain.

'Finish him off!' Cheyne urged, but Vidar didn't have the strength to haul himself out of the carcass before the stranger had expired.

'That was a mistake,' Sam said.

'There was no choice in the matter.' Cheyne cleaned his blade and added, 'Now, come.' Vidar retreated back into the beast's stinking confines, but the stranger's words still haunted him. They had unleashed something terrible, and he wondered what that would mean for all of them in the time to come.

Sam grunted and wheezed as he and Cheyne attempted to move the carcass, and eventually it shifted. Vidar clung on to the sticky insides to keep his balance as the carcass jerked forwards another few inches, and then a few inches more, and then began to slide down the bank.

Cheyne threw himself inside, followed by Sam, scrambling desperately to catch on before the carcass ran away from him. 'We'll hit a tree,' he gasped.

'There are no trees,' Cheyne replied. 'They have cleared this slope to use it for their waste disposal.'

The incline was steep and the carcass picked up speed quickly. Vidar, Cheyne, and Sam pressed themselves against the ridges of the ribs, gripping tightly as the carcass bounced over obstacles, airborne for the occasional split second before coming down hard, constantly threatening to tip over. Sam cried out with every sudden crash until Cheyne silenced him with a sharp kick of his boot.

Finally, the carcass was spinning round and round, out of control, hurtling down the slope before they all felt the land disappear beneath them. With their stomachs in their mouths, they went into free fall.

The impact threw them up to the top of the carcass, and was followed by a resounding splash. Cold water sluiced in one end. They were instantly caught in a current and propelled downstream quickly, the carcass continuing to bounce back and forth as it hit the sides of what Vidar guessed was a narrow gully. As they picked up speed, they had to grip even tighter to avoid being sucked out of the rear of the carcass. The sound of rushing water became deafening.

'This is insane! You're going to kill us!' Sam yelled above the roaring of the water.

Cannoning off rocks, the carcass raced faster and faster at a gradient that was getting steeper by the second. Icy water washed up to their necks, threatening to suck them out of the other end, where Sam clung on desperately, howling in terror.

They slammed into a rock with such force Vidar was afraid it was going to tear the carcass apart, and then there was another moment of hanging when Vidar feared they had gone over a waterfall. But a couple of seconds later they hit the water hard, and went down beneath the surface. The river rushed into the carcass instantly. Vidar just had a second to catch a half-breath before he was completely submerged, the carcass slowly turning so that in the freezing, inky dark it was impossible to tell which way to escape. Down, down, the carcass went. Hands tore against him, and feet kicked hard and desperate as Cheyne and Sam sought to find an exit from the carcass. Trapped, and drowning.

Vidar's last breath seared his lungs and colours flashed across his vision. Just when he was convinced they were all going to die, the current sucked the carcass back up to the surface.

Vidar thrust his head up until he found air and sucked in a mouthful. Enough water washed out so that they could all catch a breath, and then Cheyne was helping him out of the carcass with Sam just ahead. The river was wider and slower moving at that point, and they were close enough to the bank to wade out.

Collapsing on to the grass, they forced the water from their lungs and breathed deeply. 'We can't wait here long,' Vidar gasped. 'The forest people aren't going to give us any time to rest.'

'Then come.' Cheyne helped him to his feet.

But as he struggled to stand, Vidar realised that his hoped-for burst of energy was not going to come. Either the strain of their escape, or the mysterious repercussions of Greer an' Lokh's spell for Asgrim, had thrust him into the last stage. Death was closing fast.

Cheyne helped him along the bank a little way, but it was clear that he would not be able to progress very far. While a shivering Sam sat recovering his nerves, Vidar pulled Cheyne down so he could whisper to him conspiratorially.

'You have to get out of here as soon as possible,' he said.

'And leave you here? How could any Huntsman abandon their leader?'

'You know the situation, Cheyne. I'll never make it back to Idriss like this, and very soon the only thing on my mind will be surviving. You know what that means.'

Cheyne nodded thoughtfully. 'But that time has not yet arrived.'

'And you don't know when it will,' Vidar said, frustrated.

'I am very good at defending myself.'

'The Elorhim are going to be tearing the forest apart to find us now. They hated us before, but now they'll never rest until we're dead. The leader of the Berex army wants the jewel and the map-cube and he's going to be hunting for us continually. Then there are the beasts roaming everywhere–'

'Well, when you put it like that...' Cheyne examined the smaller saplings that grew among the large oaks along the river bank. 'I can cut some of these and build you a bier. We can drag you. Admittedly, woodworking is not one of my best skills, but I am sure I can improvise.'

Vidar cursed, but in his weakened state there was nothing he could do. He listened to the rumbles and shrieks of the forest beasts passing nearby as Cheyne cut down saplings, forcing a complaining Sam to help. They all understood the futility of it, but to do nothing would have meant owning up to the inevitable.

After a while, exhaustion claimed them and Cheyne and Sam took an opportunity for a brief rest while Vidar kept watch. They made their beds on the edge of the river so that if any predators or enemies came they could throw themselves in the water and hope the current would help take them away from immediate danger.

Hot needles burned in all Vidar's joints and his skin felt raw to the touch. In his chest, each slowing pulse of the jewel was like a hammer blow driving the life out of him. The ghost-whispering had become a constant, like the

sound of the sea washing in and out of his consciousness, and occasionally he thought he
glimpsed them flickering on the edges of his
vision, throwing their arms high in praise of
the impending end. His constant companions,
never letting him forget, never forgiving. Their
simple message – that he had decided his life
meant more than theirs – tormented him, for
he knew they were right.

The experience was horrific, like slowly
being pressed beneath the waters, and
although it had become familiar over the last
three years, the terrors had never eased. On
several occasions he wondered if it would be
easier to let himself die, but a fundamental
part of him would not take that step. At the
point when death was a breath away, the drive
to survive crushed every rational thought,
every good intention, every single piece of
decency within him. He would kill to live. He
would always kill.

That certain knowledge dominated his
thoughts as he watched Cheyne and Sam
sleeping. When the black tunnel closed around
his vision and the only light was the faint glimmer of moonlight on the river, like a beacon
about to wink out, he would cut another slice
from his own soul. But which one would he
choose? For all his aesthetics and his education, Cheyne was damaged beyond all hope.

He had stated on many occasions that he could kill everyone he knew, however close, without compunction. Yet there he was, even at the last, plotting to save Vidar's life, and his friendship had been true ever since Vidar had met him in Idriss. Cheyne had been the first one to accept him, possibly sensing that they were forced to walk the same path, though for different reasons.

And there was Sam, the key to his past, to his life. Everything Sam had told him had invigorated him with the hope that the torment of not-knowing could be wiped away and he could finally find peace. It was all he had thought of over the last three years, so many sleepless night, so many bleak days, and now it was finally in his grasp.

He watched, and he weighed, but he knew in his heart the choice he would have to make, and he knew it would haunt him for ever.

CHEYNE RESTED, BUT he didn't sleep. His brain ticked cold, registering every sound, noting every rise and fall of Sam's chest, but more than anything keeping watch on Vidar. As a student of death from an early age, Cheyne understood its capacity to transform the best of intentions in the beat of a slowly stilling heart. Vidar was a friend and a warrior he admired, but he knew sooner or later that sentiment would have to be set aside and cold calculations made. He didn't blame Vidar; he would do exactly the same under the circumstances. And so when Vidar finally dragged himself to his feet, knife gripped at his side, Cheyne's fingers closed around his own hidden knife, and he waited, ready to strike first.

VIDAR'S HEAD WAS swimming and the cries of the ghosts were finally swamped by a wave of bitter regret. Rational thoughts flickered and died, leaving just the beat of his heart and the strain it took to put one foot in front of the other. He had left it to the last possible moment to make his move, and now feared he would not have the reserves to make it at all, but he had kept hoping against hope that something, anything, would happen to prevent him having to choose – one of the Berex forces appearing from the trees, say. But he knew it was just a naïve fantasy. Life was harder than that.

He crept towards the sleeping forms as quietly as he could, hesitated only briefly to listen to the slowing beat of his heart, and then drove the knife down.

Cheyne rolled to one side and sat up. Vidar was half-aware of the puzzled expression on his friend's face, but he was consumed by the euphoric rush of the jewel drinking in Sam's life essence. Vidar was overcome by a rush of blinding white and gold driving the black from his mind; explosions of colour briefly destroyed his thoughts. Life throbbed through him, lifting the weight of exhaustion and the despair that enveloped him. His muscles surged with strength, and an unquenchable energy ran through every fibre of his being. He felt reborn, unbeatable.

As his conscious mind returned, he felt slightly sickened by the addictive exhilaration and forced himself to look deep into Sam's eyes as the light slowly died in them, and with it his own hopes of ever being whole again. In that last flicker, he saw incomprehension and betrayal, and the devastating truth that in the great story, seen from Sam's perspective *he* was the villain.

Their reflections flickering in the river water, the ghosts screamed into life all around him as they accepted the newest tormented soul into their ranks. Their cries of anguish rose up to the heavens, and all the wild beasts of the forest fell silent as one.

'Why did you kill him?' Cheyne asked, confused.

Vidar took the map-cube from Sam's pocket and then jumped to his feet, feeling as if he could run back to Idriss. 'You'd rather it had been you?'

'That would have been the logical choice. He could have transformed your life. What value do I have? I would have killed me without a moment's thought.'

Trying to mask the devastation he felt, he said, 'There's no map for this kind of business, Cheyne. You feel around in the dark and the way just opens up to you. Come on – help me bury the body.'

11

THE WAY THROUGH
THE WILD

CRACKLING BOLTS OF energy seared across Idriss from the very top of Greer an' Lokh's tower, accompanied by an orchestration of foundry-pounding and high-pitched whines. Within, clouds of acrid smoke drifted down stairwells and into chambers, eventually billowing out into the dawn sky.

At the window, Rhiannon watched the forest swaying languidly. 'It looks so peaceful,' she said with a shiver.

'You are worried about Vidar,' Asgrim said.

'If anyone can return from that hellish place…' she began, pretending not to care. She saw that Asgrim gleaned the truth and ended the comment with a pale smile. 'I fear the worst.'

'He has the map. He has Cheyne. Both those things reduce the odds considerably.'

A disturbing sound that neither of them wanted to consider echoed from the tower's uppermost floor.

'I did not thank you before. That was ungrateful of me,' she said.

There was an honesty in her voice that he found endearing, as he did so many other things about her. 'For finding you a victim?'

'I do not like that word.'

'Nevertheless.' He winced, sickened by what he had done.

Sensing the undercurrents that troubled him, she touched his arm, a simple act of understanding on her behalf, but which set his heart hammering. Yet he knew several things to be true: that she would never see past the wild exterior forged by a harsh life; that his supportive act could only make her view of him worse, a brutal barbarian who callously snatched some unfortunate to suffer at the hands of Greer an' Lokh; and that he had no choice but to help her.

The door burst inwards with a crash, and Greer an' Lokh entered, slick from head to toe with blood. He danced wildly in a state of euphoria, his eyes rolling in his head as they viewed other worlds, other places.

'Oh, the joy, the joy!' he sang.

Driven by his own frustrations, Asgrim grabbed him roughly. 'What have you found?'

'I have found the universe in a softly beating heart,' Greer an' Lokh raved.

Asgrim shook him again.

'All the secrets we need to know are there!'

Rhiannon pulled Asgrim gently away and said, 'Laurent the Seeker. Remember?'

Slowly, Greer an' Lokh's vision returned to the room. He appeared honestly upset to find himself in familiar surroundings. 'Yes, the Seeker,' he stuttered. 'He is not the Red Man.'

'But the Red Man has killed him?'

'No. The Seeker is a prisoner. The Red Man searches for secrets, as do I, as do we all. The unfolding of the universe. He keeps the Seeker in a dark place and kills him with a thousand cuts. The Seeker will not speak. But soon, perhaps, he will, and then it is the end for us all.'

'How?' Rhiannon pressed.

The sorcerer focused on her with a puzzled stare that did not seem to recognise her. Finally, he said, 'I do not know. It is gone.'

Asgrim loped around him, growling. 'How can you not know?' he snarled.

'The patterns emerge and fade just as quickly, as the life disappears into the night. But I know this: everything is at stake. If the Seeker gives up his knowledge, all is lost.'

Exhausted, Greer an' Lokh staggered to the flags and instantly went to sleep.

'All for nothing!' Asgrim snarled. 'We know no more now than before that life was taken!'

'But we do.' Rhiannon had a faraway look in her eyes as her mind turned over rapidly. 'We thought the Red Man was a ghost, flitting through Idriss, untrackable, killing at random. Now we know two things: that there is a purpose to his movements; and that there is somewhere he considers a safe place, where he keeps Laurent the Seeker while he attempts to prise information from him.'

'How do those things help?'

Rhiannon smiled. 'By understanding what motivates him, we can predict what he might do next. And now we can also begin to search for the place that he considers safe. We finally have something that is not early morning mist. Something hard, and something that I will grip on to and not let go.'

THE WINDOWS WERE covered with roughly cut wooden boards so inside the room it was impossible to define the time of day. It was sparse, with a table that looked like it had served a dual purpose as a chopping board, a rickety chair, and a greasy, sooty range on a wall where a pot bubbled. The occupant was a man with grey, wiry, mutton-chop sideburns and a florid face covered with burst capillaries from which silvery eyes peered. He wore a thick woollen coat and a stovepipe hat with a dent in the side. He smelled very sour indeed.

The man sniffed at the steam from the pot and then helped himself to a bowl of thick vegetable stew, which he carried back to the table with hands shaking as if with an ague. The stew slopped over the edge of the bowl as he spasmed and cried out, 'Nonononooooooo!'

Dropping the bowl, his hands clutched at his face. A violent tremor ran through his features before they slowly melted away, as they had done so many times. The bone-white face glowed in the room's half-light, gradually topped by the wild incarnadine mane with the bloody slash of a mouth drawn in an expression of monstrous rage. He flung the table across the room, shattering it into shards, and then destroyed the chair in his fury. Hammering on the walls, he howled, 'No more this incandescence!'

From beneath his feet came an echo of his hammering, though feebler, followed by a pitiful cry.

The Red Man tore away a board obscured by mud and dust to reveal a deep black hole. 'No more this incandescence!' he yelled into it.

'Please,' the voice carried back up. 'Once more you are not making any sense.'

Roaring like a beast, the Red Man threw himself into the hole. There was the sound of violent pounding on something soft and then silence. The Red Man clawed his way back out and sat cross-legged in the middle of the floor, sobbing gently to himself. He fought to order the fractured chain of his thoughts, and for a moment he almost succeeded. He saw a face that was not a face, and the statue of the Shepherd casting his shadow across the Store of the Ages, and the dead body of Mellias waiting for him, and then the jumbling dementia gripped him again and he said, 'These are found not now! Why? Not now!'

He dug his jagged, dirty nails into the floor and howled again. And when his throat was raw and the blood pounded in his ears, he saw another face – the woman, with the tattoo on her forehead, and the cowl that failed to cover her loneliness – and in the dim, unmappable chambers of his mind, he knew she was somehow the source of his misery and possibly the source of his salvation.

He dragged himself to his feet and went in search of a new face.

THE STORE OF the Ages had an odd atmosphere that always unsettled Rhiannon. In the entrance hall, stuffed animals looked down at her with their beady black eyes, many that she had never seen alive, barely knew their names, only that they came from a time before time when there were wonders and terrors in equal measure.

In the mounting heat of the day, the unnerving out-of-place-and-time aromas of the building rose – brick dust and parchment and leather and insect casings, warm, dusty glass, wood and bone. It whispered, *This is not a place you know; this is not a place for you.*

Rhiannon and Asgrim made their way to the top-floor scriptorium where the Keepers charted the topography of history in enormous books catalogued and cross-referenced with numbers and lines and incomprehensible codes.

Excited by the continued attention after a lifetime of insignificance, Xiang Chai-Shekh hurried from his ink-stained desk. 'Honoured Inquisitor, how may I be of assistance?' he said with a deep bow.

Rhiannon removed her cowl and gave a smile that revealed her increasing confidence since Asgrim had taken her up on the roof and showed her life from a new perspective. Despite the threat hanging over her head, she felt stronger than she had in a long time. 'There is a statue of the Shepherd on the floor where Mellias was murdered.'

Xiang Chai-Shekh nodded, unsure what lay behind her comment.

'But as far as I can tell, there are no other statues of gods from the many other religions that can be found in Idriss.'

'That is correct.'

'The path of the Shepherd is only a minor religion.'

'Now. Once it was the religion of all Idriss, and all of Gardia.'

'I have not heard that,' Asgrim said.

'It was long, long ago. Even before my own family came to Idriss, and I can name one hundred generations.'

'But still,' Rhiannon pressed, 'one religion's statue placed so prominently in the Store of the Ages–'

Xiang Chai-Shekh beckoned them over to a shelf that contained a row of books almost half his height. They were ancient, the leather worn and fraying, the edges of the yellowing pages cracked. 'When the religion went into decline, the Store of the Ages was established to keep safe the artefacts and texts of the path of the Shepherd for all time. It was feared that all the wisdom would be lost to the dust, as all things are.'

'So the Store of the Ages was established purely for the religion of the Shepherd?' Rhiannon said.

'Over time it became something greater – a store of all the ages, all the memories of Idriss,' Xiang Chai-Shekh said proudly.

'Is this common knowledge?'

'Sadly, no one cares. Everything about the Store of the Ages is irrelevant. We ourselves are a memory, a bad one, to the people of Idriss. The past, and better times, are always a threat when survival is the law of the day.'

Asgrim smiled wryly. 'All the works of the Shepherd were saved from the dust of history and are now lost in the dust of the Store of the Ages.'

'The irony is not lost on me, Huntsman,' Xiang Chai-Shekh said.

Rhiannon held up a hand to redirect the conversation. 'But in lieu of the Seeker of the Temple of the Shepherd, you can answer our questions about the religion?'

Xiang Chai-Shekh gestured to the other Keepers. 'If we do not know the answer, then we can find it, given time.'

'Find your most knowledgeable man and bring him here.'

As Xiang Chai-Shekh whispered intently to his colleagues, Rhiannon said to Asgrim, 'Everything the Red Man does leads back to the Shepherd. This religion dominates his mind. Why?'

'A fanatic, killing in the Shepherd's name?'

'No, he requires information. That is why he has captured the Seeker. Something in the teachings, or the history, is valuable to him. I thought at first it was simply the map that he wanted, a source of power for anyone in Gardia.'

'But the map is gone – though he may not know that. And he has redirected his attention to the Seeker and the religion.'

Rhiannon nodded. She undid the canvas bag containing the paintings and laid them out on the floor. 'These are ancient – you can tell by their very nature. They are unique among all the paintings in the temple. And they are of particular interest to the Red Man. He is not interested in current teachings. His attention is focused on the earliest times.'

'An ancient secret. Then why has it become of interest now, after so many generations have passed?'

'These paintings are concerned with the Shepherd, but they are not about him. If we can understand the meaning behind them, we will discover why they are important to the Red Man.'

'He wrote, "These are the one what tell you." He is saying there are clues within the paintings to explain what he is doing.'

'In the same way that *The Supplicant Praises the Power of the Visitant* revealed the existence and importance of the map-cubes,' she said.

'But why does he feel the need to communicate with us?' Asgrim mused.

Xiang Chai-Shekh returned with an overweight, bald man he introduced as Belmond. He had the pleasantly distracted air of someone who had nothing to worry about beyond sifting through history's remnants. 'Belmond has indexed many of the religious artefacts in our collection,' Xiang Chai-Shekh said.

'Do you know what these pictures represent?' Rhiannon asked.

Belmond moved along the row, bending low to study each one in detail. When he came to the one featuring the long stone box on the hillside he smiled broadly.

'You know this one?'

'It is the Tomb of the Shepherd.'

'He existed?' Asgrim said. 'He lived and died, like we all do?'

'Oh, yes.' Belmond smiled.

Asgrim snorted. 'Of what use is a god who does not retire to a shining city in the sky, filled with women and wine? And more women?'

'The texts tell us that the Shepherd died as mortals do and was interred in an unmarked stone box on a green hillside, where the sun would always praise his glory and the stars would bow down with grief.'

'So he is a man?' Asgrim struggled to comprehend.

'No,' Belmond said calmly. 'He is a god.'

'Then how can gods die?'

'He may not be truly dead, in the terms that we understand. He may only be sleeping. Waiting to be woken again.'

'Where is the tomb?' Rhiannon asked.

'Lost. Like so many of the wonders from the age of the Shepherd.'

Rhiannon studied the painting for a long moment, then said, 'The landscape includes several specific features. It echoes the smaller tomb that is just visible in *The Supplicant Praises the Power of the Visitant*. Perhaps the artist painted from life, and the two paintings taken together identify the location of the tomb.'

'Which could be filled with treasure,' Asgrim said excitedly.

Belmond shrugged dismissively. 'Perhaps. If you knew the area where the tomb lay. But there is not enough here to say whether it lies just beyond the walls of Idriss, or beyond the horizon.'

Rhiannon looked back at the other paintings – the raft at sea, the burning tree, the table, and the floating orb – but there was nothing she could see that would help explain the puzzle.

She thanked Belmond and Xiang Chai-Shekh and asked them to keep the paintings safe until they returned. Once she and Asgrim were alone beneath the staring black eyes of the stuffed animals, she said, 'Ancient secrets and ancient mysteries, Asgrim. Something lies hidden in the religion of the Shepherd that is worth slaughter.'

'But we are no closer to finding the Red Man.'

'Ah,' she replied, her eyes glittering. 'But we are.'

RABBITS SCATTERED AS Vidar and Cheyne burst from the trees and skidded down a bank alongside a brook where wild flowers grew in shafts of sunlight. They didn't look back.

It was mid-afternoon, the day at its hottest, and they had been running from the Elorhim from shortly after dawn. The forest people never tired, never slowed. They had narrowly avoided becoming meals for great beasts on several occasions, and had been pursued for more than three miles by insects as big as ponies. Mouthfuls of water had been snatched from the rivers and streams they had crossed, but they had not eaten all day.

'How much further?' Cheyne asked, red-faced and sweating.

'The next path is just through those trees.' Despite the lack of food, Vidar felt invigorated after the creeping weariness that had afflicted him for so many days.

'Are you sure? It is a long time since you snatched a glimpse at the map.'

'I'm sure.'

'But the forest people will be able to travel on the path just as easily.'

'I know, but at least that's only one thing to watch out for. My life will be easier without any of those hungry beasts at my back.'

'That is what I like about you, Vidar. Always looking on the sunny side.'

They crashed through the tree line and landed on the path, which was wide enough to accommodate twenty men walking shoulder-to-shoulder.

'What are these paths?' Cheyne said as he ran north along the route without breaking step. 'Why do they provide safe passage from the beasts of the forest? Why do they come and go like the autumn mist?'

'Why do you ask so many questions? Here's one for you: who cares? As long as it's a benefit to us, I'm not interested.'

'Hmpf. So much for an enquiring mind. I am sadly disappointed in you, Vidar. Soon you will be at the level of the sots in the Four Staves who think reasoned discourse is to count the lice that burrow in their pubic hair.'

An arrow whizzed by their heads. Glancing back, Vidar saw that six Elorhim had emerged from the forest on to the path. They carried long bows, nocking arrows as they ran.

'Damn them! How did they get so close?' Cheyne spluttered angrily.

'They wouldn't be so relentless if you hadn't killed one of them.'

'Oh, blame now, is it? I carry out my job efficiently and do I get praise–' He gulped down his final word as an arrow passed so close to his ear it sounded like the buzz of an angry insect.

They weaved from side to side as arrows whisked past on every side. It was only a matter of time until one struck home.

'Now would be good,' Cheyne said.

'For what?'

'One of your miraculous plans.'

'I have an option.'

'That does not sound as valuable as a plan.'

'It's a planned option.'

'Hmm. No. Still not valuable.'

An arrow flew directly between Cheyne's legs as he ran. He blanched, ran faster. 'Can you hear something ahead?'

They rounded a bend in the path and came up sharp against the ranks of the Berex troops, a wall of black across the path. The captain on his horse held up his hand and the warriors came to a standstill.

'Yes. It would be these.' Vidar looked from the army back along the path, waiting for the Elorhim to round the bend.

'I do not think much of this plan.'

'I did say it was more of an option.'

'These are the ones who – according to the sadly departed Sam – are particularly interested in that jewel in your chest.'

'Yes, but at least I can haggle with these people. The Elorhim want to kill me. The Berex might not.'

'What about me?'

'I didn't think that far ahead.'

Rounding the corner, the forest people came to a slow halt. They watched the army for a moment, then fixed stares on Vidar and Cheyne that chilled them both, before stepping back to the tree line and melting slowly into the shadows.

'So,' Cheyne said, 'in a choice between a burning house and the excrement pool at Greatstock, you chose…?'

'I think you know.'

His features hidden by a black bear helmet, the captain of the force rode his horse forwards.

'We are weary travellers, lost in the forest–' Cheyne began.

'Take me to Verlaine.' The whispering ghosts in Vidar's head were silent and that unnerved him even more.

The captain eyed him for a moment and then said, 'Wait here.' He trotted back to the column of warriors and leaned in to the carriage. After the curtains twitched, they glimpsed a silver gauntlet before the captain gave a loud order. The warriors fell out of formation and began to assemble a makeshift camp in the middle of the path.

Four warriors soon surrounded Vidar and Cheyne, swords drawn. 'Drop your weapons,' the captain demanded.

Vidar and Cheyne both dropped their blades, but neither made a move towards their hidden knives. Waiting in the hot sun while the camp was hastily constructed, they watched curiously as a curtained tunnel was erected from the carriage to a large black tent on which the red and black lion's-head banner flew.

At some point the carriage's occupant – Verlaine, Vidar guessed – must have made his way into the tent, for the curtained tunnel was removed. 'You stay here,' the captain said to Cheyne. 'You–' he nodded to Vidar '–in there.'

At the entrance, Vidar peered into the tent, and though it was dark apart from a hastily lit brazier in one corner, it appeared empty. 'Inside,' the captain said. He remained on his horse.

'Don't you need to guard your leader?'

'Only one will need protection in that tent. Not him.' There was a queasy quality to the captain's voice.

Inside the black tent, it was already unbearably hot from the furious force of the afternoon sun upon it, but the captain sealed the flaps so that the seething heat of the brazier was trapped inside too. Although it took a couple of seconds for Vidar's eyes to grow accustomed to the gloom, most of the tent was still lost to him in the lurid red light from the brazier.

'I apologise for the heat. I know you must find it unpleasant, but these days I just can't seem to get warm.' There was a faint sibilance to the urbane voice. It was self-assured and unthreatening with a hint of irony, educated certainly, but there was no comfort in it.

'You're Verlaine?'

Vidar just made out a hint of movement in the farthest corner of the tent. The occupant was sitting on a chair. He caught a whiff of an unpleasant, sweet smell that reminded him of rotting apples. The hairs on the back of his neck prickled – Verlaine was studying him from the dark.

'Luke. Surely you still recognise my voice.'

'I know you used to go by the name of Reichert. That's all. Most of my memory is gone.'

'A by-product of the artefact, I imagine. Which one do you have?'

'The jewel.'

'Ah.' He collated this information, and then added, 'They are wonderful things, aren't they?'

'"Curse" is the word I'd use.'

'Really? Then perhaps you are not utilising it to its full capacity.' Vidar sensed other qualities behind Verlaine's voice now – superiority and danger.

'It demands lives, and if it doesn't get them it feeds on me.'

'Yes. The Vampire Jewel. I'd heard that.' Verlaine appeared to be smiling. 'But what if you gave it not one life but ten. Twenty. A hundred. A thousand. What would it do with all that energy, eh? How would that make you feel?'

'I'd need a good reason to kill so many people.'

Verlaine laughed quietly. 'You and I have the best reasons in all the world, Luke.'

'Sam's dead.'

Silence for a long moment. 'How?'

'I killed him.'

More silence. 'Well, I can't say I'm surprised. It was coming to him sooner or later. But I truly am sorry, I hope you believe me when I say that. We shared some pleasant times together.'

'That didn't stop you tracking him across half the land.'

'You seem to have mastered a touch of bravado in the last three years, Luke. Another side effect of the jewel? Or is it a side effect of all that killing?' The shadow shifted again. Vidar imagined Verlaine clasping his hands in front of him. 'It does have a remarkable effect on the psyche. You know, some killers claim it makes them feel like a god. Not simply that power over life and death.' His tone became contemptuous. 'That would be a superficial reading. No, to look in the eyes at that final moment and to see into the infinite. It's that understanding of mystery, that specific and rare knowledge that sets you apart from the rest of the human race. How many people have killed, Luke? How many people have even thought what it means?'

'You're speaking from experience.'

'We do what we must to carry on.'

'You seem to be doing a lot more than surviving. This army. An entire city under your control, Sam said.'

'Exactly how much did Sam tell you? Before you saw fit to despatch him.' The last line was added with an uncharacteristic sharpness.

'He was less than flattering about you.'

'You can't believe everything that Samuel says. Said. He was very unreliable. Quite slippery.'

'But you did want to bring me back.'

'We were a good team, the seven of us. We deserve to be together.'

'Nothing to do with wanting this jewel in my chest.'

'Well, of course, we *all* want the artefacts, Luke. That's the whole reason for us being here. Or have you forgotten that too?'

Vidar took a step forwards.

'I wouldn't come any closer. I'm not a pretty sight. People do find it uncomfortable, even when I try to mask it with the armour.'

'A side effect of your artefacts.'

'Yes, an unpleasant one, but I can live with it.'

'Which ones do you have?'

'The gauntlet... you know all about that, of course.' When Vidar didn't respond, the note of superiority in Verlaine's voice grew stronger. Vidar knew his opponent had recognised that his information gave him power; he wouldn't be revealing too much. 'And the amulet. It's a minor one. It allows me to adopt a position of strength in negotiations with weaker minds. Wouldn't work with you, Luke, no, but it has its occasional uses. Oh, it does provide one other effect too, but there's no need to consider that now. Individually the two artefacts make demands on the body and mind. Together they take quite a toll.'

'Then how are you going to cope when you get more?'

'Oh, I'll be able to cope, don't worry about me. I'm becoming better at it. I'm not the Reichert you knew and loved.' He laughed to himself.

Vidar wanted to ask all the questions about his past that weighed so heavily on him, but he restrained himself. He knew Verlaine wouldn't tell him, or would see it as a sign of weakness, or lie to get an advantage.

'Quite a coincidence us bumping into each other here. I do have a problem with coincidences. Random events that appear meaningful are, in my experience, very rarely random.'

'My comrade and I were on an expedition to explore the forest beyond the city walls–'

'Just at the time when Sam and I were also abroad. Three members of the team, scattered across the world for so long, all coming together in the same place, at the same time.'

'I was just trying to stay one step ahead of the forest people.'

Verlaine shifted dismissively. 'Tell me, Luke – the map-cube. Do you have it? Do you have both?'

'What do you mean?'

'I could have you searched.' He paused, another shift of the shadows, perhaps a dismissive gesture. 'How rude of me. Sometimes I forget myself. One of the downsides of being supreme leader – you get so used to treating people like cattle. There'll be time to discuss this back in Berex.'

'You've got a map?'

'Yes, Luke, I've got a map. Sam had one too. And there was one in your fine city, but it seems to have disappeared at the moment. I have no idea why that would be. Sadly, my own map doesn't cover this sector so I can't really check. I do hope I won't have to send out another expedition to recover Sam's body. That map-cube is rather valuable, as I'm sure you appreciate.'

'Any map would be valuable in this world.'

Verlaine eased himself out of his chair and took a few steps to the edge of the red light leaking from the brazier. Vidar still couldn't make out much detail, apart from the unsettling sensation of movement all over his body.

'How much do you really know, Luke? About our mission here? About the team, the artefacts, even how we came to be in this godforsaken place?'

'Enough.'

Verlaine saw through his word instantly. 'That's a shame. I've missed intelligent conversation, and there's so much we really need to discuss. I look forward to a long chat when we get back to Berex. Now, if you'll excuse me, I need to rest. Samuel did lead me a merry chase and we didn't have much time for relaxation en route.'

He extended an arm. Vidar got the briefest glimpse of skin the colour of the brazier, and again that unsettling sensation of movement, before Verlaine retreated into the shadows.

'I hope you can offer us some hospitality. We haven't eaten for a long while.'

'You'll be treated well, Luke. We are old friends. And I'll even extend the hospitality to your travelling companion, though God forbid we should start treating these people like human beings.'

Heading to the tent flaps, Vidar allowed himself one glance back, but Verlaine had already disappeared into the dark. 'I'll see you in a short while, Luke. Rest easily.'

The tone of Verlaine's final comment left Vidar unsettled.

'YOU MUST HAVE stumbled across some hidden charm in your nature, for we both appear to be alive,' Cheyne said. He sat in the shade of the carriage while the warriors distributed water and hard biscuit from another wagon at the end of the column. Some of the provisions were handed out to Vidar and Cheyne, which they quickly devoured.

'He's a cautious man,' Vidar said. 'He doesn't know how much I know. He doesn't know what I'm capable of.' He tugged his shirt around the jewel. 'And he might know about this, but I'm sure he doesn't know exactly what it's capable of too.'

'It sucks the life out of everything it encounters. What more can it do?' Cheyne plucked crumbs from his beard.

'I don't know,' Vidar said uneasily.

'At least we have got a meal out of this and a moment to catch our breath. Your option seems more like a plan with each passing moment.'

'It's not going to last long. Verlaine wants this jewel. I don't know how far he's prepared to go to get it, but I can make a good guess.'

Cheyne took a swig of water and then pretended to adjust his shirt, though Vidar knew he was choosing his moment and his words. 'These people... the fat dwarf... this Verlaine. They seem on uncommon terms with you.'

'They say they know me.'

'You kept strange company.'

'I keep strange company now.'

'Where do you come from, Vidar? Berex?'

'Somewhere further away than that.' He shrugged. 'I still don't know exactly. But I'm going to find out.'

'More chats with your secretive friend?'

'Perhaps. In one form or another. Not in the foreseeable future, though.'

'Does he have body odour problems?'

'He does, actually.'

'Ah, that explains it. You would not want to be riding in this heat if you left unsightly stains on your clothes. Hiding it away... clearly a man of taste.' He hesitated, then added, 'Are you going to be rejoining your old friends?'

'I'm going back to Idriss. With you.'

A hint of a smile twitched Cheyne's lips. 'I must be addled by the heat, but it would be quite pleasant to see the face of that stinking lupine northerner. I could even cope with his body odour problems. And I presume you are aching to see the beautiful Rhiannon.'

'We're just good friends.'

'Of course. I forgot.'

'It shouldn't be too long.'

'You have a plan? Or is it more of an option?'

'No, this time I have a definite plan.'

In the cool beneath the carriage, Vidar took the opportunity to sleep, but it was fitful and haunted with images of Verlaine, his shape twisting and growing, becoming something monstrous always just beyond the edge of Vidar's vision. Vidar knew instinctively that he couldn't afford to let too much time pass. Verlaine might have spoken about returning to

Berex, but Vidar was sure a move would be made long before then.

AFTER TWO HOURS, the camp was broken up and the carriages turned around. Verlaine had taken his position in the lead carriage at some point while Vidar slept, but the smell of rotting apples hung unsettlingly close, as if Verlaine had stood over him while he was asleep, weighing if it was the right moment to make his move.

The column moved back north-east at a brisk pace. Vidar and Cheyne fell in step in the middle of the unit, aware that they had been assigned their own individual guards who always kept one hand on their swords.

They made camp again just before sunset, when the air was filled with the terrifying sounds of the beasts preparing for the night. Vidar and Cheyne were allowed their own two-man tent, but a sentry was posted at the entrance who told them, 'You must not venture out until the sun has risen.'

'Why?' Vidar asked.

'There are predators,' he replied flatly.

Once they were inside, they heard the sound of the flap being sealed with ropes and a padlock.

'When are you intending to begin your *definite plan*?' Cheyne whispered.

'Not yet.'

'How definite is definite?'

'I know when and I know where, if that's what you're worried about.'

'Worried? No. I freely rest my life in your hands. Although I may wish to pass comment at various points along the way. But I had a rather unpleasant experience at my fourteenth birthday party when one of my jovial friends leaped out from behind a curtain to wish me well and, in my shock, was unfortunately taken by the urge to bite his ear off. Since then I have been deeply troubled by the thought of surprises.'

'So you would like to know my plan?'

'I would.'

'I plan to capture Verlaine because he is a threat to us, and Idriss, while he is loose, and because he has a lot of vital information, and once I've captured him I plan to take us all back home.'

After a moment of silence, Cheyne said, 'You see, that was a surprise. I did not like it. Please do not tell me any more.'

'Go to sleep.'

'I fear I will now lie awake, worrying about you beginning your capturing and your fleeing at a time when I am not fully prepared. Or, indeed, at any time.'

'Go to sleep, Cheyne.'

* * *

THEY ROSE AT daybreak and after a brief breakfast of more hard biscuit and water, their march
recommenced. At intervals along the way, Vidar
glimpsed the forest people watching from the
trees, but they never attacked. He was convinced,
however, that their numbers were growing.

Verlaine remained behind the curtains of his
carriage, and although Vidar requested a meeting, he never received any answer, as though
he were beneath the leader's notice.

Shortly before the sun was at its highest, the
officer riding at the rear of the column gave an
insistent call. The Berex warriors instantly
broke into a run, still in step. With their
swords, the guards prodded Vidar and Cheyne
urgently to join in.

'What is this – exercise time?' Cheyne spat.
'My complexion is not suited to hard labour in
the heat of the day.'

'No. Look at that.' Vidar leaned out of the
column to indicate far behind them.

In the heat-haze, there was shimmering
movement, which they eventually realised was
the branches and vegetation altering their
position. The path was closing up. Vidar
couldn't make out at that distance if the trees
were themselves moving, for the image had a
dreamlike quality that made him feel as if
what he was seeing was not what was happening, but the result was unmistakable.

'More magic,' Cheyne snapped, but the sight clearly unnerved him.

The closing path rushed towards them at speed, and they could just about keep apace by sprinting. After half an hour, they came to a branching path, and when they turned to the east, the officer at the rear called out again and the warriors came to a halt. They rested, removing their helmets to take water and catch their breath. When Vidar looked back, it was impossible to see where the path had been. The tree line was solid, the vegetation dense and unbroken.

At one point he wandered near to Verlaine's carriage, and had the odd feeling that he was being watched by the occupant. A cryptic comment floated out from behind the curtains, but Vidar could not tell if it was directed at him: 'How fragile this existence is.'

THE AFTERNOON WAS conducted at a slower pace, and they broke for the night before the sun had set. While the warriors erected tents, built campfires, and mounted sentries along the narrow path, Vidar sat with Cheyne watching the sun, fat and red, over the treetops.

'We move soon,' Vidar said quietly, so he could not be overheard.

Cheyne moved his gaze slowly along the trees in a wide arc. 'I fail to see how now is a

better point than any other over the last two
days. You saw something on the map?'

Vidar nodded, but he still had his doubts; it
had been long ago, and he could not be wholly sure of their position. 'Listen,' he said.

They both cocked an ear. Past the birdsong
and the rustling of the leaves in the breeze,
they could just make out a distant rumble.

Cheyne narrowed his eyes. 'What is that?'

'Our way through the wild.'

Cheyne said no more. Vidar could see his
friend mentally preparing himself for what
was to come, and so left him to stake out the
surroundings. He had already chosen his ideal
time – while the warriors collected the provisions for their evening meal; all he needed to
do was identify the location of the sentries. It
was a risky strategy, but getting out of the forest was always going to be as dangerous as
getting in and, having sacrificed his past with
Sam, he was determined not to let it slip
through his fingers again.

When the warriors filed towards the quar-
termaster's wagon, Vidar surreptitiously
nodded to Cheyne. The familiar detached state
came over Vidar as he slipped along the tree
line like a ghost, drawing no attention, leaving
nothing in his passing. He didn't know if it
was truly one of the undiscovered qualities of
the jewel at which Verlaine had hinted, but

when he was in that state he felt almost dis-
embodied.

The sentry didn't hear him. Vidar stood
behind him and slipped the knife under his helmet and into his jugular, pushing the sentry
quickly to the ground to stifle the gush of
blood. The life surged into Vidar, filling his
vision with flashes of gold. Invigorated, he
retrieved the sentry's sword and moved on.
Further along the tree line, he saw Cheyne rise
up and press his needle-knife under another
helmet at the base of the sentry's skull and into
his brain.

Within a minute they had despatched the
four sentries surrounding Verlaine's carriage.
Cheyne joined Vidar as he crept towards the
curtained entrance, the pulse of vitality inside
him driving out any thought of what lay within. While Cheyne kept watch, Vidar entered
the half-light of the carriage with a single
bound, instantly taking in Verlaine's position
on a chair in one corner. In a flash, he brought
the sword tip up to Verlaine's throat and only
then realised what his eyes were telling him.

Verlaine was still clothed in black armour
from neck to foot, but he had removed his helmet to reveal a face that was not a face. There
was no sign of flesh. Insects swarmed across its
entirety, feeding, breeding, laying eggs, beetles,
maggots, flies, aphids, cockroaches. A pair of

white, lidless orbs stared out of the seething mass.

'Not a pretty sight,' Verlaine said.

Pain lanced through Vidar's head as a high-pitched scream rose up on the edge of his consciousness. His nose began to drip blood, and spasms ran through his muscles. All around him the air shimmered as the ghosts burst out into the carriage, but for once they remained in utter chilling silence, their attention focused with apprehension on Verlaine.

He raised his right hand where the silver gauntlet gleamed and hooked his fingers. Blue light shimmered around the glove until bolts of coruscating energy fizzed off like spatters of molten metal.

'Silly boy,' Verlaine said.

Feeling as if his organs were being pulled out through his skin, Vidar staggered back. His mind flipped, but somehow he held on to his thoughts. He brought the flat of his sword hard against the side of Verlaine's head, and then moved in with a furious punch. Before he fell unconscious, there was a glint of surprise in Verlaine's eyes that Vidar had overcome his attack so easily, and a suggestion that Verlaine would not underestimate him again. Vidar caught him as he fell to the floor and rammed the helmet on to his head.

Outside the carriage, Cheyne took Verlaine's weight and the two of them slipped just beyond the tree line. The last rays of the sun cast a ruddy glow along the path which only made the dark among the trees even darker. None of the warriors saw anything out of the ordinary as Vidar and Cheyne moved quickly by.

They'd gone a few hundred yards when the alarm was raised in the camp, and the air was suddenly filled with calls and whistles. Vidar led the way out from under the trees at the point where the path began a long curving arc and they could move quicker. Verlaine's bulk was slowing them more than Vidar had anticipated.

'He'll be awake soon,' Vidar said. 'We need to get to a point where we can bind him.' He indicated the length of fine but strong rope he had lifted from where it hung at the side of the carriage with the rest of the emergency supplies.

'How much further to your escape route?'

'Around this corner, and then a short break through the trees.'

Behind them, the sounds of pursuit rose up.

'You do realise we will now have the entire Berex force hunting us through the forest?' Cheyne said.

'There's not that many of them,' Vidar said.

'Oh? Was this part of your plan?' They rounded the corner at a point where the path sloped down through the trees towards an area of flatter low country. The route was blocked by an enormous army as far as the eye could see, the flag of Berex floating at the front. The last rays of the setting sun added a hellish light to the black armour, the pikes and axes, the carriages and war machines.

'An invading force,' Vidar said.

The vast army advanced slowly for its rendezvous with the unit closing on Vidar and Cheyne's backs. The sight unnerved them, but then the sun finally set and the scene became even more disturbing. Sparks of red light sprang into life along the entire length of the column. It took them a second to realise what they were seeing.

'Their eyes?' Vidar said.

'So this is why we were locked in our tent. Under cover of night, they become demons.'

'Verlaine's done something to them with the amulet artefact. But what?'

In their arms, Verlaine began to stir. Vidar forced Cheyne into the trees where the cries of the great beasts were already starting to greet the night, and together they towed Verlaine towards the distant rumbling sound.

They hadn't gone far when a crackling flash threw Vidar and Cheyne into the undergrowth, where they lay smoking. As they dragged themselves to their feet, dazed, Verlaine tore off his helmet, his huge white eyes blazing in the sea of insects.

'You have shown me great discourtesy, Luke.' Spitting, crackling energy hissed around the gauntlet. 'Dragging me from the comfort of my carriage to where these people can lay their eyes upon me.'

His ears ringing, Vidar could taste metal in his mouth.

'I've made an accommodation with my appearance in return for the power I wield, power of which you have only seen a fraction. We could perhaps have reached an accommodation between ourselves, too, but now I realise you cannot be trusted. I don't know if you ever could.'

He levelled the gauntlet.

'I can easily pick the jewel from your remains. And, I presume, the maps too,' Verlaine added.

Swiftly exchanging a glance with Cheyne, Vidar ran into the forest, zigzagging among the great trees. The same high-pitched shriek echoed in his head, and then the air appeared to catch fire all around. Trees blossomed flames along their branches, trunks igniting, soaring up to the sky, fire all around, hot air searing his lungs, all in silence until the sound

of the unleashed conflagration hit him like
thunder a fraction of a second later. The blast
knocked him to the ground, but he was up and
running instantly, ignoring the pain in his chest
and the devastating heat on every side. He
realised as he ran that Cheyne was at his side.

They broke through the trees at the edge of
a steep-sided valley. A river crashed across
rocks to create the rumbling sound they had
heard earlier. Racing along the valley edge, the
wall of fire fell behind them, and soon they
were skidding down the valley side to an area
where the river was wider and slower-moving.

When they reached the river's edge, they
could see in the gloom upstream that the
banks were too steep for any of the beasts to
come down to drink. Behind them, the sky was
bright with a wall of fire that separated them
from their pursuers.

'This is the river,' Vidar said. 'We can follow
it back to Idriss.'

'Why, we may even find one of the abandoned riverboats to make our journey easier,'
Cheyne gasped, 'before we become food for
the water monsters.'

Vidar's anger at losing Verlaine was tem-
pered by the power he had seen him wield; it
was clear now how he had seized control of a
city. If he gained more of the artefacts, the
world would be his.

Cheyne appeared to read Vidar's thoughts. 'Do not worry about leaving him behind,' he said. 'I fear we will see him again soon.'

12

OLD BONES

On the Rolling Road, not far from the edge of Ironrack where the grand homes offered views across all Idriss, a small door in a canopied stone surround was set into the wall of the winemakers' guild. Beneath a hissing lamp, Rhiannon beckoned to Asgrim to examine the padlock attached to the door. It hung limply.

'As you said,' Asgrim responded, 'but this still may not be the work of the Red Man.'

'The Seeker could not have been taken against his will from the Temple of the Shepherd without the alarm being raised,' she said. 'Somehow the Red Man removed him silently, not witnessed by any of the many people who use that area night and day.'

'But the catacombs can be reached from the temple's crypt,' Asgrim affirmed. 'You think the killer has been moving beneath our feet all this time?'

Rhiannon wrenched open the protesting door; it was rarely used. The odour of damp and dust rose up from a flight of steps disappearing into the dark. 'The catacombs run underneath a large part of central Idriss. The Red Man could use them to travel freely throughout the city. Access can be gained into many buildings with only a little effort.'

'They have been sealed off for many generations,' Asgrim mused. 'The Red Man would not be disturbed down there.'

'And the best place for him to keep the Seeker would be in a building that could be reached through the catacombs.'

Rhiannon lifted her torch and waved it above her head. Further down the Rolling Road another Inquisitor waved a torch, thereby passing the message in turn to another.

'All the Inquisitors we can spare will systematically explore the catacombs, fanning out from the Temple of the Shepherd,' Rhiannon said.

'There are still many miles of tunnels and many potential buildings off them.'

'But it is only a matter of time. Patience, care, method, and a rigorous approach to the rules of enquiry and we will have him.'

He smiled. 'That should please the Chief
Inquisitor. And keep your head on your shoulders.'

Her eyes flashed in the torchlight. 'You
know?'

Asgrim shifted uncomfortably. 'I overheard–'

'This is not about me, or my life, Asgrim,'
she said firmly. 'This is about my duty to
Idriss. I owe the citizens, and the King, and the
administration, to capture the Red Man within the time span they have decreed to prevent
a shattering blow to our home. The role I have
accepted is everything. My responsibility to
Idriss is everything.'

'Of course,' he said unconvincingly.

'I would not expect you or Vidar or Cheyne
to understand, with your loose grip on morals
and your dedication to personal achievement.'
She took one step down the flight of stairs,
then flashed him a smile. 'But thank you, once
again, for aiding me with Greer an' Lokh. I see
your motivation more clearly now. You are a
good man.'

It was a simple comment, but Asgrim was
overwhelmed. Rhiannon had already disappeared around a bend in the stairs and did not
see him puffed with joy, or she would have had
an even deeper understanding of his motivation.

In the catacombs, there was a stillness that Asgrim rarely experienced in the constantly moving city above ground. Around him lay ten thousand skulls and ten thousand more, the bones of ages piled high, spilling from vaults like the sands of the desert. The catacombs were filled with the echoes of incalculable generations, with no hint of their stories, of the history that shaped them, only a reminder of what had been forgotten.

The tunnels carried the faint echoes of other Inquisitors making slow progress, trying door handles and trapdoors and grilles, rattling chains and padlocks. Among the vaults, it sounded as if the dead were waking from a long sleep.

Asgrim sniffed the air for any sign of the Red Man's telltale sourness. 'This atmosphere is undisturbed. It holds scents well.'

'We are close to him. I can feel it,' Rhiannon affirmed.

'They say there are some parts of the catacombs that have not been explored in generations. Who knows what lurks down here?'

'You are superstitious? I am surprised. I cannot imagine anything frightening you.' She moved along the tunnel, holding the torch high so the shadows leaped away from her.

'I have seen what Greer an' Lokh can achieve. I am well acquainted with Vidar's ghosts. I know there is more to this world than the hard things we see around us.'

'Those things are fearsome, but they are also a source of wonder, for they do indeed show us that there is more to this world. More than the harshness and the struggle and the misery.' Her voice took on a wistful quality. 'There must be more than this.'

'This is a harsh world,' he agreed, 'and we must get what joy from it we can.'

At a junction of tunnels, they stopped. As Rhiannon made to follow the left-hand path, Asgrim suddenly dropped to his knees, his nostrils flaring.

'His scent?'

'Yes, but only a fragment.' The sour note was barely noticeable, but it carried with it a depth of misery. He moved along the wall, then down to the flags, lying on his belly to make sure he missed nothing.

'Can you follow it?'

'I do not know. It is old – he passed this way a while ago – and it comes and goes.' He looked up at her and grinned. 'You were right.'

'Of course.'

They were interrupted by the echoes of running boots. A lantern moved rapidly along the tunnel behind them, its beam flying across the roof and walls. It was Inquisitor Fabienne, her piercing eyes now filled with dismay.

'Inquisitor Rhiannon, you must come with me,' she said breathlessly.

'We are on the track of the killer. We must–'

'No! There has been another murder. And this time there is trouble rising. The Chief Inquisitor demands your presence, as does Administrator Ashur.'

'But we are so close!' Asgrim protested.

Grim-faced, Rhiannon pulled some chalk from the pouch at her waist and tossed it to Asgrim. 'Mark it,' she said, 'so that we may find it again.'

Reluctantly, Asgrim made a clear chalk-mark where he had identified the smell. 'I will accompany you,' he said, casting a frustrated glance into the shadows along the tunnel.

'You can–'

'No, I will accompany you. You shall not face this alone.'

THE RIOTING HAD started on the fringes of Greatstock and had quickly spread to adjoining districts. Surging through the narrow streets demanding protection, the mob soon swelled, the contagion of their fear multiplying, seeking an outlet in violence. Businesses were attacked, threatening the fragile economy. Suspects were pursued until they fell beneath fists and boots. Three people died within the first fifteen minutes. Clouds of thick black smoke hung over the city from burning buildings, and as the flames licked skywards, crowds of volunteers passed buckets of river water in an attempt to prevent the blaze from spreading.

At Fallen Spire, Rhiannon and Asgrim found a furious crowd held at bay by a small group of Huntsmen, weapons drawn, their faces reflecting their uncertainty at finding themselves facing the people they usually defended. Beyond them, a group of administrators milled, unable to hide their anxiety.

As Rhiannon and Asgrim pushed through the crowd, Ashur saw them and broke away from his intense discussion. Though his face was as emotionless as ever, his fury was evident in every movement.

'This is the result of your failure!' he bellowed at Rhiannon, pointing at the monument. 'This!'

From each of the four shattered iron columns hung a body swaying gently in the warm breeze, each bearing the unmistakable marks of the Red Man, the bloodstains like tears beneath the missing eyes. Torn strips of a purple Seeker's robe were tied around each ankle, a detail that had not been missed by the crowd. Rhiannon could hear, 'The Shepherd,' whispered repeatedly at her back.

'We are close to finding him–' she began.

'No. This has gone on long enough.' Ashur turned to Chief Inquisitor Serena and LeStrange, who hurried to join him. 'This one must be removed from the enquiry now!' he barked.

'Are you sure?' the Chief Inquisitor replied. 'The King personally requested her. Should we not–?'

'The King is in no state to make any judgement on this matter. Remove her. Now.'

Rhiannon was stunned by the revelation that she had been hand-picked by the King. But before she could process the information, a stone flew from the crowd, gashing Ashur's temple. He staggered back, blood spurting from the wound. Within seconds, stones rained from all directions.

LeStrange grabbed Ashur's arm, and together they all ran for cover behind the monument. 'Cut the bodies down!' Ashur shouted, dazed. 'It is only incensing them further.'

'They are scared for their lives, and they blame us for not protecting them,' LeStrange said.

The stones continued to fall and only the arrival of another group of Crimson Huntsmen prevented the mob from breaking through to attack the administrators.

'Take her to the cells now!' Ashur bellowed, stabbing a finger at Rhiannon. 'Let them know who is responsible!'

'No.' Asgrim stepped calmly in front of him.

'You would challenge me?'

'She is close to finding this killer. She only needs a little more time.'

'I say take her now!'

'And I say, no. You will need the Crimson Hunt to quell this riot, and to save your own neck. In the absence of Vidar and Cheyne, I am the authority here. The Hunt will only listen to me.'

Rhiannon reached out to touch his arm. 'You do not have to do this.'

Asgrim ignored her, fixing on Ashur eyes that were as cold as his northern skies. 'I was taught by my father to believe in honour above all other things. You stand by those who stand by you. You do not sacrifice them for political expediency. Inquisitor Rhiannon has been loyal to Idriss, the King, and to you and your administration. She deserves the support of everyone in this city.'

'This is treason,' Ashur hissed quietly through his teeth. 'After this is over, you will join her in the cells. Then we will talk about saving necks, or not.'

'Do not sacrifice yourself for me,' Rhiannon pleaded. 'The orders have been given. We must obey them. That is our duty.'

'These are only men, and our duty is to a higher calling,' he said before glancing back at her, his eyes warming. 'There is more than this.'

'Ignore my order,' Ashur said to the Chief Inquisitor. 'Let us do what we must this night to save Idriss.' He glared at Asgrim. 'Vidar would not have been so stupid.'

Asgrim grinned back. 'Then you do not know him.'

On the edge of the crowd their attention was caught by a surge moving towards the river path.

'Where are they going?' the Chief Inquisitor wondered.

'To the Temple of the Shepherd. They… believe the followers of that religion are implicated in these crimes,' Rhiannon replied, her dismay clear in her face.

'I will send the Huntsmen to defend the temple while the enquiry is concluded,' Asgrim said.

'I will go with them. There may still be information there that we have not found.' Pulling up her cowl, Rhiannon added to Asgrim, 'Will you continue the search in the catacombs?'

He nodded, to Ashur's bemusement. 'A role reversal?' the Administrator said contemptuously. 'You have failed in your own jobs and so attempt the other's?'

Asgrim and Rhiannon quickly moved away into the night, and so did not hear Ashur's final comment to the Chief Inquisitor: 'When the worst of this dies down, arrest her, take her to the cells, and execute her as soon as possible. Then hang the body here for all the mob to see.'

IT WAS THE choking smell that first alerted the Keepers of the Store of the Ages to the new arrival. Reeking of blood, bodily fluids, and death, Greer an' Lokh pirouetted into the chamber and sashayed around the display cabinets, humming a tune that in his head was so seductive it would win over anyone who heard it.

The Keepers watched in horror. No one could recall the last time the famed and feared sorcerer had left the security of his tower, and that troubled them greatly. Was he in search of more lives to stoke the furnaces of his magic? They could think of no other reason why he would be in a building dedicated to the past; Greer an' Lokh was only concerned with the brutal present.

Xiang Chai-Shekh met him hesitantly, hands clasped together in deferential greeting, but ready to throw the nearest object at the sorcerer and run. 'Greer an' Lokh… honoured… honoured Greer an' Lokh, how may I be of assistance?'

The sorcerer stopped dancing and peered at Xiang Chai-Shekh as if the Keeper had threatened him. 'What did you say?'

Xiang Chai-Shekh backed off a step. 'Assistance. How may I–?'

'Yes, yes, yes. The paintings. I need to see them.'

The Keeper quickly guided Greer an' Lokh to where Rhiannon had left the five paintings from the Temple of the Shepherd, and then hastily left the sorcerer on his own.

Instantly entranced, Greer an' Lokh's mind, so rarely tethered to thoughts of the here and now, began to grasp the patterns that had first presented themselves to him in his tower. He dropped to his knees, snuffling along the artworks like a pig.

'It is,' he said excitedly to himself, 'a story! Like the tales I used to hear on my mama's knee!' He backed along the line and stopped before the painting of the table bearing the mysterious objects. Mouthing the words, he counted, and when he had finished a sly smile crept across his lips.

ONLY A FEW members of the crowd made it to the Temple of the Shepherd before the Crimson Huntsmen. The doors had been barred ever since the Seeker had disappeared, and the mob hammered on them futilely, while others scoured the area for implements to break the lock. A fire was started against one wall.

The Crimson Huntsmen cleared them away as gently as they could, and then formed a defensive barrier with swords and spears raised across the doorway, a strategy they had only ever used in the defence of the city. They parted to allow Rhiannon through, and then closed like water behind her.

Unlocking the door, she slipped into the cool dark, quickly lighting a lantern in case any members of the mob had somehow found their way inside. The white walls flared in the flickering flame and then settled into a screen for the dancing shadows.

In the atmosphere of sanctity, with images of the Shepherd looking down on her, she felt at peace, and with it came a belief that everything would turn out all right. Behind the thick walls of the temple, the noise of the rioting across the city was muffled and could well have been the celebrations of the Fire Festival. She decided to keep believing that.

Examining a painting of the Shepherd, she incongruously found her thoughts turning towards Vidar. She missed him with an intensity that shocked her, and the thought that he might be dead in the forest left her desolate. She wanted him there, right then, for although she had always been strong and survived any

374 LORD OF SILENCE

hardship, the thought of standing shoulder to shoulder with someone against the world was deeply comforting.

Recovering her fortitude, she prepared to go back outside, only for the light of a lantern to fall upon dusty footprints across the marble floor. Though most would not have given them a second glance, Rhiannon was held by them until she realised why: the dust had the same silvery glint as that found along the flagstones of the catacombs, and she had noticed it in her own tracks when she had exited the tunnel system. Crouching down to examine it closely, she saw that it was fresh.

A shiver ran down her spine. Was it possible she was not alone in the temple? The Seeker had been spirited out through the catacombs, which meant it would be just as easy to gain access back into the building. Rising cautiously, she peered into the shadows at the back of the temple. Was someone watching her from the dark?

Her attention fell back on the footprints: not in the shape of the hard-wearing boots that most people in Idriss wore, but in the mark of a sandal. That gave her pause. The Red Man wore boots; she had felt the hardness of them when he had kicked her during the fight at the Order's building.

She glanced back at the door where the muffled booms and yells had grown louder. The Crimson Huntsmen were too preoccupied to aid her. Hesitating only a moment, she raised her lantern and progressed cautiously into the depths of the temple.

The floor plan of the building made it impossible to see what lay ahead. Her natural caution prevented her from moving too quickly, but she drew strength from the pictures of the Shepherd, with his kindly face and welcoming smile.

In moments of intensity, her brain responded to the training of a lifetime and slipped her into a state where every detail became heightened, the rich scent of the incense and the fragrant oil of the unlit torches, the echo of the measured tread of her boots, the cool, slick marble slipping beneath her fingertips as she trailed past a column. And there, so insignificant it would have been missed by anyone else, a purple fibre, trailing from the splintered edge of a broken chair where it had snagged. She lifted the fibre into the light of a lantern and saw that both ends were ragged; it had come from a segment of cloth that had been ripped. She recalled the torn strips bound around the ankles of the victims at Fallen Spire, and as the Unknown Shadow shifted again, a picture began to present itself to her.

She moved on, quicker now. A splatter of blood on the flags. Then the barely audible shuffle of a sandalled foot somewhere ahead. As she rounded the columns, she finally got a clear view into the sanctified area where the coloured flame flickered. Amid the shadows looming and twisting across the walls, she caught sight of a lurching figure. Her heart beat faster. Purple robes, ragged at the bottom, sandals, a shaven head.

'Laurent!' she called out.

Rushing to aid him before he stumbled, she wondered where the Red Man must now be if Laurent had escaped from his lair. More importantly, what did that mean for Asgrim?

FROM THE CHALK-MARK etched on the wall of the catacombs, Asgrim advanced quickly and decisively, his nostrils flaring. Flashes of the sour odour came and went with increasing intensity. He was heading in the right direction.

The tunnel turned, twisted, branched until he had no idea what part of the city was above his head. He had seen more bones and rats than he ever wanted to in a lifetime. It was a sobering experience to see the forgotten remnants of generation upon generation of Idriss's residents, and only added to the potency of the life he lived there and then. Everything he did mattered only in terms of the world around him. Beyond that, his deeds would only lie here, gathering dust.

The sour odour was at its strongest next to a vault of skulls, many of which lay shattered, unlike the other skulls he had seen en route, which had always been stored with respect. He pondered this for a moment, and then began to scrape the skulls to one side. When he had moved a number of them, he found a tunnel through the remainder formed by carefully stacked tibias and fibulas.

'Rhiannon would be proud of me,' he said to himself with a gentle smile.

Dropping to his belly, he wriggled into the tunnel, pushing his lantern ahead of him. The smell of the bones was like old milk, but it was nothing compared to the sour stink of the Red Man that coated everything. For a second he struggled to maintain his focus as the images conjured up by the odour flooded his head, but then he was past it and dragging himself into the depths of the vault.

At the back, the stone wall had been shattered to reveal a tunnel gently rising through the earth, barely large enough for him to enter. He forced his way in, his shoulders and back dragging tight against the earth, showers of soil falling on to his head so that he was afraid the tunnel would collapse at any moment, suffocating him there with no one ever knowing what had happened to him.

Continuing to push the lantern ahead of him with his fingertips, he dragged himself slowly upwards. He soon decided his dislike of heights was matched by his dislike of enclosed spaces. The tunnel was so small he had to keep his chin on the floor, and soon his breath was burning in his chest and he was stifling waves of panic. He fought back the sensation of being trapped with thoughts of the Red Man following the same route. What kind of a thing was the killer? Only an animal could easily endure that route more than once.

Just when he thought he could bear it no more, his head came up against something hard and for the briefest moment he was convinced that the tunnel had been blocked off and he was trapped. But then he pressed with his head and the obstacle gradually lifted. He found himself in a bare, small room that smelled of damp with yellowing, stained walls. There was a door in the wall ahead of him.

Filling his lungs with air as quietly as he could, he steadied himself, drew his knife, and listened at the door. There was no sound beyond. Grasping the handle, he gently tugged. The door dragged loudly on the floor, the echoes reverberating through the building, and then jammed just wide enough for him to squeeze through.

Asgrim cursed under his breath. The noise would have alerted anyone to his presence. Slipping through the crack, he padded across bare boards, pausing at every door with his knife raised, but all the windowless rooms were empty. The stink of the Red Man filled the house, but it was so potent Asgrim couldn't tell if it lingered from constant use, or if his prey waited to catch him unawares.

He climbed a short flight of stairs to what he guessed was the ground floor. The windows here were boarded up. Two rooms were deserted. In the third a stained bedroll lay on the floor in one corner with a chamber pot nearby. The walls, though, were scrawled with writing, inscribed by a finger dipped in soot. Most of it had the frenzied unintelligibility of madness, which made him doubt that the Red Man was operating with any rational plan, but some words and phrases were clear. *The Shepherd guides us. Save the world, kill the world. I is an angel.*

There were others, but Asgrim found it oddly unsettling to read them and he quickly left.

The final door led into a bare kitchen with a broken table and chair and a range on one wall. There was a door to the upstairs quarters, but it had been boarded shut, and another, locked, that led out. As he walked around, his heightened senses registered that the sound in the room was slightly off, suggesting a hidden space. Moving around the room slowly, he gently rapped the walls, and then turned his attention to the floor.

He found the trapdoor quickly. Opening it, he lowered the lantern to reveal a small pit filled with remnants of food and the stink of bodily functions. It was empty. From the detritus he could tell someone had been imprisoned there, probably the Seeker. Had the Red Man abandoned his hideout and moved Laurent to another location?

Frustrated, he strode towards the locked door, only to catch a familiar scent lying just beneath the overpowering odour of the Red Man. Letting his conscious thoughts settle, he attempted to sift the aromas of the room. The trace was faint but unmistakable and led him directly to the range. Kneeling down, he threw open the oven door.

Seeker Laurent's head looked back at him.

VIDAR ADJUSTED THE rudder on the boat to prevent them drifting closer to the starboard bank where something large was tracking them in the trees that came right down to the water's edge. Among the snorts of breath and the breaking of branches came the noises they had heard before, like a high-pitched child's voice talking in an unintelligible language. On occasion, it sounded as if it was almost trying to lure them to the bank to investigate, with hints of pleading and pain that chilled them both. Neither of them spoke about what might be there just beyond their perception, and they continued as if nothing out of the ordinary was occurring, but Vidar saw Cheyne's unsettled eyes repeatedly flicker towards the bank, praying whatever it was would leave them alone, or at the very least fall silent.

The boat was big enough to carry six people comfortably, with a small sail and oars, and was as river-worthy as they could have hoped for a vessel that had been half-buried in the mud among broken branches and a fallen tree. There was no sign of what had happened to the previous occupants, but they had also passed several other abandoned vessels on their journey upstream, some shattered and half-submerged as if they had been ripped apart.

It was hot and languid with flies buzzing in clouds along the river's edge. They had considered catching some of the large, silver fish that swam in shoals in the slow-moving water, but neither of them had wanted to move to the bank to light a fire.

The boat allowed them to make much faster progress than they ever could have on foot. Verlaine and the Berex army were now far behind them, though the sticky scent of burning and the occasional ashes caught in the wind would not let them forget what was at their backs.

'I hope we are amply rewarded for bringing back the second map-cube,' Cheyne muttered. 'At this moment, it appears a poor substitute for treasure.'

'That may not be top of their priorities if Verlaine brings his army to Idriss.'

'The walls are our curse and our strength. We have learned to survive within them. We cannot be starved out. The aquifers provide us with ample drinking water. The defences are robust enough to hold an army at bay for ever.'

'An army of that size? Idriss has never had to face any great numbers at the walls, because no force has ever been able to plot safe passage through the forest. The city's only ever dealt with a handful of survivors, driven half-mad by their experiences in the trees.'

Cheyne considered this for a moment, then added, 'I am slightly concerned by that gauntlet he wields. Sorcery in small measure makes life hellish. Something of that power could severely test us.' He paused. 'So it is true that there are twenty objects of such power out there, and that your jewel is one of them?'

'So it seems.'

'Could you not have got one that actually did something useful?'

'What's that up ahead?'

At a bend in the river, the water churned. It calmed quickly, although the boat rolled over large waves issuing from the disturbance.

'I would like to say a big fish,' Cheyne replied, 'but I fear it is something bigger than big, and not so fishy.'

Vidar steered the boat closer to the bank, but that only excited the thing in the trees, which jabbered more insistently in its reedy child's voice the closer they got.

'Take the rudder,' Vidar said. He drew his sword and moved to the front of the boat, searching the grey waters.

As they rounded the bend, the riverscape instantly became more menacing. Both banks were lined with the wrecks of boats small and large, their torn and broken hulls protruding from the waters like the bones of slaughtered animals. Vidar's quick calculation revealed twenty-five hulks, some almost rotted away, one or two that looked as if they had beached only recently. A grim atmosphere hung over the boats' graveyard, too still in the oppressive heat, as if it were waiting and listening.

The only route through the wrecks was along the deepest channel at the centre of the river. 'We don't have a choice,' Vidar said, pre-empting Cheyne's concerns.

'I heard tales of this place from some merchants who attempted a failed journey along the river. They made it past the dangerous shoals near Idriss, but lost their boat and half of their crew in a graveyard for other ships.'

'Did they say what stopped them?'

'Yes.' Cheyne pointedly did not elaborate.

'Then we're nearly home.'

'A little more sailing, enjoying the sun. Why, this is a relaxing pastime.' Cheyne steered the boat into the main channel. At that moment, the wind dropped and the boat slowed.

Vidar braced himself, his eyes fixed on the surface of the water. It was impossible to see far into the grey depths; anything could have been moving there. The sword felt flimsy in his hand. On solid ground, he was a ferocious fighter with a quick eye for strategy and an athletic grace. But on a boat on a river?

'Keep as close to the wrecks as you can,' he said.

They passed the first two ships without any trouble, but then, at the far end of the jumble of shattered wood, the water began to boil once more.

'Steady, now. Here it comes.'

The water continued to boil for a second, and then a wake began to move directly towards them at great speed. Two others joined it, one on either flank.

'Damn it. There's not just one,' he said under his breath. 'Get the boat against that wreck and brace it!'

Cheyne steered the boat against the hulk of a large upturned barge and lashed a rope around a jutting, broken timber. Vidar leaped on to the barge, took two steps, and propelled himself on to the next boat, which lay shattered lower in the water. As he hurried to the edge and braced himself, the wake came directly at him.

At the last a gaping jaw with rows of serrated teeth exploded from the river. It was big enough to swallow their boat whole. Taken by surprise by the thing's attack, Vidar threw himself backwards just in time. The jaws closed on the end of the vessel, ripping through planks and shattering beams.

The other two wakes circled as the beasts searched for Cheyne and the boat lost in the confusion of the other wrecks.

'We will never get past these,' Cheyne called. 'We will have to take our chances in the trees.' He didn't sound even slightly convincing.

The creature that had attacked him circled around for another go. It was huge, at least the length of ten men, its blue-grey bulk visible just beneath the surface, with one fin cutting the waters. This time it leaped out of the water with a flick of its enormous tail, a scaly mass that looked armour-plated, more like the war-machines that Greer an' Lokh sketched on his wall than any living thing. The eyes bulged and rolled, the mouth snapping as it surged towards him. Vidar threw himself on to the next boat as the hull on which he had been standing shattered beneath the creature's weight.

When the beast came at him again, Vidar launched himself off the wreck, his sword gripped in both hands ready to stab down. He half-heard Cheyne shout a shocked exclamation and then he landed hard on the beast's back, driving the sword through the thick skin.

Snapping its jaws relentlessly, the creature thrashed and almost threw him off, but he held on to the sword. Thick, purple blood flowed out from the wound around his sword, washing over him as the beast rolled from side to side. It drove out into the centre of the river at such speed that the wake almost tore him off, and then it dived down.

Gasping one ineffectual breath before he plunged beneath the surface, Vidar fought to hold on as pain erupted in his joints from the sheer force of the water. The creature went down almost to the river bottom, where an array of human bones and detritus from the ships lay half-buried in the silt.

The weight of the water thundered against Vidar's head, and his breath burned in his chest. The creature turned, and ahead through the murk, he could just make out the other two beasts swimming towards him. He pressed himself down tight against the scaly back as they tore past above him, one jaw sweeping low to try to snap him off.

The creature rushed back up to the surface, and as it broke briefly, Vidar snatched another gasp of air and then freed one hand to whip out his knife. As the creature went down again, he plunged the knife repeatedly into its side, tearing out chunks of meat and releasing a thick flow of blood that clouded the water.

His attack had some effect for the beast thrashed even more furiously. It streaked along the river bottom before surfacing sharply. Vidar continued to attack until he was suddenly smashed against one of the submerged hulls, ripping him free of the sword and knocking him unconscious.

The next thing he knew, feverish hands were dragging him from the water. Dazed, he scrambled into the boat alongside Cheyne and lay on the bottom, gasping for air.

Finally, he realised: 'I'm not dead.'

'Despite your best efforts.' Cheyne quickly untethered the boat and moved it out into the stream, keeping as close to the wrecks as he could. The boat rocked wildly.

'What are you doing? They'll tear us apart,' Vidar said.

'See for yourself.' Cheyne grabbed the oars and began to propel the boat forwards with furious strokes.

Levering himself up to peer over the edge, Vidar saw the water erupting as tail and body broke the surface. In a frenzy of feeding, the two other creatures tore chunks out of the one he had wounded. The water was purple with blood, and the wake from the fighting threatened to tear all the hulks away from the banks.

'Neither you, nor Asgrim, nor I, have a wholly reliable grip on sanity,' Cheyne said, 'but after that display I am happy to crown you King of Fools.'

'It's courage in the face of adversity, Cheyne. That's the way you get medals.'

'Or dead. Usually dead.'

Once Vidar had recovered, he helped Cheyne with the oars and soon they were past the last of the wrecks and able to move into the shallows near the bank where the enormous beasts would not be able to reach them easily. Whatever had been in the trees had fallen silent, either scared away or attracted by the fighting in the water.

As they continued upstream, they were passed on several occasions by tremendous wakes moving along the centre of the river as the scent of blood attracted other predators.

'That actually worked well,' Vidar said. 'I think I'm going to say I planned that.'

The river meandered through the forest, each bend promising so much, revealing only more dark forest. But then they glimpsed familiar landmarks and found new energy for their weary rowing. Rounding one final bend, the vast walls of Idriss hoved into view. The river flowed directly towards them, around the columns and through the iron grilles that prevented the beasts' access to the city.

Vidar and Cheyne let go of the oars and sat back in the boat, letting the wind in the sails carry them slowly the final distance. For a while they didn't speak as their eyes ranged over the rising walls, now more than ever aware of the comfort they provided.

'Home,' Vidar said.

13

UNDER SIEGE

THE FIRST THING Vidar and Cheyne noticed
was the lack of sentries along the walls. Never
to their knowledge had the walls been free of
the Crimson Hunt, and what that might mean
troubled them deeply.

They moored the boat to the grille where the
river passed under the walls, and moved
quickly along the deep shadow cast by the
towering structure, keeping one eye on the tree
line. They both knew that neither of them
would be safe until they had passed through
the Deeping Gate.

When they finally stood before the gate, the
sun was high in the afternoon sky. Cheyne
hammered heavily on the ironwood while
Vidar called out, looking up the sweep of the

walls to the guard towers. There was no sign of any movement.

'A better man than me would probably see the humour in us becoming a meal for the forest beasts right outside our own gates, after travelling safely through the very heart of their realm,' Cheyne said bitterly. 'Where are they?'

'Do you smell burning?' Vidar said. 'Not from the hearths – sharper.'

'A house has burned down,' Cheyne said. 'They always stink like that.' His tone tried to make light of the observation, but in conjunction with the missing guards they both knew it did not bode well.

They continued to call and hammer for another fifteen minutes and eventually a face appeared over the wall above them. It took another twenty minutes before enough guards could be brought together to open the gates.

They were unable to hide their relief as the gates thundered shut behind them. But their smiles quickly faded when they found a deeply troubled Asgrim waiting for them.

Vidar read the signs in Asgrim's face. 'You're going to tell me a hot bath is out of the question.'

'Or ale in the Four Staves.' Cheyne sighed. The exhaustion he had repressed for so long rose up in his features.

'Rhiannon… Inquisitor Rhiannon… she is missing. I fear the Red Man has her.'

Vidar's face gave nothing away, but both Cheyne and Asgrim recognised the intense look in his eyes. 'What happened?'

'She was seen going into the Temple of the Shepherd alone. She never came out. The Red Man had already spirited the Seeker away from there, through the catacombs. He must have taken Rhiannon the same way.'

'No body?'

Asgrim hesitated. 'Not yet.'

'And why are there no patrols on the walls?'

'We need to talk,' Asgrim said.

THE STAINED-GLASS WINDOWS along one wall of the council chamber threw a spectrum of dappled light along the room-length conference table, where generations of Idriss's leaders had thrashed out the details of history, large and small. It added an incongruously pretty tone to a sharply grim scene. The faces of the men sitting around the table were leaden with the weight of unfolding events; even the hollow look in Ashur's eyes added an unusual cast of doubt to his frozen face. It was clear they were all waiting to hear solutions, but had none to offer themselves.

The door was thrown open with a loud crash that bore the hint of theatricality, and

Vidar strode in flanked by Cheyne and Asgrim. Everyone present thought he had a gravity about him that none had seen before, hewn harder, colder.

'The Crimson Hunt thanks the administration for the invitation to address this meeting of the council,' Vidar said in a tone which, while respectful, somehow managed to convey no respect whatsoever. Asgrim and Cheyne took up positions on either wall, slowly scanning the faces of each council member.

'Vidar, how kind of you to take some time out from your gentle rides across the countryside,' Ashur said.

'I always come when I'm needed. And at this moment you need me more than ever.'

'You know, your legendary arrogance troubled me when the King said he was promoting you to the leadership of the Crimson Hunt. Frankly, I thought it was a mistake. And I still do.'

'You wouldn't be so quick to question the King's judgement if he were here, Ashur. You're much braver now he's on his deathbed.'

A concerned murmur rippled around some of the council members. Ashur shifted uncomfortably. Feigning contrition, he said, 'These are dire times and we must all put our personal concerns behind us for the future security of Idriss.'

'I disagree. Decisions have been taken that have put Idriss at risk. The Crimson Hunt isn't going to be a tool to destroy the city.'

'What?' Ashur gaped at Vidar's audacity. 'You are threatening to ignore direct orders from the administration? Treason?'

'The people are not the enemy.'

'You are correct. But the people cannot be trusted to keep the city's best interests at the heart of their decisions. They are driven by irrational concerns, the hardships of day-to-day life, the need to survive. They have to be contained, and directed—'

'Like animals?'

Ashur paused. 'You may choose to use that description. But the survival of Idriss outweighs all our concerns. The city is for ever. We come and go, and are forgotten.'

'You might think that justifies any behaviour in the here and now to keep the city safe. It doesn't.'

'I enjoy an intellectual debate, as you well know, Vidar, but this is not the time. Idriss faces unprecedented unrest at a time when there is insecurity in the succession. There have been deaths and destruction. It would take only the slightest catalyst, perhaps one we cannot begin to foresee at this time, to bring the entire mass of the population to anarchy. And then the walls that have protected us for so long would become a prison containing our madness as we destroy ourselves from within.'

'The people are scared, that's all. They want us to do our job and protect them.'

'And if another novice had been selected for the enquiry into the killer, that would have been the case. But in her inadequacy Rhiannon has betrayed Idriss and every single one of its citizens. She will pay the price for that. But that is a matter for later.'

Vidar hid his cold anger at Ashur's words, but from the corner of his eye, he saw Asgrim flinch, struggle to maintain his own control. 'Perhaps if the Crimson Hunt had been marshalled in the search for the Red Man instead of being used to repress the people, the citizens might have united behind you, as they always have done.'

'*You?* That is an odd choice of word. Do you not consider yourself one of us, Vidar?'

Vidar was taken aback by Ashur's question, hadn't even been aware of his phrasing, yet it gave him pause. His attention fell on LeStrange seated in a far corner, watching the exchange with surprising intensity, and he felt deep currents moving that he had not considered before.

He didn't have time to respond before Glier, one of the elder members of the council, said, 'These recriminations are not getting us anywhere. Give us solutions, leader of the Crimson Hunt, or leave us to our deliberations.'

'I have solutions.' Vidar removed the two map-cubes and pressed them against the jewel in his chest. Flooding out across the council chamber, the three-dimensional map surrounded the administrators with the rich detail of forests, hills, rivers, ruins, encampments, harbours, mountains.

There were shrieks of panic, chairs thrown over backwards, council members sprawling on the floor muttering prayers to a variety of gods. LeStrange stood on his chair, watching with awe.

'What is this?' Ashur raged. 'Sorcery?'

'It's a map,' Vidar said.

Silence fell instantly across the room. The council members froze where they stood or had fallen, seeing the rich colours and astonishing detail with new eyes. Though recognising it for what it was, they could barely believe it, but all were fully aware of the monumental repercussions.

'A... map?' Ashur repeated.

'Half of one, anyway. Two more parts complete it. But it's more than just a map. What you see is happening now. It is a picture-view of the world beyond the walls that changes as the world changes.'

Dazed, Ashur moved slowly through the topography, reaching out to hill forts and waterfalls that he could never touch. 'Remarkable.' The word was barely a breath.

'Idriss is not there,' LeStrange said from the corner. He stood on tiptoe on the chair to get a better view, a fascinated smile curving his lips.

'When the maps were created, the area around Idriss was the centre of the design. That is, I think, significant,' Vidar said. 'Idriss is just beyond the edge of this map.'

'Why, with this, the world is ours,' Ashur said.

'This map represents freedom,' Vidar said. 'The people don't have to be trapped within the walls. We can find safe passage through the forest.' He flashed a glance at Cheyne. 'Reasonably safe passage.'

'This is the reason you went on your expedition?' Ashur asked.

Vidar nodded.

'Why did you not inform the council?'

'I wasn't wholly sure what I was searching for until I found it.'

Glier had tears in his eyes. 'You are a hero, Vidar. As great as Mellias, for you have not only preserved the glory of Idriss in the here and now, but for all time. This achievement will have the musicians on the Rolling Road singing your praises for ever.'

Vidar was unmoved. 'Living on in song. I'd prefer to do it in this world.'

'What is that?' LeStrange indicated the two white spikes and the two coloured ones.

'That's the reason I'm showing you this.' Vidar manipulated the map to centre the spikes. 'The two white ones are the remaining pieces of the map. The two coloured spikes are weapons. Very powerful weapons.'

'Then we can recover the rest of the map,' Ashur said.

Vidar pointed just off the edge of the map. 'Idriss is here. The maps and the weapons are moving towards it. They're being held by an invading army from a city called Berex.'

'On its way to Idriss?' Ashur gaped.

'Looks like it to me.'

'But... we will not be able to defend ourselves with the city in turmoil,' Ashur said in horror.

The council members took their seats, their mood now subdued. Only LeStrange remained thoughtful, his attention hanging on Vidar's response.

'We must keep this from the people,' Ashur said, 'else they will lose all hope.'

'No. We must trust the people.' Vidar's tone was defiant. 'As we always should have done.'

'Madness! That will guarantee the end of the city!'

Vidar clasped his hands around the cubes and the map winked out. The mood in the room became noticeably darker. 'I'm ordering the Crimson Hunt to leave the streets and return to the walls, effective immediately.'

'That is not the wish of this council,' Ashur growled. 'If you follow that course, you will be considered a traitor. You will be removed from the leadership of the Crimson Hunt and conveyed to the cells in preparation for your execution.'

'Don't pick fights you can't win, Ashur.'

An audible gasp rose up from the council members. Eyes flickered towards Cheyne and Asgrim, who kept their attention focused on the administrators.

'You seem to be branding everyone a traitor these days. I don't think you'll be happy until you're the only one left. Now, here's what's going to happen,' Vidar continued. 'The Huntsmen are going to stop attacking the people they are charged with defending. They will instigate the Chief Defensive Strategy along the walls. The Berex army will be here soon, and before it arrives I'm going to address the citizens and tell them the extent of the threat facing us all.'

'And then they will tear the city apart, in the height of their fear-induced madness.'

'And then they'll unite behind us against a common enemy.'

'You are a dreamer... a child.'

'If we can't trust the people – if it's us and them – then Idriss is a myth. And it doesn't deserve to survive.'

An outcry erupted among the administrators. They jumped to their feet, shouting and hammering the ancient table. Over their shoulders, Vidar could see LeStrange smiling.

'This is a revolution,' Ashur bellowed. 'You are seizing control of Idriss from the duly selected officiators. The King will be informed–'

'I'm going from this chamber to tell him myself.'

'The word must go out from this room. Anyone who follows your orders will be considered a traitor and will face the penalty.'

'Send out your messengers. We're all going to have to live – or not – with the outcome. But I have to do what I believe is right.'

Vidar turned and marched out of the room with Cheyne and Asgrim close behind, slamming the doors on a deafening confusion of fearful yells and angry shouts.

'That went better than expected,' Cheyne said. 'I imagined I would now be looking at your head on a stick.'

'Thanks for your confidence.'

'Oh, there is still plenty of time for that,' Asgrim said. 'And it will be three sticks, and three heads.'

'I want to thank both of you for your loyalty and trust,' Vidar said honestly. 'I didn't expect you to put your lives at risk.'

'Why, we are friends,' Cheyne said, puzzled. 'What else could we do?'

'If you didn't have such a confused relationship with death, you might have discovered a few more options,' Vidar replied.

'Options are overrated,' Cheyne replied. 'I prefer a good, solid plan, as you well know, and this plan is better than any other I hear.'

'I would be interested to hear what happened on your journey through the forest,' Asgrim said thoughtfully, 'as we appear to have a different Vidar here.'

'Different how?'

'There appears to be a strange and troubling streak of honour and unselfish dedication to the public good. I am struggling to find any opportunities for personal advancement. Where is the treasure? The free beer at the Four Staves? I cannot believe you would leave these vital matters out of your great plan.' His grin emphasised the irony in his words.

'I've been concentrating on looking after my interests for too long. If I hadn't gone into the forest on my own personal quest, Rhiannon wouldn't be with the Red Man now.'

'You must not blame yourself for that. I was accompanying her,' Asgrim protested.

'Everything we do has consequences, however much we try to ignore them. If Rhiannon is killed, that's something I'm going to have to live with.'

'She may already be dead,' Cheyne said.

Asgrim glared at him.

'What? I am only being pragmatic.'

Vidar turned to Asgrim. 'Now I'm putting my trust in you. Find Rhiannon. Bring her back safely. Protect her with your life.'

Vidar was puzzled by an odd expression that crossed Asgrim's face. 'I will do that. With my life.'

Vidar nodded, reassured by what he saw in Asgrim's face. To Cheyne, he said, 'We have plans to make, and a city to defend. And I hope you're right about the Crimson Hunt.'

'Be reassured: they will follow you to the ends of Gardia,' Cheyne replied, adding thoughtfully, 'or was that to the end of the Rolling Road?'

VIDAR IGNORED THE protesting guards and marched directly into the King's bedchamber. Lud was as insubstantial as autumn leaves beneath the piled sheets and mountainous pillows, his skin a deep yellow, his breathing loud and ragged, punctuated by occasional hacking coughs.

But when Vidar approached, his eyes flickered open, still bright with intelligence. 'Vidar,' he croaked. 'It is good to see you.'

'And you.'

'I fear my life is draining away quickly. Sometimes I see my parents watching me, or perhaps it is a dream. I have difficulty telling the difference between life and dreams. Perhaps there is no difference.'

'The last time I saw you, you told me to break the rules to ensure Idriss remained secure.'

Lud nodded.

'I broke a few rules today. I ignored a direct command from the council and I set the Crimson Hunt against them.'

The King fell silent for so long that Vidar was prompted to check his chest was still rising and falling. 'You are certain your course is the correct one?' the King croaked eventually.

'Ashur was making decisions that put the city, and the people, at risk. This is a dangerous time. We have a new enemy.'

Lud nodded slowly. 'Then I condone your action in the defence of Idriss. But you have broken a fundamental rule, Vidar, and there must be consequences. If this stands, there can be no order here, and without order there is no Idriss.'

'I understand.'

'You must pay the price for what you have done. That is the only way to ensure order is maintained. When the next King is crowned, you must give up your leadership of the Crimson Hunt and offer yourself to him. Only your death will cleanse this act, Vidar.'

Vidar said nothing.

'I note your sacrifice in the name of our city. What you have done is a remarkable thing, and my gratitude is immeasurable. But you can never be seen as a hero after this, for that would shake the very foundations of the order that maintains our security in the face of the terrors that exist beyond the walls.'

Vidar nodded slowly. 'You've chosen your successor?'

'Have I not issued my announcement?'

'No.'

'I thought I had? Then I must think again, and quickly, for time is running away from me. Kesten–'

'He died last year.'

'Kesten is dead?'

Vidar nodded.

'I was sure he still lived. No matter. There are others. I only need to think...' His voice trailed away and his eyes flickered shut.

As Vidar made to go, Lud's hand lashed out and gripped Vidar's wrist as tightly as he had the last time Vidar visited. It felt like he had the strength of three men, not the frailty of a dying old man.

'Idriss must survive, Vidar!' he hissed. 'See that it does. Do whatever you must, but ensure Idriss survives.'

Vidar left Lud sleeping. The bell marking out the remainder of the King's life tolled the hour, and as its echoes drained away, Vidar had the sudden awareness of his own life fading too.

THE TOLLING BELL changed its tone soon after, calling the people to the forum for an important announcement. Many came, hoping it signalled the capture and execution of the killer who plagued the city; many did not, too afraid of the rioting to leave their homes and businesses unguarded.

Vidar waited in the state room of the palace, listening to the throng growing louder outside the open window doors. What he had learned about his past unnerved him. The suggestions and hints by Sam and Verlaine that he had come from somewhere much further than a distant city opened up too many troubling questions, as did the disturbing implications of Sam's statement that he had been 'inserted into this world'. But what bothered him more was that however bizarre it might seem, he didn't, and couldn't, dismiss it out of hand. Deep in his mind, his unconscious knew the truth.

Yet however much these things ate away at him, his thoughts still turned immediately to Rhiannon. It surprised him almost as much as he feared for her safety; his desire to uncover his missing past had dominated everything since his arrival in Idriss, yet now, almost overnight, it was of secondary importance. The implications of that, too, were disturbing.

He was drawn from his thoughts by LeStrange who entered with a respectful smile and said, 'It is time.'

'I appreciate your support, LeStrange. I don't imagine Ashur is making it easy for you.'

'You have always had my loyalty, Vidar.'

Vidar made his way out on to the small balcony. The large crowd filling the forum below instantly fell silent.

Looking over them for a moment, Vidar was bemused by how he had come to be in that position. He began loudly, 'You all know me. Vidar. The Ghost Warrior. I'm not Mellias, and I never will be. But what is not in doubt is that I am loyal to Idriss, to the King, and to you.

'Life here is difficult, you all know that. The threat beyond the walls. The struggle to survive within them. And over the last few days, the killer in our midst has terrified everyone and pushed the entire city to breaking point. I can assure you that a new strategy is in place. The entire Order of Inquisitors is now searching for the murderer, and I have no doubt that they will capture him soon.

'But now I have to warn you that there is an even bigger threat.'

Letting his gaze wander over the crowd, he searched for any sign of opposition or doubt, but everyone was rapt.

'An enemy approaches Idriss. The army is larger and more powerful than any we have faced before. The survival of Idriss hangs in the balance.'

An eruption of concerned mutterings and exclamations ran through the crowd. Vidar waited to see if Ashur was right, that this was the point when the citizens would break, but after a moment they grew quiet and attentive once again.

'The Crimson Hunt will be on the walls giving their lives in defence of this city, as they always have, and I will be there with them. But I need you – Idriss needs you – to join with us in the struggle that is to come. Not on the walls, but in your homes and businesses. In your hearts. You are the real strength of Idriss.

With you at their backs, the Crimson Hunt can defeat any enemy. Without you, they have lost their greatest advantage. They don't fight for themselves. They don't fight for brick and stone and mortar. They fight – and die – for you.'

A few cheers rose up here and there.

'Individually, we are weak. We suffer hardships. Our bodies and spirits are broken. But together we are strong.'

More cheers, some clapping.

'Together we are unbeatable!'

The shouts, and clapping, became one long evocation of support, rising in intensity.

'Together we shall defeat the enemy! For Idriss!'

The crowd roared its response. Vidar was overcome by the passion of their response to his call to arms, but then something happened that surprised him even more, and left his spine tingling and his heart swelling: the chant of Idriss slowly faded to be replaced by a new word, rising slowly until the force of it crashed in a wave against the palace building.

'Vidar! Vidar!'

'You have trusted the people and you have given them hope. They will never forget that,' LeStrange said at his shoulder. 'Idriss has a new hero.'

* * *

IN THE SUITE of palace rooms that Vidar had commandeered to plan the defence of the city, Cheyne lounged in one of the large leather chairs, his feet on a stool, a contented smile on his face. He closed his eyes and gave a relaxed sigh. 'How long have I been away from this place of joy and abandon? Three months? Six?'

Prowling the room, Asgrim snorted. 'The trouble with you soft city people is that you cannot cope with hardship. A few nights in the forest have you crying like a baby.'

'You cannot recall your sojourn in the forest.' Cheyne sniffed. 'I can only imagine that you were not tested as I was. It must have been a saunter along a winding path where all the little forest flowers grow. Or perhaps the great beasts recognised that a sack of bone and gristle and an empty skull was not a choice morsel.'

Asgrim laughed. 'Oh, it is good to have you back, you murderous fop! I feared I would never see you again.'

'And then who would be responsible for your education? Unfortunately, it is my burden in life to offer you the arm of friendship, an act of charity in recognition of the fact that no one else would befriend you.'

Asgrim thought for a moment. 'You know that is the only time we have been apart since I arrived in Idriss?'

Sipping the dregs of wine he had raided from the large cupboard along one wall, Cheyne said, 'I must admit my great adventure was duller for not having you there to mock.'

'I suppose if pressed I would have to admit I am glad you are back. It would indeed be a less than valuable experience sitting here alone.'

'I agree.'

'And I was for a while concerned that you might never be coming back. Well, concerned may be putting it too strongly. But the thought did flit through my mind once, very briefly.'

'And, of course, I did think of you alone here, and knew your nights would be less entertaining, and so I endeavoured to return as quickly and safely as I could,' Cheyne said.

Asgrim selected another bottle of wine and tore out the stopper. 'Here's to us, then,' he said.

'The most dashing pair ever to see the inside of the Four Staves. Together we are unstoppable.'

They drank deeply.

'It is a shame to rush this fine wine, but time is short and we may not get a chance to drink together again for a while,' Asgrim said.

'If ever.'

'You fear the worst?'

'The enemy is... challenging. We may experience difficulties.'

'Difficulties of the final battle kind?'

Cheyne thought for a moment, then said, 'Yes, that kind.'

Asgrim sighed. 'It would be a shame to break up this partnership that has served us so well. We are lesser, alone, are we not?'

'You know, I think we are.'

They sat quietly for a long moment, deep in thought, until Cheyne said, 'Still, death comes for all of us sooner or later, and the trick is to go out in a style that will match my Feegrum boots. A style that people will remember for a long time. Style is, after all, the only thing we have that separates us from the vast masses.'

Asgrim nodded in agreement, and raised his bottle. 'In style it is, then.' He drained his wine. 'Now, tell me what has happened to Vidar. He is different in some way that I cannot quite define. He may be better, he may not be, but he is different.'

'While we were travelling, we met a rather unpleasant fat dwarf.'

'Like the one who used to mine the mountain tunnels and now tumbles for coins in the market?'

Cheyne tried to picture the character. 'No. Fatter. And taller.'

'A tall dwarf?'

'A fat, tall dwarf. He came from Vidar's home, and knew him from his past life. He said Vidar's real name was Luke.'

'Where is this place?'

'Now that is the intriguing thing. From what I can gather, it is very, very distant indeed. Perhaps beyond the limits of the furthest homeland of anyone in Idriss. Vidar refused to talk about it, and I got the feeling it troubled him greatly.'

'Why would that be?'

'I have no idea,' Cheyne said, clearly baffled. 'Home is home. But it is true to say that this information changed him.'

'I am concerned. Where is the zest, the love for life? He seems too serious.'

'Yes, we cannot have that. Life is for living to the full, when death is only a whisper away.'

'I think he needs our help,' Asgrim decided.

'He needs a night of passion with that Inquisitor. Perhaps even just a kiss after dark.'

Asgrim looked deep into his empty flagon. 'Then I will find her forthwith and bring her back to make our friend forget his troubles.'

'Why, could there be a hint of a good man lurking beneath that fur?'

Asgrim glanced sharply at Cheyne.

'I know you well, you northern furball. You are my friend. I see the things you hide away.'

Asgrim bowed his head. 'Do not say anything to Vidar.'

'Of course not. But I would not see you hurt. You know there is no future there for you.'

Asgrim nodded slowly.

'We can take wounds to the body that soak us in blood and leave us at death's door. But a blow to the heart is the most devastating one of all, and I would not wish to see you suffer, Asgrim.'

'Thank you, Cheyne,' Asgrim said with a deep sigh. 'My eyes are already open. I know there is no hope. Nor would I do anything to hurt our good friend Vidar. But still, sometimes, I dream.'

'I know.'

A hot wind blew in as the door opened. Inquisitor Fabienne and three other members of the Order waited at the entrance.

'It seems a few friends have come calling,' Cheyne said.

'Finally.'

'The Order works for you now?'

'So it seems. The Chief Inquisitor clearly sensed a change in the wind. Though it took her a damnably long time to reach her decision. Every Inquisitor will now be on one enquiry: finding Rhiannon.'

Cheyne clapped his friend on the shoulder. 'If there is one person in all of Idriss who could find her it is you. Put those monstrous nostrils to good use.'

'I thank you for your faith in me,' Asgrim said as he rose to go. He flashed a lupine grin. 'You are, of course, right.'

ALL RHIANNON KNEW was that she was in a dark place that smelled of damp and dust, which were the primary odours of age-old Idriss, and so she could have been anywhere. At that time her thoughts were less on her location and more on the fact that she was still alive. One image lodged starkly in her mind: that moment when she reached out to Laurent the Seeker in the Temple of the Shepherd, only to see as he turned that it was not him, just an approximation – bald head, facial tattoos, but eyes that flashed with madness and features so distorted that they bore little resemblance to the man, as if a child had attempted to carve an image out of clay. She saw his rapid lunge for her, his snarl of ferocity, and thankfully remembered nothing more until her waking.

The Red Man had stolen Laurent's now-ragged purple robes and his sandals, but she was not even sure he was attempting to pass himself off as the Seeker. It was as if, in the depths of his insanity, he was simply putting on the things that dominated his inner thoughts.

One matter in particular struck her and sent the Unknown Shadow swirling to reveal new and startling things: the Red Man could not copy faces. He put on random features with his changes, and when he did attempt to mimic another, it failed. He would never be able to fool anyone who knew the identity he was attempting to steal. That threw up one puzzling conundrum from a past piece of evidence in her enquiry, and opened up new and surprising avenues.

But her pressing concern was survival. Why was the Red Man keeping her alive, and for how long before, in his madness, he decided to despatch her like everyone else who had crossed his path?

It was so impenetrably dark in the room that she felt as if she was blind. The chafing at her wrists told her she was tied with a rope; it had an oily smell, like the ones used by the fishermen along the river. Tensing it revealed it was fastened to the wall behind where she lay sprawled.

She made a small sound. The echoes gave her an approximation of the room's size: low ceiling, probably no more than the height of three men square.

She began to pick at the knots at her wrist as best she could without seeing them. Under her fingers, they felt as if they had not been expertly tied, and should not present too much of a problem. All she needed was time.

A faint susurration shivered on the edge of her consciousness, and she froze. Imagination? Or was someone in the room with her?

'Who is there?' she said quietly.

Light flared from an uncovered lantern, and there, only inches from her face, was the sickening, slash-mouthed, skull-white face of the Red Man.

He roared a furious declaration of insane rage and torment that almost stopped her heart, before the light winked out again.

As the pounding in her chest subsided, she lay pressed in the crook of the wall and the floor, her breath tight in her chest, wondering where he was, when he would attack. There was only silence, and that made everything even worse. She always prided herself on her ability to concentrate on her senses to pick up even the slightest detail, but it was as if the Red Man left nothing in his passing: not sound, nor heat, and she could not even register the sour odour of which Asgrim spoke.

After the shock, she found her equilibrium. Being scared would gain her nothing. She recognised that her life was hanging by a thread, and she would have to dig deep into her resources to survive.

'How can I help you?' she said calmly, choosing her words carefully.

There was a long period of silence, and then a low mewling sound emanated from the other side of the room. She realised it was the Red Man attempting to form words.

'Break-up… thoughts,' he finally said with a juddering sigh. 'When… when… you… I!' Each word was dragged out with an effort that drove him to the edge of anger. 'Like this… thoughts… like eggs–'

'Eggs?'

Another desperate sigh. 'Scrambled.' He laughed at his accidental words, but the laughter soon turned into desolate sobs.

She left him to deal with his emotions for a while, and then said carefully, 'Why have you brought me here?'

The words were birthed painfully: 'You know things.'

Rhiannon thought about this for a moment, then asked, 'What do you need to know?'

Silence, for one moment, two, until she thought he might not respond. Then: 'Where are the Tomb of the Shepherd?'

That was the last she could get out of him. Her measured questions fell into the dark unanswered, and then she heard a sound like a trapdoor opening and closing, and realised he had left her alone.

* * *

VIDAR AND CHEYNE had spent the rest of the day planning the Crimson Hunt's initial response to the arrival of Verlaine and the Berex army. Braziers had been placed along the walls south of the river next to the sluice gates where they could release the strange combustible liquid that Greer an' Lokh had spent many years developing. The Huntsmen units were given their allotted positions, and the weapons store had been unlocked and the contents allocated to easily accessible sites along the walls. More detailed strategy would have to wait until Verlaine showed his hand.

Now they waited in the warm, golden light of the afternoon sun flooding the offices of the Crimson Hunt. The map had been checked; the enemy was closing fast.

Cheyne watched the fading light. 'What are they capable of in the dark, those devil-men?'

'Whatever Verlaine's done to them, there's a price to be paid,' Vidar replied. 'Every time an artefact is used it needs fuel... energy of some kind.'

'And that is why Verlaine looks the way he does? The gauntlet and the amulet have sucked the life out of him and turned him into an insect-infested pile of mouldy vegetables.'

'The kind of power in those artefacts is too much for weak human bodies.'

'But it would be good to have one or two on our side. Can even our walls withstand the power of that gauntlet?'

Vidar swung his legs from the desk and went to the window to look out over the city. The lamplighters were already emerging to prepare for the evening's work. 'Verlaine isn't going to leave until he's got what he wants.'

'Your jewel. The maps.' A shrug. 'You could always give yourself up.'

'Let's be realistic – I'm not that selfless.'

'You would bring the whole city down with you?'

'Yes. Wouldn't you?'

'Of course.'

Vidar smiled at the wry exchange. 'You can always be guaranteed to pull me off the path of righteousness, Cheyne.'

'Thank you. I like to be of use.'

'But you know as well as I do that Verlaine wouldn't just walk away if I handed myself over to him. He'd get what he wanted from Idriss and carry on with his search for all the artefacts.'

'And they are where, exactly?'

'Unknown. He needs to find something called the Prime Locator to discover where all the artefacts are. They only show up on the map if they've been... activated.'

Cheyne made a confused expression at the word. 'And where is this Prime Locator?'

'Also unknown. He needs the map-cubes to find it, which means it's not on the two cubes he already has. But I've checked ours and I can't see anything there either. Though it would help if I knew what I was looking for.'

'If he finds that, and then the twenty artefacts—'

'He's won. He'll have the power to destroy the world, according to the Elorhim.'

'And that would not be a very good outcome for Idriss, would it? So, sooner or later, we must prevent him from achieving his aims.' Cheyne considered his words. 'It sounds quite easy when I say it like that.'

'Which brings us to the crux of the problem. We can't just hope to sit out a siege. Verlaine isn't going to get bored and ride away.'

'We need a power equal to his to drive him away. Or destroy him.'

'Which means we need to find the Prime Locator. Whatever it is. Wherever it is.'

Cheyne spotted a speck on one of his boots and began to polish it furiously. 'At least we have an ambition.' He sighed. 'I look forward to your blinding revelation as to the whys and wherefores of achieving it.'

'And with that, I can help you.'

They knew the voice, but recognised the stink a second before. Greer an' Lokh was dancing a slow twirl in the doorway.

THE KEEPERS VACATED the entire floor when they saw Greer an' Lokh return with Vidar and Cheyne. He led them directly to the five paintings and indicated the one with the twenty artefacts on the table.

'Patterns, you see,' the sorcerer said, flourishing his hands to the beat of imaginary music. 'Patterns everywhere. Close to them, they cannot be seen. But as you retreat, and retreat, and retreat, they fall into view.'

'There's my jewel,' Vidar said.

'And Verlaine's gauntlet. And, I presume, the other eighteen magical items,' Cheyne mused. 'A knife, a ring, an amulet, a… is that a compass? I have heard tell of those, but never seen one.'

'No real need in Idriss,' Vidar said, engrossed in the painting.

'All of them filled with magic,' Greer an' Lokh sang. 'Lost for generations, hidden in the stories, but now they are coming back. Because of the prophecy.'

'What prophecy?' Vidar asked.

'Oh, there is always a prophecy. I have counted three hundred and twenty-seven prophecies circulating in the tales told across Idriss.' Greer an' Lokh twirled until Vidar grabbed his shoulders to hold him still.

'What prophecy?'

Greer an' Lokh smiled. 'The one in the teachings of the Shepherd.'

'There's a book?'

The sorcerer shook his head. 'It is passed down from Seeker to Seeker.' He tapped his head. 'And locked up here. But they will tell if you ask. And I asked. *When the objects are found, the world is saved.*'

'Not destroyed?'

'Saved.'

Vidar returned his attention to the paintings. 'So these artefacts date from the time of the Shepherd. Three thousand years ago.' A revelation struck him. 'Whoever painted this must have had a good description of the artefacts. Unless they actually saw them.' He knelt down to scratch at the surface of the paintings. 'This isn't paint. What is it?'

'Something that could survive three thousand years without fading,' Cheyne said.

Greer an' Lokh did another dance, then caught himself when Vidar glared at him. 'Painted here to preserve their memory for all time,' he said. 'Oh, yes.'

'All these paintings are connected,' Vidar said. 'All from the time of the Shepherd. All important. They're telling a story. This one here, the sea journey. The man is in a foetal position, could be symbolic. Some kind of birth, the journey to life. The artefacts. The burning tree... the threat of destruction.'

Cheyne pointed to the white globe. 'If those are the artefacts, could this be the Prime Locator?'

'Yes!' Vidar said. 'That would make sense. The knowledge of it preserved. So...' He moved back and forth along the paintings and then pointed to the stone box on the hillside.

'The Tomb of the Shepherd.' Greer an' Lokh giggled. 'Would the Shepherd not want to keep something so important in a safe place?'

ALONG THE WALLS the sentries watched. The sun was a dim fire on the horizon when the first signs materialised. A terrible cry issuing from the forest as if from some enormous beast, and then a flash of flame that soared up high above the treetops. Not long after, there was another flash, nearer this time, appearing through the distant branches like lightning beneath dark clouds. After that came the thunder: armour and a heavy, marching step.

The storm was coming. The figures emerged from the forest the moment the sun fell away. In the gloom, tiny points of red light appeared, a hundred, five hundred, a thousand, more, drawing towards Idriss as relentlessly as death.

14

THE BATTLE AT
DEEPING GATE

IDRISS WAS FILLED with light, but the brassy
rumble of the approaching army beyond the
walls made every torch appear a little dimmer.
As the Order of Inquisitors gathered on the
Rolling Road, the atmosphere of anxiety in the
hot, sticky night grew more oppressive by the
moment. They all knew what was at stake, but
Asgrim thought it worth restating. He bounded on to the head of a statue of some forgotten
notary of Idriss's past and addressed the ranks
of green-cloaked women.

'I should be up there on the walls, preparing
to die for Idriss, but I am here with you
because a life is at stake,' he began. 'Every life
in Idriss is valuable. It is that belief that has
kept this city strong for so long. But here is
one life that we also hold in our hearts – yours

and mine. Know that we will not give up on Inquisitor Rhiannon as long as we have breath, whatever threat waits at our door. The Order of Inquisitors has always sought solutions to the crimes of Idriss, but here, now, is one that will challenge you to the limits of your abilities. Time runs short. The Red Man does not think like us.

'His crimes are characterised by madness, and he could be driven to kill at any moment.' He paused. 'If he has not done so already. And if he has killed, then it is vengeance we seek, and vengeance we shall have. But for now we must hold only one thought: Inquisitor Rhiannon's life is in our hands. Find her.'

As the crowd of Inquisitors broke up, Asgrim bounded down to Inquisitor Fabienne, who was waiting patiently for him.

'You wish to see me?' she said.

'To tell you that you are in charge of this enquiry.'

'Me? But Chief Inquisitor Serena would never condone that. Directing the entire Order of Inquisitors requires someone of the highest rank.'

'The Chief Inquisitor lost her right to have a voice when she failed to protect one of her own. Politics is a plague on this city, and it is time to return to higher values. Inquisitor Rhiannon always valued your abilities, and I trust her judgement.'

A flicker crossed Fabienne's hard face as she recognised and accepted the great responsibility Asgrim had placed on her shoulders. He could see then that he had made the right decision. 'Then you are sure the decision to continue the search of the catacombs is the correct one?' she asked.

'The Red Man has used them like a rat uses the sewers. It is what he knows, and it gives him access to almost the entire city. We have uncovered one of his lairs, but he will be using another, and it will be as well hidden as the last.'

Fabienne hesitated, and then said, 'Do you truly think she is still alive?'

'I dare not believe otherwise.'

In his face, Fabienne saw the meaning behind his words and nodded. 'Then I believe it too. Her sisters will find her.'

From beyond the wall came a thunderous metallic clanging. Asgrim knew what it was: the warriors of the Berex army banging the hilts of their swords against their breastplates, a sign that they had achieved formation and were ready for battle; it sounded eerily like the tolling of a funeral bell.

He nodded to Fabienne, and together they raced for the entrance to the catacombs.

* * *

IN THE DARK, Rhiannon worked feverishly at the bonds at her wrists, amid the constant fear that the Red Man was only inches away, ready to slash her throat at any moment. He had paid her four silent visits since the last time they had spoken, sometimes entering through the trapdoor without even the barest sound, alerting her to his presence only by his breath on her skin as he prowled near.

His constant returns reminded her of an animal checking its wounded prey, and there was something worryingly bestial in the way he circled her in the dark. Despite the intensity of the gloom, she also had the disturbing feeling that he could see her, catching the tiny iterations of fear that would occasionally cross her face, her fumbling with bonds knowing that he could stop her at any moment, scrutinising every aspect of her and finding her lacking.

But the last time he had visited there had been an irritation to his occasional bursts of movement that suggested impatience. She felt instinctively that time was running out.

When the trapdoor slammed shut with such force she almost cried out in shock, she knew she was right. The Red Man ran over to her and pressed his face close enough for her to feel his hot, meaty breath on her face. Small clicks and growls emanated from deep in his throat, both anxious and threatening. And now she could clearly smell the sour stink of his sweat, and she wondered if it was a sign of his state of mind, the products of his body responding to his spiralling madness.

The noises in his throat grew louder and more insistent, until they emerged in a guttural, breathless panting. The noise sounded somewhere between a mounting desperate sob and an orgasmic rush, and she feared that when it reached its peak he would strike.

Her heart thundered in her chest, but somehow she managed to keep her voice calm. 'Tell me your name,' she whispered.

Her words appeared to distract him, as she had intended. The heat of his breath pulled away as he retreated a step.

There was a long moment of silence, which to her seemed strangely as if he was trying to remember. Then he said in a juddering voice, 'J... J... Joshua.'

'Joshua,' she repeated warmly. 'Where do you come from, Joshua?'

A howl of pain that shocked her. Had she said the wrong thing?

'There!' he bellowed. 'Not here!' A whimper, then barely audibly, 'Not here.'

Rhiannon let his anxious breathing subside before asking, 'How can I help you?'

After a moment's thought, he said, 'You cannot.' Another moment passed and he added,

'Stupid. Can't think. Why you get? Why… you get? Why! Get! You! Need you don't…' His voice trailed off, and when he next spoke it was with startling and chilling clarity: 'I need a new face.'

While Rhiannon weighed the implications of this statement, he slipped silently away. The trapdoor clattered. Rhiannon returned her attention to her bonds with a furious intensity. Her time had already run out.

'IF YOU DO not stop being an obstacle,' Cheyne sighed, 'I cannot be responsible for my actions.'

Greer an' Lokh danced around his chamber, singing, and then dropped to a crouch, eyeing Cheyne slyly. 'None of us are truly responsible for our actions. We are all part of a bigger pattern.'

'Just get on with it. And do not think about palming those map-cubes. I will have your hands off at the wrists in a second.' He balanced his knife on the tip of two fingers.

The sorcerer was not in the least bit frightened. He danced across the room and threw a handful of leaves into the brazier so that a sickly pungent smoke billowed with a crackle and a spit.

'Shall we just try to get on?' Cheyne said wearily. 'We do, after all, have some things in common. A tenuous grip on morals, for one. And a complete disregard for human life, for another. It does not pay for us to be taking chunks out of ourselves with sharp objects.'

He looked out of the window, past the gleaming torches of the city and beyond the walls, where he could just make out the haze of other lights somewhere below. Occasionally a burst of Verlaine's fire would soar up into the sky, the liquid flames forming shapes by chance or design, a bird, a snake.

'They will attack soon,' Greer an' Lokh said. 'Are we strong enough to resist? Is this the end of Idriss?' He stared into the smoke from his brazier, seeing things that were beyond Cheyne's perception.

'All the more reason to find that damnable tomb quickly,' Cheyne said.

Greer an' Lokh tossed the map-cubes on to the brazier and the map rushed out to fill the room. The topography was as dark as the real landscape, but once Cheyne got among it he could begin to make out the details. It was eerie and beyond his understanding; he could even see the moonlight limning the treetops on a distant hillside.

He pointed to the painting of the Tomb of the Shepherd hanging on the wall. 'There are the features we need to find. The shape of that hill, like a ribcage when it is cracked open.

That distant mountain, like a blade protruding from a skull. And that tomb, which will be no bigger than a ripped-off fingernail on this map. What more do we need?'

Together they plunged into the midst of the forests, streams, and hills, searching for one tiny structure in a map of half the world.

VIDAR STOOD ON the walls and looked first one way, then the other. The entirety of the Crimson Hunt stretched out on either side, their colours proudly displayed. In the first instance they were armed with longbows and crossbows, but their supplies of arrows were limited. He had already sent word to every fletcher in the city to start work on new supplies, but with so few spare resources there was little they could do.

Idriss had never expected such a large attacking army to ever make it through the forest, and so they had only amassed enough weapons to deal with a force of a hundred at most; and that was believed to be excessive. The Crimson Hunt themselves were woefully outnumbered. Below, the heavy iron shutters had been lowered over the gates. As long as the walls survived, they would be safe, but with the power at Verlaine's disposal that was not guaranteed.

Vidar looked down at the eerie sight of more than a thousand flickering pinpricks of red light. The burning eyes of the enemy's warriors threatened mysterious power that was a wild card undermining any strategy he could invent.

'What is it about them?' LeStrange had appeared at his shoulder.

'You shouldn't be here. Get back to the palace where it's not so dangerous.'

'I want to help.'

'You can – by keeping an eye on Ashur and the other administrators. I don't trust them not to do anything stupid, even in the middle of a fight for our lives.'

'You can count on me. You know that. But you saved my life, and I wish to repay you.'

'In a city like this, you don't have to watch my back up here to do that. I'm just as likely to get a knife between the shoulder blades in the council chamber.'

They looked down the dizzying span of the walls to the sea of darkness that washed against the foot. The red lights, appearing then disappearing, could have been strange fish swimming in the deeps.

'The stories have already started in the court,' LeStrange began hesitantly, 'that these troops are all dead, raised up to destroy us, and thus unbeatable. Or they are creatures brought forth from the underworld.'

'They're men, that's all. Just like you and me.'

'The eyes–'

'All right, not quite like you and me. Verlaine, their leader, is feeding them some sort of power. Don't ask me what it does – we'll find out soon enough.'

Vidar tried to estimate the numbers, but the enemy was lost to the vast moon-shadow of the walls. Nor could he tell if they had any facilities for scaling the defences, but he presumed Verlaine would not have come unprepared.

'Vidar…?'

LeStrange's face had grown pale. Vidar looked around him and saw the familiar will-o'-the-wisps flicker into pallid life on every side.

'Not now,' he whispered bitterly to himself.

His ghosts, his permanent tormentors, always chose their moments to undermine him or bring about his end. He imagined that soon, with his killings spiralling, all he would see would be the spirits of his victims, stretching out to the horizon. And this time, he recognised a new face among them – Sam, staring at him with hateful, accusing eyes, trapped for ever in the miserable twilight world of the Vampire Jewel.

Screaming silently, the ghosts tore at their hair and shook their fists at the sky. And then their voices swept in with that second's delay. 'Death is coming!' they howled in voices like a gale against stone. 'You all will die!'

Vidar feared for the morale of his own men. They already faced insurmountable odds, and the last thing they needed was a portent of their own demise from one among them. But as he glanced at the Huntsmen, he was surprised to see their faces grow more resolute, some even smiling. Whispers moved rapidly along the lines: 'The ghosts are here. The dead fight on our side.'

'They are right,' LeStrange said. 'We have the Ghost Warrior.'

Vidar placed one foot on the wall and leaned over, yelling defiantly to the enemy far below: 'See! The dead are on our side! And soon you'll be joining them!'

His voice disappeared into the gulf, and a moment later a roar rose up from below. Across the sweep of the darkness, fires erupted. The attack was beginning.

TEN MINUTES AFTER LeStrange had retreated to the safety of the palace, the first fireball crashed against the walls. It did little damage, but in its sudden burst of light, Vidar saw activity at the foot of the walls. The army was massing with what looked to be some kind of expandable ladders. Vidar had never seen their like before, and guessed that Verlaine had brought their design from the distant home they both shared.

Soon after, grappling hooks rocketed out of the gloom. Vidar ordered his men to cut the ropes attached to them, but they were made out of some material that resisted the sawing of the blades.

'Hold your arrows!' Vidar ordered. 'Let them come!'

He watched as the ropes on every hook grew taut. Listened as the ladders rattled against the walls. Gradually, figures emerged from the dark, swarming up the sides like spiders.

'How the hell are they climbing so quickly in that armour?' he muttered.

Their fiery eyes glimmering, the enemy warriors drew closer right along the length of the eastern wall. Vidar knew the same scene was likely being enacted along the western and southern flanks running up to the river.

He waited until they had reached a height where any fall would kill them, and then yelled his order: 'Fire!'

Arrows rained down, slamming into the climbing warriors. Vidar waited for the screams, the bodies plummeting backwards off rope and ladder, but there was none of it. The warriors continued to climb, the arrows protruding from necks and faces and eye sockets.

Now he knew what Verlaine had given them that made their eyes burn so. 'They can't feel pain!' he called out. 'Don't rely on winging them! Take your time! Go for the kill!'

The seemingly indestructible enemy unnerved the Huntsmen and so many arrows were wasted that Vidar had to rush up and down the walls, encouraging them to hold their nerve.

When the enemy warriors were only twenty feet below the lip of the wall, he gave the order to ignite and unleash Greer an' Lokh's combustible liquid. Along the wall, the cauldrons burst into flames, sending clouds of stinking black smoke upwards. With reinforced gloves, the Huntsmen assigned to the task tipped the cauldrons and a sheet of flame rushed down the wall, lighting the no-man's-land between the city and the forest as if it were day. For the first time, Vidar saw the true extent of the army: they filled every available space of that land and stretched back into the trees. For a moment, Vidar feared Verlaine had broken the entire population of Berex on the wheel of his army.

The burning liquid washed off many of the climbers by the sheer force of the downpour. They fell, afire, and exploded on contact with the ground. But others continued to climb, oblivious that they were burning like the manikins the children threw on the bonfires at the Fire Festival. The Huntsmen watched in horror as they rose up the walls, the air thick with the smell of bubbling human flesh.

'They're already dead!' Vidar yelled. 'They just don't know it yet! Prepare to repel!'

The Huntsmen drew their swords and waited. After a moment, the burning men began to appear at the lip of the wall, climbing over and drawing their swords, even as their tendons contracted and their muscles grew inflexible with the heat.

Vidar led the attack with a frenzy that broke through the fears of the men around him. Gripping his sword two-handed, he hacked and slashed, taking down two, three, five men in half a minute.

And with each one that lost a head or was stabbed through the heart, he felt an explosion of energy rushing along his arms and into the amber jewel. His head was suffused with light, followed by a euphoria that was sickeningly addictive.

The Huntsmen followed his lead and overcame their fears, easily despatching the burning warriors. When the walls were clear, he ordered the men to step back from the edge to check their supplies. All the combustible liquid had been exhausted, and the arrows would not last another wave.

While he walked the lines, bolstering the morale of his men, the fires below were extinguished and silence returned to the no-man's-land. After a while it was broken by the lone voice of Verlaine rising up strong and tinged with irony from the deep dark.

'Do you feel that, Luke? That rush? Do you realise the potential of your artefact yet? Don't feel guilty – these people are beneath us. They're already dead. All of them. They're just waiting for their clock to run out. Don't get sentimental for the dead, Luke.'

There was silence while Verlaine waited for Vidar to respond, but then he continued, 'You're being a fool, you know. Once those memories start creeping back into your head you'll realise how much. Nothing here matters. Everything we have is back home, and they're relying on us. Beth is relying on you, Luke. Do you remember Beth?'

A jolt ran through him. The name was unfamiliar, but something inside him responded. He felt hot and queasy, and had to crouch down to catch his breath.

I'll wait for you.

'I can understand you having fun here,' Verlaine continued. 'I am! It's like looting all the riches while the shop is burning down. But sooner or later we've got to get back. We've got to complete the mission. These people here are nothing. Weak relics. Echoes of humanity. You can't see them as people. You can't. Remember the training! But you, Luke... you could be a threat to this mission. If you decide to ignore what I'm saying, if you carry on opposing me, everything is at stake. And for that reason alone, Luke, you know I have to be prepared to kill you. There's that training again! We can't let sentimentality stand in the way of our objective. This is about higher stakes than you and me. This is about the survival of a civilisation. It's about belief, and values. So I'm giving you this opportunity. Join me now. I'll tell you everything you need to know, and then you'll see that I'm telling the truth. I have to give you this chance, for old times' sake, for the hope that we can still see the mission through together. Come to me now. Order your men to open the gates. I give you my word that we won't hurt them. And then we can talk.'

Vidar knew Verlaine was lying. It was stitched into the very timbre of his voice, and in his arrogance he couldn't even bring himself to hide it. But even if he hadn't been lying, Vidar wouldn't have agreed. A while ago, perhaps; but not now.

'Last chance, Luke. After this, it'll all be over. You're as dead as they are.'

Vidar counted sixty seconds of silence and then Verlaine said, 'All right. I'm sorry, but it's your choice.'

A second later Vidar saw a single bright light in the darkness below, and then there was a feeling like a giant bubble of air rapidly expanding.

'Everybody down!' he yelled.

Many of the Huntsmen responded in time; some did not. Liquid flame flooded out at speed from Verlaine's gauntlet in a tidal wave that washed over half of Idriss. Vidar rolled on to his back on the flags of the walkway and saw the sky above him on fire as far as he could see. Superheated air rushed over them, knocking some of the Huntsmen off the walkway to the city far below, searing the lungs of others so they died in choking pain. More still were caught in the tidal wave of flames, igniting where they stood and dying in an instant, or running along the walkway screaming as the flames engulfed them.

Pulling himself into a crouching position behind the parapet, Vidar estimated they had lost nearly a third of the Huntsmen in that single attack.

He barely had time to consider the implications before the barrage began. Flaming barrels, balls of pitch-soaked material, and burning logs were propelled from no-man's-land, arcing over the walls to crash on to the nearest houses. The flames shot up through the shattered roofs instantly, threatening to tear through the closely packed buildings on the east side of Idriss.

Vidar couldn't afford to release any of the Huntsmen to tackle the blazes, but before he could call for help from within the city, people flooded from their homes with buckets to fill at the cisterns. Within minutes, they had organised into teams to fight the fires, the rioting long forgotten.

As the barrage died down, the second wave of warriors attempted to scale the walls. Grappling hooks arced up and bit into the stone of the ramparts, and the clatter of the extending ladders echoed on every side.

Examining his depleted forces, Vidar wondered if they would have enough men to repel the invaders. 'We have the advantage!' he called. 'Don't forget that! Attack the minute their heads come over the ramparts!'

As they waited, swords and axes gripped, his ghosts raged all around him, shrieking and howling and demanding the invaders kill Vidar, kill him now and save the world! For the first time that he could remember, he ignored them, focusing all his attention on the lip of the ramparts, waiting for the first movement as the sounds from below grew louder.

When they came, he responded without thinking. His sword became a blur, tearing through heads and bodies. Hot blood showered him in gouts, painting his face and hair red, running behind his armour to cover every part of him. Death was everywhere, but he was filled with a white, transcendental light, so that he felt as if he was in a dream, observing a hellish warrior who cut through things that resembled people, but were not, could not be; just echoes of humanity.

In the dream, he moved relentlessly along the ramparts, carving a path through any warriors that scrambled on to the walkway, despatching others almost without thinking. Engulfed by a joy so powerful it felt like a drug, he became a giant towering over the city, the world.

Through the haze, he had the dim recognition that a light was issuing from him, warm and amber, and that it drove the ghosts away so that they flickered and faded and fought to hold on to their foothold in the world.

'I am a furnace,' he said to himself, dreamily. 'I am a beacon.'

How many did he kill? He lost count after thirty. The Huntsmen looked to be on the brink of being overwhelmed as more and more of the Berex warriors clambered over the ramparts, but when Vidar attacked it was like receiving the reinforcements of ten men, twenty, growing with every death. His energy never faded, despite the force it took to hack through armour and bone, and the distance he covered back and forth along the ramparts. He was everywhere. He felt as if he could fight all night, never stop, ever.

In moments of clarity that broke though his dream, he was surprised to see the expressions on the faces of the Huntsmen. Every time he neared, they looked on him with an awe and respect he had never seen before. Though short in number and forced back by the enemy, they renewed their efforts, fighting as if they were fresh to battle.

And then he realised there was no more enemy left. A wave of disappointment washed over him, and he was sickened that he felt that way. Still burning with a fierce energy, he fought to contain it. But even as he did so he yearned for that elation again, and feared he would probably desire it all his life.

What Verlaine had hinted at was true: the more he killed, the more lives he drained, the more powerful he became. Killing was a drug, and he could see how addictive it might easily become if he ever lost control.

The irony was not lost on him. If he did not kill, he died, his own life consumed by the jewel. If he killed to feed it, it demanded more and more – he demanded more and more to gain the euphoric sensation of bursting life – until he became a monster. Somewhere in between was the narrow territory of his humanity, constantly under threat.

Finally, he collapsed to his knees, resting on his sword, his breath ragged, his vision blurred. But when he looked up, the Huntsmen stood proudly along the ramparts. They raised their swords and shouted to the night sky: 'Vidar! Hero of Idriss! Idriss the Strong! Never defeated!'

DEEP IN THE catacombs, the barrage sounded like distant thunder, the vibrations reaching through brick and stone and bringing showers of dust from the tunnel roof overhead. Overcome by frustration, Asgrim paced around the confluence of five tunnels, which he estimated was somewhere beneath the Fire Gardens.

Inquisitor Fabienne stood with one hand to her temple, attempting to roll back the Unknown Shadow.

'Are you sure?' he said.

'It could take us days to cover the whole of the catacombs, even with the entire Order working constantly.' She unfurled a parchment and crouched down to study it on the floor. The ink was faded and in many areas non-existent, but it was a rudimentary map of the catacombs that she had located in the Store of the Ages. 'Much of it has not even been mapped.'

'And why would it be?' Asgrim said bitterly. 'Who would want to promenade down here in the dusty dark?'

'The tunnels below the oldest part of Idriss are as shown. But I am receiving reports from the Inquisitors exploring the fringes of the network that there are newer tunnels stretching far beyond the walls.'

'There are?'

'Many. It is impossible to tell when they were built, or for what reason, though it is not in living memory. Perhaps our forebears felt that as time progressed, the original catacombs could not cope with the flow of bones.'

'A city built on the dead and excrement!' Asgrim snorted. 'Sometimes I yearn for the frozen plains of my home. Everywhere was clean, and the air was fresh, and we were never troubled by things like this!'

In his frustration, he punched the wall with his ruined hand, splitting his knuckles so that blood spattered in the dust. He didn't feel the pain.

'My Inquisitors have also discovered steps in four locations. There may be more.'

'Leading where?'

'Down to another level of tunnels, even older than these. We do not know how deep the catacombs progress.'

Asgrim cursed loudly. He realised how lucky he had been to locate the Red Man's odour in the catacombs the first time. Confident in his hideaway, the Red Man located it off one of the main arteries, but now he could well have disappeared deep into the bowels beneath the city.

After a brief lull, more tremors came from another barrage. Each jolt counted away a moment of Rhiannon's life, and escalated the fear and desperation Asgrim felt. He had never experienced its like before; it threatened to paralyse his thoughts with anxiety, but if that happened he knew he would never find Rhiannon. He punched the wall again, aware of Fabienne's concerned gaze upon him.

'I have been charged with the task of finding Inquisitor Rhiannon,' he stressed. 'I will not let Vidar down. There must be a way to find where the Red Man took her. I am but a poor northern lout with few brains, but you and your sisters have intellects like knives. Find me a path and I will follow it to the end.'

Fabienne nodded. She sat cross-legged, closed her eyes, and retreated deep into the Unknown Shadow.

* * *

BLOOD SLICKED RHIANNON'S wrists where the ropes had chafed through her skin, but she continued to work them, despite the pain. They were slippery under her fingers now, but she could feel them loosening. Soon she would be free. Did she have enough time?

From the other side of the trapdoor, she had heard the Red Man raging until his throat was raw. Sometimes the voice would spiral down into a quiet but unintelligible mutter before rising to a crescendo of pain and anger once more. His mind was more fragile than any she had experienced before, and it appeared to be deteriorating. It would not be long before something deep within him broke and he would burst in and slaughter her in a desperate, futile attempt to ease his suffering.

He had been quiet for a while, and she thought he might be sleeping. But then she started suddenly when his voice rose up in the room not far from her; once again she had not heard him enter.

'How long till this is all over?' His voice had a crystal clarity of intelligence that she had not heard before, but it was laced with a deep bitterness.

'You sound... different, Joshua–'

'Don't call me that!' he snapped. 'You're not allowed to call me that!'

She was afraid he would attack her in his rage so she hastily apologised.

'I've got a new face,' he muttered. 'I can see things clearly again.'

'Your mind calms when you get a new face?' she asked hesitantly.

'For a while. Then it all starts to break up again!' He hammered a fist on the stone flags with anger. 'It's this damned ring! Why did I ever put it on? I should never have listened to Reichert. It's eating my mind away. Soon I'll be nothing more than a mass of emotion.'

Rhiannon was almost afraid to speak to him. His feelings were so finely balanced that the faintest unintentional slight could throw him into an uncontrollable rage, but her Inquisitor's mind was desperate for answers.

'Why did you come to Idriss?' she ventured.

'We need the artefacts.' Though he answered her question, she could tell from his tone that he was speaking to himself; she was just a prompt for his shifting sanity. 'The jewel. Dead or alive, Reichert said. I mean, he was one of the team! How could Reichert be so cold-hearted?' He sighed. 'He's right, I suppose. The mission comes first.'

'What mission?'

'Shut up!' he bellowed.

He threw himself across the room and struck her with the back of his hand. Her head snapped around and cracked against the wall. She saw stars and tasted blood.

'Stop it!' he continued. 'Can't you see? The emotions are eating me up! I try to think, but they take me over. My thoughts are just drifting away like sand through a sieve. Hah! I was one of the rational ones. Not like Luke!' He started to sob, and then took a deep breath and steadied himself. 'It's these artefacts. The power in them just destroys you. Reichert can handle it. He doesn't care what it does to him. But I don't want to lose my mind!'

In the dark, Rhiannon heard him throw himself against the wall repeatedly. Already the clarity of his words was starting to fade.

'I kill and get a new face, and it's all so clear! And then when it goes, it's just an impression... like figures in the fog. Find the Tomb of the Shepherd. But then it's just the Shepherd, the Shepherd, echoing around, and I know it's something to do with the Shepherd, but I don't know what. And I see you leaving the temple, and I connect, and I bring you back, but you're nothing to do with it at all! You're no help!'

Rhiannon pressed herself back, still working her bonds, as he threw himself at another wall.

'That priest couldn't help. He knew nothing! Or if he did he wouldn't tell me! I need to find the tomb, so I can find where the Prime

Locator has been hidden. And then Reichert can gather all the artefacts and we can leave! Home! Finally! And maybe then they can get this ring off me, and I can get my mind back.'

Rhiannon forgot herself and said, 'Magic always demands a price.'

'Magic! Yes, you would say that. Magic!' He laughed coldly before adding with contempt, 'They were right. You're already dead. Why should I worry?'

She could hear his deep breathing as he fought to steady himself, but at the same time he was plucking at his clothes with mounting intensity.

Finally, he said, 'There's no point keeping you here. You're no use. You're just cluttering up the place.'

'Just forget me,' she said. 'I cannot hurt you.'

'You're already forgotten. You've been forgotten for a long time.'

'Go, search for the tomb. It must be near here somewhere. Do not wait with me. Time is short.'

He laughed. 'Time is never short. That's the whole point! We've got all the time in the world!'

'Please–'

'Shut up!'

The bonds were almost loose now. She just needed him to leave her alone for a little while longer.

'I think I'm going to kill you now,' he said calmly. 'My knife. Where is my knife?' He cursed loudly, and then leaped to the trapdoor. It crashed shut behind him, and she could hear him tearing around the room beyond, opening drawers and throwing furniture as his rage overwhelmed him. After a while, he calmed, until she could only hear sobs and loud, unintelligible mutterings once again.

THE FOURTH WAVE had passed and Vidar blazed like a star. With each new round of killing, he found it harder to delve down inside himself and find the place where his rational thoughts had retreated away from the burning light of euphoria.

When he was in his state of ecstasy, anything was impossible. But each time he escaped it, he saw that hope was receding fast. Verlaine had released several more infernos from his gauntlet. It appeared to take time for him to build the energy he needed to unleash the power, but its force was never diminished.

The last blast from the gauntlet had washed the liquid fire up the length of the walls, and now cracks had started to appear caused by the extreme heat. How long before the walls began to crumble? Vidar recalled the ruined fort in the forest, the gash in the walls that had signalled the end as the primal fury of the forest gained access to the last bastion of civilisation and crushed it in an instant.

The Huntsmen had already been reduced to half their number, and they were exhausted from repelling the attacks. Swords hung limply from leaden arms, heads were bowed, while others lay against the ramparts slick with blood, nursing wounds, from cuts that needed stitches to missing limbs. The physicians moved rapidly to stem the blood wherever they could, but there were not enough of them either.

Cheyne arrived as the glow left Vidar and his shoulders sagged from the dismal re-entry to reality. Vidar could tell from his friend's face that he had no good news.

'I have spent all night searching the map with that dancing loon and we have found nothing. I should be up here, where my skills can be put to good use.'

'You'd be a help, Cheyne, but you wouldn't make enough of a difference. There are too many of them.'

Cheyne peered over the rampart into the dark. 'Who would ever have thought an army of that size would make it through the forest? I hate it when tradition is overthrown. They should be half-eaten and mad.'

'It's not just the numbers. Verlaine's gauntlet is simply too powerful. And the army doesn't feel pain thanks to that other artefact, so however much we hurt them they just keep on coming. Only a killing blow makes any difference.'

Cheyne surveyed the depleted forces and silently agreed. 'We may need to start drafting in able-bodied men.'

'That's only going to delay the inevitable. We need something that can counter Verlaine's gauntlet.' He rested a hand on Cheyne's shoulder. 'You have to find the tomb.'

Cheyne nodded. 'I will try again. It will be a joy to spend more time with my friend the sorcerer. I have even started wearing nose plugs. But if we find this Prime Locator, there is no guarantee it will show us an artefact close enough to be of use.'

'The paintings were kept safe in Idriss. The map-cube was stored here. The city is obviously important to the Shepherd's religion and whoever hid all those magic objects away. I'd say there's a good chance there's an artefact around somewhere.'

A light came on in Cheyne's eyes. 'Of course! I missed the obvious!' He turned and ran from the battlements back in the direction of Greer an' Lokh's tower.

15

HUNTING THE RED MAN

ONE FINAL BARRAGE struck the city before dawn, setting ablaze a vast area in the lee of the walls. Crowds of people fought to contain it with buckets of water, but it had already spread through a multitude of homes before it was brought under control. A pall of thick smoke now hung over the south side of the city and a heavy smell of wet, charred wood filled the air.

But Vidar had noted that the barrage had not been as intensive, and he realised the Berex army was running low on their own supplies. They would need to hack down some of the forest to find enough projectiles for a renewed assault.

Weary now the flush of killing had worn off, he leaned on the ramparts and watched the sun come slowly up above the trees. Far below, there was no sign of the tiny red lights burning in the eyes of the enemy. Back to normal, able to feel pain like any other man; Vidar guessed they wouldn't attack again until night fell. That gave them a day's grace to find the answers they desperately needed. They wouldn't last another night.

Verlaine had sent wave after wave of his men to their deaths without a qualm. He spoke clearly about the people of Gardia being lesser – *already dead*. Vidar wondered if he was really just as callous as Verlaine, with only his lack of memory giving him an approximation of humanity.

Before he reached an answer, LeStrange walked up, grinning broadly. 'Tales of your prowess are already spinning wildly through the streets. You are now officially legendary, Vidar.'

Vidar glanced at the remaining Huntsmen who were resting and recovering along the battlements. Occasionally, they would talk to the physicians or the citizens who nervously brought them bread and water, while glancing at him with that same awed look he had seen earlier. As the citizens returned to the city streets, they took with them stories of a man who had torn through the enemy like a force of nature, not like a vampire who had sucked their lives to make himself stronger.

'We survived the night,' he said, 'but from here it's going to get harder.'

'The people have placed their trust in you. The great Vidar, the Ghost Warrior, will deliver them from the enemy.'

He ignored LeStrange's gentle teasing and said, 'Any news on Rhiannon?'

'Your deputy is still searching the catacombs with the Order of Inquisitors. If any advance has been made, I have not heard.'

'And Ashur and the administrators?'

'Sequestered in the council chamber, plotting.' He gave an embarrassed smile. 'I do not wish to appear disloyal, but—'

'Go on.'

'They face a quandary. If you lead Idriss to victory, it will be difficult for them to control you and impose their will upon the city, in terms of a successor, particularly if you wish to oppose it.'

'And if I'm defeated here, it's all over for them too.'

LeStrange nodded, smiling. 'I have never seen Ashur so torn.'

'So if I was them, I'd want a victory here on the walls, and me no longer a problem. Dead, in fact.'

'That solution would work well for them. Watch your back, Vidar. It would be easy for a knife to find the wrong mark in the middle of battle.'

'To be honest, that's the least of my worries right now.' On the cobbles below, he caught sight of groups of men walking steadily towards the walls. More joined them by the minute, swelling their numbers until they filled the streets. 'What's going on?'

'Ah, yes. That would be the volunteers.'

'I didn't call for any.'

'You did not need to. Word has already travelled through the city of the bravery of the Crimson Hunt and the losses they have incurred. The people know you will not survive the night without reinforcements, and so, here they are.'

Vidar watched the steady tread of the men, young and old, fit and carrying the excesses of the taverns and the dining houses in Red Hill. Many had probably never held a weapon in their lives. They would be of little use, presenting an impressive show of numbers along the battlements only to die in the first wave. Yet the fact that they were volunteering while aware of their shortcomings touched Vidar deeply.

'I'm not going to let them sacrifice themselves.'

'They are the strength of Idriss – you told them that, and they know it in their hearts. They will give up their own lives to preserve the safety of our city, as you are prepared to sacrifice your own life. You stand together, or fall together. They know this. You are one of them, Vidar.'

LeStrange's words struck notes deep within him, troubling him and inspiring him at the same time. Humbly, he nodded towards the volunteers. 'I'd better meet them. Thank them. But after that we find a solution that is going to save this city.'

'YOU COULD HAVE left the map-cubes with me,' Greer an' Lokh sang quietly. He stabbed a knife lazily into a hunk of indeterminate meat that was abandoned on a side table in his main chamber.

'Of course I could. If my brains had leaked out of my ears.' Cheyne marched brightly into the centre of the room and motioned for the sorcerer to join him.

'Again?'

'Again.'

Greer an' Lokh eyed him curiously. 'You are filled with the light of inspiration.'

'Patterns.' Cheyne raised an exclamatory finger. 'Have you ever thought about patterns?

Oh, yes. Then why did you not seek them here?'

Sniffily, Greer an' Lokh took the map-cubes and tossed them into the brazier. The landscape rushed out across the chamber, now bright with the morning sun.

'Idriss was the centre of the religion of the Shepherd.'

'The religion was strong here–' the sorcerer began.

'No, it was the centre. Because the paintings, dating back to the time of the Shepherd and of clear import, are kept here. As are the texts and other religious paraphernalia archived at the Store of the Ages, which, in itself, was established to keep the matters of the way of the Shepherd safe for all time.'

Greer an' Lokh considered this, and nodded thoughtfully. A little dance of joy indicated he agreed with Cheyne's analysis.

'Perhaps, in his day, the Shepherd even walked the streets of Idriss. That matters not a jot to me. Another charlatan on the streets of this city is neither here nor there. But it is entirely plausible that if his religion was here, he was here too. And if his religion remained here, for three thousand years, then it is plausible to suggest he died here too. And if he died here–'

'He is buried nearby!' Greer an' Lokh scrambled to the edge of the map where the river curved around towards Idriss on the missing section. 'Yet... we examined every area. Many times.'

Cheyne pointed towards the painting of the tomb, and indicated the landscape in the background. 'I wonder, perhaps, if my brain did leak out of my ears during the course of the night. The scenery we search... the scenery of, possibly, three thousand years ago—'

'Has changed! Yes, yes, yes, the upheaval they speak of in the stories that brought the spire to the ground!'

'And look – so few trees! This was a time before the great forest grew to its current extent. We search again, for a hill that may now lie beneath the thick forest, with a mountain that may have been laid low or thrown higher in the meantime.'

For five minutes, they eagerly manipulated the map along the edge that bordered Idriss until Greer an' Lokh exclaimed, 'Yes, yes! I have it!' With one long finger, he pushed gently through the trees to indicate a stone box, now half-crumbled, hidden by dense, thick-trunked oaks.

'That hill would once have had clear views over Idriss,' Cheyne said, 'and would have been visible to all within the city. Of course,

that would be perfect for those fools who need
the comfort of a fairy tale. The littlest lambs,
the desperate flock, always watched by their
Shepherd.'

'What now?'

'Now,' Cheyne said bitterly, 'we get Vidar
and go back into that damnable forest.'

FABIENNE CLUTCHED A sheaf of maps of the
city and the catacombs beneath as she and
Asgrim hurried down the broad marble steps
in the shadow of the Temple of the Shepherd.

'You are sure?' he asked.

'Yes. I have checked the position of our Inquisitors in the catacombs at the time that Inquisitor
Rhiannon was taken from the Temple. Most of
the main central tunnels were occupied. The Red
Man could only have taken her through a very
narrow sector of the catacombs.'

'And this should give us an even more exact
location.' They drew towards two Inquisitors
guarding a body sprawled across the cobbles,
the eyes missing. 'He has a new face.'

'He emerged from the catacombs somewhere in this vicinity,' Fabienne said. She
dropped to the cobbles to spread out the maps,
indicating a very narrow portion of an already
defined sector. 'Somewhere here.'

Asgrim turned slowly, taking in the temple,
the Store of the Ages, and the palace itself. 'I

want all Inquisitors to move in on this area.
Inform Vidar and Cheyne that we are closing
in on the Red Man... and Rhiannon.'

'Do you think there is still time?' Fabienne
asked.

Asgrim flashed a lupine glare at her. She
nodded, and moved quickly away to carry out
his orders.

RHIANNON'S HEART POUNDED so furiously
the thunder of the blood obscured the
sounds of the Red Man sharpening his knife
in the adjoining room. Her fingers tugged at
her bonds, slipping on the blood, trying to
make some sense of the knots in the dark.
She thought when she first felt them it
would have been easier, and cursed her arrogance.

Every few moments, she would think she
heard the trapdoor opening and stop, her
breath ragged. Her life could be marked in
minutes, perhaps seconds. Tears of frustration
stung her eyes. Why would the rope not come
loose? She tugged at it, but realised that was
only making it worse. She needed to remain
calm.

Taking a deep, steadying breath, she concentrated closely on the bonds, exorcising her
fears and stilling her mind. Her fingers moved
carefully and skilfully.

It was only when she broke her concentration a minute later that she realised the knife-sharpening had stopped.

Silence filled the building. Her heart began to beat faster once more. She resisted the urge to call out in apprehension and listened for even the slightest sound. Was the Red Man in the room with her?

For several long minutes, she remained still, imagining him watching her with his animal-eyes that could see in the dark. *He leaves nothing in his passing*, a nagging voice informed her from the depths of her head. *You will not hear death approaching. Silence is the tone of death. Leaving nothing in its passing.*

That warning voice made her realise it was impossible to rely on her senses. But she could always rely on her analytical Inquisitor's mind. If she attacked, from which direction would she come? The front, where she could be kicked and scratched? Or from the side?

She quickly scurried into the nearby corner so one flank was defended, and waited again. Even though she had convinced herself he was in the room with her, the rush took her by surprise. His roar was that of an animal loosed upon a vulnerable prey, and she smelled a sudden burst of sour sweat on the air rushing towards her.

At the last, she ducked from where she perceived the path of the knife to be, almost flattening herself on the floor. She came up just as quickly underneath him. He went up on her back and crashed against the wall behind her.

And then she was on her feet. Her wrists slipped free from the bonds she had loosened only a moment earlier, and she grasped the rope firmly as she spun around. She could see nothing, had no idea where the knife was, but she continued to trust her instincts. As he came up, spitting and thrashing and yelling guttural noises, she fluidly looped the rope, grabbed for his hair, and slipped it around his neck, pulling hard.

The noises became frenzied gargling as he tore at the loop around his throat. Rhiannon managed to get herself behind him and dragged him across the room, pulling tighter with each tug. The noises diminished; his movements slowed.

Just as she thought she had him, he found new energy and lashed out with the knife. It raked across her forearm, slicing through flesh. She felt the blood bubble and race down her arm to her wrist, but she did not cry out. She only pulled tighter, and finally he did halt. The knife clattered to the floor. He was not dead, she knew that, but her head was spinning from the shock of her wound and the last thing she wanted was to collapse unconscious as he recovered.

Dropping the rope, she threw herself at the wall, frantically feeling all around in the dark for the trapdoor. Along one wall, then another, she searched, her movements becoming more desperate as she lost her bearings, all the time trying to listen for sounds of the Red Man coming to consciousness. He would not let her escape again.

She felt her way along another wall, moving down, then up, down, then up, suddenly terrified she had gone all around the room and missed the trapdoor somehow. Her nails tore on the damp stone.

A moan issued behind her.

Renewing her efforts, she tried to search systematically when all she wanted to do was hammer on the wall and cry out for someone to help her.

Another moan, louder, the sound of twitching movement.

And then her hands closed on an iron ring and she wrenched it back. The trapdoor swung open. Frantically she clambered into another small room that was half-lit by a candle in the corridor beyond, slamming the trapdoor behind her.

The room was filled with shattered furniture and food scattered across the floor. She tripped over the whetstone the Red Man had been using and went sprawling, cursing even as she hit the ground hard. Though winded, she was up quickly and scrambling out of the door just as she heard the trapdoor opening.

In the corridor, she had no idea which way to run. It was a maze of tiny, empty rooms and branching, low-ceilinged corridors, only intermittently lit by torches.

Behind her, snarls and low bestial rumbles echoed as the Red Man staggered around the room, still dazed. 'Coming,' he croaked. Then louder: 'Coming!'

She chose a direction and ran, this way, then that, along corridors that doubled-back, before taking a branching route, but everywhere looked the same, and everywhere appeared to be leading nowhere, if not back to the point where she had started. Her bearings gone, she paused again and listened for the sounds of pursuit. The odd acoustics of the place sent the cracks of the Red Man's footsteps echoing so wildly it was impossible to pinpoint their location.

As she gripped the wound on her arm, a burst of anger flushed out her fear. He had wounded her twice now, and she would not be hurt again.

Finally, she came to a set of rooms filled with piles of old furniture, canvases, old cloth, and boxes. She felt weak from the blood loss and realised it was futile to keep running. She chose one room at random and threw herself inside, crawling beneath a precarious pile of tables and chairs covered by a tarpaulin. At the back, against the wall, she lay quietly and attempted to slow her breath so it would not give her away. Her heart felt as though it was about to burst from her chest.

As she peered out from under the furniture, she noticed something that made her panic flare once more. In the sliver of light from where she had left the door ajar, she could see spatters of her blood leading directly to her hiding place. If she could see it, the Red Man would too.

Minutes passed while she prayed that he had already given up and left. But then she heard a faintest tread moving along the corridor without. The footsteps drew nearer. Their softness told her he was prowling, probably smelling the air as Asgrim did. But he was not afraid, for he made no attempt to achieve his usual silence. He wanted her to hear his approach. He wanted her scared and unable to defend herself.

And she would not be afraid, she vowed to herself. She would never show him fear, even if it was her last act of defiance.

The door creaked open.

His shadow broke up the quadrant of light from the lantern hanging in the corridor. *Move on*, she thought. *Do not come in. Do not see the blood.*

A moment when he could have gone either way, and then he stepped into the room. His boots fell into her narrow field of view from beneath the tables and chairs. She saw for the first time that they were stained with the blood of his victims.

Slowly, he looked around, until he came to a halt next to the splatters of blood. Had he seen them?

His roar was deafening as he tore into the pile of furniture, throwing chairs and tables behind him as he ripped his way to her. She screamed in shock, then briefly hated herself for it. Then he was upon her, his rough hands tearing her to her feet, her head bouncing off wooden furniture.

Instinctively she brought her forearm up into his face and felt his nose break. He staggered backwards, and that was when she saw he was holding the knife.

Before she could react, the door crashed open and what she thought was a wild animal burst in. It flung itself at the Red Man, snapping and rending. As the blood flew like rain, she saw it was Asgrim and almost cried out with joy. Equally matched, they fought furiously, crashing over the furniture and tearing at each other in a frenzy.

As they brawled, Rhiannon stumbled over the chairs and tables to the door. Just as she reached it, the Red Man lunged, grabbing her ankle and dragging her back. With his knife, he attempted to slash her tendons to paralyse her.

Propelling himself to break the Red Man's grip, Asgrim thrust Rhiannon out of the way. Wrong-footed, he allowed the Red Man an opening to ram the knife to the hilt into his shoulder. Rhiannon cried out as she saw the pain lance across Asgrim's face. By then he had staggered back and the Red Man had rounded on her with his knife poised. Backed into the space behind the door, she had nowhere to turn.

As the Red Man thrust his blade towards her belly, she caught sight of Asgrim hurling himself towards them. With blood spraying from his shoulder, he arched his back and curled around the Red Man's torso. Ramming his own knife into his opponent's chest, Asgrim let his momentum carry him around so he could use his own body to shield Rhiannon from the Red Man's blow.

As Rhiannon crashed back with Asgrim's dead weight upon her, the Red Man looked down with a surprised expression at the knife embedded in his chest. Blood pumped from around the blade.

'Die!' Asgrim croaked. 'Die and go to hell!'

Seeing his life flowing away from him, the Red Man lurched to one side, and then stumbled out of the door.

'You saved me,' Rhiannon gasped when she was sure her tormentor was gone.

'You seemed to be doing a good job of saving yourself.'

Rhiannon planted a relieved kiss on Asgrim's lips. They felt cold and dry, and it was then she noticed the rapidly growing pool of blood around him. 'Oh,' she said.

He smiled. 'I fear my dreams run away from me.'

Rhiannon tried to staunch the flow from the chest wound, but the blood bubbled out rapidly around her fingers. 'I can get help.'

'It is too late.'

'No—'

'I know a lethal wound when I see one.'

His calmness made her dismay even worse. 'Greer an' Lokh can help. He did it before,' she said firmly.

'No. That was a singular experience. I lived the last few days on time that was not my own.' He smiled warmly. 'And it served its purpose, for it allowed me an experience that has made my life richer: your company.'

'Oh, Asgrim.' Trying to hold back her tears, she took his hand and gave it a squeeze. 'You should not have sacrificed your life for me. I am not worth it.'

'You are. You shine so brightly.' He coughed; blood splashed on his chin, and she wiped it away. 'There is more to life than surviving at all costs. There are higher matters to consider, of honour and duty, of morals and love. And that choice we make at the point when life and death are in the balance tells us who we truly are. Sometimes we are a mystery to ourselves, even up to that point.'

'Hush. Do not talk. Save your strength–'

'My strength is no use to me now.' He laughed weakly. 'There is something I must tell you, for I do not want you thinking badly of me.'

'Asgrim, I could never–'

He silenced her with a shake of a trembling hand. 'In the Four Staves, when I told you my secret, I did not finish my story.'

'Your father told you... how to survive.'

'He told me to eat. That my life was more important than my thoughts and memories of him. And to him it was – that is how fathers should see their children. And so I waited with him till he died, and then I buried him. Nothing more.'

'Then how did you survive your passage across the mountains without food?'

He held up his left hand, missing two fingers. 'My father's dignity in death survived intact, and so did my memory of him. It is not survival at all costs. Some things are more important.'

She could hold her tears back no longer, and quickly wiped them away with her sleeve so he would not see.

'Thank you for brightening my life,' he whispered.

Running footsteps echoed through the maze of corridors beyond the door. 'In here!' she called out. 'Help!'

Vidar and Cheyne tumbled in accompanied by Fabienne, with others close behind. Instantly, Vidar and Cheyne took in the scene and rushed to help Asgrim, lifting him off her so they could attempt to treat the wound. Soaked in blood, Rhiannon staggered next to Fabienne, her head reeling.

Asgrim laughed throatily. 'Do not make fools of yourselves, brothers! You can see with your eyes.'

Vidar reluctantly put out an arm to stop Cheyne's ministrations, but the assassin knocked it aside and continued to work. Vidar watched him sympathetically, then bent down to whisper something in Asgrim's ear. The northerner chuckled and gripped Vidar's wrist in a farewell bond.

'Will you stop playing?' Cheyne said. 'There is much to do here.'

Asgrim took his friend's bloodstained hand. 'You must swear to drink to my memory at the Four Staves.'

'This is no time for your silly games!'

Cheyne attempted to continue working on the wound until Asgrim gripped his wrist tightly to stop him. 'Swear.'

Cheyne's mouth struggled to form words, but no sound could fight through his swell of emotion. Finally, he said, 'Who will I have to mock now?'

'You will not be alone in the inn, for I will always be there beside you. You will never be alone, Cheyne.'

Cheyne looked into the furthest corners of the room, trying to see how his life would spin out now. His hands were trembling more than Asgrim's.

Asgrim struggled to moisten his dry mouth. 'You see no value in yourself, but know this: no man could want a better friend than you.'

'There is no justice in this world. I, who care not a jot for life, live on, while you... you–'

'Farewell, friend.'

Cheyne swallowed, twice, three times, then said, 'I want to cry, Asgrim. I want to, but I cannot!'

'Then laugh! It is all emotion, Cheyne, and it comes from your heart. Laugh!'

The light of revelation rose in Cheyne's eyes, and in his faint smile it was clear Asgrim had given him a gift of remarkable quality. He began to laugh, slowly and quietly at first, then louder, until his head was thrown back and tears streamed down his cheeks, the echo of his joy reverberating throughout the long, dark corridors.

And finally, when those echoes had faded, they saw Asgrim was dead.

AFTER THEY CARRIED Asgrim's body out of the complex of rooms deep in the sub-basement of the Store of the Ages, Vidar watched, hollow-eyed, as Fabienne arranged for it to be taken away and prepared for a hero's ceremony in the Fire Gardens. His guilt was etched into his features so deeply and so raw that few could bear to look at him.

Eventually Cheyne caught his arm and whispered, 'No recriminations. Only vengeance.'

'I set all this in motion, Cheyne—'

'Unknowingly. Who could lay blame on you? Asgrim would not. You know that is true.'

Vidar nodded, but his devastation was undimmed.

'Revenge,' Cheyne pressed.

Rhiannon was convinced Asgrim had struck a mortal blow, but the Red Man's body had not been discovered and a trail of blood led out into the streets, which the Order of Inquisitors was now tracking. She told them all she had learned about the Red Man – Joshua – and while much of it made little sense to her, Vidar gave her the missing information she needed.

'Another of Verlaine's team,' Vidar said, 'and another artefact twisting the body and mind.'

'I think the effect of the ring drove him to do things he would not normally have done,' Rhiannon said. 'But even so, I feel there is still a part of him that has no love of people.'

'We will find him, and then I will pay him very close attention,' Cheyne said.

Vidar drew himself together and said, 'That's for later. First we need to get to the Tomb of the Shepherd. You've got something?'

Cheyne brandished the sheaf of maps that Fabienne had collected. 'The tomb lies on a hill roughly south-west of the city. Less than a day's walk. But here–' he unfurled one of the maps '–there is a tunnel in the catacombs that leads under the walls in the direction of the hill. I believe it is a direct path to the tomb. It will get us past the enemy easily and, I hope, avoid any unnecessary experiences in the forest.'

'I'll meet you down there.'

Cheyne nodded and departed, and Vidar turned to Rhiannon, for the first time allowing himself to feel relief at her safety. 'Are you all right?'

She showed him her bandaged arm. 'Another scratch. Perhaps it is time to transfer to the Crimson Hunt.'

'It's good to see you. I was worried.'

She searched deep in his eyes for a long moment, and appeared to approve of what she found there, for she said, 'We have need of conversations, you and I, but not now. There is too much to say, and there are many distractions, not the least of which is the impending invasion of our home.'

'Later, then.'

'Later.' As she turned to go, she caught his hand and let her fingers linger in his for a moment before she moved towards three Inquisitors who were to accompany her to the physician. Vidar watched her go, enjoying the moment as much as he could before he turned to follow Cheyne.

FROM HIS VANTAGE point on a roof overlooking the Store of the Ages, the Red Man, whose hearing was as acute as his vision, paid particular attention to Cheyne's description of the location of the Tomb of the Shepherd.

The loss of blood made him weak, but the ring granted him greater strength than normal men. As the blade had missed his heart, he knew he would survive, though weakened for a while. He quickly made his way across the roofs and regained access to the catacombs not far from Greatstock, where he soon found a tunnel that allowed him to travel beyond the city walls. Locating one of the builders' air tunnels, he wriggled up through the choking dark for a long distance and finally emerged on the edge of the forest.

The artefacts called to each other, as they always did, and Verlaine sought him out. 'Joshua, you're wounded. I'll get one of the physicians to help you.'

Through his fractured mind, the Red Man eventually made known what he had learned about the tomb.

'Very good, Joshua, very good. Your sacrifice has achieved what we both hoped.' Verlaine pondered the information as he looked over the Berex army to the soaring walls of Idriss. 'The tomb is the primary objective. We can leave these things here to harry our enemy and get a head start on our adversary. I don't think Luke really understands the importance of what we're doing here. Still, that is no concern of ours at this moment. Luke is, and always was, superfluous.'

The Red Man fought with the emotions that surged into his head and turned his rational thoughts into a crackled, incomprehensible mess: fear, hatred, doubt, guilt, but no joy and little hope, he realised, which was not as it should be at this point.

Before he could attempt to raise this matter, there was a sudden outcry among the warriors along the tree line. He had the sudden impression of movement all around him in the forest where previously there had been none. Following closely behind Verlaine, he rushed out to investigate.

There was blood in the wind, and screams rising up all around. The warriors turned from Idriss, disoriented. By the time they had realised they were being attacked from the rear, bodies had already started to pile up.

'Those damn forest ghosts!' Verlaine snapped. He raised his gauntlet, then hesitated.

From out of the trees, the Elorhim moved, furious and fleet, barely registering on the vision of their victims before they had despatched them. Their features were emotionless, but the hatred in their hearts was etched in every action. Though the Red Man had been aware of their existence, there were more than he had ever seen before.

'Leave them to fight,' Verlaine said finally. 'It will distract them and give us time to make it through the forest.'

Verlaine raced among the trees, and though he really didn't want to follow, the Red Man remained close behind.

16

BURIED SECRETS

'DID YOU HEAR THAT?' Cheyne asked as they moved under the city walls and out towards the wilds. Muffled noises that sounded like fighting and screams filtered down into the long, straight tunnel extending from the catacombs.

His brow knit, Vidar listened for a moment, then shook his head. 'Our forces aren't going to be engaging them out in no-man's-land.'

'Perhaps the enemy have realised the futility of their actions and have simply turned upon themselves in their hopelessness.'

The tunnel was ancient, but not as old as the catacombs, a fact revealed in the detail of more advanced and careful construction. Flags met perfectly, and the walls and ceiling were lined with such a skill that even after the many years that had passed no damp seeped through the joins.

Vidar carried the lantern, but kept one hand on his sword. Since Asgrim's death, the questions that haunted him – about his past, and Verlaine's agenda – weighed increasingly heavily upon him. One simple fact remained sharply clear: the Red Man came to Idriss because of Vidar and the amber jewel; Asgrim would still be alive if not for him. His feelings went beyond guilt to a desire to make amends, although he knew nothing he did could ever truly right the balance.

Cheyne caught his arm and looked back suspiciously.

'What is it?'

'I thought I heard something.'

Vidar held up the lantern, but its light only stretched a little way along the tunnel. They listened for a while, but no sounds of pursuit reached them.

'Perhaps I was mistaken,' Cheyne said, not wholly convinced.

They kept one ear open as they moved quickly along the gently rising tunnel, but nothing else disturbed them, and soon it was forgotten.

'This tunnel is as straight as anything I've seen,' Vidar said. 'It can only have been built as a path to the tomb.'

'So the littlest lambs can go and bow and scrape and tear at their hair that their great and divine leader is no longer with them?'

'Something like that.'

'And now it is almost forgotten. What a cautionary tale for any would-be priests and prophets. Even if you stir the hearts of everyone in Idriss, sooner or later you will fade into the dust, like everyone else.'

'Somebody remembers his legacy enough to kill, though.'

'When that legacy is a fine collection of magical items that could help you rule all Gardia, that is hardly surprising. But the Shepherd himself? His teachings? Today they are meaningless.'

'They were important enough to ensure the Store of the Ages was built to keep them safe for all time,' Vidar mused. 'And whatever you say, the steps that were taken have kept the knowledge of him alive for three thousand years. That's got to mean something.'

'What I would like to know is how he came by the twenty magical items. Did he create them? Or did they always exist and he brought them together? And why such a mundane collection? A gauntlet? Why no magical sword that kills every enemy you fight? Now *that* would be useful.'

'I'd settle for the gauntlet. If it didn't leave me an insect-infested monster.'

'I think your own artefact causes you more than enough troubles. There is always a price to pay with magic, but the curse that accompanies these items is more than anyone should have to bear.'

'It depends how badly you want them.'

As the tunnel rose, the chill of the deep underground faded and the air became dry and dusty. The perfect construction was increasingly disrupted by tree roots breaking through the walls and ceiling, cracking the stone flags or forcing them free of their mounts.

'Remind me again why we are doing this?' Cheyne asked. 'Not for treasure. Nor, I think, for glory.'

'We're doing it because it's the right thing to do.'

'How novel.' He paused. 'And we are doing it for Asgrim. He would take great pleasure in finding a magical artefact that would blast our tormentors into a bloody smudge on the ground.'

'For Asgrim, then.'

They accepted this with a long period of silence while they both reflected on their missing friend, but there would be a time for grief later.

The tunnel ended abruptly at a large stone door. The handle failed to open it, but when Vidar put his shoulder to the door there was some give that suggested it wasn't locked. Cheyne joined him, and together they dug in their heels and heaved and strained until it began to move.

Finally, with a loud rending groan, it tore open, flooding the tunnel with sunlight. The door lay among the roots of a vast oak so big it would take twenty men to link their arms around it. Turf and fern had grown over the exit from the tunnel, sealing it shut.

Cautiously, they stepped out into a verdant forest setting on the side of a hill near the summit. It was deceptively idyllic, with shafts of sunlight breaking through the leaf cover and birds singing all around. Swords drawn, Vidar and Cheyne quickly scanned the area, but there was no sign of any of the great beasts.

'Do you feel that?' Cheyne asked. He leaned against a tree, trying to make sense of the unusual signals he was receiving.

Vidar did, but didn't know how to put it into words. There was a potent feeling of well-being that reminded him of the euphoria he had felt on the battlements. It infused the land and air, and seemed to have some material essence, for the green vegetation and the woodland flowers flourished all around.

'I think we're in the right place,' he said.

Keeping back to back so they could see an attack coming from any direction, they moved steadily away from the security of the tunnel. The area was alive with wildlife. Rabbit burrows peppered the hillside, and Vidar saw deer moving further down the slope.

'I don't think the great beasts come up here,' he said. 'Something must keep them away.'

'What could that possibly be?' Cheyne's voice had an odd tone. 'Do not start talking about superstition, Vidar. I do not want to have to consider that we really are about to break into the tomb of a god.'

'Gods don't have bones, Cheyne.'

'And you know this for a certainty?'

'There.' Vidar pointed up the slope to where grey stone peeked out from beneath fern and moss. At first glance it could have been mistaken for a rocky outcropping like the many that littered the landscape, but on closer examination some of the stone had clearly been worked.

Unsure what to expect, they approached it hesitantly. The stone box of the painting, with its symbolism and hint of hidden power, was no more, the top and one side shattered and sagging, and much of it swallowed by the land and the vegetation so that it appeared nature was reclaiming it.

'Somehow I expected... more,' Cheyne said. 'No crack of lightning? No blinding light of revelation? How disappointing.'

'Time for grave-robbing,' Vidar said. 'I always thought I'd manage to stay one notch above this level.'

Using their swords as tools, they cleared much of the vegetation from around the box. It was as plain and unassuming as it appeared in the painting. Gripping the edge of the remaining portion of the lid, they attempted to shift it, sweating in the heat of the noon sun.

The seal broke with a crack and the lid slid off, breaking into pieces as it rolled down the hillside.

'That clear lack of respect should have earned us eternal damnation at the very least,' Cheyne said.

'Say it like you care, Cheyne.'

'I would find that most difficult—'

The words caught in his throat, and when Vidar followed his gaze he could see why. Instead of old bones or dust, the bottom of the stone box gave way to a flight of steps leading down into the dark.

'That's more like it,' Vidar said. Retrieving the lantern they had brought with them, he climbed over the lip of the box. The air rising up from the depths made his mouth taste of iron.

He glanced at Cheyne, who peered apprehensively into the dark. 'Here we go – into the unknown.'

RHIANNON TRIED TO rest in her quarters after her ordeal, but she found it difficult to calm her runaway thoughts. Her own brush with mortality at the hands of the Red Man had affected her profoundly, but it was Asgrim's death, and the love she had seen in his eyes, that troubled her the most. His selfless sacrifice had been a shock. How could he value her life above his own? He was the better person, the one who served higher values. All she had to her name was quiet, steady servitude to the needs of the administration. Right or wrong.

In her confusion, her mounting feelings for Vidar only contributed to the sense of being adrift. Old certainties were fading, and she had no idea what the future held.

From her window, she could hear an outcry from the Crimson Hunt on the battlements. It sounded to her ears faintly jubilant, though she had no idea why that would be the case.

As she ventured out of her room to investigate, she was puzzled to see Chief Inquisitor Serena approaching with two other Inquisitors and Administrator Ashur, his assistant LeStrange close behind.

'Is something wrong?' she asked.

The Chief Inquisitor's face gave nothing away. 'You must come with us, Inquisitor Rhiannon.'

The two Inquisitors took Rhiannon's arms with what she considered unnecessary force. Behind the Chief Inquisitor, she saw dismay on LeStrange's face.

'After all I have suffered?' she said.

The Chief Inquisitor looked to Ashur who nodded forcefully.

'I have given my all to Idriss,' Rhiannon protested. 'The Red Man is badly wounded–'

'You failed in the task the administration set for you,' the Chief Inquisitor said. 'I informed you earlier of the consequences if that were to be the case.'

'No!' Rhiannon said in disbelief. Ashur's face gave nothing away, as always, but in his eyes she saw bitterness. It was a show of strength to prove he was not as impotent as he appeared.

'You will be taken from here to the cells,' the Chief Inquisitor said, 'and shortly thereafter you will be executed.'

AT THE FOOT of the stairs, Vidar and Cheyne found a grand corridor that belied the humble, shattered tomb above, constructed from huge blocks of stone covered with breathtakingly detailed art depicting the sacred life of the

Shepherd and the wonders he had performed. As the lantern illuminated the rich colours, Vidar saw images that resonated – a silver gauntlet, a glowing white globe – and he wondered what other secrets were hidden in this ancient art.

Cheyne had grown silent. For all his bravado, the mysteries invested in that place tugged at his superstitions.

'This is a grand tomb,' he whispered. 'Tell me – if everyone once knew this was here, surely it would have been robbed. By some unscrupulous souls. Like us.'

'Maybe it has. This could all be for nothing.'

'And if it has not been robbed–' he indicated the paintings, pristine even after three thousand years '–why would that be?'

'Let's find out, shall we?'

'I heard a story once–'

'Cheyne,' Vidar cautioned.

'Hear me out. Some mystic who had survived the passage from the east told me that all tombs have invisible guardians. The dead do not like to be disturbed.'

'Sleep is so valuable to them.'

'Do not mock. This life is harsh enough. Surely we all deserve a little rest in the next.'

'I thought you didn't believe in that kind of thing.'

'I don't. Except down here I do.'

Turning right, then left, the tunnel took them deep into the hillside. There was a majesty to the vast scale of the construction, but also an unsettling quality in angles that were not pleasing to the human eye, and colours that jarred. The intricate detail of the paintings along the wall became a distraction, pulling the attention here and there when they both wanted to keep it fixed on what lay ahead.

As they rounded another corner, Cheyne came to a sudden halt. 'Did you hear that?'

Vidar listened, and was about to berate Cheyne for giving in to superstition when a faint whisper reached his ears. It sounded like a woman's voice saying, 'Beware.'

'It's nothing,' Vidar said. 'A random echo.'

Cheyne wasn't convinced, but he continued along the tunnel at a slower pace, listening intently. They hadn't gone much further when they heard the whisper again, and another one: the same word, 'Beware.'

This time Cheyne gripped Vidar's arm and said, 'I am not easily frighted, but that does not sound like human voices.'

Handing the lantern to Cheyne, Vidar drew his sword. 'Whoever it is, we'll see how they stand up to this.'

As they moved forwards, the whispers appeared to come from everywhere, five, ten, twenty or more different voices, all warning Vidar and Cheyne to turn back, yet there was no sign of any other presence.

After a moment, Vidar reached out an arm to stop Cheyne in his tracks. Cheyne blanched as if something was about to loom out of the darkness towards him, but then Vidar took back the lantern and held it in front of Cheyne's face. The flame flickered in a strong breeze.

'A shaft to bring air for the builders?' Cheyne suggested.

'Maybe,' Vidar said suspiciously.

Searching for the source of the air current, Vidar raised the lantern to reveal tiny holes just visible along the roof of the tunnel. When the whispers started up again, he pressed his palm over one of the holes and a warning was instantly stifled.

'Clever,' he said. 'These must reach up to the surface. They've been designed so the air blowing through them sounds like a voice.'

'To scare off the superstitious.' Cheyne sniffed. 'Thankfully, we are not so primitive.'

'If their aim is to scare people away, I don't think this will be the end of it.'

They had barely gone several more yards when Vidar was proven right. As they rounded the corner, the lantern winked out, plunging them into complete darkness. Cheyne released an unnerved exclamation, then cursed under his breath, embarrassed.

'How did that happen?' he asked.

'I don't know.' Vidar prepared to relight the lantern, but every time he struck his flint not a single spark was generated.

'Stop playing games,' Cheyne hissed.

'I'm not. Something is preventing any light or heat in this area.'

'Magic,' Cheyne said bitterly. 'It was bound to happen sooner or later.'

Pressing against the wall, Vidar urged Cheyne to follow him. 'For some reason, whoever built this tomb doesn't want us to see what lies ahead.'

'I do not want to see what lies ahead.'

Edging along the wall, Vidar felt in front of him with his foot. After a few yards, the floor gave way to thin air.

'A pit,' he said, 'with no way to tell how wide it is.'

'I suppose less educated people would have blundered blindly into it in the dark,' Cheyne said superciliously. 'Clearly, we are too bright for that. And... bright enough to find a way across it?'

'The builders would have installed some way to get past this.' After a moment's thought, Vidar searched the wall until he found a hollow near the floor. He continued upwards

until he located another. 'I think there are
footholds and handholds cut into the wall.'

'"Think" is an interesting word. It makes me
feel a little like I do about "option". For
instance, it may or may not have any sub-
stance, but we will not find out the truth until
we are suspended over the pit. Possibly with
sharpened stakes at the foot of a singularly
long drop, so we can both burst our organs
and shatter our bones at once.'

'Would you like me to go first?'

'Yes, please.'

Placing one foot and hand in the shallow
holes, Vidar hauled himself off the floor. Balancing carefully, he reached out, first with an
arm and then a leg to find another set of hol-
lows. After an intense period of search, he
eventually located them and moved on to the
next. By then, he was suspended above the pit.

As he placed his foot into the next hole, he
heard a soft click and felt something give.
Quickly, he snatched his foot back. Something
hurtled across the pit and crashed into the wall
where he would have been hanging.

'Are you all right?' Cheyne called.

'Yes, but a slight rethink is necessary.'

With a gentle creaking, the crushing weight
slowly withdrew.

'Some of the holes are fake,' he continued.
'There's a switch in them that releases a block

of stone... I think. Some kind of system running behind the walls.'

'Clearly not all followers of the Shepherd are milk-blooded little lambs.'

Proceeding cautiously, Vidar tested each hole before he put his full weight in it. Eventually his foot came down on solid ground.

'It's all right,' he called, relieved. 'You can do it.'

Cursing loudly, Cheyne followed, and was soon standing next to Vidar. 'I hope this is the last of it,' he said breathlessly. 'My patience grows short.'

The tunnel turned another corner and led directly to a stone door marked with the stylised Y symbol of the Shepherd. They expected it to be locked, or hiding another trap, but it pivoted smoothly to open into an echoing chamber with torches along the walls.

'That was troublingly easy,' Cheyne said suspiciously.

Vidar lit several of the torches from the lantern, which he'd been able to rekindle as soon as they passed the pit. As the shadows rushed away from their flare, it revealed a vast burial chamber glowing with the gold designs inlaid into the marble walls. Chests, ritual ornaments, statues, works of art, and golden tributes covered the floor, and in the centre of the chamber was a raised dais of polished black stone on which lay a skeleton so aged the bones resembled dry wood.

Although the room was still, the hairs on Vidar's neck prickled and he drew his sword again. Cheyne did the same, turning slowly.

'Wait!' Cheyne warned. He indicated bones scattered across the floor among the riches. 'The remains of previous treasure hunters?'

'Looks like they've been torn apart,' Vidar noted. He quickly scanned the burial chamber, but saw nothing that could be responsible for the slaughter.

'Let us find the damnable thing and be away,' Cheyne said quietly.

Vidar walked slowly towards the dais. When he was within ten feet of it, a red light flashed at ankle height and an emotionless voice said, '*What is the word?*'

Throwing himself back, Vidar spun to see who had spoken, but the room was deserted. In the half-light, Cheyne looked bloodless, as if he had heard the voice of god. A deep, resonant hum rose up, growing more insistent.

'What is that?' Cheyne said. 'Who spoke?'

They moved together, adopting a defensive position.

'*What is the word? Forty seconds.*'

'Who is speaking?' Cheyne shouted, unnerved. 'And what will happen if we do not state the password?'

'I think you know.' Vidar backed slowly towards the door.

'*Twenty seconds.*'

'Arcadia.' The word rolled out loud and clear from the door behind them. Vidar and Cheyne whirled to see Verlaine standing proudly with the Red Man hunched behind him.

Cheyne kept his emotions under control, as ever, but his eyes grew cold and hard. 'We have a thing to discuss,' he said to the Red Man. 'Here. Now.'

'Your monkey is speaking, Luke,' Verlaine mocked. He levelled his silver gauntlet. Realising what was to come, Cheyne threw himself out of the direct line, but the fire shot forth with such force that the blast-wave spun him off his feet. His head cracked against the stone floor and he fell unconscious.

As Vidar moved to attack the two intruders, Verlaine raised a hand. 'Would you rather attack me, or clear that fug clogging up your head?'

Vidar hesitated.

'We had our differences, Luke, but you were always eminently sensible. You have a sword. I have something that could eradicate you in the blink of an eye. Let logic prevail.'

Containing his seething emotions, Vidar sheathed his sword.

'Good boy,' Verlaine said patronisingly. He looked around the chamber appreciatively. 'Do you realise this is the first time four of the artefacts have been together in one room in three thousand years?'

'Who am I?' Vidar said bluntly. 'And who are you... really?'

'Who are we? One of the great philosophical questions,' Verlaine mocked. 'Hero or villain? Saviour or guide to damnation? A backward idiot with a sword, or a clear-thinking man of intellect? All it really comes down to is a matter of perspective.'

'Who. Am. I?'

'You have a tattoo on your arm in the shape of a Y. I'd remove my armour to show you my matching tattoo, but... you know... Joshua has one too. And Sam, and the others. It's the brand of our team, a way we could recognise each other if we ever got separated, changed appearance. We had no idea how long we were going to be here. A day? Forty years? Our job was to stay as long as it took to complete the mission, and a lot of change can take place if things drag on. But of course, time isn't important.'

Clutching his head as if in pain, the Red Man sat against the wall on one side, rocking backwards and forwards, muttering to himself.

'And isn't it strange how our team brand resembles the shape the Shepherd makes in all his most iconic paintings and statues?' Verlaine continued.

Vidar's hand went back to his sword.

Verlaine sighed. 'You've been too long without cultured discourse. Who are you? Lucas Kane, a last-minute addition to our team. You weren't supposed to be one of us, and frankly I thought you were a liability, but you have very good connections. An important family – explorers, groundbreakers, transgressors – but no real, particular expertise. Not like the rest of us. Who are you? Luke Kane, engaged to the lovely Beth, a rather intelligent young woman who was quite infatuated with you. Educated, cultured even. You had quite the prospects, Luke. And you gave it all up to come here. Does that answer your existential question? I have a feeling it probably doesn't, for the hard details of our lives rarely tell us who we are.'

'If things were so good, why did I decide to leave it all behind?'

'Two reasons. Firstly, to save our world. You were as idealistic as the rest of us, Luke, more so, probably. Our world is on the brink of extinction, and we're its last hope. Bring back the artefacts, and there's a chance. Fail, and we and everyone we know and love dies. Including your lovely Beth.'

'The second reason.'

'To find your father.'

Vidar followed Verlaine's gaze towards the dais where the yellow bones lay. A shiver ran down his spine. 'My father?' he said.

'Grover Kane. The Shepherd.'

'Stop playing games with me, Verlaine.'

'Your father was the sole member of the initial mission to blast-charge the artefacts. Twenty different objects, twenty different molecular structures, because no one knew which one would most effectively hold the quantum effect we needed.' Verlaine noticed the look of incomprehension on Vidar's face and continued with mild frustration, 'But he never returned to the scheduled time and place. Our team was despatched to bring Grover and the artefacts back.'

'They waited three thousand years to mount a rescue mission?' Vidar mocked.

'There are no certainties with the forces we're dealing with. When we were inserted into this world we were three thousand years too late.'

Vidar laughed dismissively.

'We are thankful your father was a very clever man,' Verlaine continued. 'He ensured that everything we needed would survive until we got here.' He laughed. 'Until the great saviours of the Shepherd's path returned.'

Verlaine moved around the chamber, inspecting the ornate chests, lifting lids, and examining contents.

'So he founded a religion based on familiar templates from our home,' Verlaine said. 'He knew knowledge would fade and become distorted, but faith and belief were viruses that ran through generations. The Shepherd, with his seductive mythology – the paintings, the statues, the stories, the prophecies. The twenty magical artefacts. Even so, three thousand years is a long time, and even religions can become confused and lost. We got here just in time, really.'

'The prophecy about saving the world. It wasn't this world.'

Verlaine laughed quietly. 'Your father was slightly disingenuous there. Yes, the prophecy referred to saving our home. But because of the quantum effect, when the artefacts are removed from here this place will be destroyed in the process.'

The bald statement stung Vidar. 'You're sacrificing the people here to save your own. That's why you were trained to look on them as less than you – so you weren't hamstrung by the moral implications of killing an entire world.'

'That contempt in your voice is uncalled for, Luke. It's a very clear strategic decision. This is a frontier world, raw, old, sparsely populated, and not really finding its feet for a variety of reasons. Ours is a world rich with art and history and culture and science, and a large population. There's no contest, really.'

In the depths of his unconscious, Vidar could feel the echoes of Verlaine's words. He recognised the truth, however incredulous it might sound to his ears, and he felt queasy at the ramifications of what he was being told.

Verlaine smiled cruelly when he saw the thoughts play out on Vidar's face. 'That's right, Luke – you're not a hero. Far from it. You're here to destroy this world and everyone in it. Why, you're as *evil* and *twisted* as you seem to think I am. I told you – it's all a matter of perspective. If you don't destroy this place, you destroy an even greater one, and murder vastly more innocent people. How simple could the equation be?'

Vidar had a flash of a woman with long brown hair and green eyes smiling at him. Beth?

Verlaine opened a box and paused before delicately lifting out a white orb. There was nothing to distinguish it, but the atmosphere in the room instantly became more intense; Vidar felt a tingling deep in his teeth. 'Here it is,' Verlaine said with awe. 'The Prime Locator. With this, we can find all the artefacts.'

As Vidar tried to process all the new information, he understood why Sam had been so reluctant to tell him everything at once. Verlaine's words jarred so much with what he had believed about himself, his mind felt under attack.

'Luke?' Verlaine repeated, though Vidar had been too distracted to hear it first time. 'I need to know, are you with us?' He had replaced the Prime Locator in the box ready for removal.

'You're not in any hurry to save your home—'

'*Our* home, Luke.'

'You've conquered an entire city. You're enjoying all the power you're getting from the artefacts.'

'I told you, time is not an issue. I have all the time in the world to indulge myself. I just have to make it back before I die.'

'Where is *our* home? Where's Gardia?'

Verlaine removed his helmet. The insects swarmed around his smile. 'Come on, Luke. Surely you can work that out for yourself. All the clues are there. You're smart enough to make the connections.'

Shaking his head slowly, Vidar feigned ignorance, but a notion started to shift in his head: what Verlaine had said about having all the time in the world.

Verlaine saw the echoes in Vidar's face and nodded, smiling. 'That's right. You've got it.

Time, Luke. Time is the key. This world is the dismally far-flung future of our own, when everything we had built up over the millennia has fallen into nothing. It's a bit of a sinkhole, really. The ancestors of the people you've lived with for the last three years, and the beasts in the forest, and all the life you've encountered, have fallen through from our own history via some natural anomaly. Idiots stumbling into a ditch and not being able to get out. Your father was different, of course. He developed the technology that allowed him to be inserted into this era, although it was a by-product of achieving the quantum-charge that we hoped would save us from the disaster that threatened – or threatens, it's so hard to use tenses when you're dealing with time – our entire civilisation.'

'So... you're sacrificing your own world's future... our... our world's future... to... to–'

'Stop stuttering, Luke. It's unbecoming. Yes, that's exactly what we're doing. There's no point to this time. If any era has to go to save us, this is the one.'

'But there are people here. Our people.'

'Accidents, Luke. They're lucky to be alive after their ancestors plunged through to this god-forsaken era. But these are the harsh choices we have to make. Sacrifice a few here to save billions back home–'

'A few? These are people, just like you and me.'

His voice grew hard. 'I told you, harsh choices. We can't afford to be sentimental. There's too much at stake. Let me say it one more time, Luke – we are not the villains here. We truly are saviours. When we return with the artefacts, suitably blast-charged and empowered, we deliver all of Earth to salvation.' Verlaine calmed himself and allowed his smile to return, though it was a freakish grimace in his ruined face. 'It's your job to help bring the silence of death to one world, Luke. Will it be this one, with its rough-hewn, small-minded people, barely eking out an existence in this harsh place? Or will it be our world, with its rich culture, vast population... and, let's not forget, the people we love? The woman you love? Simple, really. Are you telling me you have trouble making that choice? If so, I'm baffled. What has happened to you during the last three years?'

Steadying himself, Vidar attempted to assimilate everything Verlaine had said, but it was too much. Instead he saw through his opponent's façade. 'You're not noble, Verlaine. You're collecting the artefacts to build up your own personal power in this world. Yes, if time isn't an issue, you can rule over Gardia for as long as you want and still return to be the hero of the hour. But to be prepared to take your time and exert that power here over these people... that reveals something very unpleasant about your psyche. You're treating them, and this era, like your toys, before you wipe them all out for good.'

Verlaine said nothing.

'Idriss...?'

'Oh, it was there in our time, but you knew it by a different name. A great European city.'

A sound echoed along the tunnel outside the chamber. Verlaine looked towards the door suspiciously before returning his attention to Vidar. 'Time's up. I need an answer.'

'The people in this world don't deserve to die.'

'Perhaps not. Sadly that isn't an option.'

'They're no different from you... from me. They suffer through all the problems that life throws at them and try to do their best.' His thoughts see-sawed wildly.

'Give me an answer, Luke.'

Vidar thought of Rhiannon, even Cheyne, and how much they meant to him; he pictured the Red Man killing Asgrim, the contempt for another life, and his disorientation turned to an anger that blazed with a fury that surprised him. Drawing his sword, he moved for cover before Verlaine had a chance to use his gauntlet.

'Joshua,' Verlaine called. 'We need to put an end to this quickly.'

Vidar noticed two things in rapid succession: firstly, Cheyne was no longer lying where he had fallen; and secondly, a potent stink of death told him who had followed them along the tunnel from the catacombs.

'A balance, I think.' Cheyne's voice was low and measured, but barely hid a wealth of emotion. He stood behind the Red Man, who was not even aware of him. In one fluid movement, he inserted his needle-knife into the Red Man's ear and forced it through his brain and out the other side. It took a second before the Red Man realised he was dead.

As he fell to the floor, Verlaine gave a roar of anger that was accompanied by a loud buzzing from the insects feeding on him. A crackling sheet of flame washed up the wall where Cheyne no longer stood. As Verlaine staggered back a pace, Vidar could see how much the artefact took out of him.

With his sword high, Vidar rushed forwards; not fast enough. Gauntlet raised, Verlaine faced him, his eyes wide and white and filled with anger. For a brief moment, Vidar saw his own death clearly, and then Verlaine staggered back as the insects lifted from his raw flesh in an incessantly buzzing cloud. He screamed from the pain of removal of his false skin.

At the doorway, Greer an' Lokh danced wildly, consumed by his madness, every step a ritual movement, every turn of hand and limb a silent incantation. In response, the insects turned on their host with a fury, burrowing deep into flesh. Verlaine's cry tore at his throat.

Unable to concentrate on the gauntlet, he grabbed the box containing the Prime Locator and ran for the door, knocking Greer an' Lokh to one side. Vidar gave pursuit, with Cheyne close behind.

The area that dampened all light slowed them, but they caught up with Verlaine on the hillside as he clambered out of the shattered stone box. He gripped the chest tightly to him, the insects calm once again, now Greer an' Lokh was too far away to influence them. Turning slowly with the gauntlet levelled, he silently urged Vidar to attack.

'I was right, Luke – you're a liability. You're prepared to destroy your home for these hopeless already-dead people.'

'The only thing on my mind is stopping you, Verlaine. There's no justification for the kind of misery you're inflicting.'

Verlaine made to release the fire from his gauntlet, only to stop, mid-action, blinking stupidly. Vidar was no longer standing where he had been. It took Verlaine a second to realise what had happened, and then he gave a mean smile. 'So you're learning that your little gem has a few more qualities than you first imagined. That doesn't matter. Wherever you're hiding, you can still burn.'

As Vidar slipped from tree to tree, he realised Verlaine was right. The stealth he had always exhibited had been the result of him unconsciously drawing on the gem. Now he could feel the ability with his mind, manipulate it, like bending light with a prism. It felt as though he was sliding across the surface of the world.

Verlaine had no time to unleash the power of the gauntlet. Vidar emerged in the blink of the eye, fluidly carving downwards with his sword. Verlaine's gauntlet, and the hand it encased, fell to the leaf-mould before he even realised he had been attacked. Thin grey blood spurted from the wrist stump.

As Verlaine stared at it in mute shock, Vidar threw him to the ground and pressed the tip of his sword against the insect-seething neck. 'Tie off the wound,' Vidar ordered.

Cheyne stepped up with a supercilious expression and little sign of urgency, and used his wire garrotte as a tourniquet to stem the arterial flow. 'Look,' he said, 'this monkey can do tricks.'

'I think you've still got a lot to tell us,' Vidar said, striving to keep his voice free of emotion.

'I'm taking you back to Idriss, and then we'll let Cheyne see what he can get out of you. I'll attempt to persuade him to control his enthusiasm.' He searched Verlaine's armour till he found the two map-cubes and the amulet.

Verlaine stared at Vidar hatefully, but said nothing.

'No, no, no,' Greer an' Lokh called out. 'Time to hide!'

'What are you gibbering about?' Cheyne said uncharitably.

Greer an' Lokh pointed down the slope to where pale shapes moved quickly among the trees.

'The Elorhim,' Vidar said. He turned to the sorcerer and said, 'Can't you do something?'

'So little of the life-energy left, so little,' Greer an' Lokh whined, but he began to make his ritual patterns with his hands and feet, singing to himself under his breath.

The Elorhim emerged silently from the greenwood, their skin gleaming in the shafts of sunlight, their eyes dark and murderous.

One of them wore a silver necklace that appeared to bestow some authority. He stepped forwards as the other Elorhim formed a wide arc behind him. Vidar and Cheyne edged back to the Tomb of the Shepherd where Greer an' Lokh continued to dance, seemingly oblivious.

'You are intruders in this land,' the leader of the group said, 'and no longer will we tolerate your presence.'

Weak from his injuries, Verlaine finally appeared to realise the Elorhim were all around him. He forced himself to his knees and attempted to crawl away into the trees until three of the forest people picked him up and effortlessly held him tight. He struggled, cried out, his eyes lighting with fear for the first time.

'Help me,' he called out to Vidar. 'You don't know what they're like.'

'I know,' Vidar replied.

The leader of the Elorhim plucked the gauntlet from where it had fallen and examined it. The faint smile that played across his lips suggested he knew exactly what it was. 'The end of your days is coming, with the blazing heat of the sun. And when your kind are all gone, there will finally be silence, and peace, and the unending cool green forest.'

He looked into their eyes in turn, holding Vidar's gaze last of all, and then he motioned for the other Elorhim to move forwards.

'Quickly, quickly!' Greer an' Lokh shouted. He dived down the steps in the Tomb of the Shepherd as the ground began to shake, then shift.

Vidar and Cheyne followed amid the deafening crack of stone. As they stumbled into the burial chamber, the entrance way collapsed, blocking it completely. When the rumbles faded away, the only thing they could hear were Verlaine's screams growing fainter and fainter until they finally disappeared into the deep forest.

Cheyne examined the pile of rubble and said, 'I hope you are not expecting me to congratulate you on that rescue, sorcerer.'

'We'll move that in no time,' Vidar said. 'Better trapped in here for an hour or so than torn to pieces and left as a snack for the forest animals.'

Cheyne fixed Greer an' Lokh with a cold eye. 'Now, perhaps you would like to explain why you were around to rescue us.'

'Is the fact that I was here when you needed me not enough?' The sorcerer squatted on the rubble and eyed them both like a bird of prey.

'And if an object of power tumbled into your pocket, or at the very least a map-cube, all the better, eh?' Cheyne pressed.

Leaving them to their sharp exchange, Vidar kept hold of the chest containing the Prime Locator and walked back into the burial chamber to stand next to the remains of the Shepherd. He saw old bones, displayed reverently for future generations to find; at best, a lie in human form.

The paintings from the Temple of the Shepherd now made perfect sense. The sea journey, the man in the foetal position – a symbolic representation of the Shepherd's birth into this world from the place he called home, the longest and most perilous journey of all. The artefacts on the table, the Prime Locator, the Tomb itself – all vital clues for the next team coming after him. Vidar had thought the Tomb was the last in the sequence, but it was actually the burning tree, the symbolic destruction of this green world.

Vidar wondered what the Shepherd's last thoughts were, alone, on a world primed for destruction. Were they for his son? Were they a desperate hope for the survival of the place he called home? Was he a man ready to sacrifice himself for a greater good, or someone engineering the greatest crime ever, the genocide of an entire world's population? Verlaine said it was a matter of perspective, but whose view counted the most? Who could pass judgement?

And what, in the end, did it mean for him? He had found the map of his life, but all it showed him was a forbidding territory filled with dilemmas and heartache, lies and death on a grand scale. He was more lost than he ever had been.

17

EXECUTION

Rhiannon sat in her cell, listening to the note of the bells change. Through her window she could see the sun making its downward arc towards the horizon, but not the block or the hooded swordsman. That would have been too cruel, even for a city like Idriss where she had come to realise there was a thick vein of cruelty lying just behind the lies of honour and duty and sacrifice. The City of Lights had darkness at its core.

After her ordeal, she didn't feel terrified, only bitter. Her life had been gifted to her by the true sacrifice of a decent man, a new life, free of her blinkered view of responsibility to the city's administration, and with a belief that she was finally on the brink of ending the loneliness that had always haunted her. And within moments of Vidar leaving, all of it had been taken away from her again.

Ashur would never have dared attempt it while Vidar was there, she knew. The administrator was as weak as he was vindictive. She was surprised by how much she hated him, and everything for which he stood.

There was a polite knock at the door, which she found faintly humorous, considering her predicament. LeStrange slipped in, looking embarrassed, as if he had been personally responsible for her impending death.

'What do you want?' she snapped, and then felt guilty, for he looked honestly upset.

'They are coming to collect you. For the execution.'

'I know. I heard the bells.'

'Of course. I am sorry.' He looked around the tiny cell impotently, and then said, 'This is wrong. It is a betrayal of the very principles of Idriss.'

'There are two Idrisses, LeStrange. There is the idea, in which the people believe. And there is the Idriss designed to support the lives and ambitions of the administration. I always thought they were one and the same. Now I know the truth.'

'I serve one,' he said. 'Not the other. Is there something I can–'

He was interrupted by the sound of marching boots as Chief Inquisitor Serena and three other Inquisitors arrived at the cell.

'It is time,' the Chief Inquisitor said.

THE SUN WAS low in the sky as Vidar, Cheyne, and Greer an' Lokh emerged from the catacombs close to the Store of the Ages, dusty and exhausted.

'I need a bath, and some clean and beautiful clothes,' Cheyne said. 'But I suppose we ought to clear the Berex army from our front door first.'

Vidar was distracted by the bells. 'The call to execution?'

'Who would they be despatching at a time like this?' Cheyne said. 'An execution with an enemy at the gate? Unless there is a traitor, but I find it hard to believe any citizen of Idriss would betray this city in its time of greatest need.'

Greer an' Lokh suddenly became animated. He tore the tiny bones from his neck and sat down on the cobbles before throwing them feverishly, poring over the results, and then throwing them again. He looked up at them, unsettled. 'This is wrong. The patterns are being disturbed.'

Vidar and Cheyne rushed towards the forum, only to be intercepted by Ashur and three other council members ambling along, deep in conversation.

'Who's being executed?' Vidar snapped.

'Ah, yes,' Ashur said, giving nothing away. Vidar could tell he was about to dissemble, but then a cheer rose up from the crowd in the forum.

'It is done,' Ashur said. 'The price has been paid for failing Idriss at a time of great need.'

There was a note of cruel victory in his voice that made Vidar shiver. He thrust Ashur to one side and raced towards the forum, trying not to imagine what he would find, knowing in his heart what it would be.

The executioner's block was hidden by a large crowd, all cheering and clapping and calling out with an exultation that sickened Vidar. Roughly, he pushed his way past them and broke through to a sight that left him stunned.

The executioner lay unconscious in the middle of the forum with a defiant Rhiannon standing over him. Her shackles hung loose, and beside her LeStrange shifted uneasily, looking for a way out as the Chief Inquisitor and her aides moved towards them. The crowd continued to cheer what they had seen.

'Leave her!' Vidar yelled to the Chief Inquisitor.

The crowd fell silent. Then, when they recognised Vidar, their cheers rose up louder than ever. Vidar strode into the middle of the forum and took Rhiannon's arm, facing the Chief Inquisitor rebelliously.

'Thank you for the prompt rescue,' Rhiannon said tartly.

'I knew you wouldn't need me.'

'Please do not make any grand romantic gesture. It would be so embarrassing.'

'Wouldn't dream of it.'

He slipped a protective arm around Rhiannon's waist and raised his sword towards the Chief Inquisitor.

'She has been duly processed for execution by the Council of Administrators. What you are doing is treason,' the Chief Inquisitor stated.

Vidar fought to contain his anger and said, 'She's as much a hero of Idriss as Mellias. Nobody did more than her to catch the murderer.'

'She failed–'

'No, you, and Ashur, and all the administrators have failed. Failed her. Failed the people. Failed the city.'

'Take her,' the Chief Inquisitor ordered.

The Inquisitors stepped forwards hesitantly until Vidar turned his sword towards them. Silence fell across the crowd as they watched the stand-off, before Cheyne pushed his way through to stand beside Vidar.

'You have a plan?' he whispered to Vidar.

'Options.'

'Ah.'

The Chief Inquisitor prepared to press the matter until she saw the inevitable outcome in Vidar's eyes. Uneasy, she motioned for the other Inquisitors to stand down. 'This is an issue for later. There is an enemy at the gate who needs your attention.' She turned and marched away, red-faced at the rising cheers of the crowd.

'Vidar, there is no going back from this,' Rhiannon said. 'You have made her lose face in front of the people. That will not be allowed to stand, for the sake of order.'

'So, the options are... death... or find a new home very quickly? Am I correct?' Cheyne said.

Ignoring him, Vidar turned to LeStrange. 'You helped her?'

LeStrange nodded. He forced a smile, but his eyes were scared. Vidar knew how much he had sacrificed to make his stand.

'Then you've paid me back for saving your life,' Vidar said.

Taken aback, LeStrange shrugged. 'But... it was the right thing to do.'

'As was saving your life. We won't let them harass you for this.'

LeStrange smiled shyly. 'I fear there is more difficulty ahead for us before this reaches a conclusion.'

'Vidar, thank you,' Rhiannon interjected, 'but you should not have–' The words caught in her throat as she looked into his eyes. 'What has happened to you? You are changed.'

'My perspective has altered,' he said cryptically. 'I never thought they would stoop this low.' His cold anger at Rhiannon's treatment was barely contained.

'There is something else… something important,' Rhiannon began. 'When the Red Man changed identities, he did not copy the features of people he had seen. The faces were random.'

Vidar instantly knew where Rhiannon was leading him. 'Mellias was murdered by someone he knew.'

'It could not have been the Red Man. I think he found Mellias's body, and in his madness arranged it, and cut out the eyes, but he did not commit the original crime.'

As Vidar let this information sink in, the connections began to form in his mind. He knew who had killed Mellias, and he thought he knew why. His anger boiling over, he turned to Cheyne and said, 'Now I have a plan.'

* * *

STILL REELING FROM the assault by the Elorhim, the decimated Berex force watched in amazement as the Deeping Gate cranked open. Thoughts that Idriss was surrendering were dismissed moments later when the Crimson Hunt stormed out in formation, howling their bloodthirsty calls of death for the glory of Idriss.

But, as fearsome as they were, it was not the Hunt that terrified the Berex warriors, but the man who led them, surrounded by a shrieking host of pearly spectres, a hint of what was to come for any who opposed him. Vidar was already spoken of in whispers by those who had seen his terrifying slaughter on the battlements the previous night, but on the ground he proved even worse than they imagined. All who faced him realised he was consumed by a monstrous rage. As the bodies piled up around him, he became even more intense so that many felt he was not even seeing them. A euphoric light glowed in his eyes, and with each death it grew brighter and drove him on to a more furious attack.

By the end, he was slaked from head to toe in blood, a wild-eyed demon that had accompanied the ghosts from the depths of hell. All who crossed his path fell. Nothing could diminish his anger; nothing could stop him.

Without Verlaine to drive them on, the Berex force was torn apart by the Crimson Hunt's ferocious attack. Many preferred the terrors of the forest to death at the hands of their enemy. Others threw down their weapons and surrendered. By the time night had fallen, the prisoners were trooped back through the Deeping Gate to hear the ecstatic reception for Vidar and the Crimson Hunt.

The city had survived. Idriss the Strong, Idriss the Unvanquished.

STILL DRENCHED IN blood, Vidar marched from the cheering crowds into the quiet of the palace. Many of the court were joining in the celebrations that now ran wildly through the streets and had led to an impromptu festival at Fallen Spire, but the council had been holding an emergency meeting at Ashur's prompting.

It was just breaking up as Vidar climbed the stairs towards the royal quarters. Many of the council members recoiled from his hellish appearance, and others made no attempt to hide their fear and suspicion of him, but Ashur came up to him defiantly.

'I want you to be the first to hear this most important news,' Ashur said. 'The King has agreed that I should be his successor. He will make the official proclamation within the hour.'

'Congratulations,' Vidar replied emotionlessly.

'We will, of course, require a meeting shortly afterwards to discuss your bizarre behaviour and flaunting of the authority of this administration. There will be consequences: for you, your man Cheyne, the failed Inquisitor, and–' he swallowed to contain his anger '–LeStrange. You do understand that?'

'There will be consequences,' Vidar repeated. His wry tone unsettled Ashur, who nodded and moved away to accept the congratulations of his fellow council members.

Forgotten, Vidar continued into the royal quarters and the King's bedchamber. Lud was fading fast, but his eyes remained bright. He looked Vidar up and down appreciatively. 'The survival of Idriss always demands blood.'

'So I'm learning.' Vidar looked around to ensure they were alone, then said, 'Ashur tells me you're going to name him as your successor.'

'Reluctantly. There is no other choice, Vidar. Of course, I would have liked to appoint you, but the people would never agree to it.'

'You know your people well.'

Vidar's odd tone puzzled the King.

'You know what's best for them,' Vidar continued. 'Like staying trapped here in Idriss for ever.'

'What are you saying?' Lud's tone was measured; he could see what Vidar had discovered.

'You knew about the map-cube in the Store of the Ages. You knew it could provide safe passage through the forest, trade routes, new lives for the people here. Freedom.'

The King nodded slowly. 'That information was passed down through the generations, but I decided – as my father decided, and his father before him – that the map was a seductive lie. It promised much for the people, but ultimately it would have led to the destruction of Idriss.'

'How?'

'The longevity of this city has been built on the strength of our great, defensive walls, the nurturing, protective mother of Idriss's life, and on the strength of the people, united against the threat that lies just beyond the Deeping Gate.'

'The threat of the real world out there.'

'If the people were not united, our strength would fade and the city would ultimately fall.'

'This wasn't about the city's survival, it was about yours. You were afraid that once the people started interacting with the wider world they might come to look less favourably on the long, stagnant rule of the royal family. They might want change. And your kind always thinks change is dangerous.'

'But it is, Vidar. You are young, but when you have reached my age you will see how dangerous change truly is. Change means destruction, and death. It is both real, and symbolic.'

'So you denied the people their freedom and their chance of a better life to keep things safe for yourself, and everyone else trapped in this great prison.'

'Safe, as they always have been,' Lud stressed.

'And then Mellias found out about the map-cube.'

The King hesitated. 'We had learned that an outside force was at large in Idriss, searching for a valuable item. Naturally I could not risk the map-cube falling into the hands of the enemy. It cannot be destroyed. So the only alternative was to keep it safe, lost for ever in the vast, ringing vaults of the Store of the Ages.'

'And you told Mellias what it was?'

'No, he discovered that for himself. He had begun to be drawn towards the path of the Shepherd, and once I told him there was a need to find and destroy the enemy who sought out an item of incredible value, he made his own enquiries.'

'Which drew him to the Store of the Ages that night, to protect the map-cube from the

Red Man. And that was when you killed him.'

Lud flinched as if Vidar had struck him. After a moment of recovery, he said, 'Mellias was determined to reveal the existence of the map-cube. He thought it would be a boon for the people. He did not understand–'

'And so you killed him,' Vidar repeated coldly. 'I've seen how much strength still exists in that frail body when you feel your beloved city is under threat.'

'Do not judge me, Vidar. I told you – sometimes kings have to do terrible things. I killed our greatest hero for the survival of Idriss. The White Warrior, my son in all but blood. It was a choice no man should have to make, but that is why only some are able to be kings. A balance... a choice, stark, clear. One man's life, or the survival of an entire city.'

Vidar watched him for a moment, weighing his own emotions as they rose inside him: there was anger, for all the hardship the King had perpetuated over the years, and contempt for the manipulations of the ruling class, but no sympathy, no pity.

'You're right about one thing,' Vidar said. 'Sometimes you have to do terrible things for the greater good, even though you know it's going to haunt you for ever.'

Vidar clamped his hand over Lud's mouth. There was a moment of shock in the King's eyes, and then he began to fight and claw with the last of the strength that had plunged the knife into Mellias, and left him dying on the floor of the Store of the Ages. Mellias had gone to great lengths to ensure some good would come out of his death; and now it had.

Vidar held his hand tightly in place as the King's struggles slowed, and eventually stopped, and only silence remained.

THE LIGHTS OF the great city of Idriss flooded through the stained-glass windows of the council chamber and painted the stern, concerned faces of the administrators in familiar shades. But there was one colour that dominated: that of blood, the colour of the cloaks of the Crimson Hunt who lined the walls, hands on swords.

Vidar entered, still covered in blood himself, followed closely by Cheyne, LeStrange, and Rhiannon.

Ashur jumped to his feet, his rage barely masking the fear that was clear in his eyes. 'Your days of disrespect for this council will be over shortly when the King announces his successor,' he shouted.

'The King is dead,' Vidar said calmly, 'and I am his successor.'

A stunned silence fell on the room for a brief moment, until all the administrators started shouting as one. Vidar motioned and the Huntsmen drew their swords. The administrators fell silent, eyeing the Hunt, and then all but Ashur gradually resumed their seats.

'A revolution,' Ashur said.

'If you like.' Vidar motioned to Ashur to sit. 'This is what will happen. The council will approve my succession – not that it matters if you do or don't, but it's always good for the people to see that the administration and King are on the same side. Then we will go straight to the King's Chamber for the ceremony, after which I will announce the start of a new age for Idriss.'

'The age of Vidar, the Ghost Warrior,' Ashur said contemptuously.

'The age of freedom. I now have in my possession the complete map of Gardia.'

The outcry from the administrators was tumultuous. 'Is this true?' Ashur shouted above the throng.

'It is. This will be a new age. Of trade, and travel, and of Idriss exerting its influence across the world.'

Ashur held his head, stunned, and then briefly joined an intense, hushed debate with the other council members. Vidar waited patiently.

Eventually, Ashur said, 'This council recognises your succession.'

'King Ghost Warrior,' Cheyne muttered. 'How novel.'

Vidar could see that Ashur realised he had no other options, and he also knew the Administrator would remain a threat, but for now the most dangerous moment had passed.

'One other thing.' Vidar motioned for Rhiannon to step forwards. 'Welcome your new Chief Inquisitor.'

Rhiannon exuded strength as she looked around the council. She had initially resisted Vidar's request, uneasy at the responsibility, but her desire for change in Idriss soon overcame her doubts.

'Together the Crimson Hunt and the Order of Inquisitors will ensure the people will be free from fear and able to enjoy the riches of this new age,' Vidar stated boldly.

'Oh,' Cheyne said archly at Vidar's shoulder. 'All hail you.'

As THEY LEFT the council chamber, Vidar quickly pulled Rhiannon into an alcove behind thick velvet curtains, ignoring Cheyne's lascivious wink.

'These are going to be difficult times,' he said. 'I'm glad you'll be there with me.'

'A little while ago you would never have convinced me to get involved in your madcap scheme. If you can call seizing control of power, threatening the administration, decapitating the Order of Inquisitors, and overthrowing generations of tradition and stultifying oppression a madcap scheme. But you are a changed man, Vidar. Changed in some profound way that I still cannot quite divine. I think you are a better man.'

'I don't feel it.'

'But it shows in your actions. I know you have been deeply troubled by whatever you discovered in the Tomb of the Shepherd, and I hope you will find it within you to tell me about it one day, but some good has come out of it, though you may not be able to see it at this moment.'

He wanted to tell her everything – of the awful burden he carried, and the lives that hung in the balance, the weight of questions still haunting him and the emptiness he felt – but it wouldn't be fair.

She saw some of it in his face for she said, 'That jewel has made you walk alone for too long. You always feared those close to you were at risk from its hunger, and your own perceived weakness, but I know now that a man like you would rather die than sacrifice his friends. I trust you completely. And you should trust yourself. Whatever lies ahead, you will make the right decision.'

Her belief in him was deeply touching, and though it meant he would have to live up to it, he knew he wouldn't have to face the future alone.

'I'm glad you survived,' he said.

'And I, you.'

She hesitated before giving him the briefest of kisses that promised more, then she slipped quickly through the curtains.

THE CELEBRATIONS OF the citizens still echoed across Idriss as Vidar entered the King's Chamber for the first time as monarch. Cheyne, Rhiannon, LeStrange, and Greer an' Lokh waited for him there.

'How does it feel?' Cheyne asked.

'It feels like I just made the worst decision of my life.'

'But think of the treasure. Now you only have to clap your hands and people will bring it to your feet. They may prostrate themselves. And you do not even have to ask nicely.'

'I'm sure the novelty will wear off quickly.' He turned to LeStrange. 'You work for me now. Tomorrow Asgrim gets the ceremony he deserves at the Fire Gardens. The people here are never going to forget his sacrifice. Make the arrangements.' LeStrange nodded. 'After that, we have a lot of plans to make.'

Cheyne eyed him suspiciously, but said nothing.

'We need to establish a team of explorers, and diplomats, and trade delegations. Transport. Warriors who can protect travellers from the forest people and any other threats they meet en route. I want Xiang Chai-Shekh to turn the Store of the Ages into a place of study so we can finally start to learn something about this city where we live–' He noticed Rhiannon was smiling, 'What?'

'I do not believe you think this is the worst decision of your life at all,' she chided.

When LeStrange had left to make the necessary arrangements, Greer an' Lokh became animated. 'Show me!' he said, dancing more excitedly than he ever had. 'There are new patterns to explore! New things to discover!'

'Still keeping your eye on power, I see,' Cheyne said caustically.

'Why not? Power will bring me happiness. Is that not a perfectly rational thing to want?' Greer an' Lokh leaped to one side of the room and squatted, hands clasped eagerly, releasing little gulps of excitement every few seconds.

Vidar removed the map-cubes from his pocket and weighed them in the palm of his hand before opening his shirt. Amber light washed out over the room.

'Oh,' Rhiannon exclaimed. 'I have never seen the jewel like that. It appears so bright.'

A shadow of regret crossed Vidar's face. 'I'm starting to discover the extent of its appetite.'

He pressed the cubes against the jewel and the map rushed out across the room, for the first time revealing the full splendour of the entire world. The others were caught in awe, but Vidar found his attention turning to his father, who had bequeathed the map to Gardia. He wondered what kind of man he had been, if they had loved each other, if Grover, the Shepherd, would be proud of his son this day, or contemptuous.

Rhiannon surreptitiously took his hand and pulled him into the midst of the map. 'You may be the King, but you do not have to stand apart from us,' she whispered. 'You have friends here to share your burden.'

It was the right thing to say, and it briefly stilled his troubled heart.

'Look,' Cheyne said, 'are they pirates?' He indicated a fleet of ramshackle ships with crimson sails on the azure sea.

'And what are these strange buildings?' Rhiannon asked. 'What kind of people could possibly live there?'

Wonders beyond their imagining unfolded as they passed through the map, cities of glass and gold perched on the top of mountains, others burrowed deep into the earth in the entrances to caves, lone towers, river-towns, places that gleamed and winked and suggested strange powers and stranger inhabitants.

Rhiannon gasped, tears in her eyes. 'I never imagined what could be out there.'

Vidar removed the Prime Locator from its box and placed it in the centre of the map. 'This stays our secret,' he said. 'Whatever we do when we move out into the world, finding these artefacts will always lie behind it.'

'To keep them out of dangerous hands,' Greer an' Lokh said pointedly, 'or to bring them into yours?'

Vidar ignored him. The Prime Locator was triggered in the same way as the cubes and within a moment coloured spikes burned across the map, appearing from the azure sea to the white caps of mountains.

'Wait,' Cheyne said, counting and counting again. 'There are only nineteen. Where is the final one?'

'That's something we're going to have to discover,' Vidar replied. 'For now, the important thing is that we've gained a world.'

They spent another half-hour luxuriating in the wonders of their new frontier, and then

Cheyne and Rhiannon left to prepare for their new roles. Rhiannon paused at the door and cast him one look that suggested there were as many mysteries and wonders ahead for the two of them as there were beyond the walls.

'You have gained a world, Ghost Warrior, but what have you lost?' Greer an' Lokh said when Vidar closed the map.

Vidar took a seat where he could look out over the lights of the city. 'What do you mean?'

'I overheard everything in the Shepherd's burial chamber. Who you are. The mission you were sent here to achieve.' For the first time there was a note of lucidity in the sorcerer's voice, and Vidar had the disturbing feeling that Greer an' Lokh now felt a connection with him on some level.

'All that happened to someone called Luke. My name is Vidar. Different life, different rules.'

'So you say now,' the sorcerer pressed. 'But what if your memory returns completely? What if you recall a woman named Beth, and what she and her world meant to you? What then, Ghost Warrior? Will you choose to be the saviour of this world and damn your own kind? Or will you choose to be the destroyer here, the lord who oversees the long, silent rule of death?'

Vidar couldn't answer.

Bowing, the sorcerer left with a strange look of sympathy on his face.

Deep in his chest, Vidar felt the dim pulse of the amber jewel, still hungry, always hungry, and in his head the ghosts whispered and laughed; and they told him he was becoming death, the destroyer of worlds, the Lord of Silence.

And he listened to them for a while, but for the first time he did not give in to their message of despair. Somewhere there was an answer to his terrible dilemma, whether it was across the opening frontiers of this world or buried deep inside him. If it took every resource he had, he would seek it out.

There in Idriss, the City of Lights in the vast gulf of the night, he had finally mapped the contours of his heart, and he knew he was ready for whatever challenge lay ahead.

About the Author
A two-time winner of the British
Fantasy Award, Mark Chadbourn
is the author of eleven novels and
one non-fiction book. A former
journalist, he is now a screenwriter
for BBC television drama. His
other jobs have included running
an independent record company,
managing rock bands, working on
a production line, and as an
engineer's 'mate'. He lives in a
forest in the English Midlands.

"Attractive characters and an imaginative setting combine in an excellent, fast-moving quest novel."
— David Drake, author of the Lord of the Isles series

GAIL Z. MARTIN

THE SUMMONER

Book One of the
CHRONICLES OF THE NECROMANCER

www.solarisbooks.com ISBN: 978-1-84416-468-4

The world of Prince Martris Drayke is thrown into sudden chaos and disorder when his brother murders their father and seizes the throne. Cast out, Martris and a small band of trusted friends are forced to flee to a neighbouring kingdom to plot their retaliation. But if the living are arrayed against him, Martris must call on a different set of allies: the ranks of the dead...

SOLARIS FANTASY

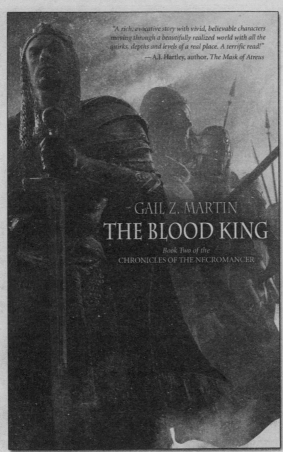

"A rich, evocative story with vivid, believable characters moving through a beautifully realized world with all the quirks, depths and levels of a real place. A terrific read!"
— A.J. Hartley, author, *The Mask of Atreus*

GAIL Z. MARTIN

THE BLOOD KING

Book Two of the
CHRONICLES OF THE NECROMANCER

www.solarisbooks.com   ISBN: 978-1-84416-531-5

Having narrowly escaped being murdered by his evil brother, Jared, Prince Martris Drayke must take control of his magical abilities to summon the dead, and gather an army big enough to claim back the throne of his dead father. But it isn't merely Jared that Tris must combat. The dark mage, Foor Arontala, has schemes to cause an inbalance in the currents of magic and raise the Obsidian King...

SOLARIS FANTASY

FALCONFAR

Dark Lord

"A master of fantasy world-building.
His magic and wizardry are wondrous
to all."—Margaret Weis, New York
Times best-selling author

ED GREENWOOD

BOOK ONE

www.solarisbooks.com   ISBN: 978-1-84416-584-1

When writer Rod Evalar is drawn into a world of his own devising, he is
confronted by a shocking truth—he has lost control of his creation to a
brooding cabal of evil. He must seize Falconfar and halt the spread of
corruption before it's too late.

Dark Lord is the first installment in The Falconfar Saga, from bestselling
author Ed Greenwood.

 SOLARIS FANTASY

UK ISBN: 978-1-84416-651-0 US ISBN: 978-1-84416-588-9

www.solarisbooks.com

Arch Wizard is the second thrilling adventure in The Falconfar Saga. Having been drawn into a fantasy world of his own creation, Rod Everlar continues his quest to defeat the corruption he has discovered within. He sets off in pursuit of the dark wizard Malraun, only to find that he has raised an army of monsters and mercenaries in order to conquer the world...

 SOLARIS FANTASY